ELLEANDER MORNING

ELLEANDER MORNING

A Novel

by Jerry Yulsman

ST. MARTIN'S/MAREK
NEW YORK

Design by Manuela Paul

Library of Congress Cataloging in Publication Data

Yulsman, Jerry.
    Elleander Morning.

    I. Title.
PS3575.U4E4   1984   813'.54   83-16139
ISBN 0-312-24369-3

First Edition

10 9 8 7 6 5 4 3 2 1

To Lesley Dormen
and
Linda Raskin
and
Barbara Woike

History is bunk!

—Henry Ford

ELLEANDER
MORNING

Vienna: 1913

The young man woke up angry. The window was closed. It had been open when he went to bed last night, so once again the old Jew was trying to suffocate him. He lay glaring at the clapboard partition that separated his tiny cubicle from Goldman's and divided their mutual window into two equal parts. It was an arrangement once characterized by Kanya, the hostel's proprietor, a parlor-Marxist, as "democratic compromise." Kanya's hackneyed utterances infuriated him.

He kicked out viciously, striking the thin, unpainted partition just under a narrow shelf holding some of his art supplies. A tumbler containing watercolor brushes crashed to the floor. His rage ripened. He kicked again as he heard his neighbor come awake with a hacking, liquid cough. Slime! He sat up, pounding the wall with both fists. He cried out in a shrill falsetto, "Goldman! I will not inhale your Jew filth!"

Someone down the corridor shouted for silence. He continued pounding, and was rewarded with a drawn-out groan from the other side of the wall, then a shuffling sound and a series of Yiddish curses as the window slowly opened.

The young man unbuttoned his long gray underwear to expose the thin flesh of his chest and belly to the rush of cold March air. From the window, he watched as a taxi slowed to a stop across the street. He could not remember ever having seen one parked on the Meldemennstrasse before. Taxis were a rare sight in the district; no one could afford them.

He counted the scattered pfennigs on his small table. There were seven of them, all that remained of nine crowns he had received the previous week for a poster advertising Teddy's Perspiration Powder. He would have to sell something. Searching through the litter, he found two small pen-and-ink sketches of St. Stephen's Cathedral. He smoothed out the creases, then slid them into a battered portfolio.

As an artist he was incapable of drawing from life. The little sketches and paintings he did of Viennese landmarks were copied from picture postcards or existing renderings of one type or another he found in galleries and museums. His work was stilted and lifeless, much like the carelessly drawn, rough sketches of neophyte architects. The human figures he sometimes added resembled cartoon characters, tiny stuffed sacks, and grotesque dwarfs superimposed in front of monuments, churches, and palaces.

He stood in his sagging underwear gazing out the window at the Vienna rooftops. Beyond the canted roofs of the Twentieth District, the monumental buildings of the Ringstrasse punctuated the horizon, symbols of an imperial city attempting to rule a now crumbling, ramshackle empire of fifty million souls.

In the near distance, the overcast rendered everything in colorless shades of gray like an underdeveloped photograph. The view augmented his depression. He swallowed deeply, fighting back nausea.

After almost four years he was sick of Vienna. They had been miserable years, beginning with his rejection from the academy, then ending here, in a hovel shared by Jews, Czechs, and other rabble. But there had been, he recalled, even worse times than these. During the summer in which his orphan's pension had been terminated, he had slept miserably in doorways or under the trees of Schönbrunn Park. The following winter he had spent his nights on lice-infested straw mattresses in a dosshouse behind the Meidling Station. He would never forget the constant chilblains and chronic nasal catarrh he had suffered after being forced to sell his overcoat for food in this, the most prosperous city in Europe.

Vienna, though basking in the twilight of the Empire, remained unique. It was the envy of Europe, a charming baroque city even more exciting, it was said, than Paris. Its people, under the now benign Hapsburgs, reveled in its art, its soaring music, its majestic rococo architecture. A burgeoning middle class gorged itself on cinnamon-flavored coffee and heavy-cream cakes in a hundred convivial cafés. During the long evenings they took delight in the opera, the theater, the ballet. They danced, flirted and made love, leaving politics to the working classes whose social-democratic trade unionism was eroding the Hapsburg power. Vienna was not only the most romantic city in Europe, but also the most democratic.

The young artist hated it all.

For him, the Empire had become the embodiment of racial desecration. Its capital, once an important center of the "true German culture," was now eroded by this detestable foreign mixture. Everywhere, he thought, as he gazed down at the taxi still parked below, behind each and every degradation, stood the Jews.

He retched. The sour taste was still with him, counterpoint to a spasmodic pounding in both temples.

He had slept badly on a stomach that, throughout the entire previous day, had known but a single serving of soup-kitchen slop. Then in the evening there had been three mugs of bitter coffee at the German workers' tavern near the Danube. His companions had been drinking tall seidels of beer. As always, he had abstained, foolishly substituting coffee for his usual mineral water.

It was a tavern he preferred over all the others in the district, a smoke-filled cave alive with boisterous chatter and disharmonious attempts at group singing. Frequented entirely by Germans, the place was an echo of a nation he had never seen but had dreamed of since his adolescence in Linz.

There were five of them around the table. They spoke for a time of politics, then Kranze, the tubercular ex-teacher, told an anti-Semitic joke. The young artist remained silent and morose through the laughter.

Plumb, a huge ape of a man, looked at him curiously. "You don't find it funny?"

"No. I find nothing funny about the Jew. To me, it would be like laughing at a plague."

Franz Schilling, the bankrupt businessman, said, "I employed some and they were just like everyone else. They got on with their work and minded their business and made no trouble." He leaned back in his chair smugly, hooking his thumbs into the vest pockets of his threadbare suit.

"Some of them are even good socialists . . . Jews," said Plumb.

Schilling rested his elbows on the table and leaned forward, the smoldering tip of his cigar just inches away from the young artist's face. "I even know one who converted—became a good Catholic."

The young artist engaged Schilling's eyes through the smoke. "Only a fool defines a Jew in terms of economics or religion or politics." He twisted his head around slowly, looking carefully at each one of them.

They were all social democrats, naive children. Plumb, he suspected, might even be an anarchist. It was futile. He felt suddenly deflated.

They sat around the table in silence. Kranze diverted his eyes upward so that his collar, no longer shadowed by a long chin, revealed a darkened yellow where it met the loose, pinched skin of his neck. He muttered, "Perhaps . . ." Kranze's voice was quiet, as if he did not really want to be heard. "I've never really trusted them."

Stahlmann, only eighteen, a waiter at Popples during the day, toyed nervously with his silk cravat and seemed to have forgotten how to blink. Plumb looked thoughtful, his mouth gaping like a drowned fish.

Finally, Schilling raised his stein and broke the tension. "Ah, but the women," he said lightly. "Surely you'll make that exception?"

"A Jewess is still a Jew."

Grinning broadly, Kranze exposed a gold tooth that lit up his emaciated face. "So! In that case we will talk about women who aren't Jewish, if it will make you feel any better. Though when you turn them upside-down, they are all the same. Is that not so?" He looked about for approval.

Plumb shook with laughter, wedging himself even tighter into a chair that was too small for him. "Bravo, Kranze! It's what they hide in their bloomers that's important!" He raised his stein in a jubilant toast, slopping beer onto his trousers. "Here's to *all* the little darlings, no matter what they are!"

It was said that Plumb, working as a porter in the West Station, had once broken a purse snatcher's spine with a single blow. The young artist watched him warily as one by one the others shouted mock toasts over the general hilarity. Finally, Plumb glanced at him questioningly. Then the big man, about to say something, seemed to change his mind. He looked away quickly, the grin frozen on his face.

Though the topic remained sex and women, the conversation grew serious. The young artist stayed out of it, gazing into the dregs in the bottom of his cup. He had little interest in women, being shy and uncomfortable in their presence. He was aware that his lack of wit bored them. He had no small talk, no feeling for the inconsequential. As for his need, he masturbated a few times a week to vague fantasies of silent Nordic goddesses, plump and blond, like scaled-up cherubs stretched out beneath him.

He'd left the tavern early, feeling sour. Now he sat on the edge of the bed in the chill morning breeze from the open window, examining his toes. His feet were black to the ankles. He would bathe late tonight when everyone was asleep, so that there would be little chance of his having to share the large shower stall behind the hostel. The thought of exposing his body to others filled him with dread.

He retrieved a pair of black wool stockings from the floor that were stiff to the touch. He blew into them, put them on.

Standing in the cramped space between his bed and the small table, he dressed in the same soiled trousers, shirt and jacket he had worn yesterday and the day before and the weeks and months before that. They were all he had except for a greasy black derby and a threadbare, ankle-length coat given him out of pity the previous winter by his neighbor Goldman, the old-clothes peddler.

A conceited German is the worst of them all, and the most hardened of all, and the most repulsive of all; for he imagines that he possesses the truth in a science of his own invention, which is to him absolute truth.

—Count Leo Tolstoi

2

1913

As requested by his fashionably dressed female passenger, the taxi driver pulled up to the curb across from 27 Meldemennstrasse, a hulking, four-storied building of gray stone that took up the whole block. A large sign over the entrance read:

MÄNNERHEIM HOSTEL FOR MEN

The driver studied the woman in his rear-view mirror, certain that there was some mistake. A *lady* had no business in this sort of neighborhood. She would soon realize her error, then order him to return to central Vienna, where, out of embarrassment, she would overtip. They always did. With luck he could be back in the Hotel Bristol rank just in time for the morning tourist rush.

He eyed her questioningly through the glass partition as she unshipped the brass speaking tube to say in halting German, "We will wait here, please."

"For how long, madam?"

"I don't know. Perhaps an hour or more . . . maybe less. It's all right, I'll pay you for your trouble."

His sigh of resignation synchronized with the dying cough of the taxi's engine as he switched it off. It was eight twenty-two, according to his large Swiss pocket watch. The following morning, under police interrogation, he would take pride in the fact that he was easily able to recall everything in precise detail, even the long fox fur draped over the lady's shoulders, framing the perfect profile he now viewed in the driving mirror. Though a trifle underfleshed for his taste, she was indeed beautiful, especially for an English or American woman of a certain age.

Staring out through the drawn windows of the taxi, she compared the drab landscape with the slums of London. What she saw here was benign compared to those; almost sanitary, like an old cadaver, preserved and rendered germ-free. Quite soon all of Vienna would be a preserved corpse. The knowledge saddened her.

She sat and waited, attempting to bring reality into focus while anxiously wondering if she would recognize the young man at first glance. There were many years separating him from the photographs she had studied. If doubt existed, she must begin again, possibly with the help of a private inquiry agent. She had come too far. She and Bertie had invested too much. . . .

Twenty minutes later she caught her first glimpse of him as he descended the few steps leading from the hostel. He was walking slowly, carrying a large, battered portfolio. At a distance of thirty meters she was sure it was he, despite the wan and hungry face, half-hidden behind a ragged black stubble.

He crossed the street to her side, eyeing the taxi with what she took to be curiosity. Surely he'd seen taxis before, she thought, gripping the soft worn leather of the seat with such force that a long, exquisitely burnished fingernail split through a seam.

On the sidewalk within an arm's length of the taxi, he turned briskly, like a well-drilled soldier, then looked directly at her. It was a brief, inquisitive glance that drained the blood from her head. Trembling, she turned from his pale-blue eyes. She felt she might faint.

Then he was past, walking faster now down the Meldemenn-strasse. From the rear he looked every bit the melancholy tramp, his shabby coat flapping about his ankles, long, unkempt hair hanging over his collar, the ludicrous, battered black derby, which was a size too large, covering part of his ears.

She waited a full minute, and then, with a steady voice, ordered the driver to follow the retreating figure, keeping a block from him.

They proceeded thus for a kilometer or so, making only one turn. Pedestrian traffic increased quickly as the decrepit structures of the workers' district became fewer and fewer.

Finally, her quarry turned left onto a wide avenue bustling with commuters and morning shoppers. At the intersection, she hurriedly paid off the driver, tipping him liberally, exiting the taxi as quickly as ladylike demeanor would allow. The young man was nowhere in sight.

She couldn't lose him; it must be today. She doubted she had the courage or dedication to go through it all again.

The corner was occupied by a lady's milliner, the building next to it was a new block of flats, presided over by a doorman who was costumed as a general officer commanding a regiment of hussars. Next was a large furniture shop, then a barber and finally a book merchant. It was this last that caught her attention. She knew her twenty-four-year-old quarry to be a voracious reader. The book shop seemed his most likely destination.

With long strides, made possible by a skirt that was somewhat wider at the hem than was currently dictated by fashion, she hurried down the avenue. When she passed the furniture shop, a glance told her she had miscalculated. In the window, a portly, tail-coated gentleman was tacking a pen-and-ink sketch of St. Stephen's Cathedral onto an ornate wooden screen. She had no doubts now, the sketch was in the style of another she had seen. She stepped to the curb and waited.

The young artist emerged a few minutes later, the now empty oilcloth portfolio folded and tucked under his arm. He stood for a moment, rubbing his palms together in a hand-washing gesture, uncertain in which direction to turn. As if reluctantly obeying an arbitrary order, he pivoted slowly to head back the way he had come. As he did so, his eyes swept past her, hesitated, then returned to rest on her face. He had, she was certain, recognized her as the woman in the taxi. This time she held his gaze and was surprised at her lack of anxiety. He was, she reasoned, just an ordinary man, surprisingly young and presently of no importance to anyone but her. She felt a sudden excitement, a feeling of superiority as his eyes wavered, expressing bewilderment.

With a shrug, he turned away, moving rapidly now, his shoulders characteristically hunched forward. With a light step, she followed.

He stopped at a newspaper kiosk in the Square and purchased two papers, then stepped off the curb to work his way quickly through the traffic out to the center island, where he swung aboard the second car of a double tram that had just begun to move.

His action caught her by surprise. Thirty meters behind him she battled her handicap and, oblivious to the turmoil of traffic, raced out into the street. The trolley car was gathering speed. She ran, holding her skirt high, gaining ground, despite inadequate shoes that caused her ankles to twist inward on the uneven cobblestones.

Then suddenly she was on the ground, her left leg curled painfully under her body. For the first time she was aware of a discordant orchestra of auto horns and shouted warnings. A police whistle was trilling. Dazed, she glanced around to see men converging on her from out of a confusion of stalled vehicles. The brief confidence she had experienced only moments ago was gone. She had failed. Dimly, she wondered once again if she would have the courage to try again tomorrow or perhaps the next day.

A few seconds later, the double tram, spewing sparks from its overhead trolley wheel, slowed to a crawl to begin its sharp, laborious turn into the Magramstrasse.

Breathing deeply, she rose awkwardly to her feet and was running again, shoes in hand, in a desperate attempt to cut the angle and intercept the trolley before its rear car cleared the turn.

She raced wildly across the tracks into oncoming traffic, closing the gap, each step on the bare stones a separate agony. On the rear platform, a man was reaching out for her. Vaguely she sensed a handsome young face, a military uniform, as the streetcar began its acceleration into the straightaway.

Suddenly she felt her arms being gripped. She was lifted free, her naked feet barely clearing the cobblestones.

On board, she clung to him, fighting for breath, the brass

buttons of his tunic pressing into her cheek. He was complimenting her on her stamina, her beautiful legs, inviting her to a champagne breakfast to celebrate her victory. Thanking him, she
pulled away.

He said, "Are you English?"

"Yes." She felt lightheaded, almost giddy.

"Then perhaps tea?"

"No, thank you."

As the young officer paid her fare, she stepped into her
shoes. A moment later, she saw the now familiar derby bobbing
amidst the strap-hanging passengers. He was standing in the
front of the car, separated from her by more than a dozen people.

She smiled gratefully at her gallant chevalier, then brushed
past him to move farther into the car, closer to her quarry. It was
crowded. A stout, middle-aged burgher in a black frock coat
tipped his hat and half-rose to his feet. She shook her head
negatively, attempting still another grateful smile. Seated, there
would be the danger of losing sight of the derby. The gentleman's solicitous expression turned sour. Her refusal, she knew,
was somehow scandalous: *a gentleman offers, a lady accepts.* Fatigue
washed over her. It was obvious that for the moment, she was no
lady, but rather a wretch—soaked with perspiration, her makeup
smeared, her hair down in ugly strands.

She squeezed her way through the mass of standing passengers, refusing two more seat offers, but finally accepting the gift
of a leather strap loop. With eyes half closed, she swayed gently.
The chase had sapped her energy; her ankle throbbed now in
cadence with a still pounding heartbeat.

The tram had stopped. The derby was gone. She fought her
way through to the exit. Finally, she was on the street and in the
center island. The departing streetcar cleared her view; her
quarry had reached the sidewalk. Favoring a weak ankle, she
followed, vaguely surprised at her own sense of purpose.

He entered Popples, a large café taking up almost half the
streetfront. There was no hurry now. She thought it best that he
be seated when she entered. Limping slightly, she paced the
length of the street twice, giving him five minutes.

The cavernous interior of Popples was a rococo hothouse
made fragrant by the warm aroma of roasting coffee and fresh

baking. Chairs and tables grew out of a dense jungle of potted palms and giant rubber plants. Overhead a vast skylight bathed the large area in diffuse north light, bringing to life the painting and sculpture crowding the walls.

It was early, a slow period. With less than ten customers scattered about at remote tables, Popples seemed empty. He sat alone at a small corner table, even younger-looking now without the coat and derby, and, she thought, pathetically vulnerable.

The headwaiter was busy elsewhere. She seated herself at a table facing the young artist. Only a few meters separated them. He was eating cream cakes and chatting amiably with a waiter. At one point he glanced at her curiously, then looked away.

She ordered streusel and café au lait, then sat staring absently into the green filigree of a palm an arm's length away. She was light-headed as if she had drunk the champagne so chivarously offered by the handsome officer on the streetcar. It would have been, she mused sadly, a wonderful way to spend the day. She had been in Vienna less than twenty-four hours and had seen little of it.

When her order came, she found herself suddenly hungry. She finished off the streusel quickly, then sipped her coffee, all the time looking at him as he sat half hidden behind the large printed pages of the *Arbeiter Zeitung*.

Unsnapping the catch on her small beaded bag, she reached in, running fingers across the smooth ivory handgrip of the ladylike 25-caliber Baretta automatic. She removed her compact from the bag and repaired her makeup. Then, dabbing a spot of L'Heure Bleu behind each ear and another at the base of her throat, she surveyed herself in the small mirror.

She set the compact on the table and removed the pistol from her bag, flicking up the safety as she did so. Placing both elbows on the table, she sighted along the barrel and squeezed the trigger.

The sound was not much louder than that of a child's cap pistol. A small hole appeared miraculously in the center of the newspaper.

He dropped the paper and she saw that the hole was echoed in his shirtfront a few centimeters to the right of the second button. As she watched, a patch of deep red surrounded it, then began to spread. He was, she thought, about to speak, but instead his startled eyes drifted down to her long fox fur piece, which he stared at intently, as if it were a deadly snake about to strangle her.

She fired again. The small projectile, spinning rapidly, struck his head at a velocity of 420 meters per second, drilling its way neatly through the skull just above his right eye ridge. Thus flattened, it pushed before it a mass of compacted gray tissue, punching out a large piece of the back of the skull before falling, spent, under his jacket collar.

She flicked the safety back up and placed the pistol carefully in the bottom of her bag. Oblivious to the growing tumult around her, she quickly reviewed her makeup in the small mirror, then, dropping some money onto the table, she turned for a final glance. Like a tired old man, his body was slumped deep in his chair. A small black hole punctuated his forehead. Beneath it his eyes, wide, unblinking, stared intently into hers. She felt nothing. It was as if she were viewing the dead man from a remote distance through a pair of cheap binoculars.

She stood. Her commitment had been fulfilled. It was time to leave, to escape, in order to return to Bertie.

Favoring her left leg, she approached the door leading to the streets of Vienna. As she reached out to open it, she was knocked to the floor by a frightened Jewish waiter named Stahlmann.

3

1983

Lesley Bauman parked the Packard in the lot behind Union Station, put the top up, then removed her two pieces of luggage from the trunk. She stepped back and looked at her car with sad, admiring eyes. It was a bright red '81, the last of the breed. She walked around to place her hand affectionately on the tall traditional V-shaped radiator grill. It was, she reflected, the only machinery she had ever developed an affection for.

In the station she tossed the car keys into a trash can, then bought a ticket and checked her luggage through. *Twenty-three dollars and eighty cents, one way, L.A. to New York.* She had seventeen minutes until boarding.

In a public booth she obtained Gloria Gold's number from information. She dialed, hoping Ralph would answer. He didn't. He was out, gone for the afternoon. His girlfriend Gloria, seemed nervous, her phrasing and diction turning awkwardly formal as the tremolo increased. Lesley told her that the Packard was parked behind Union Station. A set of keys was on the foyer table at the beach house. Ralph could keep both the car and the house. Gloria responded with stunned silence and heavy breathing, then finally blurted out a dumbfounded "thank you."

Lesley hung up abruptly, thinking that the little twenty-three-year-old blonde was just right for Ralph, at least for a while. Gloria probably knew the difference between Olympic and Budweiser and would more than likely learn to love baby oil and the Los Angeles Cowboys.

As for herself, Lesley would miss the Packard. It had been home away from home for months, a sanctuary. But nothing lasts forever, neither cars nor husbands.

The magnitrain was crowded almost to capacity, but she managed to find a seat on the aisle. She buckled up both lap and shoulder straps as, moments later, they trundled out of the station, turned into the west-east tube and began accelerating.

The large speedometer mounted on the bulkhead in the front of the car read 400-plus miles per hour as they wound their way through the Rockies. The smaller acceleration meter just below it varied alternately between 1 and 1.12 gravities as the centrifugal force generated by long shallow turns and climbs made itself felt.

Finally, in the clear just west of Flagstaff, Arizona, the 65-foot-long, windowless capsule was free to begin its 2,000-mile straightaway.

Both indicators began climbing. After just a minute the acceleration meter was holding at 1.5 Gs. Lesley was pressed gently into the now totally resilient seat back, which folded around her like a feather bed. The skin on her face felt tight, as if she were grimacing. She was heavier—188 pounds—instead of her usual 125.

The magnitrain sped silently through its seamless, airless tube, suspended in the center by a potential induced by electromagnetic rings that encircled the inside circumference. They were placed 27 yards apart, charged sequentially by massive capacitors, which on this stretch of acceleration fired an ever-increasing amount of current. As the capsule was thrust out of the field of one electromagnetic ring, it was drawn into the field of the next—in effect, a simple linear electric motor, with the magnitrain capsule itself acting as the armature.

After a minute of acceleration, the speedometer held at 4,200 miles per hour and the accelerometer dropped rapidly back to normal 1 G.

Lesley relaxed and ordered a Dewers and soda from the stewardess. The seat was once again firm against her back.

South of Dayton, Ohio, the magnitrain's seats were rotated to face the rear as it began its long deceleration. This time the effects were less severe, the acceleration meter hovered at only 1.23 Gs. for a few minutes, then leveled off close to normal.

Shortly afterward, the capsule, now rolling on its own retractable wheels, pulled into Pennsylvania Station in New York, just one hour and three minutes after departing Los Angeles. The cab ride through evening traffic to her mother's house on East Eighty-seventh Street lasted almost as long.

"Were there other men?" Lena Morning lowered her brandy glass and arched an eyebrow at her daughter Lesley.

"One."

"And?"

"Just one time. It was awful, but at least it was spontaneous —a new experience for me—really new."

Her mother turned to speak to the wall: "I have a daughter who's a total sex maniac!"

"I don't know," said Lesley, sighing, resting her cheek against the comforting velvet of the chair, thinking it could be true. It had been her husband's business partner, less than a month ago. He had come to the house to speak with Ralph, who was at a ballgame. She was stretched out on her belly next to the pool, the bra strap of her riviera hanging loose. It was the tiniest one she owned, white against her deeply tanned skin, one of the

newer ones this year, with an extremely high-cut V at the crotch.
She sensed his interest through half-closed eyes even before she
heard his voice. He threw himself into a camp chair and they
talked for a few minutes while the idea percolated in her mind.
It was simply a matter of sitting up to let the top fall. A *grudge fuck*,
she reflected. For just a moment it had given her a sense of
power. But he was inept as a lover, leaving her high and dry—
empty.

"Did Ralph find out?" said her mother.

"Yes, I told him."

"Lesley!"

"He was not only boring me to death, Mother, but he also
had another woman. There's a parlay for you. Anyway, it was with
Bob."

"Good God!"

"They had a fight, but later it got kind of crazy. I mean,
Ralph kept asking for details. I lied, told him how terrific it was,
invented all sorts of raunchy detail. I was angry but it got to be
a game . . . it turned him on." She laughed bitterly. "Might have
saved our marriage if I'd wanted to hang around."

She closed her eyes, trying to go over some of it. Ralph had
been in real estate. Lots of shop talk and football and *his* friends
and *their* wives and empty gossip on the telephone. And sex. The
game plan had called for Wednesday and Saturday nights. There
had been a *sensible reason* for that particular schedule, but she
couldn't remember what it was. Ralph kept score and there was
even a half time—he'd have a beer, she'd have a cigarette. A little
TV. It was paced well; Ralph was out for a record. But last
summer she stopped faking orgasms, which caused him to go
off his feed. His backhand suffered. Then, the incident with
Bob. . . .

Her mother was saying, "Men aren't all that bad, you know.
They open doors and send flowers and light our cigarettes and
pay the bills." Lena Morning could think of nothing else to say.
She shrugged and looked up at the ceiling. It was a different
world now.

"That's nice," Lesley said, not quite managing to suppress
a compulsive giggle. It all seemed so absurd. She'd have to get
organized. She felt as if she were going through her thirty's
trauma four years after the fact.

"You're laughing at me—your mother."

"No," she said, grinning, "I just flashed Ralph lying in bed reading 'The Importance of Foreplay in Marriage.' It was a *Reader's Digest* article. I mean really! It became the official rule book, the Bible."

"It must be the genes," said her mother sourly.

"What?"

"Sometimes it worries me."

"What are you talking about?"

"Never mind . . ."

"You said genes—you mean from you and Father?"

"Just from your father; leave me out of it."

"Okay, I'm hooked," Lesley said, thinking how typical it was of her mother to distill a complex reality into a few concentrated drops of predestination. This time it was genetic, usually it was astrological. "Come on, Mother, *what* worries you?"

"It's not important."

Lesley knew the game, the disclaimers indicated a fragmentation bomb was about to be dropped. She drew deeply on her cork-tipped Marvel, leaning forward. "You mean, the world is just dandy, but something is a little off-kilter about Lesley, some nasty, mysterious genetic inheritance that nobody ever talks about?"

"Your grandmother . . ."

"Which one?" she said. She had met neither of them.

"Your father's mother, of course." The older woman stared into the fire, using a little time to put the words together. "I really shouldn't have brought it up. It was a scandal of your father's family, long before I knew him. Naturally, I wouldn't have married him if I'd known. But your father was one hell of a good-looking man—handsome is the word, you don't hear it much these days. And money, and a dry humor—you know how they are—I was swept off my feet." Lena Morning held up the brandy snifter and squinted at her daughter through the golden pool. "Of course, I didn't know too much about his personality, they used to call it *character* in those days. He seemed charming at the time in his blazer and straw hat and black-and-white wingtips." She lapsed into silence, gazing down at her feet, as if expecting to find his shoes there. "He was a solitary man, it was his nature. I mean, I really don't know why he married. In the years we lived together, there were no relatives, no friends, nothing but two horrible old ladies—twins—who would come to tea every few weeks." She looked up, her eyes misting over, focusing on nothing.

Lesley sighed. She had heard it all before, this superficial description of a father who remained, for her, merely a dim childhood memory. She rose from her chair and, feeling a deep pang of sympathy, laid an affectionate hand on her mother's arm. She realized for the hundredth time that Lena Morning's knowledge and understanding of Harry Morning was just as vague and unformed as her own.

But here, she realized, was something new: her grandmother. In the past, her mother had always avoided the subject. In a concerned voice, Lesley asked, "Mother . . . what are you getting at?"

"Your father's mother . . . your paternal grandmother, killed a man, shot him dead. She was a murderer. It happened in Europe; your father was an infant at the time."

"Good God!"

"And there were other rumors. Of course, it was all a long time ago, but as I said, I've always been a little worried about the genes."

"I don't think you're joking."

"I'm not, dear."

"Well, for God's sake, tell me about it!"

"I don't know much, really. Your grandmother's name was Elleander. You'll have to get the rest from your father."

Later, lying in bed, she thought about him for the first time in years. She was just about three years old in 1952, when her mother packed her up and moved to New York. After that, she had only dim memories of a tall, thin man who, when she was ten, visited from England to take her to the Museum of Natural History and Radio City Music Hall. There had been, down through the years, greeting cards on traditional occasions and, just once, an overseas phone call. It was on the day of her wedding in the spring of 1975. Her father's voice, she remembered, had been deep and resonant, his words formal, as if he were delivering a speech. She sensed the effort he was making and was touched by it. She called him Dad, then the phone seemed to go dead with shared guilt. There were moments of agonized silence. She felt relieved when they rang off. She sprinted from the phone into the arms of her brand-new husband with a show of affection that brought cheers from the reception guests and the day's first and only tears from her mother's eyes.

With those exceptions, the only reminders she had of her father's existence were the monthly remittances she received from the trust fund he had set up for her. The checks had been arriving regularly since she was twenty-one and were quite liberal. The first one had included a handwritten note:

> *Daughter: Drafts to this amount will be sent to you every month from now on. It is my wish that you use the money, however wisely or unwisely, as you see fit, to ensure both your personal pleasure and your independence from the damnable coercion of insolvency. Your father, Harry Morning.*

Yet it was the memory of her father's telephone voice that haunted her. She felt that there was something important he had wanted to tell her, some intimate confidence that she had somehow forestalled.

She rolled over on her back to stare wide-eyed at the darkened ceiling. It was, she thought, all nonsense. Typical filial guilt toward an absent father, textbook stuff. She should know better. She sat up and lit a cigarette.

As a child, she had idolized him, building romantic fantasies, first of an ancient castle and a handsome prince, then, later, of an industrial empire and a rich and powerful businessman escorting glamorous, befurred women hither and yon in a white chauffeured Rolls-Royce. Later still, in college art class, she had done him in oils from memory.

She thought, where am I? It was as if, for most of her life, she had been anesthetized and was now just coming out of it. It explained her disorientation, her anger.

Until the incident with Bob, she had always been a good girl, always did what she was told, did what others had programmed for her. Leaving Ralph had been the only major decision of her life. Marrying him had not been. That had been the result of the coercive approval of her friends and her mother. Marriage, the big wedding and happy-ever-after was the major goal of her social peers. But she had never loved Ralph. She had never loved any man. Love, hate, fear were emotions she only knew of from movies and books and the tube.

She thought of her grandmother. Her mother's talk about a murder was probably nonsense. But what if it wasn't? Suddenly, Lesley found herself enthralled with the idea that a blood relative might have exhibited the passion necessary to kill someone. Real emotions she could only imagine . . . there was, it seemed, a secret part of her in England.

Now, quite suddenly, she knew she would go to London. Why not? There was nothing to keep her here. *Father and daughter —Harry Morning—flesh and blood.* Surely they could share things she was never able to share with her mother.

Feeling a sudden burst of excitement, she punched out her cigarette in the ashtray. Tomorrow morning she would cab to Idlewild and catch one of those new jets to London. By dinner time she would be in her father's house on Highcastle Road.

But in the morning, she felt differently. She needed time to sort things out. Time by herself, she decided, a week, or at least a few days to go shopping, if nothing else. At breakfast her mother chatted amiably through the orange juice, soft-boiled eggs and toast. Lesley paid little attention. She gazed out the window, her mind drifting. She should have kept the car.

Over coffee her mother was saying, ". . . old job back?"

"No," she said. She felt she was on a seesaw.

"Well, you've got to do *something,* dear."

"Mother, I've been home less than twenty-four hours, for God's sake!"

"Don't yell, dear." Lena Morning smiled at her daughter tolerantly. "I mean later, when you sort of get on your feet—a few weeks, maybe. They're sure to remember you."

"Don't be silly. I was a very junior editor, the job I had was probably filled a dozen times since I left. Girls come and go so fast, it's like a relay race."

"They do? Why is that, dear?"

"I don't know—they pay so little that no one takes the job seriously. It's half of what a man gets. A woman editor only makes a few more dollars than a secretary. And then I guess a lot of the girls get married." She sipped her coffee, feeling a growing, unaccustomed anger and wondering at its source.

"Well, that's not so bad," said her mother.

Lesley looked up sharply. "Oh no, you don't!"

"Don't yell, dear."

"I'm not yelling," said Lesley, her voice tight, the three short words clipped and defined. "You're really marvelous, Mother! You should be in the fucking government—a genius at leading interviews exactly where you want them to go."

"Don't be silly and watch your language."

"I learned it from Ralph."

"Well, you're in New York now, Lesley, not California."

"I'm sorry, I forgot." Lesley felt a pang of guilt. She was, she realized, using her mother for a punching bag.

"I have a friend at Bendel's, maybe he can find something for you in the advertising department. Or, if you'd like, you can come to work at the shop. Anything."

She tried unsuccessfully to visualize herself selling lingerie at her mother's shop on Lexington Avenue. Sighing, she picked up her empty coffee cup to stare into it. "Mother," she said quietly. "Please try to understand. I woke up this morning with a hangover and I haven't been drinking."

"I understand, dear."

"I mean, it's not every day that I walk away from a marriage."

"Poor dear. Believe me, I know the feeling."

"I need some time."

"Take all the time you need, darling."

"I'd like to be alone for a few days, a week maybe. What about Saltair?"

"Fire Island would be freezing now," said Lena Morning, feeling suddenly left out. "There's no heat in the house and you'd freeze. Wait until late April, early May—five, six weeks."

"I should have kept the car. I could have driven from Los Angeles, just me and the Packard and the open road. It would have been a psychic physic."

"You sold the car?"

"No, I gave it back to Ralph."

"You're a crazed person!"

"The Malibu house too—I just wanted to get out, I don't

want any souvenirs. Nothing! I don't even want his cockamamy name; I'm changing it back to Morning."

"And I don't even want to *think* about it!" said her mother, rising abruptly. "A girl gives everything back from the settlement —it's cuckoo! There are people starving all over and you give back a car and a house?"

"Mother . . ."

"I've got to get to the shop," Lena Morning said, turning her back on her daughter and leaving the room.

Lesley sat at the table barely breathing. She followed her mother into the foyer. The older woman had donned a small mink jacket and was pulling on her gloves.

"I've just never heard of anything like that," she said. "But of course, I'm from the older generation, I don't think modern."

"Mother," said Lesley, laying a hand on her shoulder. "I don't need money. I get all the money I need, and so do you."

"Famous last words."

"It's not the *money* that I *need* right now," Lesley repeated, leaning back against the mirrored wall.

"Then what do you need?"

"I have to find out who I am. Something!"

"Everybody has to find out who they are—from the very first caveman crawling out of his tree. *Who am I?* It's the national pastime. Listen, you are who you are, so wake up!" Lena Morning turned to find her daughter in tears. She softened. Then she had Lesley in her arms, comforting her, running a hand gently over her full blond hair.

Lesley pulled back, straightened up to take her mother's hand. "I'm sorry, Mom." She forced a tiny, embarrassed laugh. "I'm really acting like a teenager. I don't know what's wrong with me."

"Well, maybe another cup of coffee, we could talk some more."

"I'm okay now, honest. Go ahead."

"You sure?" Her mother placed a reluctant hand on the doorknob.

"Sure." Lesley smiled. "I'm fine, I can feel the manic state beginning to take hold."

"Go for a nice walk and look in the windows. It's almost like spring." She opened the door. "Buy a new hat, or a pretty little riviera for Fire Island, something cute; it won't be that long to beach weather. And Saks, by the way, is showing some pretty cruise things."

"Mother—good-bye."

"Maybe we can get some theater tickets for tonight. There's a revival of *My Fair Lady,* I hear it's lovely."

Later Lesley took her mother's suggestion and walked down Madison Avenue. At Fifty-third she turned west toward Rockefeller Plaza. She'd have a nice quiet lunch at Conrad's, then maybe some shopping after all.

It was an unusual day for this time in March, beautiful, with a warm, exhilarating feeling of spring in the air. I'm a yo-yo, she thought, from depression to euphoria in three easy hours. But maybe it was the town. New York in the spring always did that for her.

She glanced into the French Line window on the corner of Fifty-first and Fifth. The display was dominated by a large, detailed model of the liner *Normandie.* A small, tastefully lettered sign below it read:

—*COMPAGNIE GENERALE TRANSATLANTIQUE*—
*S/S *NORMANDIE**
Now back in service
Weekly service to
Southampton
and
Le Havre
World's largest passenger ship.
79,000 tons gross registered.

The next crossing was in three days' time, but there were only two first-class accommodations available. The *Normandie* was popular. It would be her fourth Atlantic crossing after sitting in mothballs through eighteen years of French revolution and counterrevolution.

Of the two, Lesley chose the luxurious main-deck suite in preference to a single cabin on A deck. With no attempt to rationalize the $800 expense, she paid up with her American Express

Card, exited quickly, then went around the corner to the RCA
cable office, where she sent a brief message to her father. After
that, she crossed Fifth to Best and Company, where she proceeded to spend another three hundred dollars on a summer
wardrobe. When she emerged, the sky was clouded over and a
raw chill was setting in. Nevertheless, she was feeling better.

That night, Lesley went with her mother to see the *My Fair
Lady* revival. It was presented with all the richness of the original.
Henry Higgins emerged more phlegmatic, less introspective,
with the aging but still handsome Rex Harrison in the role. It was
difficult to compare him to Leslie Howard, who had played Higgins in the original production, though, over a late supper at
Sardi's, they tried.

The following afternoon she received a cable from her father. He was looking forward to her arrival.

The *Normandie* lifted anchor at 9:10 P.M., Saturday, March
26. Lesley waved to her mother through miles of multicolored
confetti as the brawny little Moran tugs eased the massive ship
out into the Hudson. She stayed forward on the lifeboat deck
until they cleared the Verrazano Bridge, at which time she went
to her quarters, where for two hours she sat in her sitting room
gazing out a large porthole and sipping the Piper Heidsieck provided by a gracious porter. She had dinner in her cabin, took a
bath and went to bed early with the latest Ernie Pyle novel.

The following morning she awakened before dawn to do
four circuits of the promenade deck before breakfast. Then a
sumptuous feast that, as the first diner of the day, she consumed
in elegant solitude in the aft sundeck buffet. Later, under a light
blanket, she read, stretched out on a deck chair, until noon. She
gently rebuffed the men seeking conversation. They included a
somewhat portly but well-turned-out businessman from Budapest. There were others, younger, much better-looking, but none
so charmingly insistent.

She kept to herself for the next three days, enjoying early
morning jogs around the deck and light suppers in her sitting
room. From time to time, when lying on her deck chair, or making use of the swimming pool, she was aware of the Hungarian
businessman just slightly offstage, observing her. All the other
young French officers and single men in first class had long since

given up. Both she and the ship seemed to be floating on a sea of ennui.

On Wednesday night, Lesley Morning dressed and took dinner for the first time at her assigned table in the salon. She made polite conversation, then went to the bar, where she allowed herself to be picked up by the Hungarian. They danced until midnight. He spoke English well. She told him of Los Angeles, and he talked at length of the Paris of the East, Budapest. He was funny and made her laugh. They took a stroll, arm in arm on the boat deck, where he kissed her. Shortly after 1 A.M. they went to her quarters.

His name was Breyer. He was in the printing business. He folded his clothes neatly, placing them over a chair, leaving his protective horn-rims on until the last moment. She was touched by the quality of giving and the affection he displayed. But despite this, she lay there afterward wondering why, for the second time in her life, she had gone to bed with a man for whom she had felt no sexual attraction.

At Southampton, she was greeted by a tall, loose-limbed man, roughly her own age, who sported a tousled shock of sandy hair and a shy smile. He introduced himself as Fred Hayworth, her father's solicitor. They exchanged small talk while he placed her luggage in the boot of a battered green TR4. When they were seated, he reached back to pull the top up, before turning to her. His smile was gone.

"I am afraid I have some bad news, Mrs. Bauman," he said, resting his hand lightly on her arm. "Your father suffered a heart attack—a massive coronary—on Wednesday night." His words were strung together in a single breath, like a child hurriedly reciting a memorized poem.

"No."

"I'm sorry. It's a terrible way to greet you, but I thought it better than a wireless to the ship."

"Where is he? How . . . ?" She knew the answer before she could finish stating the question.

She felt the increasing pressure of his hand, then he said softly, "He died this morning in hospital. They did everything possible."

Lesley sat erect on the seat, fishing in her bag for a cigarette, fumbling for what seemed like minutes before accepting one from him. He lit it with a Zippo, while holding her hand steady with his own. A charming man, she thought, with an endearing boyish quality she had found common to a few other homosexual men she had known. Yet she knew instinctively that here was a strong shoulder to lean on if she needed one. She felt the undertow and cautiously awaited the breaking wave.

"I didn't know him very well," he said. "I've only been with the firm two years, you see."

"I didn't know him well either," she said, staring fixedly out the windshield, wondering where the tears were, hoping they would come.

He said, "I've made all the arrangements, there's a plot reserved next to his mother—your grandmother."

A few moments later they drove off in silence. It was hours before she shed the tears that she knew, somehow, were for herself.

ELLEANDER
MORNING

THE TIME IS OUT OF JOINT,
OH CURSED SPITE,
THAT I WAS EVER BORN—
TO SET IT RIGHT.

—DEPARTED—

May 18 A.D. 1915

—Gravestone inscription
in a cemetery near
Chessington, England

4

1983

The Georgian mansion at 22 Highcastle Road consisted of eighteen rooms, not including the servants' quarters, which, in their heyday, had housed a butler, a head housekeeper, a cook, a pantry boy, a kitchen maid, a scullery maid, a gardener, a liveryman, a coachman, two housemaids, two lady's maids, a gentleman's valet and a governess.

For sixty-six years, beginning with its initial occupancy, a brass plate just to the left of the front door carried the name Harcourt. By 1902, three generations of Harcourts had occupied the premises. The first of these, Gerald, had died suddenly in the billiard room at the age of sixty-three during an argument concerning Napier's Ethiopian expedition.

The next Harcourt, Jason, blew his brains out in the sanctity of his study on New Year's morning 1898, over a maritime insurance misunderstanding. He left behind a second wife not quite thirty-seven, two sons from his first, and a spinster sister. The youngest of his sons opted for Canada shortly after impregnating his aunt's personal maid. The other, James Harcourt, was killed at Ladysmith by a seventeen-year-old Boer sniper who had spent nine terrified hours hidden in a tree just sixty-five yards from the British command headquarters. It was to be the boy's only shot of the war.

In 1902, the two remaining Harcourt women moved to a smaller country place in Buckinghamshire, and in 1909, the house was sold to one Elleander Morning, who auctioned off the furnishings and had the house completely redecorated.

By 1983, one hundred and forty-seven years after its first tenant had moved in, Harry Morning's house was a survivor, the only one of its kind left intact on all of Highcastle Road. Conservative, stately and well-kept, it stood unblemished by any exterior improvements, like a grand old lady dressed in dignified, moneyed gray.

Until his very recent death, Harry Morning's house was one of the few in the area that still performed its original function, that of housing a single family and a staff to service it. (Though it could be argued that one individual does not constitute a family and that a staff of two is hardly adequate to maintain, in the old sense, a mansion of eighteen rooms.) Many of the stately homes in the area had long since been carved up into blocks of flats. Some housed commercial ventures, management firms, restaurants and even a few small and exclusive gambling clubs, while the well-proportioned rooms of a few others were graced with the embassies of obscure nations known only to the League of Nations.

For the third morning in a row, Lesley awoke to the sound of Mrs. Green's incessant sniffling. In the far corner of the bedroom the woman was flicking her perpetual feather duster with one pudgy hand while wiping away dribble from under her nose with the other. Mrs. Green was the late Harry Morning's housekeeper, a rotund woman in her late sixties who, for three days, Lesley observed, had been roaming aimlessly through the house, dressed in the same tattered pink bathrobe and waving the same ineffectual duster.

Now, ignoring Lesley's feigned sleep, the elderly woman stared at the bed out of anxious wet eyes, to say, for the tenth or twentieth time, "I was with your father all me life, and me mum was with his mum."

Lesley, admitting defeat, opened one eye and with a yawn acknowledged Mrs. Green's presence. "Did you know her . . . my grandmother?"

"Oh, no, miss, I was just a baby then." Mrs. Green stared intently at the floor and made a valiant effort to stop weeping.

"I'm sorry."

The housekeeper nodded, then straightened and resumed her circuit of the bedroom, waving the feather duster in a desultory fashion at odd pieces of furniture. Once again she said, "Your dad, he was a fine gentleman."

"I know," said Lesley, thinking she'd have to get out of the house, walk about the West End, visit the Tate, anything. She sat on the edge of the bed for a moment, then stood, her nightgown clinging with static electricity. She would dress and leave before Mrs. Green had the opportunity to insist on making breakfast.

The old woman looked at her and smiled sadly. "You've got a fine figure, that's plain to see."

Returning a nervous grin, Lesley crossed the room to her suitcase.

"Your father, he had an appreciation."

"What?" She felt suddenly aware of her near nakedness.

"An eye for the ladies, so to speak. He would have liked *that*, all right." Mrs. Green gestured in Lesley's general direction, then sniffled and continued, "I don't mean to say . . . you being his daughter and all, if you know what I mean." Mrs. Green's troubled gray face turned grayer. Her sniffling segued into a full-scale sob as Lesley nervously gathered some clothing out of her suitcase, then walked briskly to the bathroom.

She bathed in a very hot tub, dressed, applied makeup, then fifteen minutes later emerged into the bedroom to find Mrs. Green still dusting. The elderly housekeeper looked up at her. "I'll make some nice scrambled eggs and kidneys."

"I'm sorry, Mrs. Green, but I've got to go out."

"It's cats and dogs; you'll catch your death!"

"I have an umbrella. It's important," she lied, starting for the bedroom door.

"Your father," whined Mrs. Green, "he never went out . . ." The last few words changed pitch like a cat's wail.

Lesley raced down the stairs. As she approached the study on her way to the front door, Rose Parker, her late father's personal secretary, emerged, blocking the way. Rose was a thirty-five-year-old, pale, redheaded woman, with terrible posture. She dressed exclusively in ankle-length garden-party dresses, and sang to herself.

"Are you going out, Miss Morning?" Her voice was high-pitched and cultured.

"Yes."

Rose blew on her nails. "Can I go with?"

"I have an appointment, Rose, I'm sorry," said Lesley, lying once again, reflecting on the fact that she had never seen the woman with dry nails. "Maybe next time."

"It's raining anyway."

"Yes, well, I have no choice, you see . . ."

"I want to thank you again," said Rose, her slump-shouldered body still blocking the way. "I mean to say, for your consideration and so on, in helping me to move my things."

"You're welcome," said Lesley, recalling how terrified Rose had been to enter Harry Morning's bedroom. "I must be going."

"You're very nice—I mean, really." It was the tenth time Rose Parker had expressed her gratitude. The other efforts had been orchestrated with bursts of tears even more voluble than Mrs. Green's. In Rose's case the tears invariably streamed down her face depositing streaks of mascara. Lesley eyed the door, thinking of herself as a ball carrier searching for a hole in the line.

"Mrs. Green has talked about some lovely boiled eggs and kidneys for breakfast. You really should have something fortifying before you go out." The tears were starting.

"Sorry, no time." Lesley pushed past her, grasping an umbrella from the stand. Finally she was out the door and onto the portico.

A solid wall of rain descended out of a leaden sky that seemed little higher than the houses across the way. With no specific final destination in mind she raised her umbrella, descended the three short steps to the pavement and, turning left, splashed her way toward the square. A phone box stood on the corner, a haven in the pouring rain. On impulse, she consulted a card from her bag, then dialed Fred Hayworth.

Twenty minutes later she was seated in her stockinged feet in his comfortable office, sipping a cup of hot tea. Her shoes, soles up, lay drying in front of the electric fire. The room, she thought, was everything an American could expect from a London law office. The paneling was dark mahogany on all but one wall, which was lined floor to ceiling with glassed-in law books. The heavy walls were graced with Daumier lithographs, the floor, with a respectably worn Sovonnerie carpet.

Fred Hayworth caught her roving eye and smiled. "I had nothing to do with any of it," he said. "All inherited. My grandfather is the culprit, the office was his originally. I represent the third generation. It takes a while for one to leave his mark on this room, and I'm afraid I'm an infant where that's concerned. Even the tennis trophies on the mantel aren't mine; I believe my grandfather won them after the war. Wimbleton, Forest Lawn and so on."

"Forest Hills," said Lesley, liking him. "Don't you have any of your own?"

"Good Lord, no. I'm a reasonably sedentary fellow, except for a little nonsense with billiards and karate. But then my great-grandfather's ghost would probably knock me about with his chains if I dared to hang a Purple Belt on these walls. They believed strongly in the yellow peril in his day. Do you play billiards, Mrs. Bauman?"

"Lesley . . ."

"Lesley, then. And I wish you'd call me Fred."

"Freddie." She smiled.

"If you must."

Their small talk was interrupted by Hayworth's secretary, a horse-faced, middle-aged woman, who glanced at Lesley's bare feet with obvious disapproval. There were papers to sign and other small matters of business. After a few minutes, she left.

"How are you getting on at the house?" Hayworth said, his interest once more centered on her.

On the couch, Lesley tucked her legs up. "Lousy," she said.
"Aren't Mrs. Green and Miss . . . what's her name?"

"Parker," said Lesley. "Rose Parker."

"Aren't they taking care of you?"

"It's the other way around."

"I'm sorry." He seemed confused. "I've only seen them a
few times, and then just briefly when I was at the house getting
papers signed. I just assumed you'd prefer to be with people
rather than alone in a hotel—I mean, under the circumstances."

"Freddie," she said, sitting up now, "my father's house is a
loony bin, and those two lost souls are the loonies. My father was
probably the chief loony, that's the way it's beginning to seem to
me. I mean, maybe my mother was right—she was worried about
genes."

"Genes?" He tilted his head questioningly. "Whose?"

"Mine."

"Perhaps you should start at the beginning."

"I'll try." Lesley padded to the desk in her stockinged feet
and seated herself on the edge. "My mother just recently mentioned in passing that my paternal grandmother was a murderess
—shot a man in Europe. Now, after being here awhile, I can
almost believe it." She closed her eyes, then opened them again,
on his. "Everybody else is off-kilter, why not my grandmother?
And, according to my mother, why not me? She may have a
point."

"Nonsense." He was smiling now. "Your mother probably
has an overactive imagination, or somebody once pulled her leg.
Or maybe she savors the idea of a skeleton in the closet. A good
many people do, you know. And the two ladies at the house,
assuming they *are* loony, as you say, have nothing to do with you;
you're not even related. As for your father, well, perhaps he
might have been somewhat eccentric. I've been told he was a bit
solitary, as they say, but certainly not . . . crazy."

"Maybe not, but if I have to stay there for even one more day,
they'll have to cart *me* away. I'll probably be singing harmony with
Rose when they do."

"Harmony?"

"She hums 'Tea for Two' all day long. She never lets up, not for a minute, unless of course she's crying, or thanking me. She thanks me a lot, that girl. Jesus, am I getting hysterical?"

"A little," said Hayworth. "Sit down."

"I'm sorry," she said. "I just had to get out of there for a while—I mean, even in the pouring rain. Mrs. Green never stops talking about my father and she has a perpetually running nose. Everything . . . I felt I had to speak to someone other than those two or I'd go ape. Three days! Anybody!"

"Flattery will get you nowhere." Hayworth went over to her and put his hand on her shoulder.

"Forgive me," she said, attempting a smile. "It's just that I don't know anyone else in London, anyone who's sane, that is. I've no right to dump all this on you, and you're being very nice."

"As your late father's solicitor, I'm also acting as yours."

"Thank you." She straightened up, feeling a tiny bit better about it all.

He said, "What are your plans?"

"They consist of getting back to New York as fast as one of those new jets can carry me. Right after the funeral tomorrow."

"There's a will reading in a few days."

"I'm afraid you'll have to mail me the check."

"It's important that you stay. You're going to come into a considerable amount of money, and—don't let this throw you— the house. We'll need you here for a few weeks. Without you it would be far more complicated. If you would like, we can book you a suite in a hotel, or find a furnished flat nearby."

"A lot of money?"

"Yes—even, we hope, after inheritance taxes."

"So quite suddenly I'll have responsibilities, is that it?"

"As the saying goes. . . ."

Lesley Morning spent the rest of the day lost in art and antiquities at the Tate and the British Museum. She decided to stick it out in London. Fred Hayworth, she realized, had contributed much to that decision.

The funeral took place the following morning, a perfect day for it. The light was flat, a soft placid gray filtered through tiny water droplets that coalesced into an all-pervasive mist. It was a light found only in Britain. Polarized, it created no highlights on the manicured cemetery grass that in the gentle radiance looked like green felt.

The priest, in a voice perfectly suited to read BBC stock quotations, said, "It has been my misfortune that I have never, in my lifetime, enjoyed the pleasure of meeting the deceased. He was, I have been informed, a solitary man, a scholar, a serious historian. But, above all, Harry Morning, throughout his days, exhibited the highest moral values and behavior. . . ."

Lesley glanced to her left, wondering at the source of his information. Rose Parker stood veiled and hunched forward. Through the diaphanous material she could see the woman's lips moving, singing softly to herself—"Tea for Two."

Lesley shut out the priest's words, hearing rather the oboe-like tones, the musical timbre of his voice. He was far too young for a priest, and much too muscular and fit. More like a football —or rather, she thought—a rugby player than a priest. He failed to dominate the proceedings. It was obvious that her late father did not rate someone from the first team. Each of his congregation of six seemed isolated from the priest and from one another. Even Mrs. Green's interest lay elsewhere—her lips, like Rose's, moved out of synch with the priest's. Her eyes were vacant, focused on nothing.

They lowered the coffin to further incantations. A few handfuls of dirt and it was over. Lesley started to leave with the others, but instead veered five short steps to the left, to stare at the fresh flowers ornamenting the base of her grandmother's headstone. For the third time that day, she read the curious inscription.

The pair of graves were bordered on one side by a large willow and on the other by a hedge that separated two sections of the cemetery. Thus her father and grandmother were isolated from all the thousands of others in a kind of little park of their own.

Between the two graves was what seemed to be ample space for a third. *Room for one more,* thought Lesley, confirmed by a tiny, numbered metal marker, half-hidden in the grass. A reserved grave between mother and son—booked for whom?

She shuddered, then turned away, finding herself face-to-face with the pair of elderly women who had stood across from her during the proceedings. Ancient twins, they were shrunken with age, unveiled but dressed in black silk from head to foot.

"She was a sweet and wonderful woman, your grandmum," said one of them. "I'm Fawn Fowler, and this is my sister Clara. We know who you are, dear." She held out a black gloved hand, displaying the grace and suppleness of a woman sixty years younger.

"You knew my grandmother?"

"Quite well."

"She looks just like her, you know," said Clara, turning to her sister. "Beautiful."

"A mirror image, if you ask me," said Fawn. "It's uncanny."

"It was a long time ago; your father was just a pup," said Clara.

The three of them turned and walked slowly toward the access road.

Clara Fowler said, "You'll come take tea with us when you get settled, dear, and we'll tell you all about your grandmother, and the good olden times."

"There was no one like her," said Fawn.

"How well did you know her?"

"Worked with her. She governed the best establishment in the British Empire, bar none."

"In the world," said Fawn.

"Establishment?"

"Well yes, dear."

"Never been anything near that sort of quality, before or since," said Fawn. "And the Lord only knows what goes on these bloody days!"

"What kind of establishment?"

"She doesn't know, poor dear," said Clara.

"Not exactly."

Clara grinned, displaying perfect dentures. "Everybody knows."

"No, Clara," said the other woman, "everybody's dead now, except us." Her short laugh was childlike.

"What do you mean?" Lesley glanced from one to the other. They were perfect duplicates.

"We mean, that since your dearest father has been taken from us, there's no one else left who was ever there."

"Except us."

"No one else who was *where?*" said Lesley, managing to keep her tone conversational.

"At the club," said Clara, "in the very house you're staying in now."

"A lovely house," said Fawn.

"Club?"

"House of assignation, dear," said Clara.

"Brothel," said Fawn.

"But we didn't use words of that sort. Everything was quite proper, as it should always be. We had a membership, nothing off the street, mind you. The finest gentlemen. There isn't a man alive today, anywhere in the world, who could even polish their shoes, our gentlemen. Half of them were listed in Burke's and the other half were the crème de la crème."

"Posh."

"Exclusive."

Lesley brought them to an abrupt stop in the path.

"You mean," she said, "that my grandmother—that lady— Elleander Morning, buried over there next to my father's fresh grave, was a hooker?"

"Hooker?"

"A prostitute? A common whore?"

They were silent for seconds, and then Fawn, her head erect, her eyes blazing with offended dignity, said, "Common indeed! Your grandmother was the most distinguished madam in all of bloody Britain!" She glanced over at the twin graves and seemed to grow six inches in the process. "If they knew what she'd done, they would have awarded her the bleeding Victoria Cross!"

"No doubt of it," said Clara.

"I didn't mean . . ." Lesley began.

"Her own flesh and blood," said Clara. "Shame, she's certainly not her father's daughter."

Clara snapped her umbrella into the crook of her arm like a brigadier on inspection. The two sisters turned in unison and proceeded in lockstep up the path, leaving Lesley standing in place, her pulse racing. She heard a movement behind her and turned abruptly to find Fred Hayworth staring at her.

"You heard all of that?" she said.

"Inadvertently." He seemed embarrassed.

"Dirty old broads," she said. Then, after a pause, "Actually, I'm sort of proud of my Grandmother Elleander. It sounds to me like she was the only one in the family with any class."

He was laughing. "Bravo, Mrs. Bauman!"

"Lesley—never ever again *Mrs. Bauman,*" she said. "I'm in the middle of my first divorce, and I want to change my name back to the same one my father and grandmother had—*Morning.* From now on, I'm Lesley Morning all over again."

He took her arm and they started toward the access road. "You seem to be in much better spirits than yesterday."

"Well, there's nothing like a nice, happy-jolly funeral to cheer up a girl, and besides, why should I feel miserable? I'm living in my grandmother's eighteen-room whorehouse along with two prematurely senile women who spend all their time mooning over a father whom I practically never knew. I've been put down by two old harlots and I face either starvation or food poisoning—pick one."

"Starvation."

"Fine, what are you doing this evening?"

"Taking you to dinner."

"Thanks, Freddy. Another meal out of Mrs. Green's pixilated kitchen would do me in for sure."

"Not first-rate, I take it?"

"Only if you go for boiled chicken, boiled cabbage, and boiled chops."

"*Boiled* chops?"

"Mrs. Green carries grief and melancholy a little too far. I haven't eaten any of it for days. I'm famished." She felt happy, a little giddy, headed up toward the top of the curve again, she thought.

He opened the curbside door of the battered Triumph. "The Savoy Grill? I don't think they boil anything there."

She mused on the similarity between him and his car. British, somewhat disheveled, lightweight, unobtrusive, but quick on its feet.

When he entered the car on his side, she reached over to impulsively kiss him. It was a brief but thorough kiss. He didn't seem to mind. For a brief moment she found herself wishing that he weren't so thoroughly homosexual. He seemed to read her thoughts and suddenly they were both laughing.

Later that night, she thought about the reserved cemetery plot. Could it be for her grandfather? Who was he? She closed her eyes and tried some mental arithmetic. Her father when he died had been seventy-two; born in 1911. Therefore, unless he had been a boy wonder, her grandfather would now have to be at least ninety-two and possibly over a hundred years old, and somewhat ancient, she thought, to be still unburied. Then, moments before she was about to fall asleep, she permitted a chilling thought to rise to the surface: Perhaps the empty grave was meant for her.

5

1983

Less than a week later, Harry Morning's will was read to the
same congregation who had attended his funeral. Mrs. Green
received a trust fund paying an annual £1,000, and Rose Parker,
"for her loyalty and superb secretarial services," was the recepient of
a like amount. The Fowler sisters received the sum of £2,500,
"in order to do what they will, in whatever naughty way suits their fancies."
The sum of £200,000 was to go to St. Verna's Benevolent Sisters
of Mercy in Woolwich.

The remainder of the estate went to Lesley Bauman, née
Morning. It consisted of three commercial properties in the West
End, the house in Mayfair and *all the contents thereof,* including a
1944 Jaguar MKIV convertible, currently sitting on blocks in a
small garage. There was also a portfolio of securities and stocks,
and a personal letter from her late father.

Later, over tea, Lesley, seated strategically between Clara
and Fawn, attempted to correct the misunderstanding that had

occurred between them at the cemetery. After a few futile minutes of this, she gave up and just apologized. It was simpler. The sisters then became very understanding. She would come to tea just as soon as they returned from their four-month round-the-world trip.

When everyone had left, Hayworth informed her that the stocks and securities she had inherited had a face value of approximately half a million pounds, or, according to the current rate of exchange, $2.5 million.

She flopped down onto the overstuffed leather couch and attempted to cope with it.

Freddy said, "Money isn't everything, you know."

"Do I still have my looks? I mean, I wouldn't want to make *that* trade, even though I know I'm going to have to pay for this with something."

"No, you still look satisfactory," he said with mock seriousness.

As she left the office, Fred Hayworth handed her the letter from her father. It was in a large, buff-colored envelope sealed with wax. She put it in her pocketbook.

Later that night, after Mrs. Green had gone to bed and Rose was safely in her room, probably, thought Lesley, doing her nails, she seated herself in the big leather armchair in her late father's study, where, under the light of a fringed Victorian floor lamp, she broke the seal on the envelope. The letter was written in precise, black chancery script.

May 5, 1968

My Dearest Daughter,
   When you read this, I will have gone to my reward.
(An archaic phrase, perhaps, but certainly no more
moss-covered than the hand that wields this pen.)
   As you know by now, I have provided for you and
have also satisfied those responsibilities I feel toward the few
others who have gained my affection. That, of course, does
little to diminish the guilt I feel as I write this. For being
less than a good father, even allowing for the difficult
geographic circumstances, I have no valid excuse. I am

*truly sorry, my daughter. You were such an adorable little
girl and, understanding myself well, I realize I will never
have the pleasure of seeing you as a beautiful woman.
Perhaps the punishment fits the crime.*

*Now I must tell you of your second legacy. It is a kind
of rebus that I pass on to you with the hope that you will
be more successful at solving it than I have been. I must
add at this point that I haven't been entirely unsuccessful,
and though I have no hard evidence, years of conjecture
have led me to a conclusion so bizarre and frightening that
I refrain from stating it, lest you think me, as they say,
starkers. Therefore, I believe it best for you to work out
your own conclusion. To get on with it:*

*I was born a bastard child of the early twentieth
century, on February 8, 1911. This auspicious event took
place in a small cottage in Cornwall, where I spent the first
few years of my life in the care, I've been told, of a nanny.
Most of the remainder I spent in the very house where you
now sit reading this letter. It was, at that time, a house of
some repute—ill repute, as they used to say. In short, my
darling daughter, a brothel. And your grandmother was its
notorious madam.*

*My mother launched herself on this illustrious purple
career just a few years before my birth. Her success was
immediate, first as a prostitute, then a mistress and
courtesan, and finally as the madam of what I've been told
was the most "important" house in London. One can only
take pride in such resolute endeavour. (I pray you join me
in this.)*

*Her amatory adventures, plus a handful of
well-advised and astute investments, proved successful
enough to provide me (and you, my daughter) with a more
than adequate education and a life devoid of some of the
harsher realities.*

*Despite her profession, and despite the fact that she
died while I was still an infant, I have always felt close to
her. She was, I assume, to the best of her ability, a good
mother. I realize you might find that difficult to accept, you
being a modern woman brought up on Freud and all that*

other nonsense (forgive me), but even as a youth I felt no animosity toward her memory, nor do I now in retrospect. This, despite the fact that I learned early not to develop friendships of any depth, as they were bound to end disastrously in embarrassment.

To put it another way: It is not generally acceptable behaviour during school holidays to invite one's friends home to a bordello to meet one's "aunts." So be it. I simply learned to live without close friends, and such lack troubles me not, even today. Women, however (your mother included), have remained a problem. I speak of course of serious *women pursuing* respectable *goals. As for the other variety, God bless them and reward them. They have fit into my life quite well as, unlike their more august sisters, they have never asked me for what I was incapable of giving. I married only because Mother's last words to them elicited a promise from my two young guardians that I do so and have children. I remained puzzled as to her insistence on continuing a blood line of such little distinction, but Fawn and Clara, in my name, had given their word and I felt a duty to honor my mother's final wish.*

On a summer morning in 1913, when I was two years old, my mother, Elleander Morning, crossed the Channel, entrained for Vienna, and there on the morning of August 15, she shot to death a twenty-four-year-old art student. Neither the police, the court, nor the press could suggest a reasonable motive for what seemed so gratuitous, and as my mother did nothing to aid them in their quest for a tidy conclusion, her crime was finally ascribed to "the result of an instantaneous mental aberration."

I found it impossible to accept that conclusion, and, at the same time, impossible to accept the idea that Mother shot a total stranger without either provocation or motive. The trial record states that she admitted to travelling from London to Vienna for the express purpose of murdering the young painter. Such premeditation usually entails motive. What motive? I was determined to find out!

According to her wishes, my mother's remains were

transported back to England, after the Great War, for burial.

I quit Cambridge and passed into official adulthood as a neurotic and relatively wealthy young man, with no living relations, and weighted down with a compulsion to solve a rather complex puzzle.

 Having come up with little more than a confusing and frightening paradox in all these years, I now pass the task on to you.

 In the larger of the two bookcases in the study, you will find a volume entitled The Intimate Diary of a London Gentleman. *When you have digested this letter, read the final chapter. Then another book on the second shelf awaits your attention: the Time-Life* History of the Second World War.

 I leave you, my dear, by quoting great words by a great Englishman who was never given the opportunity to enunciate them: "It is a riddle wrapped in a mystery inside an enigma."

Your (late) Father,
Harry Morning

P.S. Please keep an eye on Mrs. Green and Miss Parker, those two gentle souls. If you are somewhat skeptical concerning the function of Rose Parker in my household, allow me to inform you that, as an old man, I retain a residual though hardy capacity. Rose Parker is very kind.

H.M.

Lesley found she had to read the letter through three or four times before she was able to accept its reality.

She poured herself a cognac and found the books her father had spoken of. *The Intimate Diary of a London Gentleman* was a volume of 215 pages bound traditionally in moroccan leather, its cover embossed in gold leaf and its paper of a quality rarely seen these days. The Time-Life *History of the Second World War* consisted of two large-format volumes encased in a slipcase that was illustrated with photographs of a few dozen colorful flags.

She laid the large volumes aside and opened the *Diary*, thumbing through it tentatively before turning to the title page.

THE INTIMATE DIARY OF A LONDON GENTLEMAN

By "B."

Published Privately

by

The Turtle Press

Glasgow, 1910

6

1983/1910

*Being the adventures both intellectual and amatory of a young
gentleman in the most civilized of cities.*

VOLUME ONE
January 1st., 1907 to June 1st., 1910

Lesley downed the cognac remaining in her glass, then poured
another to savor. Slowly she thumbed through the book until, as
directed, she found the final chapter. She read:

CHAPTER 22

May 31st. & June 1st., 1910.

A cab ride with a mad harridan of
great beauty and sincere talents.
A sudden brainfever.
A confused and disturbing dinner with Herbert W——.

Less than a fortnight after the event in Covent
Garden, I found myself strolling The Embankment
late at night, when quite suddenly I was aware of footsteps seeming to trail my own. Footpads being not
uncommon at that place and time, I refrained from
looking back, but rather increased my pace as I turned
off toward The Strand. In moments, however, it became obvious to me that my shadow possessed a pair
of mincing female boots. Relieved, I slowed, then
turned to observe the source.

The woman, tall, with blond tresses peeking out
from the edges of a large, ornate but rather tastefully
trimmed hat, stared me straight in the eye from a
distance of less than six or seven yards. Her pace
slowed to a stop, but then, as if coming to a decision,
she resumed a purposeful but delicate tread in my
direction. She approached to within a foot of me, her
eyes continuing to lock onto my own. She was quite
brazen, straight as a dart, well turned out—a splen-
didly shaped *fille de nuit* who, it seemed to me, was of
an age somewhere between twenty-five and thirty. As
a lie to her obvious calling, her features displayed a
singular character and breeding, marked by high
cheekbones and wide, spacious eyes. I looked into
them and smiled.

"Good evening, madam," said I, my gaze descending to her lips, now gleaming wetly in the glow
of streetlights from The Strand. Her mouth, though
well formed and expressive, was a mite too full-lipped
for my taste; a minor deformity exaggerated by the
application of a coating of lip rouge. (A "high fashion"
once characterized by my American friend, Sam, as
being suggestive of clotted blood.) Nevertheless, the
rest more than made up for this trivial blemish on a
female configuration as close to perfection as any I
had ever seen.

Now much like an experienced general surveying
a future field of battle, she directed her eyes down the
length of me.

"It's so nice to see you again," she said through an asymmetrical smile of such consummate lewdness that I found myself instantaneously fetched. This, too, she noted, allowing once again her luminous eyes to travel downward.

"To see me *again,* madam?" I asked.

"Yes, it's been a while. A long . . . time."

I feel I must state at this point that I have a keen faculty for remembering both the faces and the intimate physiognomy of women I have known, even including those whose association with me have been little more than brief encounters. It is an avocation I take some pride in, a talent, actually. Therefore, it is quite inconceivable that a female such as this could have evaded my memory. It occurred to me that perhaps this was her way of legitimatizing what might otherwise be a purely commercial transaction with a total stranger. I'd play her game.

"Ah yes, I do remember now," said I. "Perhaps it is the hat . . ."

"Liar," she said softly, her voice underscored by a cryptic tonality contradicting the warm smile on her lips.

I raised my eyes to find them trapped in hers. From behind their screen of long, spiked lashes, they reflected a wisdom far beyond either her years or mine, a weird prescience that unnerved me. Then suddenly the temperate London night turned glacial. I shuddered as an inexplicable wave of anxiety washed over me, drowning in its wake even those libidinous intentions so easily aroused just moments before. I stood, bewildered for seconds or minutes, I know not which, struggling with a powerful aberration, the source of which eluded me completely. I felt as if I had just been awakened from some monstrous nightmare, already half forgotten—a déjà vu that slipped away even as I struggled to recall its horrors.

I must add at this point that at no time in my life had I ever before been subjected to sudden brain fevers, false memories, or passing fits of hysteria or melancholy. As the reader has no doubt judged by now, I possess a stability of character plus a clarity of purpose equal to any of my age and class. Nevertheless, the memory of that brief but severe dysphoria continues to haunt me! Even now, more than a month later, the recollection can cause me to pass into a state of despondency that might hold me in its debilitating clutches for hours. Yet, try as I may, I can recall none of the images or insights I experienced in that flash of time.

The whore moved closer, as if in sympathy with my mental predicament, placing a soft gloved hand on my arm and her lips within inches of mine. I had passed briefly through the cold black tunnel of inexplicable despair at great velocity and now stood, once again, in the open. I shivered briefly in wonder of it.

"I'm sorry," I said. "I honestly don't know what came over me. . . ."

Without a word she bridged the short gap separating our lips. Hers, parted in fervent submission beneath my own, were soft, pliable, intoxicating, despite the somewhat greasy texture of her lip rouge.

Shaken, I was nevertheless suddenly as randy as ever! Once again, the tail, so to speak, was wagging the dog. I forgot everything else and pressed against her, drawing her closer. To my surprise, she giggled nervously and pulled away.

"Forgive me," she said, attempting sobriety but not quite succeeding. "I don't mean to laugh, it's just that I'm reminded of something."

"May I take you home?" I asked, not sure whether the trembling in my voice was due to passion or shock.

"Certainly. Yours or mine?"

"Whichever you desire." I thought her cheeky but evocative.

"Yours, then," she said, in a voice suddenly displaying a dim Cockney undertone.

As we proceeded, I felt myself regaining control,

thrusting from my mind the momentary derangement of just minutes ago. I would deal with it later. For now, I was determined to concentrate exclusively on what I was certain would be the more rewarding events of the evening.

In a state of high excitement, I patted her arse. She appreciated the gesture, snuggling closer, pressing her hand into the small of my back.

I hailed a cab from the Savoy rank, giving the coachman my address. As we clobbered through the dark London streets, she leaned back and sighed with pleasure.

"Madam . . ." I began.

"Elleander."

"Elleander," I repeated, savoring the sweet sound of the unusual name. "Perhaps now we should dispose with amenities?"

"Ten pounds will do quite nicely."

I was astonished! "Good Lord!" I cried, sitting erect. "Not a bawd in London asks for a third of that!"

"I am not just any bawd in London."

"No doubt, you are not, madam," I said, preparing to knock on the roof of the cab to alert our coachman to stop so that she could safely disembark.

"Look at me. Tell me I'm not worth ten pounds."

I was in a snit, about to speak out again, when I felt her hand in my lap. Without a moment of hesitation, with a will of its very own, not giving even a thought to the indignant state of its sometimes proud squire, my traitorous pogo sprang up once more to attention.

"Ah . . . you see . . ." she said.

I turned to her. Never in my life had I seen such a lascivious expression grace the female countenance! If theatrically motivated, it was a performance far superior to any currently on the London boards.

"No one," she whispered, "can make love as *we* can."

I thought it an extraordinary remark for a prosti-

tute. *We!* It aroused my lust to even higher levels. The
sheer intensity of her expression convinced me of its
authenticity. Here, I thought, was a whore even *more*
than dedicated to her calling. She was a sainted rarity,
a woman who enjoyed sexual play fully and honestly
for its own sake, much like a man. As the reader of this
no doubt realizes by now, I am expert in these matters.
It is impossible for a woman, even the most talented
whore, to fool me. Even now, she was toying with the
monstrous bulge in my trousers.

From my billfold I extracted a ten-pound note.
With her left hand she hiked up her skirt, revealing a
captivating thigh of unimaginable symmetry encased
in silk to a point somewhat more than halfway up, and
gartered in the French style. She took the bill from my
hand and stuffed it under the lace.

"For our son, my darling," she said, her voice
throaty and hushed.

I disregarded the remark. I was coming to realize
that, despite her extraordinary attributes, the woman
was quite daft.

She sighed and said, "It's the same lovely prick."
Then she laughed and, squeezing affectionately, said,
with a voice like music, "Would you care to fuck me
now?"

"Here, madam? Here in the cab?"

She was a singularly frank and outspoken creature
even for a harlot, quite unusual, with a peculiar, cultivated accent. Though I usually dislike coarse-ton-
gued women, her manner now amused me.

Her perfume I recognized as L'Heure Bleu, sophisticated and Parisian. It suited her, echoing no
other scent in nature, a musky aura that spoke of the
intrigue of love. It had existed nowhere in the universe
prior to its inspired invention by man. It was unique,
and unlike purely floral perfumes, it reacted to the
mercurial chemistry of the female body. My keen ol-
factory sense told me that even now it was doing so as

her lustful juices flowed. (What other miracles will science produce in this new century!)

I was intoxicated with her, ready for anything, and the sooner the better! The mysterious and melancholy déjà vu I had suffered such a short time ago was now suppressed in my memory, at least for the present.

I reached under her skirt and fondled a smooth, pneumatic thigh. Then, while she frigged me lightly through the rough texture of my trousers, she spread her legs to accommodate my probing hand, which, now given free access, ascended through an opening in her silken French knickers all the way to the warm junction. The mons veneris was plump, voluptuous. I fingered gently. The pads of sweet moist flesh were firm and elastic—perfection, the clitoris well proportioned and, as I quickly ascertained, totally responsive (particularly on the underside of its exquisitely plump base).

A few moments of this and it dawned on me somewhat belatedly that there was no hair! What sort of fashion was this? Did whores now clip and shave their pubic tresses? If so, why?

She moaned, frigged me faster, exclaiming, "Fuck me!"

I felt the fingers of her other hand working at my trouser buttons, and in just seconds she had me free. Then, brazenly, she raised herself, hiked her skirt up around a smooth, firm, milk-white arse, then, straddling my legs, her back to me, engulfed my iron-hard tool clear to the bullocks in one swift, downward plunge!

"You bawdy devil!" I gasped, as she sat, wiggling her bum in a wide circular motion.

"Fuck . . ."

I lifted her slightly, so that I might have greater facility to drive into her from below. I could sense a rising ecstasy telegraphed through quickening tremors of her oscillating bum. A low-pitched murmur es-

caped her lips, climbed the scale rapidly, then peaked
as she called out my name! "B——!"

It was loud enough to capture the attention of the
coachman, whom I found staring down at us, a lascivious sneer distorting his features. I caught his eye, shot
him a disapproving scowl. The trap slammed shut immediately. A moment later, the carriage slowed. The
clever fellow, in an attempt to make up for his rude
voyeurism, reduced speed to give me sufficient time
with my whore and thus qualify himself for a larger tip.

The woman now descended from her plateau and
sat solidly on my lap, exercising the most extraordinary muscles I had ever encountered. It was as if a
hand were alternately clutching and unclutching, frig-
ging me at an ever increasing tempo. I had come on
such talent previously—the little Chinese tart in Lime-
house, for one, but never with the efficacious vigor
and energetic cadence of this experience. It is known
to me that such vaginal machinations are a valued
tradition in the East and that certain oriental women
spend years developing these hidden Paphian muscles, until they are capable of projecting an iron ball
to a target eight to ten feet away! There was little
doubt that the young woman who was now clipping
me with such amorous intensity could hold her own in
competition with the most gifted of her oriental sisters!

I was fast approaching the climactic moment,
grasping her tightly against me, my right hand knead-
ing mercilessly a full, firm breast (now bare), my
breath racing, my heart pounding . . . all of this without either of us moving a muscle that would be visible
to an onlooker.

"Ahh . . . you're close, B——," she whispered,
slowing the tempo while increasing the vigor and
power of each individual contraction.

"Spunk . . . fuck!" I cried as I burst deep inside
her. She twisted her body to find my lips.

It took us a few minutes to right ourselves. As I

fell back into the cornering, breathing deeply to regain my energy, she said, "Once again I have your
seed inside me."

"Once again, madam?" I was tired of her game
now, and wished to tell her so. "Once and for all," said
I, breathlessly, "we have never met!"

"Poor B——"

"I can only assume that you are familiar with my
name because you asked it of some mutual acquaintance. I was pointed out to you somewhere, probably
in the recent past. It is quite late—"

"You are," she interrupted, "twenty-seven years
old . . ." She paused, staring into space, then continued, her eyes on mine ". . . at this time. Hidden
under your whiskers is a birthmark, a large one, dia-
mond-shaped. In your sleep you twitch and snore—
quite disconcerting." She smiled briefly. "Enough to
wake a regiment!" The smile became a hearty laugh.
"You are a writer and you will soon publish all of this
in a diary. And in a few years, London will be applaud-
ing the plays you write . . . *The Remaking of Angela*,
March Hare."

I was astonished. Though her mistaken description of my sleeping habits was obviously no more
than a glib invention, and knowledge of my age easy
to come by, the mention of a birthmark represented
something much more specific. There was simply no
way she could know of it! I had worn the beard since
attaining maturity. Nor could she have obtained the
information from any of my current friends in London, for none of them had ever seen me beardless.
But most astonishing was her knowledge of this very
diary! Only one other person knew of it, my friend
Herbert W——, and he was sworn to secrecy. Then
how?

I grasped her shoulders, swung her around to me
and said firmly, "Tell me how you acquired knowledge
of my birthmark—and the diary! Through trickery, of
course, but I want to know."

I felt her fingers on my lips. "I know you more fully than does any woman in your life, past or present." Her voice was hushed, almost blending with the rumble of the cab. "Poor B—— I have a mission and I won't see you again, but I want you to know that I love you."

A few tears were washing down her cheeks, depositing black streaks of dissolved kohl around her eyes. The woman was certainly crazed, weeping over I know not what. Surely her grief was not the result of any action of mine. My behaviour had been quite correct throughout. Nevertheless, despite my earlier feelings of annoyance, I was touched. I handed over my handkerchief.

"Madam," I began, "please allow me to . . ."

"Elleander!"

"Elleander, then, may I escort you home?"

"Elleander Morning. Remember it, B——, darling." She wiped away her tears, leaving a dark smudge on her cheek.

I felt quite discomforted by her presumptions. It was time for us to part.

In order to find out where we were, I peered under the drawn curtain on my side of the carriage. The thickening fog barely revealed Grosvenor Place. The coachman, as mentioned earlier, aware of our activities in his cab, had wisely held his horse to a slow walk. He would be tipped well for his thoughtfulness, but now I desired all possible speed in order to rid myself of this madwoman.

I turned to ask her for her address. She was gone! The coach door was open. It had been seconds!

I pounded on the cab roof, ordered the driver to stop, then vaulted out the door only to find myself walled in by the impenetrable fog. In the gloom, I could hear night sounds; the hoofbeats of a nearby carriage, a foghorn on the Thames, a distant blur of coarse conversation and women's laughter. Then, barely perceptible as they dissolved into the obscure

din, the fragile *tip-tap* of her heels on the cobblestones. It would be senseless to follow her.

I stood by the cab for minutes, straining to hear
her footsteps. She'd vanished. I mused on the fact that
both my first and last sight of her had begun and
ended with this same delicate, feminine cadence. A
crazed woman and good riddance. Yet it troubled me.
Elleander Morning . . .

The following evening at my club, I spoke of the
escapade to my friend Herbert W——. "She said her
name was Elleander Morning. I remember it well because she insisted that I do so."

Herbert W—— lowered his fork, then, looking up
slowly from the as yet untouched Dover sole on his
plate, asked me to repeat her name.

"Elleander Morning," said I. "A most unusual
whore."

"In what way?" He seemed very interested. "Start
from the beginning, B——."

During the next hour, prodded constantly by
Herbert W——, I retold the story three or four times.
He asked innumerable questions, every word the
woman had said seemed important to him. Finally,
when there was nothing more he could learn from me,
he fell back in his chair to stare at the high, orna-
mented ceiling.

After demonstrating a superhuman show of pa-
tience, I broke into his brown study, saying, "Why is
this woman so important to you?"

"I knew her mother." He remained distant, his
attention riveted on the chandelier overhead, as if
hypnotized by its crystal facets.

"Pamela Morning—we had been lovers, you see.
I met her daughter—Elleander Morning—just once. It
was at the theatre, an Oscar Wilde play. It was the
child's birthday . . . her first theatrical experience. The
pretty little thing was quite excited. She wanted to be
an actress." He pushed his plate away and lifted his
wineglass. "Pamela Morning died at an early age."

"I'm sorry."

"It was a long time ago. But the daughter . . . I would have helped her if she had come to me." A look of sad confusion passed over his face. "What's peculiar about this entire episode, B——, is that I feel I *did* help her. It's a strong feeling, but for the life of me, I have no idea how or when."

Lesley lowered the book slowly. She closed her eyes for a moment, feeling that she was at an important crossroad. Either she would believe what she had just read and by doing so share in the madness, or she could discard all of it, just forget about it and get on with her life.

She flipped back through the pages: . . . *the bills from my hand and stuffed them under the lace. "For our son . . ."*

Was "B." her grandfather? She paced the room, suddenly recalling the empty gravesite between her father and grandmother. *Her grandmother, Elleander Morning.* The connection between the woman lying under the strangely inscribed headstone and the Elleander Morning in "B." 's diary was difficult to accept. Had she remembered to ask Freddy to check out the plot reservation with the cemetery management? Was it reserved for "B."?

Dumbly, her mind in a turmoil, she poured another cognac and, flopping down onto the floor, pulled one of the Time-Life volumes out of its slipcase.

Time-Life *History of the Second World War.* She stared at the title, trying to make sense of it. Underneath, in smaller type, she read: *Volume Two—Pearl Harbor to Nuremberg.* She flipped the pages of the large-format volume back to front—a kaleidoscope of war pictures. Ships, soldiers, aircraft, explosions, ruins flowed one into the other like a jerky movie montage. She paused for a sip of brandy, then glanced down again. Something had caught her eye. She thumbed the pages back to a photograph of a large passenger ship lying on its side. In the near background was New York's West Side Highway; beyond that, the skyline with the Empire State Building predominate. She sipped slowly, reading the caption: *February 9, 1942. The eighty-thousand-ton French liner Normandie is burned out at her berth in the Hudson. Sabotage was suspected but never proved. The capsized vessel, later rechristened the United States troopship* Lafayette, *was eventually scrapped.*

Lesley Morning surveyed the photograph carefully. The cars on the elevated highway seemed to be out of the proper vintage, there were no tall boxlike buildings disfiguring the cityscape. Then, looking even closer, she confirmed the caption. In barely discernible letters on the bow of the great capsized ship was spelled out the name, *Normandie.*

She stared at the photograph for minutes, rereading the caption. It was the ship she had come over on. Could there have been two *Normandies?* If that were the case, she would surely know of it. The *Normandie* was a "monument," practically a household word. Surely, if there had been a second *Normandie,* she would have heard of it, just as she would have heard of a second Nelson's Column or a second Eiffel Tower or a second Statue of Liberty. Her thoughts developed into a wave of anxious bewilderment.

She considered calling Fred Hayworth, but it was nearly four A.M. Perhaps it should wait until morning, where in the clear light a simple explanation would present itself. She was suddenly very sleepy.

In bed, Lesley's desire for sleep was overwhelmed by the anxiety of unanswered questions. She stared into the darkness, doing battle with her exhaustion. The glowing face of the bedside clock showed four-thirty when she lifted the phone and dialed Fred Hayworth.

Less than an hour later, Hayworth stood in her entrance hall, his hat dripping rain. He glared at her. "This had better be worth it!"

"I'm sure someone said that about the Rosetta Stone," she said, taking his things. She was wide awake now, relieved to have an ally, albeit a reluctant one, on the scene. Someone whose judgment she trusted, who could validate her own confusion.

In the study, he read her father's letter, then, with no comment, the last chapter of the diary. As he set it down, Mrs. Green materialized in her tattered pink bathrobe to present them with a pot of her usual misguided coffee.

Freddy said, "Your mother was right; there is a skeleton in

the closet." He sipped his coffee, grimaced, then gulped the rest. "Good God, an entire community of skeletons!"

"What do you make of it?"

"The man who wrote the diary—published it privately— might very well be your grandfather. There's something very strange about all of this. . . ." He paused for a moment, reflecting. "I think that's a gross understatement."

Lesley handed him both volumes of the Time-Life *History of the Second World War*. She watched as he thumbed through one of them, a sense of excitement displacing the confusion and anxiety she had felt earlier. It came to her suddenly, in an almost euphoric rush, that she was about to step off into a new life that would bear not the slightest resemblance to the old one. She shivered as with a chill.

After just a few minutes, Freddy Hayworth looked up. Stunned, he spoke in a voice half an octave above its usual tone. "What in the bloody hell is the Second World War!"

March 25, 1910

Jean François Reynaud
École des Beaux Arts,
Paris, France

Dear Mr. Reynaud:

My friend, Miss Elleander Morning, will once again be visiting Paris and would appreciate your arranging a collection from which she can choose. Her interest, as you must recall, centers on young artists, this time Georges Rouault, who was a student of Gustave's at the same time as was Henri.

Because she remains that rare and beautiful thing, the true patron, she will, as usual, pay at least double the asking price. (Enough said.) The third week in April will be satisfactory. If at that time I am free to do so, I will accompany her.

Yours,

John Singer Sargent

 7

1983

The following morning, Lesley caught the day's first magni-train to Glasgow. In the station she consulted the Glasgow classified phone directory but could find no listing for Turtle Press. Then, using a public telephone, she began calling at random those other publishers that were listed. On the seventh inquiry, she was successful. From Central Station it was a short taxi ride to a two-story structure that huddled protectively between an abandoned warehouse and the corpulent hulk of an omnibus garage.

The building looked as if it had received its last coat of paint sometime during the reign of George the Fifth. Now, a few large patches of flaking gray still clung bravely to an expanse of crumbling brick. There was little other adornment, except for a highly polished brass plaque on which were engraved the words:

MACFENNEL AND DART, LTD
PRINTERS
&
PUBLISHERS

The plaque hung to the right of the entrance, above which, embossed in the aging cement of a mock pediment, was the barely visible, eroded image of a turtle.

Inside, a receptionist asked her to wait, graciously offering coffee. Lesley held it while eyeing a glass case in which were displayed a dozen paperback novels bearing logos that announced them as Dartbooks. Young, garter-belted females in various postures of erotic agony illustrated such titles as *Uncle Harry's Little Girls, Hot, Wet and Ready, Passion's Septette.*

Then, minutes later, Lesley Morning was seated in the overstuffed office of Michael Dart, a somewhat husky blond in his early forties who appeared to have spent most of those years lying under a sunlamp. He was explaining that Turtle Press had been harassed to a point close to bankruptcy by the Lord Mayor's censor more than fifty years ago. They finally had been bought out by MacFennel and Sons, a predecessor to the current firm, of which, Dart was happy to state, he was now the sole proprietor. "Turtle," said Dart, "wasn't much, but they managed to survive in business for almost a century. We've got a roomful of stuff they left behind. Some of it, a few choice literary items, are quite interesting. I have a thing, you see, against tossing out old books and galleys and the like. Feels almost like it would be sinful, if you understand what I mean, and, between you and me, I might even republish some of it one day. Why not? It's all part of our British cultural heritage, and most of the copyrights ran out ages ago." Michael Dart smiled broadly, revealing a set of perfect, pearly

white caps, which, in conjunction with his light-blond hair and
deeply tanned skin, gave him the appearance of a fully exposed
photographic negative. He said, "But I really can't fathom why
anyone else would show any interest in the old firm."

Lesley explained the problem in simple terms, leaving out
some of the more dramatic details.

"I have," she said, by way of reinforcement, "a book in
search of an author."

"And now you want to know his name, is that it?" said Dart.

"If it's possible."

"It might be." He leaned back in his desk chair, making a
church steeple of his fingers. "You know, in those days there were
a large number of privately printed personal diaries. Turtle had
quite a little business going along those lines. Most of them, of
course, were what one might call intimate—some more than others."

He asked for pertinent details, then was gone for less than
ten minutes. He returned with a large, somewhat battered green
ledger. On the binding appeared the words, "Turtle Press—
Accounts 1908–1911." He set it on the desk as a deep rumble
shook the walls. The presses had started up.

Dart leafed through the book, running a thick thumb down
the pages. Within seconds, he found what he was looking for.
Wordlessly he swung the book around to his guest, his index
finger indicating a point about midway down the page. Lesley
read:

AUTHOR . . . . "B." (anonymous)
TITLE. . . . *The Intimate Diary of a London Gentleman.*
    Book One.
480 COPIES . . . . Printing and Binding
£386 . . . . Received from Bertram Trasker,
    June 25, 1910.

"Bertram Trasker . . ." Lesley breathed the name rather than
said it.

"Who was he?" said Dart. "Anyone important?"

"Very important," said Lesley. "I think he was my grandfather."

In less than an hour, she was back in Euston Station, from which she cabbed to the Time-Life Bureau on Bond Street. Their book catalogue contained no mention of the Time-Life *History of the Second World War.* She considered asking someone but thought better of it—such an inquiry, she was certain, would raise nothing but eyebrows.

At one o'clock, after a quick lunch, she kept her appointment for a haircut at Michal's. She was becoming a regular there. She wondered if her pleasure at being recognized at this and a few other establishments indicated that she was setting roots down in London.

She called Freddy to tell him the results of her research. "Bertram Trasker," she said. " 'B.' in the diary. I now know who my grandfather was, or at least I know his name. I can finally hold my head up like any other red-blooded American girl."

"Good work," said Hayworth. "That's one mystery solved. I wish I could say the same."

"The cemetery. You checked . . ."

"Yes. The gentleman in Chesington consulted his documents and informed me that the third and still unoccupied burial plot had been reserved for one Elleander Morning of 22 Highcastle Road, London."

"But my grandmother is already buried—they must have their wires crossed. . . ." She reassured herself of this, but nevertheless found that she was left with an anxious feeling about it. "A clerical mistake," she added weakly.

"The three plots were bought and paid for in 1913, according to their records, by Miss Elleander Morning, one for her son Harry and two for herself. The cemetery manager insisted that the record was quite clear. He seemed a little surprised himself."

Hayworth paused for a moment in expectation of a response. There was none. Even the sound of Lesley's breathing had stopped. "It would seem," he said, "that your grandmother expected to die twice."

BEST-SELLERS

This Week	FICTION	Last Week	Weeks on List
1	*FROM HERE TO ETERNITY* by James Jones. (Harper & Brace, $4.50) A regular army private deals with love and personal rebellion in the days just before the outbreak of the Civil War.	1	13

8

1983

Mark Kowan was forty-six years old and twenty pounds over-weight. His jogging route on this pleasant spring morning carried him across Seventy-first Street, through the park and out onto Sixth Avenue. He stopped for breakfast at the large Horn & Hardart Automat on Fifty-seventh Street, where he consumed roughly four times the number of calories he had expended en route.

At his office in Rockefeller Center, Kowan spent the next few hours viewing 420 Ektachrome slides dealing with America's re-born craze for ballroom dancing. He edited them down to just eight for a five-page feature, rushed them up to an impatient art director, and then turned to his mail.

The pile was topped with a cablegram that had arrived after he left the office the previous evening. It was a frantic request for additional expense funds from a *Life* staffer covering the fighting in partitioned Palestine. Kowan filled out a requisition for a thousand dollars to be transferred through First National City Bank to Haifa, then phoned down to Finance to make certain it was expedited.

The rest of the mail consisted of an invitation from MGM to a film preview and invoices and story ideas from free-lance photographers. *Life* magazine depended on outside suggestions for a good deal of its editorial content. At the bottom of the pile was a large manila envelope bearing a London postmark. It contained a dozen glossy eight-by-ten-inch prints and a covering letter. He leafed through the prints, then read the letter. When he had finished, he buzzed his secretary and told her to cancel his lunch date and all his afternoon appointments.

> *22 High Castle Road*
> *London W.1.*
> *England*
>
> *May 17, 1983*

Life *Magazine*
20 Rockefeller Plaza
New York, N.Y.

Dear Sir:
    The twelve photographs enclosed are copy prints from a two-volume set of books entitled The Time-Life History of the Second World War. *They are a random sampling of over three hundred images found in the books.*
    I have inquired at the Life Bureau in London regarding the books, only to find that no such title has ever appeared on the Time-Life list. The books came to me as part of a recent legacy from my father. They are obviously counterfeit. But are the photographs genuine? Most of them carry a magazine accreditation plus, in practically all cases,

*a photographer's credit. I have penciled these, and the
original captions, on the back of each print.*

*I would greatly appreciate any effort you could make to
check their authenticity. (At this point, I'm not even sure
what I mean by that.)*

Thank you,
Lesley Morning

LIFE MAGAZINE
20 Rockefeller Plaza
New York, New York

May 20, 1983

*Lesley Morning
22 Highcastle Road
London W.1.
England*

Dear Madam:
No prints or negatives of your pictures exist in the
Life *magazine files. Furthermore, two of the photographers,
Robert Capa and Eugene Smith, were shown the
photographs credited to them and both denied ever having
made them.*

*I share your confusion. If a hoax, it is certainly an
ingenious one. At first glance, the photographs show no
obvious signs of negative or positive retouching or
manipulation. Of course, we have been looking at copies of
halftone originals. Viewing the books themselves would get
us one generation closer to the original print.*

*Both I and our editor in chief, Michael Hand, are of
the opinion that there is an interesting story in this for* Life
if you would make the material available to us.

Waiting to hear from you, I remain,

Yours sincerely,
Mark Kowan
Picture Editor

Sidney Shulberg watched intently as the three astronauts made their way across the thickly powdered surface of the moon. Behind them, the blue planet Earth hung brilliantly in its second quarter against a deep-black sky punctured by a million stars. Awesome, he thought; incredibly beautiful—but not quite right. He stood up, jammed both hands into his chino pockets and called out for them to stop.

The astronauts halted in mid-stride, flopped down onto the lunar surface. It had been a long day. One of them pushed his visor up to light a cigarette.

Shulberg walked out onto the gray surface with Paddy Duff. "Christ, Paddy, you've got this lit up like midnight in Picadilly," he said.

Paddy Duff, BSC, attached the flat disk to his Spectra meter and read the key light. With ludicrous delicacy, he removed the soggy wreck of a cigar from his face. "There's no atmosphere, no skylight, no fill. It's naked sun, Sid."

Shulberg frowned at him. They had worked together on four films. Paddy had been a tough, stubborn bastard on all of them. Despite that, he was one of the best in the business, an old-timer who had started his career on this very sound stage as a nineteen-year-old "best boy," brewing tea for grips and gaffers and running errands. Since then, there had been five Academy Award nominations for photography, resulting in two Oscars that Paddy Duff kept polished and hidden in his liquor cabinet. One of them was for Shulberg's own remake of *All Quiet on the Western Front.*

Shulberg said, "What about bounce light off the ground?"

"I'm betting," said Paddy, "that even with the bounce, the ratio on the moon would still be over six to one—deep black shadows. Stark, cold and brilliant, Sid."

"Okay, but just for the long shots. After we establish it, switch to a lower ratio. We don't want to blind the audience for two whole hours . . . or do we?"

Sidney turned to the three astronauts. He explained the probable effects of one-sixth Earth gravity, then ran across the lunar landscape to demonstrate the long, hopping strides he required from them. They tried it three times before he was satisfied. With the camera cranked up to thirty-six frames per second, the awkward running gait would translate to a kind of fast, floating walk on the screen. Another educated guess.

The shop foreman warned him that just fifteen minutes remained until overtime. They executed one take, then wrapped it. It was all Shulberg needed. The following morning he would check the rushes and, if it looked all right, they would spend the next two days shooting random moon walks for intercutting.

He accepted a Havana from Paddy and collapsed into his director's chair. He needed some time to digest the fact that the months of pre-production research and design were over. They were finally running film through the camera. He looked out over Mare Nubium and wondered for the hundredth time if they had it right. They'd all know for sure in a little while. The Germans with their Project Galileo were already practicing docking maneuvers in Earth orbit and the Anglo-Americans were about a year behind. (The Japanese were nowhere in sight with their two unmanned, orbiting soccer balls.) *Moon War* was scheduled for theater release within a few weeks after the world viewed, on television, the actual first manned landing on the surface of the moon . . . if the Germans made it in one piece.

The shooting lights were killed, destroying the magic, turning a few acres of lunar landscape into just another lifeless movie set. In the artificial glare of the single worklight, a couple was treading its way toward him through the tangled spaghetti of electrical cable. Exhaling a sigh of annoyance, he remembered an appointment he had made the previous day and wondered if this could be it. A mutual acquaintance had set it up—something to do with pictures, unusual stills of some kind. The name, he recalled, was Haywood or some-such.

The man approaching him exhibited a kind of shaggy British charm that he was certain many women found irresistible—particularly foreign women, most particularly American women. And, he wagered, the woman on Haywood's arm was indeed American. She had the look of an American female: streamlined, trimmed down to essentials. Shulberg watched with appreciation as she carried herself forward with a lean, graceful stride that orchestrated an ebb and flow of soft blond hair.

They introduced themselves as Lesley Morning and Fred Hayworth. He had been close. In unmistakable Yankee tones, which won him his solitary wager concerning her nationality, she suggested that if he was amiable, it would be nice to have their discussion over a quiet supper. He agreed, pointed out that the two or three neat whiskeys that would precede it were perhaps the ideal conveyance for a pleasant voyage from the cold surface of the moon back down to good old Mother Earth. He reasoned silently that a little refreshment might also ease the tedium of having to deal with two total strangers, no matter how charming, whose interest in him was probably related to a "wonderful idea for a film" that hitherto had been moldering away for years in a Chelsea closet. He was tired. He remembered that he had agreed to the meeting simply because of a vague and probably mistaken idea that he owed their mutual acquaintance a favor.

The restaurant was a steak house in Borham Wood that looked as if it had been decorated out of stock from the Warner Brothers' property shop. Merrie Olde England was evoked in the form of dark plywood paneling and fiberglass armor. In its cool and comforting gloom, Shulberg hoped for the best as he accepted the first of his pre-dinner drinks from a dour young woman done up in a seventeenth-century wench's costume, complete with nylon-net panty hose. After a few preliminary sips he began to answer their polite questions about *Moon War*. It carried them through the prawn cocktails and halfway into the filet mignons.

He wondered if they were lovers. His own life had been an interminable strip of sprocketed celluloid stretching back through four marriages and God only knew how many affairs. Now, at sixty-one, there was time left to make a few more films and experience, if he was lucky, just one more important love affair and perhaps a little pain. He looked up from his third glass of red wine, realizing that he had already drunk too much.

Lesley Morning was staring at him out of wide-set eyes. She raised her wineglass, saying, "To your moon, Mr. Shulberg. Here's hoping that it will prove to be even more authentic than the real one."

In time-honored tradition, it was not until dessert and coffee that they came around to the matter at hand. There were twelve photographs that, even in the dim light of the tabletop candles,

Shulberg could see were unique. He ruffled through them quickly, picked out three and laid them on top of the pile.

"We'd like to know what you think of them," said Fred Hayworth.

"The light's bad."

Hayworth stole two additional candles from the adjoining tables. "All we really want to do is whet your appetite," he said.

"You have." Shulberg was studying a photograph taken from the deck of a stricken aircraft carrier. "Where did you get these?"

"They're from a book, a two-volume set called the Time-Life *History of the Second World War,*" said Hayworth. "I made photocopies myself—actually, a kind of random choice. There are, all told, about three hundred."

"Second World War?" He laughed. "I'm not unfamiliar with the first." He glanced down at the pictures. In the near foreground a damage-control party was attempting to deal with the flaming carnage on deck. Beyond them, the midday sky was mottled with ugly black puffs of flak. A single-engined monoplane was falling toward the sea, trailing a quarter mile of white smoke.

"This is a combat photograph from the Russo-Japanese War of 1953." He looked up at Hayworth. "It is, isn't it?"

"No," said Hayworth. "I looked it up. There were no Soviet aircraft carriers at the battle of Tatar Strait and no hits on any of the Japanese flattops. The Russians lost all their ground-based aircraft to Japanese preemptive strikes and their big guns were never in range."

"So this is a photograph of a naval battle that never took place?"

"Captions are on the back," said Lesley. "I copied them from the original."

Shulberg turned the picture over. He read the handwritten caption twice, then, confused, looked up at Hayworth. "The *Lexington,* that's got to be an American ship. They name their carriers after historical battles. And the Coral Sea is somewhere in the central Pacific. What is all this in aid of?" He wondered if someone had prepared a monstrous joke on him. But who? And why?

Lesley studied him over the rim of her coffee cup. Some of Shulberg's films had been considered classics when she was barely in high school: *The Big Money, Doctor Faustus, Gettysburg, Falcon of France*. And later: *One Hundred Years of Solitude, Messalina, The Trial of Mata Hari, Absalom, All Quiet on the Western Front*. He had retained, she noted, most of his hair and, despite a softening of once craggy features, a fair portion of his good looks. He seemed to her a bitter man, sad, she thought, despite his success. She felt a pang of sympathy. She said, "The books were in my father's library. I don't know where they came from originally; they might even be some sort of hoax. At least that was our first thought. But I'm beginning to think differently. They're too massive an undertaking for that, too well done. The two books have the look and feel of authenticity." She smiled, encouraged by the look of interest on his face. "When you see them, I'm sure you'll agree. There are seven hundred and fifty pages of pictures, maps and text, all beautifully printed and reproduced . . . but none of it ever happened."

"The text," said Hayworth, "is well-written history, all of it; tactics, politics, strategy, the lot. All done up as if someone had conducted years of research."

"We feel you can help," said Lesley. She leaned forward, the candlelight causing her eyes to gleam.

"How?" He felt intrigued by her beauty and wondered again if Hayworth was her lover.

"Well, most of your films depend on projecting an authentic sense of time and place; the sights and sounds, the real essence of past events." She paused to glance at Freddy.

"It's simple, Mr. Shulberg," he said. "We need an expert, someone who can examine the pictures and determine if they've been doctored; created through the use of miniatures or models, or with special photographic effects—trick photography or whatever you chaps do. Are the people in the photographs real participants, or are they actors playing parts? In short, are the pictures authentic? You're the expert, the only one available to us."

"By authentic, do you mean photographs of actual happenings?"

"I'm not sure what I mean."

"But they couldn't be authentic. . . ."

"Suppose you determined that they were?"

"Then I'd assume I was mistaken." Shulberg gulped his

drink. He was doing his damnedest to remain skeptical but was failing at it. He realized suddenly that Hayworth was homosexual, then briefly wondered what had given him away.

"Sidney," said Lesley, using his given name for the first time, "could any of these be movie stills?"

He shuffled through them again. "I don't think so. I not only make movies, I also see a lot of them. Not one of these is familiar to me." He shuffled through them again. "None of them. This one, for example . . ." He picked up another one. It showed a flotilla of warships dotting the horizon. Peculiar-looking boats were debarking men and machines down lowered ramps into a shallow surf amidst a forest of deadly, spiked objects that looked like monstrously scaled-up children's jacks. Dead soldiers lay in grotesque attitudes at water's edge while live ones rushed forward or sought cover on the rocky beach. "Extras," he said. "If that's what these chaps are." He bent forward to examine the photograph closer. "I've never had any working for me who were this good. I mean these chaps are actually being shot at with real bullets!" He laughed. "I wonder what the Screen Actors Guild would have to say about that?"

"You mean it's not from a movie," said Hayworth.

"Not from a theatrical film; I'd wager anything on that." He leaned back in his chair. "There are thousands of men on this beach and all kinds of expensive paraphernalia and pyrotechnics. In this light it's hard to tell if it's a process shot, but one way or another, it would have been a major production with a huge budget. I'd certainly know about it. It would look familiar. As far as I know, there's never been a war movie that looked like this. The nearest anyone's come to this sort of seaborn invasion in film was David Lean's *Gallipoli*, but that was totally different—uniforms, weapons, all World War stuff, circa 1915. The ships were different and there were horses." He struck the table with his hand, almost upsetting his glass. "Damnedest thing I've ever seen!"

"I'm glad you think so," said Lesley brightly.

Sidney Shulberg turned the photograph over to read the caption on the back: "Fortress Europe is finally breached as men of the U.S. First Infantry Division land on Omaha Beach on the coast of Normandy during the early morning hours of June 6,

1944." He set the print down on top of the others and laughed
humorlessly. "I was in Europe in 1944, and the only Americans
invading France that year were tourists fighting their way into the
fleshpots of Paris." He laughed again. "It's absolutely crazy!"

"Everything has an explanation," said Lesley, adding
weakly, "I think . . ."

"But they're asking too much. The chap who concocted all
of this would have us believe that the Americans, bent on world
conquest, attempted to make a colony of France!" He raised both
hands to the level of his face, palms outspread, as if asking God
for confirmation. "Worse yet, it seems that in the process they
went around naming French coastal areas after provincial inland
towns in Kansas!"

"Nebraska, I believe," said Hayworth. "And the Americans
were not at war with the French. The common enemy was Germany, just as it was in the Great War."

"That's a relief, I must say." Shulberg realized he had taken
a liking to both of them.

They ordered cognac with their coffee.

Hayworth continued. "According to our Time-Life *History of
the Second World War,* France and England went to war with Germany after the German invasion of Poland. The Hun came
through Belgium, same as in 1914, but this time they were successful. Paris fell and France capitulated."

He paused for a moment to sip his coffee, then went on to
recount the rest of it. At one point, during the Battle of Britain,
Sidney Shulberg broke in with a toast to "our gallant boys in
blue," and at another, Lesley interrupted to correct a mistake in
the sequence, pointing out that Germany invaded Russia *before*
the Japanese surprise attack on the American fleet in Hawaii.

Afterward, Shulberg said, "Not a bad bit of fiction, though
there are a few odds and ends that stretch the imagination. You
say the books have the Soviets defeating massive German armies.
That's a joke. In real life the poor Ruskies even had problems
defeating little Finland, and a decade or so later, they lost deci-
sively to the Japanese in only fourteen days! And then there's the
idea of Britain and Communist Russia as allies. Who were the
respective leaders?" He was aware now that he was actually taking the whole thing seriously.

"Churchill and Stalin."

"Winston Churchill?"

"Old Winnie himself."

"Unthinkable! It doesn't even make for good fiction. Winston Churchill in bed with Stalin? It would be just as easy to believe in Britain changing sides and allying itself with the Germans!"

"If you consider the nature of the enemy . . ." Hayworth reached out, leafed through the photographs, and laid one on top of the pile. "There was no question as to who was the lesser of two evils."

Shulberg stared at the picture in the flickering candlelight. He spoke in a quiet voice. "Good God! What is it? Who were they?"

"Jews," said Lesley. "European Jews."

Shulberg read the caption on the back and then once more turned the print over and studied it closely. They were real people, not actors or models. He was sure of it. He felt his stomach turn over. Finally, he said, "This has ceased to be funny. . . ."

"It never was," said Lesley Morning. "There are more photographs like that. In my father's books there is a man named Hitler who ruled Germany . . . he attempted to wipe out the Jews and nearly succeeded. He murdered six million. It's unbelievable, yet the pictures are so real that once you see them you're haunted. It's grotesque. Help us figure it out, Sidney." She laid her hand on his arm.

"I think you should see the books," said Hayworth quietly.

"Where are they?"

"In my office safe."

"I must say I'm intrigued." His excitement was tinged with a peculiar apprehension. "You make it sound like it all happened. It's insane. . . ."

"It would be less so," said Lesley, "if we could figure out where it all came from, or, as you asked earlier, what it's all in aid of."

They drove to the West End in two cars. Seated next to Shulberg in the front seat of his big American Lincoln, Lesley told him all about her father's letter and the diary. He remained curiously quiet. In Hayworth's office he spent the night leafing through the two books. Shortly before dawn he looked up and, every bit the movie director, set the course of their action. Hayworth was to make the books available to a photographer who, on orders from Shulberg, would make slide copies of the photographs from both volumes. They were also to Xerox the entire text. Before he left, he suggested the need for additional expert opinion. Lesley agreed.

"In that case," Shulberg said, "I intend to recruit four new members into our exclusive little club." His eyes were red from lack of sleep and from too much booze. "There must be a rational explanation for all of this. If we can't find it, I'm simply going to conclude that I've been hallucinating . . . and I think you should also." He laughed, then sobered. "On second thought, I think not. Only a raving lunatic could even begin to imagine some of these horrors." He tapped the two volumes with his knuckles.

"The strange thing," said the angel, "is the readiness of you human beings—the zest with which you inflict pain. Everyone seems to be giving pain."

"Or avoiding it," said the Vicar.

"Yes, of course. They're fighting everywhere. The whole living world is a battlefield—the whole world. We are driven by pain."

—H.G. Wells
The Wonderful Visit

9

1983

The meeting took place on Saturday afternoon two weeks later. First to arrive at the house on Highcastle Road were Sidney Shulberg and Paddy Duff.

The two of them, steering clear of Mrs. Green's tea sandwiches, proceeded, drinks in hand, to set up a Carousel slide projector and screen.

The other guests arrived within the half hour. First of these was retired Field Marshal Rudolph von Seydlitz, ex-chief of the German General Staff. Lesley, feeling Seydlitz's dry, inflexible lips on the back of her hand, was amused by his ruthless polish. His body, locked into an erect Prussian stance, was spare, efficient, seemingly that of a much younger man. He was, she conjectured, the type of hatefully imperious male who never sweated, who could clean a stable and then emerge as he had entered, immaculate, his tailoring crisp, his manicure unblemished.

Gallantly correct, the field marshal passed Lesley's hand to

Brigadier James Entwistle, who held it weakly for a moment, as if it were some particularly unappetizing breed of fish. The brigadier was a loose-limbed Englishman whose ungainly height was at least partially offset by a permanently hunched posture. It was, thought Lesley, a most unmilitary bearing, brought on, according to Sidney Shulberg, by ducking little else but low-flying chandeliers.

Then she was introduced to Paul Bauer. He smiled, took her hand. She found him an attractive man she judged to be in his early forties. She glanced down, taking momentary pleasure in the sight of her hand in his. They seemed complementary. His was well used, the hand of an active, vital man. Yet it was nicely groomed, possessing long, sensitive fingers.

"I'm afraid," he said, "that I'm by way of being an uninvited guest. The field marshal insisted I come."

"It's nice to have you."

"Thank you," he said. "I was told we're going to look at some old photographs. I have a kind of interest in that sort of thing."

She felt vaguely self-conscious and wondered why. "You're a photographer. . . ."

"No. I wish I were." He smiled broadly, emphasizing strong laugh lines. "I'm the information officer at the German Embassy."

"I would have taken you for an Australian."

"Australians usually think I'm a Yankee." The broad smile continued to animate his face. "And my compatriots have accused me of speaking my native language with a British accent." His wide blue, questioning eyes locked with hers for a moment, then descended to her lips. "You have a lovely house."

"Thank you." She found herself approving of his shaggy tweed jacket, his striped shirt, red tie and cavalry-twill trousers. "You're a good friend of Field Marshal von Seydlitz?"

"He's my uncle."

They were interrupted by Mrs. Green, who insisted on consulting Lesley about tea. It was then she noticed that Paul Bauer still held her hand. She removed it gently, smiling at him, charmed at the slight blush in his cheeks as he too became aware of it.

Last to arrive was Frances J. Boardman. Shulberg met her at the front door, kissing her affectionately on the cheek.

Lesley, who had imagined the well-known historian to be a remotely austere matron—portly, tweedy and sensibly shod—was pleasantly surprised to find herself being introduced to a somewhat petite, outgoing woman who sported a tasteful beige knit dress that showed off a trim, athletic figure. Frances Boardman's face, which at the moment exhibited an open smile, was modestly made up, maturely attractive and framed by carefully coiffed silver-gray hair. Lesley took an immediate liking to her.

In just over a decade, Frances Boardman had written three best-sellers, an impressive feat for a historian. Each had earned her critical acclaim and even grudging praise from some of her more academic peers. *The Humbled Obelisk*, which dealt with a defeated Germany after the Armistice of November 1918, had won her the Pulitzer Prize. It was while working on this, her first major book, that she had met Brigadier Entwistle in his capacity as associate curator of the Imperial War Museum. Subsequently, the research facility had, on many occasions, proved invaluable to her. The brigadier himself had been consistently helpful. He was, she acknowledged, a brilliant tactician, despite the fact that he had never heard a shot fired in anger. She had met neither Rudolph von Seydlitz nor Paul Bauer before, but she recalled that Sidney Shulberg had spoken of the German officer's helpfulness in clearing a way through a maze of Luftwaffe restrictions to enable him to view, first-hand, the German space effort, Project Galileo.

Now, Frances Boardman sipped tea and wondered about the contents of the sandwich in her left hand. She looked up, momentarily startled by Von Seydlitz's head, hovering just inches from her own. He was seated casually on the arm of her chair, smiling from a face that was minimally fleshed, its skin stretched tautly over delicate bones.

"It has been my pleasure, Miss Boardman, to have read all of your books."

She thanked him, wondering at the source of her distaste as he engaged her in inconsequential small talk. Germans, she thought. She had never felt this way about them before. It was, she realized, a newborn prejudice, engendered by the books.

Shuddering inwardly, she recognized the bizarre unreality, but was still unable to shake the revulsion.

Just a week earlier, the package of Xeroxed pages had been delivered, via special delivery, to her home on Philadelphia's Rittenhouse Square. Sid Shulberg's covering letter projected a sense of urgency. She took it seriously. He was one of her very few close friends.

> *Sweetheart [he wrote],*
>> *A two-volume set of books, entitled the Time-Life* History of the Second World War, *is here Xeroxed. The books represent a complete history of a war that never occurred. Comprehensive, my sweet. Monumental!*
>> *They were part of a legacy from her father to an attractive young lady named Lesley Morning, who has not an inkling as to their actual origin. Nor have I. The Time-Life people are also mystified, though the book carries their imprint. (Copyright 1970.) There is no evidence of any other copies having surfaced.*
>> *Your guess is as good as mine. Someone has gone to a good deal of trouble. Why? Read it right now, then ring me up.*
>
>> *Love,*
>> *Sid*
>
> *P.S. Sorry about the pictures, they don't take well to Xeroxing. You'll have to see the real thing in the books when you get to London.*

She had read far into the night, slept a few hours, then arose shortly before dawn. Sustained by little more than a pot of strong coffee, she spent the next day reading in her garden. She was bewildered by the text. Its tempo of events was just too haphazard, too irregular, to have been orchestrated out of the raw material of a writer's ordered imagination. She had to remind herself constantly that what she was reading was not the actual panoramic history of a monstrous war, but was indeed fiction—an awesome work.

By evening, Frances Boardman was finding it almost impossible to keep herself from believing in the factual reality of what she knew to be a nonevent. The conflict depressed her. Later in bed, she suffered nightmares based on the partially solarized, indistinct, Xeroxed photographs. The holocaust . . .

She awoke in a sweat, her mouth dry, acrid-tasting. A dull headache stayed with her for most of the morning.

She spent the afternoon and evening of the third day re-reading what she considered to be key portions of the books, and then, sometime after nine o'clock, in a fit of confused petulance, she dialed London. Sidney Shulberg greeted her out of a sound sleep.

"You read it?" he said, muttering through a fit of wake-up coughing.

"Yes. What are you up to, Sidney? What in the hell is this all about?"

"You just read what it's all about. You know as much as I do."

"It's a film scenario."

"C'mon, Fran, you know better than that. And what are you so bloody angry about?"

"It's a joke, a bad joke that you're pulling on the writers, or somebody."

"Not a joke. Try again, darling."

She was silent for a moment, then, in a small voice: "I feel there's a Rasputin in the works somewhere."

"It's only a book."

"No . . ."

"You've got to come here to see the original."

"Sidney, there's something wrong about this. I'm a historian. I can tell the difference between history and fiction. Those books are impossible, they're neither one nor the other . . . or maybe they're both. Jesus! What in the hell are you up to?"

"Come to London, Frances, I need your help with this project."

"Project?"

"Yes. I want to get to the bottom of this damned thing."

"So do I. . . ."

Over the next few days, Frances Boardman studied the text, accumulating copious notes in the process, in much the same way she prepared research for her own books. On Thursday she

Xeroxed her notes and also made another copy of the Xeroxed books themselves. These she packed along with her clothes in two small suitcases, locking one set of copies in her desk drawer. Then, early Friday morning, Frances Boardman cabbed down Broad Street to Philadelphia's International Marine Air Terminal, where she caught Imperial Airways' daily nonstop jet to London.

Now she sat in Lesley Morning's warmly furnished sitting room, staring at her old friend Sidney Shulberg. The affection she felt for him had its roots twenty years in the past, when for a short time they had been lovers. Since then, despite a hundred stormy disagreements, they had remained intimate friends. She watched him now as he stood before them, speaking much in the manner of a teacher at his podium. He was, she thought, aging well, not a sign of paunch, jowls or baldness. Hurrah for Sidney, she thought.

"You will be seeing," said Sidney Shulberg, "eighty slides, edited down from roughly three hundred we made from the halftoned originals published in a set of two books. Field Marshal, you and Brigadier Entwistle, and you, Mr. Bauer, have not seen the books yet. Bear with me; you'll see them soon. But first, the pictures. I want you to view them with no pre-conditioning —cold. Your reactions and opinions are important. None of us who have seen them have any idea where the books came from, or why and how they even exist." He glanced at Von Seydlitz, who nodded, a tight grin of acknowledgment creasing his face. "The question is, are these photographs authentic? And if they are, how can they be?"

Fred Hayworth walked through the room, clicking off lamps. In the dark, Lesley felt a growing excitement as she switched on the projector, then pushed the forward button. The first slide flashed onto a seven-foot screen at the other end of the room. Lesley focused, causing the image to coalesce into a black-and-white photograph of three aircraft in V formation as seen from above.

"Spitfires," said Brigadier Entwistle. "Lovely birds, they were."

"What year would you say it was?" said Shulberg.

"Let's see . . . the RAF had a few squadrons of them from

about 1940 until '54 or '55. Marvelous machines, beyond a doubt
the best fighter of its day. Royal Navy used them too. Wizard scale
models here, I must say."

Paul Bauer said, "Model aircraft? Miniatures?"

"Couldn't be anything else," said the brigadier. "Color's all
wrong, unit markings never existed, and those eight guns would
have torn her wings off in real life."

Lesley Morning flicked on her penlight and read, "August
1940: Spitfires of Number Nineteen Squadron rise to meet the
enemy. The Supermarine Spitfire and Hawker Hurricane—see
opposite page—formed the gallant backbone of British defense
during the Battle of Britain."

After a pause, Entwistle, his voice quiet, said, "Hawker Hurricane? No such thing. Hawker Aircraft went out of business in
1940." Then, "What's the Battle of Britain?"

"Air battle," said Frances Boardman.

The screen was lit with a different picture now; a group of
three figures involved in what seemed to be amiable conversation. Behind them on the tarmac was a line of single-engined
aircraft.

"They're German," said Entwistle. "The Maltese Cross
. . . but what in the devil are they?"

"Field Marshal?" said Shulberg.

"I must admit to ignorance," said Von Seydlitz, "though I
am, of course, familiar with the old British Spitfire. The new
Luftwaffe purchased some in the late forties and I myself flew
them. But these . . ."

"Curious insignia on the tail surfaces," said Paul Bauer.

"*Hakenkreuz*—crooked cross," said the field marshal. "Austrian, I believe, though I've seen it in photographs taken in Germany during the twenties."

In the semidarkness, Frances Boardman uncrossed her legs,
leaned forward. "It was the Kapp Putsch, 1920 or '21. The Er-
hardt Brigade wore it on their helmets."

"Ah yes," said Von Seydlitz.

"Indians," said Lesley. "American Indians."

"That's true," said Boardman. "Though I don't recall the
particular tribe. But it's always been around. The Trojans
marched under the crooked cross. The ancient Chinese, the

Egyptians, the Buddhists used it to decorate their tombs and temples and artifacts. In the books it's referred to as a swastika."

Von Seydlitz had risen from the settee and was standing a few feet from the screen, staring at it intently. "The man in the center, the one holding the baton—that's Göring, Hermann Göring."

"Familiar," said Paul Bauer. "You mean the German ace from the 1914 War?"

"Hermann Göring took over the Flying Circus when the Red Baron was shot down in 1917. After the war he married a wealthy Swedish woman, moved to Sweden."

"I guess the fat came from good living."

"Göring," said Von Seydlitz, "was a drug addict. I believe the corpulence was a result of his cure. I saw him in person once when he returned to Germany for a reunion. I was a youngster at the time, in love with flying, and he was one of my heroes. He died in an auto accident, three or four years later, long before this picture could have been made. If you are looking for proof of fakery, Sidney, you now have it."

"Why," said Shulberg, "do you say *before* this picture could have been made?"

"The photograph gives itself away. Göring was killed in 1929. The aircraft in the background of this photograph are definitely too advanced for that year. There were no production cantilevered monoplanes of this type. Much too modern— fighter aircraft like these were not even on the drawing boards in 1929."

Lesley Morning asked, "Is there anyone else in the photograph familiar to you?"

"Ernst Udet, on Göring's left," said Von Seydlitz, once again approaching the screen. Then, after a pause, "And that young officer there on the right . . . I've seen him somewhere."

"It's you," said Shulberg.

The German officer's laugh was like a strangled cough. "Preposterous!"

"Why?"

"Because this young man seems to be about thirty years old. He's standing next to Göring—talking to him. Hermann Göring was dead before I reached the age of twenty. I could never have posed for such a photograph. And, I must add, neither have I ever worn such a uniform."

"But it does indeed look like you, old man," said the brigadier, chuckling.

Once again Lesley read from her caption sheet: "Reichsmarshal Hermann Göring, head of the Luftwaffe (center), Ernst Udet (right), and General Rudolph von Seydlitz confer at a forward air base in France, during the Battle of Britain. The fighter planes in the backround are Messerschmitt Bf 109s, the mainstay of the Luftwaffe Fighter Arm at that time."

"Someone," said Von Seydlitz, "possesses a grotesque sense of humor. But I must say, I find it quite fascinating. I'll go along with the joke, yes? What year was this supposed to be?"

"Nineteen hundred forty," said Lesley. She found herself perversely pleased with Von Seydlitz's obvious confusion.

"Ah, yes. Then that's Hermann Göring up there, ten years after his death, speaking with me, who had never even met him, in front of an entire squadron of fighters that never existed!"

"According to the text," said Frances Boardman, "you took over command of Fighters after the deaths of Udet and Molders."

"Incredible! I must tell Herr Udet the good news. He's a jolly old man living in Dortmund now. How did he die?"

"Suicide."

"And Molders?"

"Crashed."

"You seem to know all about it, madam."

"I went over the books thoroughly."

"You'll have the same opportunity," said Shulberg. "Quite soon."

Brigadier Entwistle's high-pitched voice pierced the darkness. "I say, about this so-called Battle of Britain—who won it?"

"Britain."

"Capital!"

"Ah," said Von Seydlitz, "these ridiculous books you speak of must have been written by a Britisher, no?"

"They were published in America."

"Well then, birds of a feather, as you say."

To Frances Boardman, the field marshal's accent seemed even more guttural than usual. She muttered, "Thank God," exchanging smiles with Lesley, who was the only person near enough to hear the remark.

Paddy Duff stepped up to the screen, examined it closely. "The reproduction is good. It looks like a standard hundred thirty-three dots to the inch, and I can make out the grain quite easily."

"The photograph is most certainly a paste-up," said Entwistle. "Trick photography of some kind."

Paddy Duff, inches from the screen, said, "It's not a paste-up. Hair is very well defined against the background and the grain pattern is continuous right through the three heads. And it's not rear projection. This flat overcast foreground lighting would have degraded the projected background image. And there's no hairline shadow around the foreground subjects, which would indicate front projection. I'd bet a fiver it's authentic."

"Nevertheless," said Von Seydlitz, "it must have been counterfeited in some way—probably actors in makeup."

Next was an aerial shot, taken from what appeared to be two or three thousand feet. The screen reflected a few square miles of total urban destruction. The burned-out skeletons of building blocks alternated with areas of mountainous debris. Here and there an untouched structure, a church or commercial building, stood as a sullen monument in a wasteland of rubble from which wisps of gray smoke climbed into a dirty sky.

There was a stunned silence as Lesley read, "The result of the first fire storm in history. Hamburg, shortly after being visited by one thousand aircraft of the RAF Bomber Command on the night of July 29, 1943."

Brigadier Entwistle, in a voice higher-pitched than usual, said, "Good Lord . . . a thousand bombers! Someone was having a nightmare!"

"It's a model," said the retired field marshal.

"Maybe," said Sidney Shulberg. "But if it is, it's the best and most detailed I've ever seen."

"I don't think you'd see smoke acting like this in miniature scale," said Paddy Duff.

"Rubbish," said Entwistle. "Amateurish fiction. Everyone knows that in 1943, the entire British Empire, from Gatwick to Rangoon, could not have flown even five hundred aircraft off the ground—RAF, Royal Navy, the lot." He turned to Von Seydlitz for confirmation. "And you could have thrown in British Imperial Airways."

The German nodded. "There's no doubt that our friend, Herr Shulberg, is having a bit of fun with us." In the dim light from the screen, Von Seydlitz's smile was a tight grimace activating deeply etched lines of dissent around his mouth. "These are, of course, stills from a film he is making. Isn't that correct, Sidney?"

"You know exactly what film I'm making," said Shulberg. Lesley advanced the projector to the next slide. It was a photograph taken from the deck of a stricken aircraft carrier, the same picture Shulberg had first seen in the restaurant two weeks earlier.

"Obvious fake," said Entwistle. "There has never been, in naval history, as much as a single hit scored on an aircraft carrier. Sidney, you are having us on!"

"Maybe it's a montage," said Paul Bauer. "Or what you film people call a process shot."

While the others discussed it, Paddy Duff examined the screen. He turned in the light of the projector, black puffs of flak mottling his face. "I doubt it's a process shot. There's no softening of the line where a mask would have been. As for the possibility of a montage, or the use of two or more negatives, despite the halftone screen I can still see the original grain quite clearly. It's uniform across the entire photograph, background to foreground. There's no secondary pattern. This picture was made on the scene, on one piece of film."

"Grain?" said Entwistle.

"Grains of silver that make up the photographic image. Some photographic emulsions are course-grained, some are fine-grained. This picture was made on a film that was moderately coarse-grained. My guess is Eastman's old Super X. If two or more photographs had been combined—montaged—the grain pattern would be broken up where they meet. There'd be an unevenness. There isn't here. No, it looks like some bloke just picked up a thirty-five millimeter camera and took the picture."

"It could be a model."

"No," said Paddy Duff. "The foreground and background

are sharply focused. A miniature shot this close could never carry focus back to those attacking aircraft. Depth of field would be much too shallow at any usable f stop."

"Then," said Paul Bauer, "it's a picture of a naval battle that never took place?"

"It took place in a film," said the brigadier. "It's obviously from some movie or other, despite what Mr. Duff says."

"Have any of us seen this movie?" asked Lesley.

There were a few minutes of silence. Then, in precise cadence, Field Marshal von Seydlitz said, "It's time for Herr Shulberg to tell us exactly what it is we're looking at."

"We are looking, gentlemen, at the Second World War," said Sidney Shulberg quietly. "From 1939 to 1945."

"Aha! A second world war!" said Brigadier Entwistle, cackling. "Then one can assume that there might be a third, a fourth, even a fifth world war? And what of the Second War of the Roses? That must also be an interesting book. I'd like to reserve a copy."

Disregarding Entwistle's joviality, Von Seydlitz asked, "I assume this book is not in general circulation?"

"There's only one copy, as far as we know."

"What's the copyright date?"

"Nineteen seventy," said Shulberg.

"Through the looking glass," said Paul Bauer.

Entwistle, somewhat sobered now, said, "Then what is this all about?"

"We have present in this room a considerable body of military, historical and photographic expertise," said Sidney Shulberg. "Between us, I hope to reach some sort of conclusion regarding the source of these photographs—and the text too, of course."

A photograph of the Champs-Élysées flashed on the screen. The broad avenue was filled, curb to curb, with ranks of soldiers caught in mid-goose-step. In the background, the Arc de Triomphe.

"The helmets—German troops," said the field marshal. "And the flags, the *Hakenkreuz* again—what did you call them?"

"Swastikas," said Lesley.

Paddy Duff stepped up to the screen. "This one doesn't look manipulated either."

"Impossible . . ."

"Paris was occupied," read Lesley, "on June 14, 1940, by troops of General von Kuechler's Eighteenth Army. Here, victorious German troops marched down a Champs-Élysées empty of Parisians. It was to be the start of a long and agonizing occupation."

Lesley Morning said, "Poor Paris . . . what a horrid fate."

"Worse than death," said Frances Boardman.

"Frances, it's only a book," said Shulberg.

"I know . . . I find that hard to remember."

"So do I," said Lesley quietly, feeling herself drawn to the older woman.

"The text," said Frances Boardman, "is just so damned matter-of-fact about background events of which we have no knowledge. And, as in real life, so much is left unresolved. It just doesn't read like fiction. It's journalism. I know that sounds ridiculous, but . . ."

"I believe, madam," said Field Marshal von Seydlitz, "you are taking this too seriously. I haven't seen it yet, but it is, after all, as Sidney said, just a book. It is a very clever book, no doubt, written in obvious jest by a talented and cunning fellow."

"No," said Frances Boardman. "The book was not written by one person. My feeling is that there were a dozen writers— possibly even more. The writing style changes from chapter to chapter." She paused to light a cigarette. The flame from her Zippo cast flickering highlights onto her face, causing her eyes to gleam as if they themselves were projecting some inner radiance. "The text has the feeling of having been put together under strong editorial control, making use of researchers, writers, historians and reporters who were on the scene."

"I hadn't thought of that," said Shulberg, "but you're right. And now that you mention it, the photographs also vary. Some have a modern photo-journalistic look, others are formal studio portraits, old-fashioned newspaper flashbulb shots, professional aerial photographs, even a few amateur snapshots, as if made by soldiers on the scene. The books, as you will soon see for yourselves, could not have been the work of one individual, no matter how cunning."

Lesley Morning, staring at the older woman, felt a chill ascend her spine. She said, "And there are those words that are used over and over again, like *GI . . .*"

"What's GI?" said Bauer.

"American soldiers."

"It replaced the term *doughboy,* from the 1914 war," said Fred Hayworth. "But I don't know what the letters stand for."

"There are others," said Frances Boardman. "At least twenty or so, all undefined. The writers seem to take it for granted that they are in common usage. It's as if the books had been written for a public that possesses an underlying body of knowledge unknown to us."

"*Jeep, napalm, genocide, blockbuster, snafu,*" said Lesley. "The definitions become clear as you read on."

"What in heaven's name is jeep?" said Entwistle.

"The jeep," said Frances Boardman, "was a marvelous little American-made four-seater vehicle, very maneuverable and versatile and, from what I gather, practically indestructible. There must have been millions of them used by the Allies—British, Chinese, Free French, Free Poles, Russians and others. But essentially it was basic transportation for the American GI—it was his horse."

"*Nazi* was quite important," said Lesley. "At first, just thumbing through the books, I got the impression that the word referred to some country or other that I'd never heard of. There were terms like 'Nazi panzer division,' and 'Nazi concentration camp.' I thought they referred to a Naziland or Nazi Republic. Of course, after a few minutes of reading, it becomes clear that 'Nazi' is simply synonymous with the word 'German.' "

"It was a derisive term?" said Paul Bauer.

"Depended on what side you were on, I guess," said Lesley.

Frances Boardman said, "The Germans themselves invented it. The word is actually an acronym for the National Socialist party, which ruled the country under a man named Adolf Hitler. For thirteen years, Germany was Nazi Germany and Adolf Hitler was its god."

Lesley advanced the projector.

It was a full-length photograph. The subject wore a military uniform; head high, heels together, hands clasped in front as if protecting his groin.

In a louder voice than usual, Brigadier Entwistle called out, "Begad, Sidney, someone is pulling our leg! The man's a bleeding double for Charlie Chaplin!"

"You'll change your mind about that when you read the books."

"You're really beginning to believe this claptrap!"

"Don't be silly, James," said Shulberg. "It's just that some of the facts have made me, well, a little nervous."

"Facts? What bloody facts? This business is beginning to send you round the bend!" Entwistle turned to Frances Boardman. "That applies to you too, old girl. And as for facts, the only one I can see clearly is that fact on the screen, that face. This man is a music-hall turn, if you ask me." The brigadier slapped his thigh. "Adolf . . . what's-his-name?"

"Hitler."

"Ridiculous."

Frances Boardman ignored him, staring fixedly instead into the deep-set eyes of Adolf Hitler. She was aware that Brigadier Entwistle's attitude, despite its stridency, was rational. Hers, she realized, was not. She felt herself being drawn progressively deeper into a nonexistent world whose palpability frightened her.

Von Seydlitz was speaking. She caught the word "napalm," turned in her chair to find him staring at her questioningly, his bald head gleaming in the semidarkness like a nodule of polished wood. She heard herself say, "Napalm was a term used for a kind of jellied gasoline. I'm sure we all know what that is; the Arab Legion dropped enough of it on Tel Aviv last year."

The brigadier said, "Jellied gasoline, or napalm, as you call it, is very effective against heavy industrial targets, more so in some situations than demolition bombs, which just knock things about. Jellied gasoline dropped on machine tools, for example, sets the surface oil burning."

"And genocide?" said Rudolph von Seydlitz.

Frances Boardman turned her head slowly until her eyes connected with Lesley's. The younger woman projected a shy smile.

Shulberg, filling the breech, said in a low voice, "The word 'genocide' is first used in a chapter in Volume Two titled 'The

Holocaust.' It means the purposeful or systematic destruction of a race or ethnic minority—in this particular case, the eradication, through mass murder, of the Jews. The holocaust refers to a period of a few years during which six million were put to death."

. "By whom?" said Bauer.

"Nazi Germans."

Before anyone could react, Lesley advanced the magazine. On the screen now were hundreds of bodies, piled like naked tree limbs in a deep trench. On the muddy banks, a half-dozen soldiers squatted, feeding belts of ammunition into tripod-mounted light machine guns.

Then a kaleidoscope series: a barrack room of death stacked with five-tiered bunks from which cadaverous faces peered at the camera with large, hungering eyes; a heap of gold dental appliances—teeth, fillings, bridgework; a monstrous bakery of over-sized ovens, their steel doors gaping; a long queue of naked men, the obscene deformity of starvation implicit in protruding hip-bones and matchstick limbs.

". . . quite enough," the brigadier was saying. "The joke has gone far enough, Sidney."

The others remained quiet as Lesley's deadened voice intoned captions: "The shrunken head of a young Polish Jew serves as a paperweight for a Nazi administrator at Buchenwald . . . crematoria at Weimar . . . gas chambers in Lublin filled, wall to wall, with naked dead."

Frances Boardman said, "Oh God."

But it was Von Seydlitz's voice that fractured the heavy silence. "Enough!" It was a guttural command that darkened the screen. "I believe we have all seen quite enough pictures."

"Yes, there's a good fellow," said the brigadier in a hoarse vibrato as the room lights came on. Then they all sat silently for a while, not looking at each other.

Brigadier Entwistle was the first to speak. "Surely, Sidney, if for whatever reason you felt you had to perpetrate a hoax, you could have invented one in better taste."

"I swear to you," said Shulberg staunchly, "if this is a hoax, I've had nothing whatever to do with it."

Von Seydlitz spoke stiffly, barely moving his lips. "I believe it's time we saw the books you've been speaking of."

Lesley opened a small gate-legged table on which she placed, side by side, the two volumes of the Time-Life *History*. Next to them, she put a stack of cardboard boxes in which were Xeroxes of the original. Von Seydlitz, Entwistle, Paddy Duff and Paul Bauer were each presented with one of these. Individually they began reading, while the others, drinks in hand, clustered around the originals, thumbing through pages and discussing them in hushed tones.

For the next three quarters of an hour, Rudolph von Seydlitz, seated in a comfortable chair in the corner of the room, was accepting it all on its own terms: the grand strategy, the dazzling tactics of a phantom war—a new kind of war. He leafed through the Xeroxed pages of Volume One, experiencing sweet moments of satisfaction in the clean, surgical victories of blitzkrieg in Poland and France, the billiant successes in the North Atlantic, Norway and Denmark, then Barbarossa, code name for the invasion of Russia, and the lightning drive to the gates of Moscow; the delightful prospect of a Greater Germany extending from the Channel to the Caucasus. The field marshal was enjoying himself.

Glancing up for the first time, he turned to Brigadier Entwistle, saying in conspiratorial tones, "The material seems well organized."

"And the cast of characters well chosen, Rudy," said Entwistle. "Fascinating, I must say. Churchill, if you can imagine it, and Roosevelt, conveniently elected four times. Stalin, of course, and Zhukov, Chiang Kai-shek, Marshal Pétain, and a large number of more obscure types whose names ring bells; MacArthur, Tojo, Mao Tse-tung, Bernard Montgomery." The brigadier riffled through his pages. "Monty would have been delighted to know of the part he played here, although, as I recall, he hadn't much of a sense of humor. And there's a Frenchy named DeGaulle. Met him back in the early forties, a captain—impressive fellow. We have a book of his in the museum library—bit dusty now, I'd say —*War of the Future,* or some-such. It deals with armored tactics —brilliant for its time. I believe he was governor-general of one of their colonies—French Indochina, I think."

"It's fascinating," said Von Seydlitz. "It's all so well researched."

"Researched, Rudy? Researched from what?"

Von Seydlitz frowned, turned back to his Xerox. Within minutes, he was reading of Hitler's suicidal obstinacy at Stalingrad. There were other failures. The earlier satisfaction he had felt over German triumphs dissolved in the angry acid of stomach constriction—El-Alamein, Kursk, the traitorous Italian surrender, Normandy, the Luftwaffe's blunders under his childhood hero, Hermann Göring, the catastrophic defeats due to wishful thinking and arrogance. Even the assassination plots against the madman Hitler had been botched. Then finally, Von Seydlitz found himself staring down at a photograph of accused prisoner Hermann Göring, in faded uniform, sitting in the "Allied war crimes dock at Nuremberg." He was leaning forward as if listening intently to testimony, a headset clamped loosely over his ears, a deprecating grin spread across the sagging flesh of his face. War crimes, thought the field marshal, how dare they! A taut redness distorted his features. He looked up at the others. "This is malignant fiction. It is a damnable insult to the German nation!"

"Steady, Rudy," said Brigadier Entwistle, his short burst of laughter sharply pointed. "Just moments ago you were complimenting the authors on their excellent research!"

"And you were the ones who accused Frances of taking it all too seriously," said Shulberg.

"Monstrous!"

"Every story has its villains and heroes," said Bauer. "It is usually the victors who are the heroes because they write the histories—the stories. Had this been written by Germans, it would have been the other side, the Anglo-Saxons, who would have been portrayed as villains."

Entwistle, his expression sober now, drummed his fingers across Volume One. "I'm certainly willing to concede now that the chaps who put this together were quite adroit, most thorough despite a few errors in judgment and some inconsistencies. Nonetheless, it fails as a prediction of the future—1939 came and went with no war. Some of us seem to have a problem accepting that!" He laughed briefly, cutting it short when he realized none of them had joined him. "Science fiction," he said.

"They don't read like science fiction, James," said Frances

Boardman. "They read as if they'd been written *after* the fact, the way history is written."

"What fact this time, Frances?"

"The Second World War . . ."

"Ahh, that fact."

"The copyright reads 1970," said Lesley.

"I've spent a good deal of my life browsing in bookshops," said Paul Bauer, "and I've never seen a copy."

"Well, when were they actually published?" said Lesley.

"It had to be after 1941," said Paddy Duff. "Otherwise, how would they know about radar? It wasn't used until then."

"In the books, its first practical use was in 1938," said Shulberg.

Bauer said, "The theory existed as far back as the twenties, and radar was a common device in science fiction."

Frances Boardman smiled for the first time since the start of the slide show, over three hours earlier. "We've got the wrong end of the mule. It's not the device or even the theory that's important in this context, it's the term . . . *radar*. It's an English acronym for 'Radio Detection and Ranging,' —in real life, a word that wasn't even coined until 1940. The writers might very well have envisioned the device—the technology—but they would have had to be clairvoyant to predict the *term!*"

"Are you saying that the books had to be written after 1940?"

"No, much later. We all saw the photograph of an atomic bomb detonating over a city in Japan—Hiroshima. The caption tells us that it ended the war in 1945." She paused for effect, then went on. "There is also considerable text about this bomb. The authors knew what they were talking about."

"So did many people," said Paul Bauer. "It was no great feat to predict. H. G. Wells, for example, wrote of an atomic bomb in 1914."

"True, but neither Wells nor any other prognosticator was ever able to describe what it would *look like!* I mean, the explosion, the visual appearance of a mushroom. It looked almost exactly like the photographs of the world's first nuclear explosion when it was detonated by the Germans in Antarctica in 1980! I have read that even the physicists who worked on the device itself were surprised by the shape and scope of the explosion. So how could writers and photographers predict it with such great accuracy? They just couldn't. The idea defies logic."

Lesley Morning turned to Fred Hayworth, who stood leaning against the mantel on the other side of the room. "My father's letter . . . the wax seal was impressed with the date . . . 1968—*before* the first bomb."

Hayworth straightened, a thoughtful frown on his face. "The letter resided in a safety deposit box until the day before I handed it to you. It couldn't have been altered. It's all impossible."

"Yes," said Lesley, turning to the others. "It was my father's letter that directed me to the books—a letter written twelve years before the first real atomic bomb was set off." She paused, contemplating her hands. "And two years before the publication date." Then quietly, as if to herself, "It is a riddle wrapped in a mystery inside an enigma."

"Total contradiction," said Shulberg. "You say that because of your father's letter the books had to exist in 1968, yet it's clear that because of the knowledge required concerning the bomb, they would have had to be published after 1980! Therefore the publication date of 1970 is meaningless. In fact, the whole damned thing is meaningless. They don't exist!"

"Yet here they are," said Frances Boardman, slapping the books with an emphatic open hand. She took a deep breath, expelling it slowly. "The only logical explanation is that this represents the history of an actual event."

"Nonsense!" said the brigadier. "We're playing games with reality. All that we have here is a damned interesting puzzle. That's all it is, and there is most certainly a rational solution."

"Perhaps that's true . . ."

"Perhaps!" Entwistle's laugh was sharp. "You mean," he said, "that there was a monstrous war—a world war, forty years ago, that everybody has forgotten about?"

"Well . . . no, of course not." She paused, smiled at him. He meant well. Then her smile was gone and she said, "But there is a reality and it frightens me. The photographs, the accurate description—precise in every detail—of weapons we know were

developed after the books were printed, the cast of characters . . ."

"There has to be a rational explanation," said Paul Bauer.
"Something we've overlooked. We've accepted the fact that the
books had to be published after 1980, yet they existed in 1970,
or earlier. A contradiction. But how do we know they *actually*
existed then?"

"My father's letter," said Lesley. "In a sealed vault . . ."

"The letter was in a vault, not the books."

The others were silent, as if digesting the idea. Paul Bauer
continued, "Miss Morning, just what did your father write about
the books?"

"That they were in a certain place on the bookshelf."

"Did he mention the title?"

"Yes, of course."

"What are you getting at, Bauer?" said Shulberg.

"Just this. For whatever reason, the books had to be written
and produced not before, but *after*, the letter was written. In fact,
the part dealing with the atom bomb must have been written after
1980. We have been confusing two things here. It is not the letter
that speaks of the war in great detail; it is the books. The letter
stopped short with just a title. The books must have been printed
later, *after* the letter was sealed in its lock-box."

"A good point," said Shulberg. "But why?"

"I don't know." Bauer grinned briefly at Lesley. "Perhaps to
get some unusual free publicity for eventual publication."

"I can understand your thinking that," said Lesley, "but I
assure you it's not so." In spite of his words, she felt a sudden
attraction to him.

"It's a hoax," said Von Seydlitz. "A hellish plot to discredit
the German people."

"Even assuming that's the case," said Freddy, "why? Who
would go to that much trouble? And to what end?"

"Jealousy. They envy us our hard-won success, our superiority in science," said the field marshal; "in art, technology, com-
merce . . ."

"I think that's madness," said Bauer quietly.

"Perhaps, but it's the only possible explanation."

"Nonsense," said Frances Boardman. "And how would you account for all those photographs? We still haven't discredited them. With just those alone in evidence, it becomes impossible to prove that there hasn't actually been a second world war!"

"Do you, madam," said Von Seydlitz, "think there has been?"

Frances Boardman was silent. She fumbled for a Lucky in an empty pack, then crumpled the pack into a green ball and dropped it into a crystal ashtray. Lesley offered her a cigarette, saying, "I wonder what the world would be like now, if there had been."

Brigadier Entwistle said, "You ladies would probably have higher hemlines." He laughed. "Or lower ones."

"There's one thing we could be certain of," said Sidney Shulberg. "There would have been forty or fifty million fewer people in the world."

"And fewer Jews." Frances Boardman moved her glass about in front of the light, staring into it as if it were a faceted crystal ball. "Hitler murdered one third of us."

Von Seydlitz glanced up, an angry frown on his face. "There was no Hitler, madam, no Nazis, and no massacre of Jews or anyone else. I'd like to remind you that we've had no Jewish problem in my country for a century. If that's your interest, I suggest you make a trip to Poland, Latvia or Russia!"

"I think it's time we changed the subject," said Sidney Shulberg, a wary eye on Frances.

She laid a hand on his arm. "Not yet," she said, crossing frozen glances with Von Seydlitz, who now stood erect, as if on parade. "German culture and social traditions," she said, "the very structure of the German language, the cult of blood and iron, the Teutonic talent for cold efficiency and discipline . . . forgive me, Field Marshal, but your compatriots are the most ideally equipped of all the Europeans to declare themselves a master race. Your own Thomas Mann said that Germans were catapulted into a Christianity that was never to experience a Renaissance. Nazis . . . it's all possible. You're the most heavily armed country in the world, and you could hold us all at ransom. It's a possibility, perhaps a probability." She paused, then in a single breath said, "At times the books seem so real to me, I find myself believing it all happened. At other times it seems as if it's about to happen."

"Madam, you're mad."

"Only Germany, of all the nations in the world, would be capable of creating a realpolitik out of anti-Semitism. The final solution, sir, it frightens me."

He glared at her in icy silence, then dismissed her abruptly, turning to the others. "We must keep this to ourselves."

"The books?" said Lesley.

"Of course."

"But why?"

"They insult my country—the German people. There will be trouble, I assure you."

"It's only fiction, Rudy," said Shulberg. "You said that yourself—a made-up story."

"And one you are no doubt considering for a film?"

"It's crossed my mind."

"Frightfully expensive," said Entwistle.

"At the very least," said Frances Boardman, "they should be published, or should I say re-published. A warning . . ."

Entwistle looked pained. "Aren't you being a trifle over-dramatic? A warning against what?"

Frances Boardman ignored the question. The short hairs on the back of her neck were bristling. She turned sharply to find Von Seydlitz's eyes boring into hers. He seemed even more rigid now, ossified, cast in ancient gray cement.

Brigadier Entwistle said, "The public would never understand these books. They're way beyond them. Nevertheless, if they are published, they will beyond a doubt find their way into military libraries and war colleges around the world. If one overlooks the occasional political nonsense and concentrates instead on the military material, there is probably much to be learned from them."

Five minutes later, most of the guests were leaving, each with a blue cardboard portfolio containing a Xerox of the Time-Life books tucked under his arm. At the door, Paul Bauer took Lesley's hand once again, saying, "I hope you don't think I was accusing you of attempting a hoax; it was just a kind of objective hypothesis, you see . . ."

"I think it's a very logical hypothesis—but mistaken. Are you in London often?" She found his grin infectious.

"I seldom leave it. May I ring you up?"

"Please do . . ."

She shared a dispirited dinner with Sidney Shulberg, Freddy and Frances Boardman. They tried unsuccessfully to speak of other things. Then later, as she lay alone in bed, she reflected on what had occurred. The eight of them had reached no consensus, no conclusion. The puzzle still remained to be solved. But the meeting, despite that, had been far from a failure. The horrors of a second world war were no longer beyond the capabilities of her imagination. They seemed very real—very possible. There was, she realized now, sufficient madness and stupidity in the world to have brought it about. It seemed to her that only the catalyst had been missing—Adolf Hitler.

A while later, half asleep, she thought about Paul Bauer. She smiled to herself in expectation of his call and what she hoped would follow it.

➤ 10 ◄

1983

After they had left Highcastle Road and were making their way through the evening rush of Londoners, Paul Bauer found he had nothing to say to his uncle. They were heading back to the embassy, the aging field marshal lost in thought, while setting a brisk pace as if on parade.

Paul, rather than increase his pace to keep up, increased the length of his stride, thus managing to stay out of step. He had been, he reminded himself, out of step with Uncle Rudolph since his tenth birthday, when, much to his mother's horror, the field marshal had presented him with a scaled-down replica of a wartime army rifle. The miniature, old-fashioned Mauser came complete with functioning parts and a sharpened steel bayonet. His uncle taught him how to field-strip the weapon, how to load and fire it and, using a sack stuffed with straw, how to parry and thrust with the bayonet. Young Paul was to suffer recurrent nightmares for weeks, based on the field marshal's graphic explanation of the anatomical function of the bayonet's "blood gutter."

Later there was Prussian military drill and almost incomprehensible lectures about blood and iron, will and discipline. "The Fatherland above all," quoted Field Marshal von Seydlitz. "Duty before self. Stand straight! Eyes front! There is no place for weakness!"

Paul's mother, attempting to reason with her overbearing older brother, was told to mind her own business—woman's business. Paul's father expressed the opinion that it was all quite harmless and, if anything, excellent exercise.

Paul recalled the chilled autumn when, as a young boy, he had spent afternoons goose-stepping back and forth across the barren forest clearing near his home. With his head all but lost in the commodious iron confines of a Teutonic coal-skuttle helmet, he had reacted with anxiety to the clipped, shouted military commands of the field marshal, who stood tall and erect; martially gorgeous in gleaming black boots and precisely tailored uniform.

The weekly "educational" sessions with his uncle were a dreadful chore to Paul. For months he hid what he considered to be this shameful weakness, only once feigning illness—a bogus bellyache that quickly developed into a self-induced reality when, with a rush of guilt, he realized the field marshal might find him out.

His salvation arrived in midwinter when his father was appointed German consul general in Toronto. At the foot of the floating ramp leading to the Lufthansa Condor IV that was to take Paul to Canada, Field Marshal von Seydlitz grasped him firmly by the shoulders, saying, "Remember at all times that you are a German." Paul nodded assurance and then with a light step ascended the ramp under the giant eight-bladed, counterrotating propellers with his mother and father.

In Toronto, he adapted quickly, developing his rudimentary English so that within a year he had lost most of his accent. He learned to ice skate, became a rabid Toronto Maple Leaf fan and tried out successfully for the goalie position on his school hockey team.

Then on a bright summer afternoon, while watching a parade, he found himself fascinated with the marching style of a company of Canadian soldiers. Wearing helmets fashioned as dapper steel derbies, their arms swinging in long, graceful arcs, they strode jauntily down Yonge Street behind fluttering banners and the discordant, yet somehow stirring music of massed bagpipes. They swaggered rather than strutted. How different, thought the young Paul, from the brutish goose-step he had learned so well. The Canadians seemed human figures of flesh and blood rather than mechanical men of blood and iron.

Now striding up Regent Street next to his uncle, he smiled grimly to himself. The old man had changed not a bit since Paul's childhood. He was still the hard-shelled, humorless Prussian. Nevertheless, Paul Bauer had felt for him an occasional flush of proprietary affection. Field Marshal Rudolph von Seydlitz was his only living relative.

"Jews," said his uncle, his eyes glazed over in thought.

Paul frowned quizzically.

"Sidney Shulberg and that horrible woman—Boardman. And it wouldn't surprise me if the other woman . . . the young one, was also a Jewess."

"Miss Morning," said Paul. "Lesley Morning." He wondered what his uncle was getting at.

"It's an iceberg and they are merely the tip. A monstrous conspiracy."

"Toward what end?"

"You are a naive young man. You've spent too much time away from Germany. We are hated and envied. Those books are merely an artful manifestation of that . . . very clever. . . . But they'll soon see that we are even more clever." The field marshal's mouth came to rest in a thin-lipped line.

Paul Bauer remained silent. He had come to consider his uncle's views to be amusing—an archaic, paranoid old fox, convinced that Germany was under mortal siege and that only an all-pervasive strength and constant vigilance could save it. An old story. In one form or another, he had been hearing it from Uncle Rudolph since he was a child.

Later in his apartment, Paul Bauer realized that the participants that afternoon had taken it all much too seriously. Each of them had drawn from *History of the Second World War* a reality that suited them: Entwistle, a lesson in tactics; Boardman, a dread of the possible; the field marshal, a threat to the Fatherland. But to Paul it was only a book, a book that, despite its cleverness, had little to do with the real world. Others had also been clever: Nostradamus, Wells, Huxley. But there, too, it had been only books.

He darkened the room, crawled into bed and then, smiling softly to himself, realized that even he had accepted a reality that afternoon, the reality of Lesley Morning. He closed his eyes in order to see her. Paul Bauer liked what he saw, just as he had earlier in the day. He would call her. . . .

Once again the Democratic party is being called upon to rescue the nation from the results of four disastrous Republican years . . . and we will do it, my friends. We will do it!

Our first priority must be to repair the damage. Repair the damage of three million lost jobs, of an economy in tatters; plowed under by President Dewey's love affair with nineteenth-century economics. . . .

—Excerpt from acceptance speech given by Presidential candidate Joseph Kennedy, Jr., to the Democratic National Convention meeting in Philadelphia, August 7, 1952

◆━━ 11 ━━◆

1983

They had dinner at The Tandoori Restaurant on Fulham Road. Lesley ordered the vindaloo curry, Paul Bauer a mild kurma. They shared an order of pakora and a quantity of poori and dhall, all washed down with cool glasses of draft lager. At one point he had tasted a bit of her fiery vindaloo and, after recovering, congratulated her heartily on her fortitude.

"And other things as well," he said, raising his glass to her.

"Such as?" The words, as she uttered them, sounded coy. She cringed inwardly, hoping he thought otherwise.

"You have a way with you, a self-confidence, a sureness." Did she? she wondered. And what about *beautiful, charming, sensuous, exquisite?* She had spent hours readying herself for this, their first date. Her perfume had cost forty pounds an ounce. She had invested three valuable afternoons choosing a dress. Even her choice of underwear (just in case) had been the result of agonizing calculation. She presented him with a wry smile.

Over tea, he said, "Would you care to go dancing?"

"I'd love to."

"In that case, we have a choice—your choice. We can look in on a phlegm parlor; Cecil's is the most fun. They have an American group, I believe—the Rambams. All the rage."

"Rum Bums," she said, grinning at him. He had, she guessed, done some homework—a little research—then got it all wrong. She wondered what the other choice might be. She had experienced all the phlegm she cared to with Ralph. The pounding drums, amplified harmonicas and shrill voices had been an almost constant diet on the record player when he was home. She said, "But I understand it's difficult to get in, particularly on a weekend night."

"I know the doorman."

"I had no idea that you were a man about town." She felt she couldn't get her eyes off his face.

"I'm not. His name is Tommy, he used to be employed at a French cleaning establishment near the embassy."

His grin was slightly lopsided, distorting the symmetry of what she considered to be an ideal male face. It was a weathered face with a strong dimpled chin and soft, questioning blue eyes. She smiled back at it and said, "We don't have dance-clogs with us, and the ones they rent never fit properly."

"Good," he said. "I'm in agreement. Your other choice is Glenn Miller's band. Everything seems to be American tonight."

"I think that's a lovely idea." A little while later, as they awaited the check, she said, "It's amazing . . ."

"What's amazing?"

"That neither of us has uttered a word about the meeting

. . . the pictures, the books . . ." As she spoke the words, she regretted them. There were, she realized, more important things to talk about tonight, namely, Paul Bauer and Lesley Morning. But feeling driven to get the subject out of the way, she added, "Aren't you curious?"

"Yes. But at the moment I'm more curious about you."

With a sense of relief, she sipped the last of her tea. Her grandmother and the Second World War could await the light of day. Lesley felt a sudden delicious desire to be kissed.

In the taxi, he rested his hand on her knee. It was, she realized, much too casual an action for it to have been casual. She could, if she cared to, ask him "casually" for a cigarette or the time, either of which would create other employment for his right hand. She reflected on this for a few seconds, deciding finally on neither of the two options, and then fighting off a third, that of placing her hand on his.

He said, "Do you like martinis?"

"American-style martinis?"

"Yes. Dry. Cold and clean and clear, like liquid pearls."

"Made with gin and vermouth and an olive?"

"A pitted olive," he said, with great seriousness. "With a very thin coating of its essential oil floating on top."

His voice seemed to resonate through her body. She said, "I love martinis. The only form of alcohol fit for civilized—cultured —human beings." She dropped her hand casually on top of his.

"You don't seem German," she said, and was suddenly aware of the faux pas. She attempted to cover it quickly by adding, "I mean, your accent, your use of the idiom . . . it's marvelous . . ."

Paul Bauer laughed. "I come from a diplomatic family. My father held various posts in Canada, the U.S., and for two years he was the ambassador to Australia. I grew up with the English language and many of the attitudes that go with it . . . but I'm still a German." He shifted his body in the seat, placed his left hand on her shoulder. "And we're really not that bad, Lesley . . . some of us." He laughed.

She smiled at him, wondering how she could have become so attracted to a man in such a short time. They were passing Grosvenor Place. Suddenly, she found herself thinking about her grandmother. It had been right here, seventy years ago, in another cab, a hansom, where her father had been conceived.

They sat at a ringside table drinking martinis out of cone-shaped footed glasses. An aging Glenn Miller led his band through a Gershwin medley, the reeds sounding like polished titanium.

She said, "What do you do when you're not busy being press secretary?"

"I write."

"Books?"

"One book. I've been at it forever. A novel. God knows if I'll ever finish it. It's about down-at-the-heels Russian aristocracy in Paris after the war. Early twenties; I love the time and place."

"May I read some of it?" She smiled gratefully at the waiter as he set up another round of drinks.

"Nothing would delight me more. And you?"

"Me?"

"What do you do when you're not pursuing elusive wars?"

"I want to paint." Her answer came as a surprise to her. It was something she had not considered since her college days. Perhaps, she thought, it was an idea that had come home to roost. "Yes," she said, this time more emphatically. "I want to paint again."

"When you do, I'd like to see your work."

He caught her eye and she sensed a ripening sexual tension. He said, "Most of the women seem to be wearing pants; you're one of the few wearing a dress."

"Do you like it?" She was aware that her eyes were making misty promises over the top of her glass.

"I love it . . . may I touch?"

"Within reason."

She stood before he had the chance to pull her chair back. In his arms, she let herself drift to the music and the martinis. She buried her face in his neck. They swayed, taking tiny shuffling steps. His hand dropped from her waist to the swell of her hip. He said, "Silk."

"Yes." She caressed the back of his neck. ". . . they're writing songs of love, but not for me . . ."

"Biology."

"Yes," she said. "Good old biology."

"Biological love at first sight."

"An explosion . . . stars . . ."

"Astronomical love at first sight . . . super-nova love, black-hole, expanding-universe love at first sight."

She pulled her head back, murmured into his mouth, "You're an ideal madman! Where did you come from so suddenly? Who are you, really?"

"A world-famous sex maniac. I want you. I've wanted you since the moment I first saw you. And right now I'm visualizing all the things I want to do to you. Some of them are unspeakable."

"Just keep doing what you're doing, for now."

He pulled her even closer. Her lips roamed his neck. She felt a sharp spasm of joy, laughed quietly, then whispered, "Do you think anything will come of this?"

"Yes, everything . . ."

She felt his arousal and pressed against him, rotating her hips in a slow rhumba, counter tempo to the music. It occurred to her that she was acting outrageously. For an instant she wondered how she would feel about it in the morning.

An hour later, in his flat, their first kiss seemed to require a hundred hours to bring to fruition.

In the morning, Lesley awoke to breakfast in bed; orange juice, sweet rolls and coffee. He said, "You're beautiful." It was a coldly dispassionate statement.

Not quite awake, she wondered if he had approved of her underwear, her perfume. "I'm self-confident and, as you said, self-assured. So flattery will get you nowhere now. Where were you yesterday evening when I needed you?"

He reached over to kiss her, almost upsetting the orange juice. "You were trying then. Most women are beautiful when they try to be . . . but now you're just you—unwashed, unadorned, your hair a mess . . . and you are beautiful beyond reason."

Lesley smiled, felt herself go limp. She was thirty-four years old, she had experienced sex with four different men, but had only been made love to by one. He stood before her now in a navy-blue dressing gown and worn slippers, a smile on his lips, but something more in his gentle blue eyes. It was an expression she had never seen in a man's eyes before. She parted his robe, stared fondly for a moment, then leaned forward to engulf him. His low-pitched moan of pleasure thrilled her. In moments, she felt that she too was about to burst.

* * *NEWSBREAK* * *

Joseph Stalin, born Josif Vissarionovich Dzhu-
gashvili, in Gori, Georgia, the tyrannical leader of the
Soviet Union since Lenin's death in 1924, is dead. He
fell in the Kremlin itself, the victim of an assassin's
bullets, along with the hated NKVD leader L. P. Beria
and Politburo members Molotov, Khrushchev, Malen-
kov and others. An informed source has stated that the
murders were part of a coup organized and led by
General Ivan Stepanovch Konev of the Red Army.
Less than fifteen minutes ago, Konev himself announced the formation of an interim military government to restore order. At the moment we are out of
touch with our Moscow bureau, but a few minutes ago
Douglas Manners reached us by telephone to describe
the deadly chaos taking place in the streets of Moscow. Here is a wire recording of his report. . . .

—BBC News
March 5, 1953

1983

Frances Boardman chewed thoughtfully on her toast. "Mrs.
Green's technique seems improved," she said. "The bacon is
crisp, the eggs are perfect . . ."

"And the coffee," said Lesley, "if you'll notice, is palatable."

"A miracle. What happened?"

"I've convinced Mrs. Green that she's been overworked, and

that we should have an additional person to share her duties.
Rose is useless. It took a little doing, but now we have a Mrs.
DeLange. She's just a little younger than Mrs. Green and will be
good company for her. Actually, that's even more important than
decent bacon and eggs in the morning." She leaned back in her
chair, sipping her coffee. "I just rattle around in this place. It's
ridiculous—eighteen, twenty rooms. It comes out different each
time I count them. If I can ever get Mrs. Green and Rose settled
comfortably, I'll sell it and buy a human-sized flat in Chelsea and
do my own bacon and eggs." She leaned back in her chair. "You
have plans? If you're going to stay in London, I have plenty of
room here."

"Thank you," said Frances Boardman. "A few days, maybe
a week. But sooner or later I have to get back to Philadelphia—
back to work."

In the short time she had known her, Lesley had developed
an affection for the older woman. She smiled at her. "I know
nothing about your life, Frances. Were you ever married? Children?"

"No marriages, but I was a mother for three days. It was a
boy—premature. Sidney was the father."

Lesley wondered if it had been a deliberate pregnancy, but
then realized that perhaps it was too intimate a question. She
said, "I'm sorry . . . ."

"Thank you, dear," said Frances Boardman. "But don't be.
It was a long time ago and far away." She poured another cup of
coffee.

Later, Lesley said, "I was with him Saturday night."

"Paul Bauer?"

"Yes. I really like him."

"He's charming," said Frances Boardman, setting down her
coffee cup and splashing an ice cube into an inch of Scotch. "But
that uncle of his is a coiled snake."

"I think I'm going to fall in love with Paul."

"Going to?"

"Well, it's a little early . . . ."

"How do you feel?"

"Unbelievably happy . . . just glorious!"

"Then you don't have to think about it at all," said the older
woman with a gentle laugh. "You're in love."

That night in the warm glow of her bedside lamp, Lesley reread the last chapter of her grandfather's diary. There was something on the edge of memory eluding her, something about a medal—a military decoration. She closed her eyes . . . one of the Fowler twins at her father's funeral. The Victoria Cross? Finally, her father's words, not as written in neat chancery script, but rather heard, deeply resonant, in her mind . . . *a riddle wrapped in a mystery inside an enigma.* . . .

She felt free-floating excitement that kept her awake for most of the night. Her thoughts flitted back and forth between the mystery of her grandmother and vivid images of her night with Paul Bauer. Was she, she wondered, actually in love with him? She hoped so.

The following morning, Lesley cabbed to the offices of *The Illustrated London News* in Bloomsbury Square. With a shock she found what she was looking for in the edition of June 20, 1913. Elleander Morning gazed out at her from the bound, yellowing pages. There was no mistaking the face.

Lesley fumbled in her bag for her makeup mirror and held it before her, eyes flicking back and forth across seventy years, from ancient brittle paper to silvered glass. She stared into her dead grandmother's eyes. They were the same as her own, widely spaced under arched eyebrows, the lashes naturally long. The nose was shared—aquiline. The lips were full, the cheekbones high, as were hers. Elleander Morning was a ghost image of herself. Only the hairdo was different.

For a fleeting moment she felt one with the woman in the photograph. Then her eyes dropped to the caption. She read it through three times before it registered.

COFFEE HOUSE MURDER

CONVICTED MURDERESS, Miss Elleander Morning, British, of Highcastle Road, London, awaits sentencing by the High Court in Vienna for the murder of an indigent Austro-Hungarian artist, whom she had shot to death in a Viennese coffee house five weeks earlier. Miss Morning refused to testify in her own defense. The victim, one Adolf Hitler, was twenty-four years old and a resident of Vienna. A love triangle is suspected.

Dazed, Lesley Morning spent the next few hours at the Mayfair Gym, where she swam eleven vigorous laps in the pool, then
lay for half an hour in the sauna. It helped. The reality of her
body was reassuring.

She ate a hearty lunch at Harrods, following it up with a
whirlwind orgy of compulsive shopping. At five, she strolled into
Michal's, where the tall, sibilant proprietor scolded her for arriving without an appointment, then cleared his time and took her
on for a set and comb-out.

She felt surprisingly calm, to the point, she thought, of being
tranquilized. She smiled to herself. Perhaps it was something
they were putting in the tea these days. She felt there was nothing
that was impossible.

That evening over dinner in Sid Shulberg's sprawling bache-
lor flat, Lesley turned to him and said, "Hitler. Adolf Hitler."

"Adolf Hitler what?"

"Adolf Hitler existed."

The director pointed at her with a limp asparagus stalk.
"You're around the bend, old girl."

"I saw it this morning in a back number of *The Illustrated
London News*. There was a photograph of Elleander Morning and
a caption, stating she shot him in a café."

Frances Boardman's voice was pitched low. "Your grandmother . . ."

"Yes," said Lesley. "Miss Elleander Morning, British, of
Highcastle Road, London. She shot him dead. Except for some
nonsense about a love triangle, it was all just as my father said
in his letter."

Sid Shulberg slumped in his chair. "But Hitler? I just can't
believe he was a real person—flesh and blood. I mean, he was a
made-up name in the books!"

"He *was* flesh and blood," said Lesley. "It's confirmed in
black and white; *Illustrated London News*, June 20, 1913. You can
check it out yourself. It's true, all of it is true!" Smiling nervously,
she folded her napkin. "Both my father's letter and the photo
caption mention that the court was provided with no motive. My
father stated in his letter that the judges finally termed it 'a result
of instantaneous mental aberration.' Put simply, that means that
my grandmother went suddenly berserk—homicidal—and
crossed the Channel, booked passage on a train to Vienna, then

picked at random a total stranger, barely beyond his teens, in order to kill him in cold blood. My God! If Elleander Morning was a crazed killer, she would have been satisfied to find her victims right here in London like all those other mad English rippers! That's the tradition, isn't it?"

"But she must have been at least temporarily insane," said Freddy. "I mean, there don't seem to be any other possibilities. How could she have known anything about him?"

Lesley Morning rose from her seat. They looked at her curiously as she crossed the room and leaned against the doorjamb. Frances Boardman said, "You all right, dear?"

"On the day of my father's funeral," said Lesley, "I met Fawn and Clara Fowler. They were twins. They had worked in my grandmother's whorehouse . . . 'club,' they called it. 'The finest establishment in the British Empire.'"

Fred Hayworth said, "That's true. I also heard it."

"Last night," said Lesley, "I suddenly remembered something one of them had said. . . . It was Fawn, I believe. We were standing in front of my grandmother's grave. 'If they knew what she did, they'd have awarded her the bleeding Victoria Cross . . .'"

"What are you getting at?" said Shulberg.

"Don't you understand?"

"Oh my God . . ." said Frances Boardman.

"And just before my grandmother left my grandfather sitting alone in that hansom cab, she said something about carrying out a mission. It was in the diary, you've all read it. And that was 1910, three years before she went to Vienna to do murder!"

"A mission?" said Shulberg.

Frances Boardman, in as calm a voice as she could manage, said, "The books. The Time-Life *History*. Elleander Morning must have read them . . . even then, before 1910!"

"Of course!" said Freddy, his voice high-pitched with excitement. "How else could she know that young Adolf was in Vienna? Or that he even existed!"

"What in the bloody hell are we talking about?" said Sidney Shulberg, slapping the table with both hands. "Radar! Atomic bombs! Roosevelt! In 1910?"

"Sidney," said the older woman, "sometimes you're just a little dense. What Lesley is telling us is that the two sisters knew

Elleander's motive. *They knew!* According to them, she deserved
to be decorated. For what, Sidney?"

It dawned on him. Now all four of them were standing. He
spoke in halting tones, as if he were having trouble reading words
from a remote teleprompter. "The Victoria Cross . . . for killing
—*assassinating*—Adolf Hitler, in order to prevent another war
. . . the Second World War."

"She knew all about the Second World War, Sidney, since at
least 1910—probably earlier."

"But how could she? It never happened, goddammit! There
has only been *one* world war! You can't prevent what's not going
to happen!" He was shouting now. "Except for those bloody
books, there was never a Second World War."

"That's right," said Freddy Hayworth.

"Because," said Lesley, "my grandmother prevented it and
so it never occurred."

In the relaxed afterglow of lovemaking, Lesley told Paul Bauer
about what she had discovered in *The Illustrated London News* files.
He lay on his back, listening to her, his finger tracing soft caressing circles on the flesh of her inner thigh. When she'd finished,
he said, "But how did your grandmother know of him—this Hitler person?"

"There can be only one answer to that." Lesley Morning
paused. "She must have read about him in the Time-Life books."

"In 1913?"

She nodded, realizing she'd never convince him.

"Impossible."

"But she shot him. She left England, went to Vienna and
shot him and there was no Second World War."

"I'll grant that. But she must have had a simpler motivation
than preventing a future war that she could know nothing about."

"What, for instance? She'd never seen him before."

"How do you know that?"

"Then where did the Time-Life books come from?"

"I don't know," said Paul, raising himself onto one elbow.
"But almost anything is easier to believe than your theory. Let me
restate it: Your grandmother, in the year 1913, prevented a major
war by shooting a young artist twenty-six years before the fact.

It was a man she read about in a book that was not published till 1970."

"Yes," she said. "But the books exist, despite the publication date. You've seen them—you even have a Xerox copy."

"That proves nothing about Elleander Morning." He lapsed into silence, finally dropping down beside her, a thoughtful frown on his face. "It seems sometimes that you're obsessed with all this."

She stared at the ceiling, feeling his eyes on her. The excitement she had felt over the past few days, the intoxication was gone, vaporized, leaving her sobered. His thinking, she realized, was reasonable, concise, intelligent. It had cast doubt on what she had considered a certainty. Lesley felt a vague sense of loss. Her search for Elleander Morning was what had been giving her life a purpose. The naked man lying beside her had not, as yet, risen to that status. She turned and caressed his face with gentle fingers, wondering what was going to happen between them in the weeks—the months—to come. She said, "I know hardly anything about you; how you grew up, what kind of little boy you were. . . ."

He was silent for a long moment, then he said, "I was born and bred a Prussian aristocrat." He spoke in a low-pitched voice, as if to himself. "I'm the end of a long line. Two of my uncles were killed on the Marne in the Great War of 1914. Two aunts and a baby cousin died of the influenza during the epidemic of 1920. Another cousin was done in by his Porsche in 1963. On my fifteenth birthday, there was an air-line disaster in Australia. I walked away from it; my parents didn't."

"My God!" said Lesley.

"My father was considered an outsider by the Von Seydlitzes. He was from Hamburg, his father had been a manufacturer of men's hats. He was a nice fellow, a pleasant, mild-mannered man, a career diplomat in the Weimar Foreign Service. I seem to remember that he was very much in love with my mother. But now, only my uncle and I are left, and for years he has been trying to get me to add Von Seydlitz to my name. *Paul Manfred Bauer von Seydlitz!* He insists that I marry well, that I perpetuate the noble line and pass on the name. It all sounds so ridiculous now, but when I was a little boy I spent more time with my uncle than with my father. The field marshal treated me like a toy soldier. He had dreams of glory for me, but they didn't take. After six years overseas with my parents I became an Anglo-Saxon by choice. I was more American, more Australian, more Canadian than I was German. I'd even lost some of the facility for my own native language . . . psychological, perhaps." Paul laughed briefly. "Then, after my parents' death, I returned to the Fatherland to live in my uncle's house. I never felt at home there. I closed my ears to his lectures about our glorious traditions and to the incessant sound of Wagner piped through the house, and read nothing but English books and went to see nothing but British and American movies. I dreamed constantly of the day when I could free myself, leave my Prussian uncle and live in London or New York or Toronto." He sat up to look at Lesley. "My fantasies came true. I made my own decision, against my uncle's wishes, to go to New York and take my master's at Columbia—journalism. Eventually I got a job with Reuter's covering the troubles in Italian Somaliland. A few years ago I accepted the press attaché job with our embassy in London . . . and here you are."

He lay back quietly, his eyes closed. Lesley stared at him in wonder for what seemed like minutes. She found it amazing that he had managed to emerge unscathed from such a background. During their short but intense relationship, she had found nothing wrong with him. He was, she was convinced, perfect; a beautiful man, intelligent, thoughtful, self-assured, sexy, witty, gentle, loving. . . . She continued to look at him, savoring his rugged but relaxed features, his slim though well-muscled body. Finally, in little more than a whisper, she said, "What are you thinking?"

Paul opened his eyes to grin happily at her. His mood had changed instantaneously from somber to joyous. He turned, wrapped his arms around her, cupping her buttocks. He spoke softly, the words running together. "I'm thinking of how beautiful you are, how happy you make me, and how I like being with you and how marvelous we are together and what exquisite things we do to each other in bed and that we should share a holiday someplace in the sun—the Canaries, the Bahamas. A long weekend." He kissed her and she thrilled to the sensation of his penis regaining its strength between her thighs. He laughed, saying, "I wonder what Uncle Rudolph would have to say about the two of us perpetuating the Seydlitz line."

She said, "That would be lovely." And then a rising pulse of excitement made her forget everything else.

They spent three more nights together, then Paul had to accompany the ambassador to Berlin for a series of conferences. On the following Thursday, *Life* magazine appeared on the newstands of the English-speaking world with a cover and eight pages devoted to the "Second World War." The traditional *Life* cover format featured a photograph of a bedraggled figure wearing a Teutonic helmet and a threadbare blanket. His arms were raised in surrender. At his feet, which were wrapped in rags, two men lay grotesquely spread-eagled in rubble that extended into the background, ultimately blending with a horizon of ruined buildings. Surrounding this tableau of defeat were a half-dozen soldiers, wearing white, ghostlike capes and holding ugly tommyguns.

—THE WAR THAT NEVER HAPPENED—
WORLD WAR TWO!

A GERMAN OFFICER SURRENDERS TO SOVIET TROOPS
—STALINGRAD, 1943—

Inside, a page of text written by Frances Boardman dealt with the discovery of the twin books and the mystery surrounding them. Then, in a few short paragraphs, she outlined the general history of the war, ending with a listing of the casualties—40 million dead, including 18 million Russians, 11 million Chinese, and 6 million Jews. Finally, America's total casualties—one million, one hundred thousand. The article went on to say that Time-Life would publish an exact replica of the original books in the spring of 1984.

The public took it for granted that the picture story was advance publicity for a forthcoming movie. There were, of course, exceptions. Among them was a group in Los Angeles who called themselves GIs and maintained that there had actually been a Second World War. Their leader, a man who called himself General Zhukov, insisted that the memory of the cataclysmic

war had been blocked from the universal consciousness and that
the only road back to peace and brotherhood lay in restoring the
memory. Within two weeks, six of the cult's members, four men
and two women, had already achieved "parity" and could remember intimate details of their lives during the Second World
War. This, despite the fact that only two of them were old enough
to have been around during that period.

Lesley Morning, staring down at the open grave, shivered in the
cold night air. There was a pervasive smell of dank, upturned
earth.

The top of the casket, matching in texture and color the
surrounding earth, was barely discernible in the moonlight. Then
from below, the sudden glare of a flashlight blinded her.

A voice from the grave said, "Miss . . . ?"

The chill was now eternal. The grave should have been
empty, reserved. There should have been no casket, despite her
intuition to the contrary. She felt suddenly light-headed. In
evenly cadenced monosyllables, sounding to her as if they came
from elsewhere, she said, "Open it, please."

She turned away, to the left, to look at her grandmother's
grave. The stone was visible in the dim light. Her father's was
obscured in shadow.

There was a sound of groaning wood. In an audible whisper
Lesley counted to three, then, once again, looked down. Highlighted in a theatrical circle of yellow light, a skull grinned up at
her. She held her breath, feeling faint. It seemed so small. Within
each of us, she thought, the bones of our childhood. She shook
herself, fought unsuccessfully to look away.

One of the workmen called up, "Do we close it now, miss?"

"Yes," she said. "And bring it up."

"Bring it up? You said nothing about that," said the other
one. "You said you only wanted a quick look."

"We're not grave robbers, you know."

"Yes, but I've changed my mind," said Lesley. "And I also
want the grave on the left . . . my grandmother, Elleander Morning."

There was a whispered conference. Then finally, "That's
highly illegal, miss. Quite serious."

"I'll make it worth your while."

There was another whispered conference, barely audible, from the grave. "Three hundred quid, miss, and mum's the word."

"I'll also want them reburied."

"That would be another hundred, miss."

"Okay . . . anything."

The two men emerged, kept their distance, looked at her queerly. She wrote down her address for them and then walked out to the road to get into the old Jag she had inherited from her father.

At home, she called Freddy, waited for him to come fully awake, then told him. At first he was uncomprehending. She repeated the story three times before he fully accepted it. He was disapproving, but intrigued. "But the cemetery chaps said it was empty. . . . Who?"

"Maybe Grandfather Bertie," she said. "But I don't think so."

"Why not?"

"There'd have been a cemetery record of his burial, a headstone. Why would he have been buried secretly?" She paused to let the logic sink in. "Freddy, you've got to do something for me. . . . Find someone, a pathologist—forensic expert, whatever they're called. I want to know everything about both corpses: sex, age, cause of death, time of death—everything."

"A moonlighter," he said, making a bad joke in an attempt to ease the tension.

Minutes later Lesley was in the kitchen pouring a cup of tea when she was struck by the full import of what she had done. She looked down at her hands to find them shaking uncontrollably.

NEWSBREAK

**FINNISH TROOPS OCCUPY LENINGRAD AND
ARCHANGEL
POLES AND HUNGARIANS ADVANCE BEYOND
KIEV
SOVIET TROOPS ROUTED ON THREE FRONTS**

**RUMANIANS MARCH
INTO MOLDAVIA**

Ukranian Rebels Pin
Down Red Army Troops

Japanese Take Sakhalin
Occupy Vladivostok

—*The New York Times*
April 6, 1953

➤➤ **13** ◄◄

1983

Dear Lesley,
    Fawn is dead. It happened suddenly on the final
homeward leg of our little journey around the world, so it
did not actually ruin our holiday. (A marvellous holiday! I
will tell you all about it when I see you.) I had Fawn
buried at sea two days out of Gibraltar. The ceremony was
quite romantic and everyone was sympathetic.
    Don't fret, dear. Fawn and I certainly had more than

our due share of good living, and from the time we were
little girls together, we have enjoyed every minute.
     Please call on me at any teatime. I am looking
forward to seeing you. You are so very much like your
grandmother.

                                        Love,
                                  Clara Fowler

P.S. I have something for you that I know you will treasure.

On Friday of that week, Lesley Morning drove north out of
London to South Mims, for tea with Clara Fowler. The cottage
was mid-thirties modernistic, poured concrete and glass brick,
flat-roofed and streamlined as if constructed to move at high
velocities. Its exterior was unadorned except for narrow strips of
bright blue tile at its roof line.

The old woman, dressed in slim, tailored white slacks topped
with a loose-fitting, pale-yellow blouse and long white silk scarf,
showed the young woman into a Bauhaus interior, dominated by
furniture of chrome and glass fixed stoically on a black-and-white
checkerboard floor.

They sat at a small round glass-topped table graced with a
tea consisting of freshly baked scones, clotted cream and black-
berry preserves. Lesley expressed her condolences for Fawn's
death. Clara Fowler clucked, reached out a withered but well-
manicured hand. She said, "My sister lived a lovely life. She went
everywhere, saw everything, tasted all the best foods and slept in
the best beds. She had a few marvelous love affairs and outlived
everyone but me. I fear we're going to miss each other . . . for
a while, at least."

"I hope it's a long, long while," said Lesley.

The old woman laughed. "Frankly, my dear, so do I." The
tea-pouring ritual required her attention for a few moments.
Finally she looked up. "I assume you saw the books—everything?"

"Everything," said Lesley. She realized that Fawn had not
seen the latest issue of *Life* magazine.

"And how do you feel about them—the books?"

"Overwhelmed," she said, feeling a rising excitement with the direction of their conversation. "Particularly now that their authenticity has been established. I mean, we've found the photographs to be real . . . actual pictures of real events." She lowered her teacup, smiling ruefully. "Events that never happened."

"Those bloody books. We should have burned them. I remember when Harry, your father, discovered them; he was about twelve at the time. We had kept them hidden for years, but you couldn't hide a pin from young Harry. Once he found them, he just wouldn't put them down. That year, for three whole weeks of a school holiday, he just sat in his room with them. Then we had a terrible row, the two of us, when he tried to carry the damnable things off to school. I should have burned them then and there. When he grew up he brooded over them, year after bloody year."

Lesley nodded, feeling an inexplicable rush of fear. Nothing good could come from any of it. Maybe *she* should burn them—and the slides—do away with it all, cancel the upcoming republishing contract; get on with her life.

Clara Fowler said, "Perhaps something a little stronger, my dear. Sherry?"

"Please." She watched with admiration as the old woman rose out of her chair with all the elegance and poise of a fashion model two-thirds of a century younger.

A few moments later she returned to set a decanter and two glasses onto the table. She said, "The day before your grandmother left on that awful trip to Vienna, she told Fawn and me that if anything were to happen to her, we were to give the books and some other items to Bertie, your grandfather. You know about that?"

"Yes, the diary. My father was conceived in a cab."

"We had never heard her speak like that before, though she tried to sound casual about it—just another trip to the Continent. It frightened me." Clara leaned back to stare at the ceiling. "Of course, as it turned out, we couldn't give the books or anything else to Bertie. He vanished, you see, disappeared off the face of the earth on the very same day that Elleander left for Vienna. We never saw nor heard from him again, poor man. He loved her." She closed her eyes for a few moments, then continued, her voice low-pitched, introspective. "Two or three weeks before she left, she drew up her will and told us that if anything ever happened to her, and Bertie, we were to take care of young Harry. Your father was only two years old at that time, poor little bloke."

"Did you know where she was going?"

"Until the day she left, we thought it was to be another trip to Paris to buy paintings. But Fawn and I were troubled about it because Elleander seemed to be putting her life in order, as if there was a possibility that she might not return. She put us off when we questioned her. Then, just hours before she left for the boat-train, she said she was going to Vienna to save the world. Fawn broke into tears. I mean, good Lord, we were not much more than children—especially Fawn. Elleander was like a mother to us."

"She actually did save the world," said Lesley.

"Yes."

Lesley felt a sudden chill. She smiled weakly, sipping her sherry.

"Bertie," said the older woman, "showed up just hours after your grandmother had left. The poor man was beside himself when we mentioned Vienna. He was frantic . . . insisted on knowing the exact time she departed, to the minute. We were all in a terrible state—near hysterics—I thought Bertie was going to fly apart before our very eyes. He left, saying he was going to Vienna to try to head her off—something about getting there before she did—though God knows how he expected to accomplish that. There was no air service in those days, you know."

"Then my grandfather knew why my grandmother was going to Vienna?"

"Oh, there was no doubt about that, though of course it was still a mystery to us. Just before he left, he said something I'll never forget. He said, 'God, if he exists, is making a bad joke, sending a whore out to unseat a linchpin.' "

Once again Lesley felt a chill ascend her spine. In a small voice, she said, "The joke was on God."

The old woman smiled gently, revealing perfect, pearl-white dentures. "Yes . . . I never thought of it that way."

"Neither did I until just now." Lesley hesitated a moment,

then said, "What happened to my father after Elleander left for Vienna?"

"When the bloody Austrians found her guilty of murder, Harry became our responsibility. After she became pregnant, Elleander had bought a cottage in Cornwall. Then later, Nanny and baby lived there and Elleander traveled down for a few days a week to be with her child. A lovely place. But we thought it best to close the cottage and bring the baby and Nanny home to Highcastle Road, where we could keep an eye on things until Elleander returned. You see, I was certain that despite her conviction and sentence, she would return within a year or two. Then when the war broke out in 1914, we resigned ourselves to her absence for the duration. Austria-Hungary was now the enemy, and we were sadly mistaken."

The old woman paused a moment to refill their glasses. "We made a lovely nursery on the top floor, but of course, the nanny didn't quite take to the idea. She hadn't been trained to practice her profession in a brothel, you see, no matter how elegant it was. I'm sure she was terrified of being mistaken for one of our ladies. Of course, if you could have seen her, you'd realize that there was little chance of that. The woman was a walking scarecrow. So, with Nanny gone, it wasn't easy. Neither Fawn nor I knew anything about babies. But our hearts were in it, and after a short while we managed quite nicely without her. And little Harry had eleven new aunties—our ladies. They loved him." Clara's deeply lined face projected a wistful smile. "Then," she continued, "in 1914 came the bloody war to end all wars, as your people called it. For the first few weeks, before it turned nasty, it seemed an exciting lark. No one ever dreamed it would last longer than six months, or that France would turn into that monstrous meat grinder. All those lovely boys . . . so many of them crossed the Channel and never came back. . . ."

The old woman stared blankly at Lesley, as if not seeing her. "Fawn and I ran the club and spent our free time, along with our ladies, rolling bandages. On weekends, we closed the doors to regular members in order to stage free entertainments for the forces. They were quite popular. We had music-hall acts and we provided the young officers with some delights not available in the more respectable voluntary institutions in London. We were

devastated when the authorities brought our weekend efforts to
a close early in 1917. 'Moral reasons,' they said. What the devil
was immoral about providing a little pleasure to some of those
lovely boys they were sending to the trenches to die? *C'est la
guerre*. . . . As you might expect, my sister Fawn had fallen madly
in love, a few years earlier. He was a beautiful young Canadian
. . . he was killed at Ypres." Clara stared down at the floor, then
raised her head to look directly at Lesley. In a brisk, businesslike
monotone, she said, "One of his comrades told me that he had
drowned in the mud. I never repeated it to Fawn."

Lesley lowered her glass, a pained expression on her face.
"Oh my God . . ."

"And the war went on," said Clara quietly. "In 1917 we
nearly lost your dad to the influenza. There wasn't much a person
could do about it in those days. For the first time in our lives,
Fawn and I prayed and, by some miracle, little Harry survived.
That was about the time that one of our regulars, a lovely gentleman with the Foreign Office, dropped by to tell us that he'd had
word of Elleander's execution. Those bloody Austrians! We had
heard that in the past they had always commuted women's death
sentences, so we took it for granted that Elleander would return
after the war . . . never for a moment questioned it. But they broke
their own tradition and carried out the sentence—killed her! She
had been an enemy alien. The court just forgot about her and no
one took the trouble to petition the emperor, as they usually did
in such cases. My sister and I were shocked out of our wits! Poor
Fawn was absolutely devastated . . . first her young officer and
then Elleander. She hardly spoke a word for months, and quite
suddenly I had two invalids to look after, Harry and Fawn. It was
a bloody awful year.

"But time, as they say, heals almost anything. After a while,
little Harry recovered completely and Fawn came back to life.
And me? Well, as with most other old fossils, if you examine me
closely, you can learn something about ancient history."

Clara Fowler laughed ruefully, then fell silent, her eyes fixed
on a decorative Vuillard hanging on the far wall. "It's been over
seventy years and I still miss her, your grandmum."

Lesley watched as the old woman inserted a Gauloise into
her long, yellowed, ivory cigarette holder. She attempted to form

an image of her grandmother, but the figure remained an elusive,
shifting mirage. It was as if she were sitting across from a living,
contemporary human being who had consorted in the dim past
with a mythical goddess. Flesh and blood, she thought. She said,
"I wish I had known her."

"I wish you had, my dear." Once again, the old woman
seemed to drift off into a sea of private thoughts. Then very
quietly, as if to herself, she said, "Men and horses were so beautiful in those days. Elleander had the winners and we all won a
packet. She used hers to buy Silver Mace. She knew he would win
the derby, and he did. What an exciting outing that was! We sat
in our box at Epsom drinking champagne and eating cold duck
and caviar with a few of our favorite gentlemen. Silver Mace came
in three lengths ahead of the pack—a long shot. Your grandmum
was on her way to being a wealthy woman, and Fawn and I didn't
do so badly either. She sold Silver Mace and used that money plus
her winnings to buy the house on Highcastle Road."

"And my grandfather . . . Bertram Trasker?"

"He showed up one summer evening at Highcastle Road.
Elleander Morning had achieved by then a kind of notoriety in
certain circles. I'm sure he remembered her from the cab ride. Of
course, at that time he knew nothing of his child, who, as I
mentioned before, was living in the cottage in Cornwall."

"When did she tell him?"

"As far as I know, she never did."

"But why not?"

"I don't know," said Clara Fowler. "It was quite sad, actually."

"Did she see him regularly?"

"Not till 1912—that would make it about two years after she
had him in that cab. He just showed up one evening at Highcastle
Road with an introduction for membership. They were in her
rooms together for an hour or two—maybe longer. It's so long
ago. . . ."

"They made love again," said Lesley quietly. "After two
years."

"I'd wager they did." She smiled broadly. "I certainly would
have. Your grandfather was a very handsome gentleman, a
charmer. After that first time with Bertie, there was never another

man, neither for pleasure nor business." She drew deeply on her Gauloise, releasing a cloud of pungent blue smoke that swirled about her head, almost obscuring it.

"They were very much in love," she continued. "They spent a lot of time together, usually at his flat, and even made some trips to Paris. Then one morning, it was a lovely Sunday, I believe, Bertie drove up in a brand-new motorcar. It was beautiful, an open American machine called a Mercer Runabout. It was bright red. Most of the ladies and even one or two of our gentlemen overnighters came out to look at it. Someone said it was the only one in England. Bertie promised all of us a ride."

Clara Fowler stood up, her legs apart as if bracing herself. "Then suddenly, from nowhere, your grandmum was there, still in her nightgown. She had a terrible expression on her face. And then she was attacking that lovely motorcar with a big fire ax— bashing it to bits, she was!" The old woman swung her arms as if wielding an invisible ax. She laughed. "It's really not the least bit funny, but your grandmum had gone starkers. Bertie grabbed her and as quick as a wink she had him on the ground with a kick in the bullocks. We all just stood there not knowing what to do while she turned that beautiful machine into a heap of ruin. Then finally, Samuel, the butler, still in his nightshirt, rushed in and grabbed the ax from her. She quieted down and he carried her into the house."

"But why?" Lesley breathed the words.

"When she was struggling with Bertie, she called out, 'This bloody machine's going to kill you!' That's all I know about it. When Bertie got over the shock—it took him ten minutes before he could stand up—he just left. They hauled the wreck away the next day, but I'm almost certain Elleander never saw him again. Poor chap was so angry—enraged—and confused. . . ."

"How awful."

"They loved each other."

"How old was my grandmother when she did that thing in Vienna?"

"She was thirty, born January ninth, 1883. We met her in 1907, when she was twenty-four and we were thirteen. You look very much like her."

"I know."

"She was beautiful."

Lesley remained silent. She closed her eyes, once again searching for a clear image of her young grandmother.

Clara said, "I have something to show you."

Lesley followed Clara Fowler into a narrow hall leading to a round chamber of glass brick. Dazzled by the sudden brilliance, she preceded the old woman up a gleaming stainless-steel circular staircase leading to the master bedroom.

Lesley stared in disbelief. The walls were a placid sea stretching to horizons graced with palmed islands. Whales and flying fish played in the gentle crests of white froth above which the sails of a dozen square-riggers were highlighted by a full moon amid scudding clouds painted on the ceiling. In the center of all this sat a massive ship of a bed, fully fifteen feet across its twin masts, fore and aft, supporting a silken Union Jack canopy. A buxom figurehead in gold leaf embellished the mahogany prow.

After a full minute of silence, Clara said, "It became Elleander's bed. Fawn and I would have nothing to do with it, we were terribly frightened by it. Later it occupied her bedroom at Highcastle Road. She called it her Ship of State. Some of the most important men in Britain, of our time, had been in it."

"God, it's . . . it's magnificent!" said Lesley. "It must weigh tons." She stared, at war with her own incredulity. "And the murals . . . ?"

"Henri Matisse. It was commissioned by Elleander in 1911. Matisse was a young man then. It's all on canvas panels." She stood in the center of the room, arms outstretched. "When I die, my dear, it will be yours, bed and all. Your grandmum would be pleased to know it's going to be kept in the family."

They returned to the living room. Lesley said, "Where did it come from?"

"That's a long story, my dear. I'd hardly know where to start."

"Please . . ."

"It's only a bed—but where to begin?" The old woman leaned back in her chair. "It would have to be when Fawn and I were children." She lit another cigarette, placing it in the long holder. "When we were only nine years old, you see, our mother disappeared. . . ."

━━━━ ➤ **14** ◀━ ━━━━

1903

It was turning dark. The twins sat on the curbstone in front
of the hovel that was their home; two little girls waiting for their
mother to finish servicing her gentleman. They were nine years
old. When their mother had a client, the door was locked. Other
than that, they had come and gone as they pleased since they
were little more than infants. Physically, they were identical, sharing the same deep-black, tangled hair, the same wide, questioning eyes, and even the same grubby, once-white dresses.

Clara, always the leader, grasped Fawn's arm, pulling her
erect. Wordlessly they strolled through the gathering night toward Barking Road, then hand in hand past the East India docks
and left to Cubitt Town where, from the deep curve of the
Thames, they could see the lights of Greenwich reflecting on the
dark water. This was a familiar place that existed on the western
rim of a radius of roughly two miles, beyond which the twins
never ventured for fear of being lost—gobbled up forever—in
the maze of an infinite London. It was a circle within which they

had wandered since they were five. They knew the area intimately and were familiar figures to the local tradesmen and to the long-shoremen at the Victoria and East India docks.

But beyond this protective circle, they knew nothing. They had never crossed the Thames nor seen the West End. Their experience with greenswards had been restricted to the tiny pocket-parks of Lyle Commons and the Millwall Recreation Grounds. They could neither write, read, nor count past twenty.

When the sisters returned home, their mother was gone. Missing also was their mother's clothing and the few personal items she possessed. On the small table in the center of the room were two single pound notes weighted down with a shiny, newly minted half crown.

"What are we going to do?" Fawn's voice was a high-pitched sob. Tears streaked her cheek.

Clara hardly heard her. She picked up the money, balanced it in the palm of her hand as if its weight were somehow relative to its value. During her short life, she had dealt from time to time with pennies and, on a few rare occasions, a shilling or two. She had never handled this amount of money before. It staggered her. Its worth was beyond her reckoning. For a moment the shock of desertion faded.

Fawn was saying, "Will she come back?" She sat forlornly on the rumpled bed, her head tilted downward as if she were study-ing the floor.

"No," said Clara. "She's gone forever and ever, she is."

To Clara, their mother had been a quiet, preoccupied woman who served them a meal every day, occasionally gave them a few pennies for sweets, and once, on a dimly remembered Christmas, a doll. Now they would have to do without her. Once again the young girl weighed the money in her hand. As if to calm her sister, she said, "It doesn't matter. Look, we're bloody rich!"

Clara slept well, awakening just a few times to comfort her sobbing twin. In the morning they dined on the stale bread re-maining in the larder. For the next three days they lived on sweets. On the fourth, they returned from the last of their inter-minable walks to find a carriage parked in front of their house. There were a young nun and a policeman. The nun smiled at them; behind her a few neighbors had congregated and were speaking quietly to each other. Clara overheard one of them say, ". . . found in the Thames she was. . . ."

The nun took their hands. In a sweet voice she said, "We're going to take lovely care of you. My name is Sister Doris."

Clara searched for a response, then found herself sobbing for the first time. For seconds, she fought a rising sea of tears. Then the nun was holding her and the young girl's face was buried in soft, well-worn black fabric. She was joined by Fawn, and both of them clung tightly to Sister Doris. As they entered the carriage, the bobby, smiling, handed Clara the doll he had found in their flat. Clara, tears streaking her face, passed it on to Fawn.

For the next three years, the twins lived at St. Verna's Home for Christian Daughters of Wayward Women in Woolich. They slept in a dormitory with thirty other young girls. The holy sisters, without exception, were kind and understanding; the food, both palatable and plentiful. The twins rounded out, grew content with their lot, made friends, learned the catechism and learned to do sums, to read and write. Clara experienced her first menstrual period five months before Fawn, and was thus able to ease the shock for her sister. It was to be thus for the rest of their lives . . . they swore to each other that they would never separate.

On a Saturday morning in May 1906, all thirty children were lined up on display for a middle-aged woman who, with the best of references, had introduced herself to the Mother Superior as Mrs. Samantha Smythe. She was there, she stated, to do her Christian duty by adopting one of these poor, unfortunate girls.

The twins were twelve and on their best behavior. Adoptions were rare at St. Verna's. Only two had taken place during the three years they had been there. They curtsied prettily when Mrs. Smythe got to them. At once, the idle smile on her round, bejowled face froze in place. "Twins!" she said, her voice at least an octave above its normal range. "Good Lord . . . you sweet, darling children!" She seemed astonished with her good fortune, held out her arms in a welcoming gesture. Clara glanced at Mother Superior, who smiled and nodded. The two girls stepped forward shyly to find themselves in the smothering embrace of the large woman.

"Oh, you little darlings . . . know what I'm going to do?" She hugged them even tighter. "I'm going to give you both a lovely home. . . ."

The twins responded sheepishly, not quite believing their good luck. Despite her lavish affection, they sensed something not quite motherly about Mrs. Samantha Smythe; perhaps the barely perceptible sour odor, the tightly clenched grip on their shoulders.

Mother Superior said, in gentle admonition, "Girls, what have you to say to the nice lady?"

"Thank you," said Clara, pulling away to curtsy.

"Thank you," said Fawn, following her sister's example, though close to tears and wondering why.

The cab took them through the West End. The twins gaped in wonder at the massive buildings, the multitude of bowler-hatted gentlemen making their way to luncheon, the well-dressed ladies with fine figures and large feathered hats, and finally, the royal palace itself. Feeling a rising excitement, Clara grasped her sister's hand. They were on their way to a new life.

The house was a small two-story affair. The twins stood in awe in a parlor of heavy dark wood and deep-red velvet. Huge potted plants created a near jungle and, wonder of wonders, there was a gramophone.

They were introduced to Mr. Earl Hammond, a thin scarecrow of a man, middle-aged, with curly red hair and deep-set, hollow eyes. "Twins," he said, his voice a deeply pitched mutter. He flashed a tight grin at them, demonstrating a mouthful of yellowed and broken teeth. Once again the girls curtsied as they had been taught.

"A matched set of sweet little virgins," said Mrs. Smythe. "Worth their weight in gold." She placed her hands on their shoulders. "Aren't you, my dears."

The twins, not understanding, nodded.

"They'll bring in a pretty penny," said Mr. Hammond, a distorted leer darkening his sallow face.

"But not if you lay so much as a finger on either of them." She pulled the twins closer to her. "I'll cut out your liver if you try. . . ."

"Wouldn't dream of it, madam."

Mr. Hammond served as a general factotum to Mrs. Smythe. Depending on circumstances, he functioned as butler, handyman, and occasional lover.

As for "Mrs. Smythe," the name itself, as she pointed out to the twins, was actually an expedient fiction she had invented for the expedition to St. Verna's. She actually called herself Madam Kooshay; a name, she insisted, that was gaining notoriety in certain circles for dealing in nothing but the loveliest authentic merchandise. The holy sisters of St. Verna's would have been shocked beyond measure to know that their delicate charges had not, in truth, been adopted, but rather had been procured. Madam Kooshay dealt in young virgins—child-women—and Clara and Fawn represented an unheard-of commodity, a double serving—a duet of innocent pubescence. A novelty, she repeated, worth its weight in solid gold. Twins. . . .

15

1906

It took Madam Kooshay three weeks to find a proper client. He was, according to her, a "rich old geezer in the fur trade." The price was to be a hundred pounds, an enormous fee. She promised the twins their share: twenty quid. But when the time came, she said, "Room and board, my dears."

"Yes, ma'am," said the girls.

"At that price," said Mr. Hammond, laughing, "they could do better at the Ritz!"

"You're a bloody animal!" said Madam Kooshay, gathering the twins to her. "Everyone knows I always take care of my girls."

When the time came, Fawn and Clara were dressed as brides in white wedding gowns and veils. Their room was painted white and decorated with lilies.

"How lovely you look, how innocent . . ." Madam Kooshay smiled sadly. "My little girls are about to become women." She held their hands, squeezing tightly. "It's so romantic, I feel I could cry." She stepped back, smoothed out a veil, straightened a seam. "You remember everything I told you?"

"Yes, ma'am . . ."

"You will do everything the gentleman wants? Anything and everything?"

"Yes, ma'am . . ."

"Like sweet young ladies? No crying or whining?"

"Yes, ma'am . . ."

"Good. But just remember, if there's any trouble, I'm going to hang you up by your toes and let Mr. Hammond beat your sweet little white arses to a bleeding pulp." She grinned at them as if she were a doting parent threatening an unlikely spanking.

Finally, with Madam Kooshay peering over his shoulder, the furrier stood in the doorway of their room, staring at his child brides through wide, puffy, unblinking eyes. He seemed in shock.

The twins faced him, holding hands, attempting to conceal their nervousness. Clara rehearsed mentally the few innocently seductive tricks she and her sister had been taught. Madam Kooshay said, "Smile prettily, children, for the nice gentleman. . . ."

The furrier's mouth was hanging open. They stared into it, smiling woodenly. Then feeling pressure from her sister's hand, Fawn fell into a curtsy next to her. When she looked up, Madam Kooshay was gone. The middle-aged furrier stood alone in front of the closed door. His words were slurred, guttural, as if he were having trouble forcing them out of a dry throat. "My name, little ladies, is Harry Lethaby . . . Mr. Lethaby."

He spent nearly an hour unbraiding their hair. Then, in order to tell them apart, he placed a solid gold bracelet on Fawn's wrist, a silver one on Clara's. (Later, Clara surreptitiously switched bracelets. As do most twins, they enjoyed such games.) Mr. Lethaby was good-natured, playful. He made it a game, playing the part of a stern master to his obedient children. "Now I want each of you to remove a shoe. . . . Fawn, undo my cravat. Mind the studs, young lady . . . now the trousers. . . . Hold it gently, dear child . . . a soft kiss . . . yes, there. . . . Ah, what pretty little things you are. . . ." Fawn watched in awe as his penis expanded. It was, she thought, magical.

Clara sensed Mr. Lethaby's nervousness as he released her from her corset. Lacking the authority of his expensive clothing, he seemed awkward, ludicrous. He was peculiarly shaped, as if, she thought, much of his inner workings had dropped into his lower torso. His face, in contrast to the ashen hue of his body, was a flushed pink. She found her remaining fears retreating and, with growing courage, she reached out to lay a gently probing index finger onto a large wart distorting an otherwise pristine member. "Mr. Lethaby," she said timidly, "do all men have this thing?"

"Only those of us, little darling, who are truly blessed."

As Fawn and Clara were to realize in later years, no woman had ever experienced a more gentle or prolonged deflowering than had they—nor a more playful one. Mr. Lethaby, despite his exotic tastes, proved to be a gentleman, in the literal sense of the word.

Later, they were scolded because of flecks of blood on Madam Kooshay's white silk coverlet. The twins had forgotten to fold it back as instructed and they were to be docked for its cost. Nevertheless, Madam was pleased. Mr. Lethaby had been profuse with glowing reports. As a reward, she took them, with Mr. Hammond as escort, on the following afternoon to tea at the Café Royal, where each twin finished off two complete, magnificent trifle desserts.

Clara and Fawn remained "twelve-year-old virgins" for six months. Every week, there was another eager, well-paying client. The girls enjoyed the game, becoming quite adroit at feigning sweet innocence. To further enhance that illusion, Madam Kooshay insisted on the use of alum to temporarily shrink the vaginal passageways. The crowning touch was provided through the use of secret, ornate finger rings from which, during the heat of passion, they would release a few drops of ox blood onto their sheets, their inner thighs and, with a bit of luck, onto their gentleman's preoccupied member. (Afterward, at Madam's insistence, there would always be a douching solution of mercuric cyanide to prevent pregnancy and possible disease.)

As the twins were to learn later, Mr. Lethaby, desperately infatuated, had been trying to see them. Sadly, the furrier's repeated requests were rejected by Madam Kooshay, who, for reasons of business, preferred to continue presenting the twins as tight little virgins. She was making her fortune with the only matched set in Britain. Fresh, young merchandise had to be shielded from unnecessary wear and tear in order to protect her "dearest investment."

When the twins had been at it for a half year, they were sold to the furrier for four hundred pounds. It was, for Madam Kooshay, a fortuitous sale, as the girls had played their role twenty-three times, and the soft, virginal innocence was going stale—somewhat brittle around the edges.

Madam Kooshay, almost three thousand pounds wealthier than she had been on the day she "adopted" the twins, retired with Mr. Hammond to a little cottage in Brighton. Until the time of her death, twelve years later, she remained in touch with her ex-charges by way of chatty letters carrying salutations such as "To My Little Darling Daughters" or "To the Sweet Lights of My Life." Clara would, from time to time, respond with a short note detailing her adventures. She and her sister retained, through the years, an abiding filial affection for their ex-"benefactress."

Mr. Lethaby installed his twin purchase in a modest West End flat, where he proceeded to provide them with just about everything that met their fancy. He referred to them as "my greedy little daughters," and had them dress for his thrice weekly visits in little-girl dresses: starched white lace with giant bows and puffy bloomers.

During the other four days of the week, they chose from an ever-expanding wardrobe of fashionable grown-up frocks and gowns made for them by a talented local dressmaker, a Miss Markle, who, after recovering from the shock of sewing adult clothing for twin children, entered wholeheartedly into the spirit of things. As they became more sophisticated, the twins took great delight in the newest French lingerie and became quite adroit in the mysterious use of cosmetics and scents.

Mr. Lethaby seemed to them to possess unlimited financial resources, for he also provided his charges with a tutor, one Miss Grimm, a wholesome-looking spinster in her late thirties who, for two hours every Tuesday and Thursday morning, instructed the twins in the cultural pursuits, in proper English diction, and in the gentle art of female etiquette.

"When you are introduced to a gentleman, you will always smile—just so—then say, 'How do you do.' Never . . . hear me carefully now . . . never take a gentleman's hand if he offers it, because if he does so, he is not a gentleman! Physical contact is always the lady's prerogative. This is quite important and you should remember it. It is always the lady's choice whether or not to extend her hand. Now, let's practice. . . ."

The girls took to going out in the evening, unescorted, first to local music halls, but then, as their confidence grew, to the theater and ballet. They flirted outrageously at every opportunity and soon there were men who took them to dinner, to the theater, to racing meets and country outings. They achieved a certain notoriety—the mysterious twins—always on the arm of a single current favorite, and finally, the double fulcrum of a circle of swells who competed for their attention and then lied about their amorous success (and excess) in order to increase their own reputations as gallant womanizers. For throughout, the twins remained faithful to Mr. Lethaby, never permitting their escorts more than a duet of playful good-night kisses before cabbing home alone.

To the gentlemen involved, it all seemed deliciously scandalous, particularly in light of Fawn and Clara's age. The girls were thirteen years old and, despite the fine feathers, if one took time to look closely, their lack of years was visible beneath the subterfuge of cosmetics and coiffure.

Out of loyalty to their benefactor, the twins told him all. Mr. Lethaby was delighted and encouraged them. His adopted daughters, he reasoned, had become celebrities, but only he, of all the men in London, had the key.

On a damp and chilly night during the second week in April, the twins, on the way home after an evening with one of their gentlemen, saw the figure of a young woman lying in the road. She was, it seemed, in the process of lifting herself laboriously onto one arm, exposing to their view a pained and bloodied face.

The coachman, who had swerved to avoid the unfortunate victim, was reluctant to turn about when Clara ordered him to do so. However, she insisted, finally convincing him of his Christian duty by offering a substantial tip.

The twins judged the woman to be young, in her early twen-

ties. The blood on her face proved to be the result of nothing
more serious than a bloodied nose. Her dress, of cheap, thin
cotton, was ripped at the bodice, revealing a full, perfectly
formed breast, above which, in the barely adequate streetlight,
the young girls could make out an ugly purple bruise. As they
kneeled at her side, she smiled weakly, saying in a quiet, husky
voice, "Thank you . . . I'm all right . . . really I am . . . if you'd
just be so kind as to help me get to my feet. . . ."

Despite her disheveled appearance, the woman on the
ground was beautiful: tall and blond, with full lips and pronounced, aristocratic cheekbones.

Fawn grasped the victim's left hand to help pull her erect.
The effort was met with a pitiful whimper. "Something," she said,
"has gone wrong with my hand. . . ." She spoke breathlessly,
struggling for air as if near fainting. The twins helped her into
the cab, brought her home. The woman seemed dazed. Her left
hand was swollen, but the nosebleed had stopped. It was much
too late to fetch a doctor, so Clara bandaged the hand the best
she could. The little finger, she noticed, seemed askew, as if
broken.

After a wash-up, the woman insisted on leaving, but the
twins insisted even more vehemently that she spend the night.
The poor thing, reasoned Clara, was still trembling and would
surely catch her death.

Then Clara, still playing mother, brewed a pot of tea, adding
to their guest's cup a dollop of Mr. Lethaby's brandy. (It was
prohibited to the girls, as Mr. Lethaby was convinced that they
were too young to drink.) With the visitor wearing one of Fawn's
many dressing gowns, they warmed themselves in front of the
fire. The woman remained silent for a time, then in a low
voice, as if she were speaking to herself, said, "You're only children. . . ."

"We're twins," said Fawn. "Thirteen. I'm Fawn and that's
Clara."

"My name," said the woman, smiling at them, "is Elleander.
Elleander Morning."

ATTRACTIVE, CULTURED, YOUNG English woman
seeks position as private secretary-companion to ma-
ture, elderly (but active) American gentleman of
means. Currently living in London but will emigrate.
Please enclose particulars.

BOX M-2216

—Personal advertisement
in *The New York
Review of Books*

16

1983

They sat over croissants and coffee at a little table on their
hotel-room terrace. It was their fourth and final day in the Bahamas. During that time, Lesley had developed a deep tan that
contrasted strongly with the white of her tiny riviera. Peering at
her over the rim of his cup, Paul laughed and said that she looked
like a photographic negative. Then he reached across the table,
taking both her hands in his to tell her for the first time that he
was in love with her. Lesley raised his fingers to her lips and felt
she was about to melt in the warmth of the sun. They had been
together now on nine separate occasions. She realized, with a
stab of pleasure, that she would no longer feel compelled to keep
track.

He stood, pulled her to her feet, kissing her lightly. "You're
very warm," he said. "I can feel it. You should go cool off in the
ocean."

She pressed her body against his. "I love you." She spoke the
words into his ear. "There's no reason to cool off."

Late that afternoon, they boarded a British Imperial Airways DeHaviland for the flight back to London. Seated in the lounge, Lesley stared through the round window at the white fume thrown up by their bow as they started their take-off run. Then the big boat was up on its retractable skis, the turbulent wake and the high-pitched whine of its six jet engines behind it. When they were airborne, Lesley released her seat belt, accepted a cool martini from the steward and acknowledged, finally, an anxiety that had been growing, unconceded, since they had left London four days ago.

Mentally she rehearsed the words, attempting to soften them, to arrange them into a sequence that would minimize their impact. How, she wondered, could she manage to belittle the fact that she was a grave robber? It was a futile effort. She abandoned the attempt, casting herself instead into a zestful geniality through a few hours of frivolous conversation over champagne and filet mignon. There was time.

She maintained the camouflage until they had entered a taxi, dockside, in London. It was now or never, and she must tell him everything, hold back nothing. They were lovers now, and it was a matter of trust. She spoke in flat tones, the words delivered quickly, matter-of-factly, with no coloring.

They sat close but apart, neither touching nor looking at one another. It seemed to her that the man she loved had suddenly been replaced by a formal acquaintance. An eternity passed before he spoke. "Horrible . . . What did you hope to accomplish?"

"I wanted to find out if anyone was occupying that other gravesite."

"But you opened both."

She detected an angry undertone in his voice. "My curiosity got the best of me . . . I thought . . ." Her voice trailed off as if she were having trouble choosing the words.

"Obsession, not curiosity."

"But there was a body—remains—in the other gravesite. It was supposed to be empty . . . the cemetery records . . ."

"Goulish," he said. "You've been obsessed with all of this since I've known you. It's as if you're living in the past. None of it is real . . . none of it. Not those damned books, or your grandmother, nor that chap she murdered . . ."

"Adolf Hitler . . ."

"None of it!"

"I had no idea you felt so strongly." Lesley's voice was tone-less. She stared straight ahead as she spoke, her hands folded primly in her lap. "If I had known . . ."

"You would have done differently? Just dropped the whole thing?"

"Yes, of course I would."

"I don't think so." He paused, finally turned to her. "I'm sorry. Perhaps I'm the one who's acting irrationally."

Paul asked the cab to wait, saw her to her door, kissed her perfunctorily with stiff, dry lips. He would call her.

In the study, she poured a glass of cognac, then absentmind-edly left it sitting on the sideboard. She sat, legs folded beneath her, in the big leather wing chair, her eyes locked on the Jackson Pollock hanging on the near wall.

She loved Paul Bauer and now maybe she would lose him. Lesley felt the tears welling up beneath her eyelids. She was not quite the same woman she had been before she met him, only six weeks earlier. Paul had opened her to new physical and emo-tional gratification, introduced her to a part of herself only he knew had existed. It was as if Paul Bauer had reinvented her. He seemed, suddenly, to have become the most important thing in her life.

Or had he? Perhaps Paul had been right and she was ob-sessed—fanatically preoccupied. "Grave robber . . . ghoul . . ." The words emerged in a barely audible whisper, horrifying her. But there were other words: "Elleander . . . Kursk . . . Omaha Beach . . . Ploesti . . . Jeep . . . Napalm . . . Dachau . . . Eisenhower . . . Bertie . . ."

She looked up to find Mrs. Green standing in the doorway. "Rose is gone," said the old woman, sniffling. She handed Lesley a small envelope and then proceeded to burst into tears. It was a note from Rose.

> *Dear Madam:*
>
> *I have found a new position as private secretary and travelling companion to an American gentleman. He is quite proper, a retired widower who came into his wealth by*

*way of the gravel business, which I understand is quite a
common thing in America.*

*Mr. Stahlmann intends to spend his last years
travelling about to places like Paris and China and Tahiti
and so on. I will send you picture postcards. We are
starting in Scotland and then on to Norway.*

*I want to thank you for all the nice things you have
done for me. Of course, I will never forget your father, who
will be forever in my heart. But sooner or later, one must
move on, mustn't one? I hope you understand.*

> *With affection,*
> *Rose Parker*

"How did they meet?" said Lesley.

"I don't know," said Mrs. Green, sniffling. "But he's elderly."

"You met him?"

"Yes. He came here to take her away. He seemed a nice
gentleman, Mr. Stahlmann."

"How elderly?"

"Very."

A week went by without a phone call from Paul. On the eighth
day, Lesley steeled herself and dialed his London flat. The phone
rang six times. His answering machine, usually triggered by the
third ring, remained silent. She repeated the process a half-dozen
times over the next two evenings, with the same results. The
following morning she rang up his office at the embassy, where
his assistant informed her that Paul Bauer was on a leave of
absence. Finally, she dialed his apartment in Berlin and was rewarded with an answer. Lesley froze, unable to speak, listening
with wildly beating heart as Paul responded repeatedly to the
silence on the other end of his line. When he finally disconnected,
she held the receiver to her ear for a full minute, fearful that
dropping it into its cradle would be the final act of their relationship.

Freddy took her to dinner that night. His good nature was
a tonic to her. He was sympathetic, but not overly so. A few nights
later they went dancing at Babe's Seventy-Nine, one of the four

currently fashionable phlegm parlors in the West End. By week's end, they had danced in all of them. Grateful, Lesley called a halt.

She fixed up one of the unused top-floor rooms as a painting studio, then spent a full day shopping for artist's supplies. Dressed in a white painter's smock, she spent the night stretching and priming three large canvases. Finally, with the new easel facing a good north light, the plump, virgin tubes of oil colors still safe in their snug compartments, she confronted the blank expanse of canvas. She could think of nothing. She applied paint haphazardly in broad, unsuccessful strokes and ugly blotches. Her second attempt was a still life of fruit she brought up from the kitchen and that, after an hour, she proceeded to eat. The third was a nude self-portrait. She stood naked before a large chennelle mirror and, after deciding she must lose five pounds, lost interest. Agitated, she paced the room for two hours, then decided to stretch and prime two more canvases. By nightfall she gave up the effort, took a long, scalding-hot shower and went to see a new Jimmy Dean movie, which for two hours and seventeen minutes managed to distract her.

She felt like a soldier on the eve of battle. She drank too much and flirted outrageously. Then on a Saturday morning, during the only serious snowstorm of the season, Lesley came awake assuming she was in bed with Paul. It took moments for her to realize that she was atop a lumpy mattress on the floor of a spare, freezing single room. A bearded young man lay snoring on his back beside her, an arm thrown carelessly across her breasts. A faded tattoo inscribed on the white flesh of his skinny bicep identified her lover as Sebastian. There had been, she recalled, exactly one too many martinis at a Soho pub the night before. He was very young.

Quietly, she slipped out from under his arm, coming erect on shaky legs, trying to remember if she'd had an orgasm. Then she gathered her clothes and, using the edge of a small folding table for support, managed to get into them. In the platen of a battered old Hermes on the table, there was a sheet of yellow foolscap. She read:

A Sense of Silence
A Time of ~~Dead~~ Dread,

A World of Violence,
And thoughts of ~~Bed Dead Bread~~ Lead.

There were others stacked next to the typewriter. A poet. She dropped a five-pound note on the table and left quietly. She felt empty.

Lesley trudged through the thickening snow to the British Imperial Airways office on Regent Street and purchased a round-trip, first-class ticket to New York. It was time, for want of something better to do, to visit with her mother for a few weeks.

Dear Miss Morning,

As per your arrangements, both coffins were retrieved last night for re-interment at Chessington. The analysis required far more of my time than I had originally planned. The reason for this is, quite simply, that I did not believe my initial conclusions. Nor did I, as matters progressed, believe any of my subsequent conclusions. I still do not.

The skeletal remains are those of two females. The older of the two died between the ages of 80 and 85. Cause of death: cancer. Date of death: 1970–1971.

The younger female died at age 29–34. Cause of death: bullet through heart (fourth and fifth ribs shattered, indicating entry and exit of large-caliber projectile). Date of death: 1912–1916.

The above data fulfils your request, but there is more that I am certain will interest you. The conclusion at which I have arrived with great reluctance is, to say the least, startling—more than that—it represents a total contradiction. In short, it is an impossibility. Yet it is, according to the evidence, an inescapable verdict. If I were ever to attempt publication of these findings, I would, in no uncertain terms, be laughed out of my profession. This despite that fact that I have used every means at my disposal.

Briefly stated: Both skeletons are those of the same woman! My first indication of this was related to badly set fractures of the small fingers of the left hands of both skeletons. *The breaks and subsequent knittings were identical in both cases. (Not merely identical, but rather, absolutely identical.)*

The dental configuration of both females is, allowing for age differential, also identical. The probability of this occurring in two separate individuals is even more remote than the probability of two identical sets of fingerprints. All of this has been confirmed by every modern means of analysis at my disposal.

Sincerely,
Lawrence Potterton, M.D.

"A stunning literary and pictorial fantasy that causes all others that preceded it to fade into insignificance."

—*Los Angeles Times*
January 8, 1984
(Review of the
Time-Life *History of the Second World War.*
Time-Life Books, two
volumes, boxed)

◄━━━ 17 ◄━━━━

1984

By the third week after publication, the Time-Life *History of the Second World War* had gone into its third printing. Time-Life itself had outbid four other publishers for the North American rights. (Random House, the runner-up, had tentatively planned to title it "The Invisible War.") Publication was simultaneous in thirteen countries (excluding, among others, Bulgaria, the Russian People's Republic, Fascist Italy, the Ukrainian Republic, the Spanish Socialist Republic, and Japan, along with its Greater-East-Asia-Co-Prosperity Sphere).

Time-Life, after much internal debate, had decided to publish the twin volumes as exact replicas of the original. Even the typeface remained the same. The only change was the actual publication date—from 1970 to 1984.

The books themselves carried no foreword. To fill that function, a slim folio was fitted into the boxed, hard-cover set. It described briefly the circumstances surrounding the discovery of the original volumes. Included also was a lengthy analysis of the political and strategic aspects of "the War That Never Was," written by Frances Boardman, plus a tactical battle analysis by Brigadier James Entwistle (retired) of the Imperial War Museum, London. The cover price in the United States was $24.95; $22.95 in Canada.

Paul Bauer permitted his shoulders to relax against the glove-leather upholstery of the high-backed wing chair. Even as he watched, the French doors on the far side of the large rococo room were darkening. It was the final illumination of a clear, unseasonably warm Berlin day. Across from him his uncle, Field Marshal Rudolph von Seydlitz, was accepting a cigar from the State Secretary. Bauer himself had graciously refused a similar offer a moment earlier. Now he observed as Field Marshal von Seydlitz clipped one end, then lit the other, using a wooden match above which he rotated the cigar as if he were roasting a piece of raw meat.

With some effort, the Secretary of State leaned forward, his bulk at least a size too large for the spindly armchair. He pointed his cigar at Field Marshal von Seydlitz. "It will please you to know, Herr Bauer, that your uncle is to be the next Chancellor of Germany."

Paul, somewhat confused, turned to his uncle and smiled politely, wondering if this announcement was the sole reason for his being there. He said, "Congratulations . . . your Excellency."

"Thank you, Paul."

The Secretary said, "The government suffers from lack of imagination . . . constipation. Your uncle is the best man to administer the laxative for us."

Field Marshal von Seydlitz tried to disguise what Paul recognized as sudden excitement. Stiffly, the elderly man said, "That is an interesting way of stating it, Herr Schmidt, but I do have certain ideas. . . ."

"I have no doubt of that." Schmidt turned to Paul. "It should be clear, my dear fellow, that I'm swearing you to absolute secrecy regarding everything that is said here. Agreed?"

"Agreed," said Paul Bauer, wondering just exactly what he was swearing to.

"Very good," said the Secretary. "You'll then be happy to

know that we have discussed your qualifications at length with the President. He was quite impressed with your background."

"Qualifications for what?"

"The cabinet post of Minister of Propaganda."

"But there is no such cabinet post. . . ."

"Ah, but you see, we have a plan." The Secretary rose ponderously out of his chair. "But first we must drink to it—and to our new Chancellor-to-be."

They gathered at the sideboard as the Secretary poured brandy into large crystal glasses. Von Seydlitz smiled at his nephew, allowing the rigid muscles of his face to relax. He raised his glass. "To the New Order!"

Feeling a rising anxiety, Paul Bauer joined them in the toast. There was a chilling familiarity to the phrase, "the New Order." He repeated it silently, suddenly realizing its origin. The Time-Life *History of the Second World War.*

The Secretary motioned for them to follow him to a glassed-in cabinet across the room. It was a display case for a large collection of hand-painted military miniatures. Schmidt opened the glass doors. "This, gentlemen, is my avocation," he said. He removed a colorful mounted figure, roughly two inches high. The horse was rearing, attached to the base by a single leg; the rider, erect in the saddle, sword drawn back to strike, helmet cockade blowing in the wind. With the base resting in a pudgy palm, Schmidt held it aloft. "King's Royal Irish, Eighth Hussars, roughly 1836. It's an English casting, they still make some of the best—took me two weeks to assemble and paint. Lovely, don't you agree?"

They nodded. The Secretary handed the figure to Von Seydlitz, saying, "Please accept this as a token of our collaboration, Field Marshal."

"I will most certainly treasure it, Herr Secretary."

State Secretary Schmidt reached in for another. It was of the same scale but involving three figures. A soldier wearing an open tunic held down a buxom, half-naked woman, while the third, his military trousers bunched below his knees, his minute penis at the ready, hovered over her. "French foot soldiers," said the Secretary, "probably around 1808. The young female is most likely Spanish."

"Exquisite," said Field Marshal von Seydlitz.

Schmidt handed Paul a jeweler's loupe. "If you look closely under magnification, you can make out individual pubic hairs. It's a most unusual piece."

Paul placed the loupe to his eye, twisted the piece to the light. Terror-filled tiny metallic eyes, the pupils the size of pinpoints, stared into his.

"Rape," said Schmidt, "is endemic to war. Many men pay in blood, just a few women with the carnal use of their bodies. *C'est la guerre,* wouldn't you say, Von Seydlitz?"

"It's always the losers who are raped."

"Precisely!" said State Secretary Schmidt. He turned to Paul. "But they are not always losers because of a lack of gallantry, or just cause, or fighting spirit. We were, as everyone knows, betrayed . . . raped, my dear Bauer. The Saar, Alsace-Lorraine, the Sudetenland, Upper Silesia, the Polish Corridor and more."

"But that was over sixty years ago," said Paul.

"It matters not," said Von Seydlitz. "The lost territories, for the most part, remain German to this day. They belong to us."

The Secretary closed the cabinet, leaving Paul holding the rape miniature. "A gift," he said. "I have signed it on the bottom."

"Thank you." Paul, puzzled at the turn of conversation, returned to the wing chair.

State Secretary Schmidt stood to the side, his hands clasped behind his back, huge belly thrust forward, encased in what seemed to be yards of navy-blue chalk-striped fabric. "I mentioned earlier, Herr Bauer, that there was a plan. Put simply, we intend to win back those territories that were stolen from us. We will do it without firing a shot. Without a single casualty on either side. A bloodless war, my dear fellow, the first in history." He paced forward, stood directly in front of Paul, his overwhelming bulk filling the younger man's entire view. "We intend to convince France, Poland and Czechoslovakia to return what is rightfully ours."

"And the annexation of Austria," said Von Seydlitz, his voice high-pitched.

"Not annexation, my dear Von Seydlitz, but rather peaceful

reunification of two German peoples into a greater Germany."

"Convince them how?" said Paul.

"We are the only nation in the world with atomic capability and the means to deliver."

"Are you saying that we'll launch our missiles if the demands are not met?"

"One rocket at a time, Herr Bauer," said the Secretary earnestly, "until they realize their foolhardiness. Of course, that's purely theoretical. The threat alone will ensure victory. The means simply do not exist to counter our demands. Delay or foolish provocation on their part would be more than stupid; it would be criminal. And they're sensible politicians presiding over, thank God, responsible representative governments, every bit as democratic as our own."

"But the Americans also have the bomb. . . ."

"Devices, not bombs. The Anglo-Americans are at least two years from an atomic arsenal. Even if it were otherwise, they have nothing to fear from us. Their treaties with Poland, Czechoslovakia and France ceased having teeth a long time ago. Nevertheless, if the Americans, the British, the French, or anyone else attempts the madness of conventional airborne attack, our Luftwaffe will stop them in their tracks." The Secretary paused, as if catching his breath. "When all is said and done, Bauer, we are reasonable men, not asking for much—just a few thousand square miles, inhabited for the most part by Germans, areas that are historically, culturally, and geographically ours—stolen from us sixty years ago through the use of an arbitrary and punishing treaty."

"I'm familiar with it," said Paul Bauer dryly, not quite believing what he was hearing.

"It is time." His uncle, the field marshal, spoke tonelessly through billows of acrid blue cigar smoke. "We have the will and the means. We're the strongest military power in the world. We alone will have been to the moon—soon the planets too will be ours. Yet we permit German territory to be occupied by thick-headed Slavs and infantile Frenchmen."

Von Seydlitz paced the room, stopping momentarily at the French doors to stare out into the interior courtyard. Paul watched him in stunned silence, then turned to find Schmidt once again seated, staring at him curiously. "Any questions, Herr Bauer?"

Paul, caught unawares, took his time lighting a cigarette. "Who else is involved?"

"The plan is shared by only those who are important to its political, logistical and technological development. That includes the President of the Republic, some dozen Reichstag members, four members of the Reichsrat, the Deputy Chief of State Intelligence, most of the key figures in the Army, Navy and Luftwaffe, a few media people, and Herr Bosch and his National People's party, which in a few weeks your uncle will take over. Little by little, we will involve others as the need arises."

"It sounds," said Paul, "as though a coup d'état might be a necessary prerequisite to the plan."

"Do I take it," said the Secretary, "that you would disapprove, if such were the case?"

"Wholeheartedly," said Paul. "My allegiance is to the constitution."

A soft smile spread across the Secretary's moon face. "Then you are certainly the right man for us. Your idealism and patriotism seem beyond reproach." He chuckled, as if he were a fat, kindly uncle addressing the naiveté of a schoolboy. "But you need have no fear of anything so crude or misanthropic as a coup, military or political. We are all believers in the constitution."

From across the room, Von Seydlitz faced them, his eyes locked with Paul's, his feet apart, splayed out, his hands clasped behind his back like a soldier standing at ease. "What the Secretary means," he said grimly, "is that we have every intention of following the letter of the law. It is quite simple. There will be a convenient cabinet crisis and a new Chancellor—me. The battle plan requires a strong commitment from the top, something we could not get from the current leadership. The country requires a leader."

Hitler, thought Paul, feeling a chill of apprehension.

"And if the Reichstag refuses to go along," said Schmidt, "there will be elections. It will all be very democratic."

"I take it," said Paul Bauer, "that it will be you who will precipitate the cabinet crisis?"

"God forbid . . . not I!" said Schmidt.

"Who then?"

"The Jews," said Von Seydlitz, matter-of-factly.

Paul thought for a moment that he had heard incorrectly. "Jews?" he said.

"Yes," said Schmidt. "But we plan nothing overt. Nature will simply take its course."

"Has any of this been suggested by the Time-Life books?" Paul fought to keep his tone conversational.

"Tactics," said his uncle. "Trappings . . . and more, much more." He seemed reluctant to go on.

Paul said, "The concept of Teutonic racial superiority?"

"That concept is not totally out of the question." The field marshal's gaze shifted from Paul's eyes to the knot in his tie. "The author, whoever he was, possessed a certain genius. So I was mistaken, you see . . . the strong feeling I had about the German masses reacting violently to those books . . . the Second World War . . . You expressed the same concern . . ."

"Yes . . ."

"We all make mistakes," said Schmidt. "Nevertheless, it worked out well in the long run. The people need stirring up. The books will now serve our cause well. They're invaluable, both as a textbook and a tool."

"Invaluable," echoed Field Marshal von Seydlitz.

Paul felt as if he had been struck. It required seconds for the full implications to surface. He breathed deeply, attempting to relax his tensed facial muscles into a bland, deceptive mask. The shadowy image of a flattened, smoldering city coalesced in his mind. Hiroshima, from the Time-Life books.

"The field marshal has assured me that you are the man for us."

"Yes," said Paul somberly.

The fat man peered at him from over a church steeple of pudgy fingers. "You will, as we've told you, be in the cabinet. But you are to remain uninvolved politically until after the party has assumed power. We want you to do nothing public that might compromise your present situation as press attaché with the London Embassy. You are one of a number whom we prefer to remain in the closet until the new government takes office. Anything you do for the party must remain confidential until then. At that time you will be asked officially to join the government. Thus it will appear that you come to us fresh from the outside, perhaps from another political persuasion. It will serve the public as an example of political harmony, unity."

"And legitimacy," said Paul.

"Precisely." Schmidt grinned broadly. "Your example, along with some others, might induce similar conservative young men to emulate you. The party, you see, must recruit all the talent it can."

"It must be expanded a thousandfold," said Von Seydlitz.

"And now," said Schmidt, his eyes locked onto Paul's, "you can speak freely. If you have any objections, we will simply forget about this meeting. Though, of course, I will hold you to your pledge of silence. I am a man who does not equivocate and I trust you are likewise. Are you with us?"

"Wholeheartedly, Herr Secretary," said Paul Bauer, once again concealing his horror, this time behind an expression of ardent commitment.

His uncle, Field Marshal Rudolph von Seydlitz, rewarded him with a thin-lipped smile and said, "Welcome, Paul, to the New Order."

Herbert W——turned to me. He spoke sadly in sotto voice, though there was no one in the billiard room to hear him other than myself. "History's inevitable fate," he said, "is entropy, and no amount of twisting and turning can divert it from that final destination."

—*The Intimate Diary of a London Gentleman* (Chapter 6) by "B." Turtle Press, Glasgow, 1910

18

1970

The old woman was dying in a huge bed shaped like a ship. She knew she was dying, and though she appreciated the concern of two friends seated near her, she was annoyed by their repetitive encouragements. She said, "I'm going to die. You know it and I know it. A little truth will clear the air."

"Nonsense," said one of them, smiling weakly. "In a few weeks you'll be fit as a fiddle."

"All right," said the old woman, "I'm eighty-seven years old, I've got a terminal disease, and I'm going to live forever." She laughed, then was quiet. Her friends stared blankly, disconcerted by her candid behavior, feeling discomfort over the fact that they both wished to be elsewhere.

Once again the old woman found herself drifting. The transit from conscious to semiconscious was pleasant; a soft cruise on quiet waters. She had been an actress for most of her life, and now the curtain was descending. *Finis,* she thought. But the second act had been horrid. . . . If only she could run through it just once more.

Her voice was barely audible to the visitors as she spoke intimately to them via the ceiling. "It was a Mercer Runabout and it was beautiful, an American motorcar, bright red. The bloody machine smashed him."

She was silent for minutes, then she turned her head, her eyes focusing on the visitors. "I'm sorry," she said. "It's the drugs; I come and go quite regularly—doze off, you see. I was telling you about Bertie and the 1912 Mercer?"

"It was red," said one of them self-consciously.

"Yes," she said. "It was a gift on my twenty-ninth birthday. He was teaching me to drive it and something went wrong— horribly wrong. There was a horse and I swerved to the right . . ." She turned away from them, the brief speech had left her tired. "Poor Bertie . . ." She felt herself drifting off again. Dimly, she heard the nurse, Sister Bartlett, asking the visitors to leave.

Her son, Harry, was less than two when his father was killed. He had been an adorable child; bright, cheerful, two attributes that saw him through his life. She flashed a picture of an older Captain Harry Trasker, tall, his hair red like his grandmother, his sincere eyes, deep-set in a rugged, rough-hewn face like his father. Her son, Captain Harry Scott Trasker, D.S.O. born in London, February 8, 1911, died on Sword Beach, Normandy Beachhead, June 6, 1944, the victim of a Messerschmitt Bf 109 that had broken through the Allied air umbrella. Poor Harry . . . poor Bertie . . . like father, like son.

She awoke in her darkened bedroom. Through the french doors opening into her garden, the soft hills of Sussex were bathed in moonlight. Sister Bartlett, across the room in her chair, emitted quiet, ladylike snores. The bedside clock read 3:00 A.M. The old woman felt that hers was the only consciousness alive in the room, in the house, in the two square miles surrounding it —perhaps in all of England.

She thought of her parents, the images sharper, clearer than they had been in decades. Her mother had been a tall, proud woman with flaming red hair and an attitude of defiance toward the mores and customs of her time and class. "Elleander . . . no flowers or saints or people are called by that name. That's why I gave it to you, a new name for the new century that's coming. Your father and I, we had a terrible quarrel about it, he believed it to be un-Christian. . . ."

Her mother, Pamela Morning, was one of three daughters and a son born to a London omnibus driver. She had married early and somewhat above her station. Her husband, Jonathan Morning, was by way of being in trade, the proprietor of a small tobacco shop in Whitechapel.

Though he loved her, Jonathan Morning remained, throughout his life, confused by his wife's "unusual notions" and "stubborn attitudes." In a world where members of her class considered four, possibly five children to be right and proper, she would argue, "One perfect child, dear Jonathan, is quite enough. If other women want to be breeding mares, then let them . . . cows . . ." Unbeknown to him, she had aborted five times in nine years, with commonly used lead plaster. Nevertheless, in typical ignorance, Jonathan Morning took it for granted that she possessed some means or other—probably strong will over her own bodily functions—that enabled her to deny him additional children. He'd say, "All right then, but one more, a boy. Surely, as a God-fearing man, I'm entitled to at least that."

"There's going to be a new century," she'd reply. "Boys, girls, it won't matter. Women will be in trade, just like men. They'll be cabinet ministers, women of the cloth, solicitors, soldiers, even admirals. Your daughter might do you proud, she might be the first woman judge or member of Parliament."

"Outrageous poppycock! You've gone daft! It's all those damnable books you read! Diabolical anarchy, that's what it's all coming to. Blast your new century! I'd as soon be dead as live to see it!"

He would stomp off to dig furiously in their small vegetable garden, leaving her to practice, along with her daughter Elleander, the art of retaining one's *h*'s and broadening one's *a*'s. It was a process, she was certain, that would enhance her daughter's social potential, ensuring her of a place in the world far above the one that she herself currently occupied. Religiously, they learned from a large dictionary, one new word a day.

On January 8, 1895, the eve of her twelfth birthday, Elleander Morning was treated by her mother to an evening at the theater. The two of them attended Oscar Wilde's new play *An Ideal Husband.*

Throughout the performance, the young girl sat spellbound, gripping the arms of her seat, soaking up the richness of her first serious theatrical experience. By intermission she had developed a burning ambition: she would be an actress. She would be on the stage bathed in brilliant light, graciously accepting the applause, just as these actors did. She would, despite her mother's arguments, leave Parliament and His Majesty's Forces to their current male practitioners. She was convinced now, beyond a doubt, that the theater was to be her future. She applauded the many curtain calls furiously, standing on her seat until after the stage lights were dimmed and the audience was in the aisles.

Finally, her mother's gentle prodding had its effect, and they were seeking an exit along with the other patrons. Elleander seemed dazed, responding in monosyllables to her mother's concern. It was in this state that the young girl walked full-tilt into the back of a man at the top of the aisle. He turned abruptly, revealing himself to be a young man of less than average height, with large, questioning eyes and a deep, black, full mustache set off against a pale, almost sallow complexion.

"Elleander," said her mother. "So clumsy . . ."

"Pardon me, sir."

"You dropped your program," said the man. He bent to pick it up, then, smiling, handed it to Elleander. "I'm sure you will value this as a souvenir one day." As he spoke, his eyes locked with Pamela Morning's. She colored, saying, "My daughter is not usually so clumsy. I believe she was affected by the play."

He turned once again to Elleander. "You liked the play?"

"Very much," she said, brightening. "It was my very first, you see."

"Ah, then happy birthday and I wish you many more such exciting evenings." He nodded, and in doing so, surveyed Pamela Morning from head to foot. "Good night, then. . . ."

To Elleander's surprise, he placed a tentatively affectionate hand on her mother's arm. Then he was gone. Later that night as she lay in bed it occurred to her that somehow he had known it was her birthday.

> If the will of man were free, that is, if every man could act as he chose, the whole of history would be a tissue of disconnected accidents.
>
> —Count Leo Tolstoi
> *War and Peace*

→ 19 ←

1970/(1900)

In the huge bed-that-was-a-ship, the old woman stiffened her resolve against increasing pain. Drugs would dim her sensibilities, launch her consciousness into the cool waters of serenity. She had much to think about, to relive, and little time in which to do it. It must all be clear, sharply edged.

Her own life span, she realized, had been twice that of her mother, who had died at the age of thirty-seven on a midwinter day in 1902. Nevertheless, Pamela Morning had survived both the old century and the old Queen who had shaped it. She had lived into the dawn of what she frequently stated would be "Elleander's century."

The young girl had been seventeen when her mother died. Dazed, she permitted herself to be led through the formalities of church service and funeral rites. It was after she returned home from the decrepit little cemetery in Leyton that she was struck by the full impact of her loss. Inconsolable, she locked herself in her room, refused her meals. For hours on end she stared blindly out the window at a stone wall just a few feet away.

Late on the morning of the third day, with her father away

at his shop, Elleander emerged. She roamed through the small
house, collecting things that had been her mother's: icons, an
embroidered eyeglass case, a small sewing kit, a leather-bound
copy of Elizabeth Barrett Browning's *Aurora Leigh,* a stere-
opticon, complete with "Artistic Views of the Mysterious
Orient" . . .

It was while she was staring, unseeing, at a three-dimen-
sional view of the Taj Mahal when suddenly, no longer dazed,
Elleander Morning saw her situation with a clarity even exceeding that of the twin photographs before her. *She was alone.* There
was no one. There were, in her life, no intimate friends; no
close family who cared beyond the point demanded of them by
social convention and "good Christian morality" . . . *alone.* Her
father would supply her with food and shelter but little else.
She was to be little more than a boarder in a dry and loveless
house.

She slid the mechanism to the next photographic pair.
Through a mist of tears she looked at the familiar image of British
gunners posing by their cannon in Afghanistan; behind them, the
mighty Hindu Kush reaching for the sky.

Upstairs, she went through her mother's chest. Buried under
a mass of carelessly folded silk hose she discovered a packet of
letters. Sitting on the edge of the bed, she untied the blue ribbon.
There were eight thick envelopes addressed to her mother in a
concise copperplate script. She began reading at random.

> . . . *very early in our marriage, Isabel stated her opinion*
> *that "lovemaking was nothing more than an outrage*
> *inflicted upon reluctant womankind." You, my dear*
> *Pamela, are certainly not of that breed! You, in fact, are*
> *that rare woman who takes delight in the conjugal act for*
> *its own sake, for the exquisite pleasure it affords both you*
> *and the partner of your affections. How marvellous it would*
> *be if all women bore this similarity to men. A fruitless wish*
> *—God, according to popular thinking, intended otherwise.*
> *Genesis, I am told, explains it all, though I for one have*
> *never understood who was being punished or for what.*
> *Despite all that, the new century, just eight years away, will*

*see the beginning of change. The old Queen cannot last
forever, and if Edward, the next monarch, as did this one,
sets the moral tone, then make way for the "New Woman"!
Venus Urania! (Of which you, my dearest Pamela, are a
prototype.)*

> *With best wishes,*
> *Yours very faithfully,*

> *H. G. Wells*

*Dearest Pamela,
Same place and time? Wednesday? Your unworthy admirer
is finally on his feet after studying his ceiling all these
weeks. Despite that, I am remarkably cheerful and
clear-headed. Chest diseases seem to have this effect, or is it
perhaps a function of ice bags and opium pills?
Nevertheless, I have not been in pain, though you will, I
am sure, find me haggard—a happy shadow of my former
self. Under those circumstances, we will, of course, have
need to be cautious and restrict our pleasures to sharing tea
and conversation. . . .*

*. . . Queen Victoria is like a great paperweight who, for
half a century now, has sat on men's minds, and when she
goes their ideas will begin to blow about all over the place,
haphazardly. Women too, I might add. The new century
will see them gaining their liberty, not only the vote but
everything else as well. There might even someday be a
female First Lord of the Admiralty! (Or rather, First
Lady.) . . .*

*December 27, 1895
Dearest Pamela:
Cust has made a terrible mistake. I am to be drama critic
for the* **Pall Mall Gazette.** *I told him he could not find
anyone less qualified, but he insists. (My experience with the
theatre has been limited to Gilbert and Sullivan and the
Crystal Palace annual pantomime.) The play is* **An Ideal**

Husband. *I have managed to wrangle two extra tickets on
the assumption that it might be nice to bring your daughter
to the show as a birthday gift. Of course, I shall remain
anonymous for her sake, even if we should happen to run
into each other. The tickets are enclosed. . . .*

There were more letters. Elleander read them all half a
dozen times. Wells wrote of politics, of sexual passion, of
women's rights, of past and future history. The young girl felt
herself carried away on the strong currents of his ideas, just as,
she was now certain, her mother had been. In Wells' last letter,
dated October 17, 1899, he wrote: "*. . . and if you or your daughter
should ever require aid that I am capable of giving, please seek me
out. . . .*"

Elleander resolved that she too would become a "new
woman." Venus Urania! As a virgin, she had just a dim understanding of "exquisite pleasure," but she would seek it out, culti-
vate it. She would be independent of the restrictive world shaped
by the old Queen—her father's world. She would be an autono-
mous woman with her own income and control over her own
destiny.

In her mother's closet she found a shoebox containing a pair
of delicate white evening slippers. They were unadorned and
elequent, sporting daring two-inch heels. Elleander held them in
the palms of both hands; they seemed weightless, like two exquisite, wingless birds.

She sat on the floor to try them on, noting that the soles were
unmarred. They had never been worn. Her mother, she reasoned, had been saving them for a special occasion. Elleander
was surprised to find that they fit; Pamela Morning had worn a
different size.

She stood and took a few tentative steps. They would, she
decided, be hers. She would emulate her mother and lay them
aside for a special occasion. As she returned them to their nest
in the pink pasteboard box, she went even further, vowing to
wear them only on the single most important day of her life. She
wondered what it would be.

Almost a year to the day after the death of his first wife,

Jonathan Morning remarried. His bride was an ample woman of thirty-one, simple and undemanding, replete with "Christian virtues." In a manner of months, she was pregnant. Elleander's father prayed for a boy and in due course his prayers were answered. The following year, much to his satisfaction, the process was repeated.

Elleander, her schooling finished, took employment with a millinery shop in the West End. Saving what she could, she began to plan independence from her father's household, in which she had become little more than a tolerated guest.

By the winter of 1903, she had accumulated enough savings to enroll in a typewriting course. Then in the spring, she answered an advertisement and found employment in her new specialty with a newly elected young member of Parliament, a liberal, Mr. Ian Gilbert, to whom, with a joyful feeling of liberation, Elleander lost her virginity.

Thus she became, in a short time, Mr. Ian Gilbert's valued assistant and equally valued mistress. They were together one or two nights a week. To explain his absence from home on these occasions, the young liberal M.P. informed his wife that he was visiting his constituency in the Midlands.

Elleander's intuitive grasp of politics was soon honed to a much sharper edge than that of her politically naive employer. Within a year, she was guiding him through the rocks and shoals of the House of Commons, advising him as to which party-supported issues to concentrate on and with whom to ally himself. She wrote the few speeches he delivered, coached his expositions and made enthusiastic love to him in the small house he had rented for her in Chelsea. Elleander had realized at last her fondest wish, an escape both from her father's house and an end to a stultifying existence. She knew that no matter what happened, she would never return to that. For the first time since the death of her mother, she was happy.

Then, on a particular April evening, everything changed. The man, a Mr. Stock, or so he introduced himself, appeared at her door shortly after 10:00 P.M. He was middle-aged, barely an inch taller than she, possessing, in her eyes, both the physiognomy and the stance of a bulldog.

"Miss Elleander Morning?" He tipped his hat, a derby he wore as if it were an iron helmet.

"Yes . . ."

"I've been sent by Mr. Ian Gilbert to fetch you."

She felt a moment's panic. "Is something wrong . . . ?"

"No, miss. I mean, nothing serious. It will all be explained, but we must hurry."

She was ready in minutes. He had a cab waiting. As they entered, she said, "I'm not an hysterical woman, Mr. Stock, I promise you. You must tell me if there's been an accident . . . is Mr. Gilbert all right?" She felt surprisingly calm, prepared to cope. "Please . . ."

"Nothing like that, miss. Mr. Gilbert is fine, I assure you."

They were moving at a rapid clip through the darkened streets. Mr. Stock turned to glance out the window. She marveled at the sight of his massive bull neck, conjecturing that it was probably as big around as her waist. He sighed audibly, turned to her. "Actually, Miss Morning, I'm here at the behest of Mrs. Gilbert, rather than Mr. Gilbert." He spoke precisely, as if attempting to lend an official dignity to his accent. "Mrs. Eleanore Gilbert has retained me to pass on certain information to you."

Elleander felt as if she'd been struck. Shocked, she stared at him openmouthed. Mr. Stock seemed to wait patiently as she balled her fists, tensed every muscle in her body in order to regain her composure. Then finally, in a small but steady voice, she said, "Yes . . . what is it Mrs. Gilbert has to tell me?"

"That you are not to see *Mister* Gilbert again."

Elleander felt a rising anger displacing the near panic. In a louder voice now, she said, "She can damn well tell me that in person! Take me home, please."

"I do sympathize with you." He spoke in low, sincere tones now. "It is most cowardly of her to approach you this way."

"Thank you, Mr. Stock. Now take me home at once."

He reached around her to open the carriage door on her side. "I'm afraid I'm unable to do that, miss. I've also been instructed to inform you that the premises we just left are no longer to be considered your home. I'm sorry, Miss Morning. But if you attempt to return, or attempt to see or speak to Mr. Gilbert ever again, it will be my job to break your neck—which, mind you, I will do, if paid the proper fee." He turned his hands palms upward, glanced down at them and sighed, as if at two naughty children.

Elleander pounded on the roof. "Stop the cab!"

The overhead trap opened, revealing a thin, leering face. Mr. Stock gestured with an outthrust hand. "A little faster, Nick, there's a good fellow."

"Please," she said. "I will speak with Mrs. Gilbert in the morning and we'll settle this as civilized human beings." She glanced quickly over her shoulder through the open door. The ground was passing beneath them at an alarming rate. Her heart, too, was racing. She fought back a wave of panic, steeled herself and glared at him.

He grasped her shoulder with one huge muscular hand, an arm with the other. "I too believe it would be civilized, Miss Morning, but out you go, as instructed. Nothing personal, mind you." He twisted, turning her cruelly toward the door. "It's to convince you of Mrs. Gilbert's sincerity."

He shoved, as with her free hand she raked her fingers down the side of his face, leaving behind them three bloody tracks. She was aware of no other sound but her heavy breathing as he released her to run a hand across his cheek. He held it before him, staring curiously at the blood. In a rage of self-defense, she grasped his arm, dug a spiked heel cruelly into the soft flesh of his calf. Then, with all the strength she could muster, she thrust her fist into his groin. Mr. Stock screamed in pain as she grasped even tighter to an arm that shook rapidly up and down as if it were attempting to dislodge some clinging insect. Then, with no warning, his open hand smashed across her face.

The blow was stunning. A thousand bright fireflies, orchestrated by a single high-pitched, strident tone, danced about in her head. Yet still she clung to him as if to a life raft in a turbulent, blood-red sea, incapable of any other reaction—paralyzed.

She felt him prying open her fingers. There was a sudden snap of pain, and then blackness.

Awareness returned slowly with the feel of hard, cold stone pressing against her cheek. Her hand throbbed painfully, there was a taste of blood. She raised herself onto one elbow, dimly conscious of the near sound of horses' hooves on the cobblestones. A hansom swerved around her, continued on for ten yards or so, then stopped. She fell back, attempted to rally her strength. There were two figures kneeling beside her, two identical, beautiful young girls. She heard herself mutter, "Thank you, but I'm all right . . . really I am . . . if you'd just be so kind as to help me to my feet. . . ."

"How are you?" he said.

"Poorly, Barker, poorly."

"What are you doing?"

"Writing my epitaph."

"What is it to be?"

"Quite short," said Wells. "Just this—'God damn you all. I told you so. . . .' "

—*Age and Youth*
Sir Ernest Barker, 1953

20

1970/(1907)

In her straight-backed chair, the nurse, Sister Bartlett, snored gently, twitching in her sleep. Across the room, the old woman closed her eyes, the names Fawn and Clara barely audible on lips stiffened in pain.

How long had it been since she had last seen them? The old woman fought for clarity . . . a ship . . . They had sailed for New York in the spring of 1912—an unsuccessful emigration to the Golden Land. Fawn and Clara Fowler shared a frigid North Atlantic grave with fifteen hundred other passengers of the world's largest ship.

In the dull gray noon light of Southampton, they had waved happily to her from the deck of the departing White Star Liner, *Titanic*. The twins wore identical hobble-skirted sable coats, designed by Paquin, a bon voyage gift from a wealthy admirer. They were sophisticated, well-spoken young ladies now, grown up, matured from the precocious children they had been when El-leander first set eyes on them that horrid night during the winter of 1907.

The twins had rescued her, helped her into their cab, took her home with them. She had been in shock, bruised, the small finger of her left hand fractured. Fawn and Clara served her hot tea, provided her with dry clothing, a warming fire and the comfort of new friends.

In the light of day the next morning, Elleander told them her story. The girls invited her to stay indefinitely, assured her that Mr. Lethaby, the kindly old pervert who was keeping them in what they considered to be magnificent luxury, was certain to help her. She was grateful, as she had no other choice. She could not, after four years, return to her father's house, and she viewed seriously the threat made by the efficiently sadistic Mr. Stock. She would never see her ex-employer—her ex-lover—again. Nor could she complain to the police, an action that would surely result in scandal and the end of Gilbert's career. She was destitute, with no one to turn to other than a pair of compassionate twins, strangers, barely out of their childhood. She would, she vowed, be forever grateful to them.

Then things went from bad to worse. Three days passed with neither word nor visit from Mr. Lethaby. The young sisters, nervous about this unusual absence, journeyed to his fur shop, a modestly sized but elegantly stocked Regent Street establishment. It was closed; the wooden mannequin in the window, usually clothed in fashionable sable or fox, was draped demurely in a white sheet.

Fawn and Clara turned to Elleander. They were beside themselves with anxious concern about the mysterious fate of their beloved benefactor and with fear for their own futures without him. Thus, in a very short time, she found herself cast in the unlikely role of "aunty."

Elleander accepted the responsibility. She took it on herself to inquire of the Metropolitan Police and was informed that Harrison Bartlett Lethaby had been arrested and charged with "criminal exposure in-toto." Place of arrest: Kensington Gardens. The victims: two young girls and their nanny.

The following morning Elleander awoke with the name H. G. Wells on her lips. Her letter was brief.

> Dear Mr. Wells:
>   In a letter to my mother Pamela, you stated that if ever either of us required your help, we were merely to ask for it. I do that now. May I see you?
>
>   Elleander Morning

Wells' reply was immediate and equally brief:

> Dear Elleander:
>   I will call on you Saturday next, in the afternoon.
>
>   H.G.W.

His first words to her were, "You are even more beautiful than your mother." He stood in the doorway, his hat dripping rain.

"And you," said Elleander, smiling broadly, "look exactly like the gentleman in the aisle." She took his hand. "A trifle damper, perhaps."

"Ah, then the little girl knew her mother's secret all along."

"No, your subterfuge worked. I really thought you to be a total stranger. It was only later . . . your letters."

She served him tea. They sat facing one another. The twins were conveniently out for the afternoon at the music hall. Starting at the beginning, Elleander told Wells everything that had happened since her mother's death.

Finally he said, "Do you have any money?"

"None. The twins have a few pounds. After that . . ."

"You'll need some, then."

"Thank you. A loan. But there's something more important." She put her cup down, leaned toward him. "You see, I feel I can earn enough to keep myself and my newly adopted nieces." She laughed nervously. "In your position, you must know some people in the theater."

"A few."

She felt strangely confident, an attitude that surprised her, considering her precarious circumstances. Quietly, she said,

"I've always known I have talent as an actress. Perhaps there's someone I can audition for."

Wells thought a moment. "Yes, there is someone."

"Then it's settled."

"You're quite sure of yourself." Wells smiled at her.

"I have a strong impression that my life is about to change again . . . that it will all work out for the best. I feel I can do anything."

"I believe you can." Wells looked at her curiously. "His name is Bertram Trasker, a playwright. His first play will open in the West End next season—they should be casting now. I've read the script and there are a number of small female parts. You might be right for one of them." He paused for a moment, then said, "I'll ask Bertie to arrange an audition with the director. That's the limit of my influence. Beyond that, it's up to you."

Elleander auditioned three weeks later. The play was *The Remaking of Angela.* It was a small role, less than ten lines. She was the first woman to audition for it and the last. The director was convinced before she was halfway through the reading that he couldn't do better for the part.

As he told her so, she glanced at Wells, who was sitting with the author in an otherwise empty third row. Wells beamed, as if she had been his own personal discovery. Bertram Trasker smiled at her, making a silent applause gesture. She had been introduced to him by Wells minutes before the reading, and had been drawn to him immediately. She suspected from his reaction to her that he might have shared that feeling.

He had. That evening she went to dinner with Wells and Trasker. Bertie was attentive, couldn't seem to keep his eyes off her. A week later, after the first rehearsal, they had dinner alone. They danced the brand-new one-step to a lively orchestra, holding each other while taking quick but graceful walking steps back and forth in two-quarter time. It was during this, their first evening alone together, that Elleander felt she was falling in love.

Later that night, feeling like a giddy schoolgirl, she told Fawn and Clara about Bertie Trasker. They were delighted and joked about being flower girls at the wedding.

Elleander spent four or five evenings with Bertie before he

told her he had fallen in love. Their first kiss was consummated
in the wings during rehearsal. A few days later, while picnicking
in the nearby countryside, Bertie asked her to marry him. Her
answer was immediate.

"Oh yes . . . yes, Bertie . . ."

They embraced in the warm sunshine. He was about to say
something. She placed a hand over his mouth. "But . . ." she said.

"But?"

"But I don't want to give up the theater, Bertie. Not just yet.
I've had a small taste of it and find it glorious. It's really what I
wanted to do since I was a little girl."

"You mean you want to work?"

"Yes."

"And be married at the same time?"

"Of course . . ." She threw herself back on the grass.

"It isn't done, you know."

"Yes, it is. More and more women are becoming independent. My mother used to tell me that the new century would
be different, better. Well, the new century is seven years old.
And I'm in love and I'm an actress. Why can't I have everything?"

"You can . . ."

"I can?"

"Of course."

She threw herself on him, raining kisses on his face. They
rolled in the grass, laughing at each other.

Three days before opening night, the leading lady of *The Remaking of Angela* walked off the stage after a violent argument with the
director. Elleander pleaded for an audition.

The Remaking of Angela opened, starring Elleander Morning,
to good notices. It ran in the West End for two years.

On opening night, Elleander and Bertie made love amid
empty champagne bottles and floral tributes in her dressing
room. They were married two months later. Fawn and Clara gave
the bride away.

In the dim light coming from the gaping bathroom door, the old
woman gazed about the bedroom, her pain receding to the bare

edge of perception. The muscle tension used to support it relaxed, leaving her limp, euphoric.

Just beyond the foot of the bed, the nurse slumped in her chair, stockinged feet propped up on the matching loveseat. Above, a large Jackson Pollock dominated the wall. The room and almost everything in it—the blue-saturated wall-to-wall carpeting, the light peach-colored walls, the profusion of get-well flowers—were rendered in shades of gray like an underexposed photographic print. Only the remarkable color of the Pollock masterpiece survived the gloom.

She stared at the painting for minutes, losing herself in its nonlinear complexity, as she often did. Then her eyes moved to the other end of the room, to the mirror hanging above a long chest of drawers. It reflected the massive bed on which she could just make out a dark figure, its arms splayed out, its head supported by a mass of pillows. "My soon-to-be-mortal remains," she said in a hoarse whisper.

On the other side of the french doors, the half-moon swung back and forth in a long, slow arc, as if suspended from a chain. The old woman whispered, "Mare Nubium." Her eyes, like searchlights, locked on the target.

Her friends, Fawn and Clara, she thought, drowned in the freezing waters of the North Atlantic. Her husband Bertie, crushed by a beautiful red machine. Her son Harry, ripped open by a deadly spray of 7.92 mm machine-gun bullets. The four who meant everything to her, who, except for her mother, constituted the sum total of her love for eighty-seven years, cut down by random circumstance—coincidence. If she could just live it over again, change only a few minor details. . . .

The bed that was a ship, finally afloat, rocked gently. Now the moon, no longer a hypnotic icon, had become a navigational beacon. Lunar winds and currents would speed her to her destination.

Then suddenly, reality: an explosion of pain. The old woman glanced once again around the familiar, dimly lit bedroom. The clarity of her vision astonished her. There were, the old woman perceived, only moments left. Perhaps some of it could have been different . . . perhaps still. . . .

With sudden purpose, she commanded the sum of her

strength. A powerful current raced inward from vital organs, muscles, viscera: an enormous potential, accumulating in some secret capacitor. She willed herself back. Then, with the last residue of strength, she whispered, "Perhaps . . ." tripping the tiny switch in her mind. The stored energy was discharged in a millisecond—a psychic detonation. It thrust the essence of her being outward, backward. . . . In the next instant, the little that was left of Elleander Morning Trasker died. But by then, her consciousness was elsewhere; a dimly familiar place.

"Good evening, ladies and germs, I just blew in from the East Coast . . . and I really mean *blew in.* That new magnitrain got me here from New York in fifty-one minutes and twenty-seven seconds . . . Marvelous! A miracle! And there was even a second miracle . . . it took them only four hours, nine minutes and twenty-nine seconds to find my luggage! But seriously, folks, . . ."

—Milton Berle at Jack
Lerner's Panthenon
Club
Hollywood, California
Summer 1955

─────── **21** ───────

1907

Elleander Morning awoke just before dawn. She shuffled into the bathroom, leaving the door ajar to take advantage of the minimal light it afforded. Her broken finger throbbed painfully, but despite the violent events of the previous evening and the unfamiliar surroundings, she had slept well, an unusually deep, dreamless sleep, devoid of its customary fits and starts.

She reached up for the flushing chain, waving her hand back and forth in a futile effort to locate it. Dimly, she recalled that the chain had been hanging within easy reach the night before. She glanced upward. The familiar, oblong flushing tank was also missing.

Feeling a vague disquiet, the young woman automatically reached behind her to fumble for a small porcelain handle. Mindlessly, she pressed it downward and was startled fully awake by the sound of rushing water.

Confused, she stepped backward into the bathroom doorway. She had never seen nor heard of such a device before. There was always a chain connected to an overhead wooden tank. Yet she had flushed this strange water closet without a moment's hesitation. A small handle . . .

She turned, halted in mid-step. The cold blue light of false dawn illuminated a bed that was far different from that of last night. It was an awesome giant that took up half the room. A ship! There was a buxom figurehead, a high canopy supported by two masts, fore and aft. Beneath it, the slumbering fetal shapes of Fawn and Clara seemed lost on the quilted deck.

She stared, a tight constriction growing in her chest. Perhaps she was still asleep—she would awake in seconds to find the same simple brass bed that had been there the previous night and, she thought, glancing to the right, the same red silk chaise that had served as her bed, rather than the long, low-slung, unadorned chest of drawers that had miraculously replaced it. The red chaise . . . gone! Yet just a few minutes earlier she had arisen from it to use the loo. Surely this was a dream, she reasoned. There was no other explanation. . . .

Elleander stepped haltingly through the bathroom door into the large room, her mind a turmoil of conflicting impressions. She felt the soft pile of a rug under her bare feet where shortly before there had been cold, wooden flooring. A carpet stretched in all directions like a well-manicured blue lawn. Once again, she froze in place. If all of this was indeed a nightmare, she had no alternative to dreaming on till it ended and she found herself being nudged awake by the reassuring hand of Ian Gilbert in her own bed, in her own little house in Chelsea.

She found matches, but there were no gaslight jets. They had vanished, to be replaced by what she recognized to be electrical lights. She inspected a shaded lamp sitting on the low table next to the bed. The bulb was smoothly rounded at the top rather than pointed as were others she had seen, and there was no pullcord to turn it on. With an instinct that surprised her, she pressed an unfamiliar switch. There was a click, but no light.

The sun was rising. Its rays, having used up a good deal of their actinic energy in piercing the heavy overcast, illuminated the room in dull highlights and tired gray shadows. Dazed, she turned slowly in a full circle, her eyes flitting from one point to another. The fireplace was gone. Just in front of where it had been, a low love seat upholstered in beige, a straight-backed chair in the same fabric, a small, cluttered table. Except for the bed, all of the furniture was hideously unadorned, as if function were the sole reason for its existence. She found it frightening—furniture for bodies without souls.

On the peach-colored wall to her right hung a large painting whose artistic substance seemed to have been created by some-one's arbitrarily dribbling large quantities of vari-colored pig-ments over its surface. Against the far wall, a long chest of draw-ers squatted beneath a mirror, into which was reflected her own figure and, behind it, the bed-that-was-a-ship.

In a state more of bewilderment than fear, she surveyed herself in the glass, expecting that here too she might discover a transformation. But no. Unlike the room, she remained un-changed. Her face was the same, her hair, as always, long and golden, her body slim, still supple under a shocking example of black silk "French" lingerie, lent to her the previous evening out of Fawn's extensive wardrobe. She was Elleander Morning as she had always been. It was the world that had changed . . . miracu-lously, frighteningly.

Hearing a rustling sound behind her, she shifted her gaze in the large mirror. One of the twins was sitting rigidly upright, hands braced on the bed with stiffened arms, eyes wide, unblink-ing. Elleander, confused as to which twin it was, turned to face her. As she did so, the girl screamed.

"It's all right," said Elleander, moving quickly to the bed to grasp the girl's hand in an effort to calm her.

"No! Where are we . . . ? How'd we get here?!"

"It's all right. . . ."

The girl swiveled her head from side to side. She shuddered, turned to the left, where her twin was struggling into wakefulness. "Clara . . . !" She enunciated her sister's name in a high-pitched, hysterical whine, shrill enough, observed Elleander, to shatter glass.

Clara squirmed to a sitting position, rubbing her eyes—well-manicured child's fingers attempting to wipe out an aberrant illusion. She wore black silk, in contrast to her twin sister's virginal pink lace. For Elleander, the difference in nightgowns served as a tentative means of identification. (Later she would learn to tell them apart through differences in expression and gesture.)

"Where are we?" said Fawn, this time in a tiny voice, her free hand grasping her sister's shoulder, shaking her.

Clara, coming awake, surveyed the room slowly. Her hands were spread open across the lower part of her face as if attempting to quell the pain of a toothache. "Blimey . . ." Clara uttered the word much in the manner of a member of an appreciative audience acknowledging the wonder of a magician's sleight of hand.

"It's all right," said Elleander, looking down at Fawn to see tears streaking her face. Dimly, she felt a vague responsibility for this grotesque phenomenon, as if she, the stranger, had somehow brought it on. Had she?

Clara was out of bed. In seconds she stood at the window, staring into the gray dawn. "Good old Porchcote Road," she said. "We're still here where we belong, not in bloody Arabia or some-such; we haven't moved an inch. Father Christmas just changed the furniture—that's what."

"Father Christmas?" Fawn echoed mindlessly, as if she had forgotten who the old gentleman was. She looked down toward the bow, where the giant mattress came to a rounded point. It was fenced in by a sturdy mahogany rail, above which the towering mast spread its yardarm. "It's horrible!" She pulled away from Elleander, leaped from the bed, then stood, gaping at the bulbous, hand-carved breasts of its gilded figurehead. "Horrible," she said, her voice a quiet whimper.

Clara watched her for a moment, then once again her eyes swept the room, coming to rest on Elleander, as if their guest were a part of the weird metamorphosis. "Somebody is having us on," she said. "I'll wager it's some kind of lark."

"We should," said Fawn, "fetch Mr. Lethaby. He'd know what all this is in aid of."

Elleander stood up. She felt faint, grasped the mahogany rail. The twins were conversing, but for a few minutes she found it impossible to decipher their words. First the toilet, the electric lamp, and now everything seemed strangely familiar. Could she have been in such a room before and not remembered? Hardly possible. She fought for breath. A dream? Déjà vu? There was difficulty in organizing her thoughts. Then, miraculously, the indisposition was gone, replaced by a feeling of well-being, an almost languorous tranquillity. A word formed itself on her lips, "polyester." Though it was meaningless, she repeated it several times, savoring its sound.

"Who's that?" said Clara.

"Who?"

"Polly Esther."

"I don't know," said Elleander Morning. Her broken finger was throbbing.

Fawn, standing like a lost child in the center of the room, said, "The wardrobe chest, it's gone."

"So is everything else," said Clara.

"But our clothes . . ." Fawn looked around frantically, turning in circles. "Our money . . . my purse! Everything . . . shoes. . . ."

Clara pointed to the new chest of drawers. "We'll look in there."

They searched through the drawers, but there was nothing at first glance that seemed fit for street wear. Undergarments, hose, blouses, nightgowns, but no dresses or skirts long enough to be worn in public. At one point, Clara held up a pair of sheer stockings that were attached at the crotch to form underpants. "Ugly," she said. "Knicker-hose . . ." She laughed briefly, balled the stockings in her fist, and tossed them back into the drawer. "It's so very awful! All of it . . ."

Elleander peered into the drawer and reached past a white slipper to retrieve a worn, yellowed theater program. "St. James

Theatre," she read quietly. "*An Ideal Husband.* A New Play by Mr. Oscar Wilde." She felt a sudden chill. Trembling, she lowered herself into the love seat. Incomprehensible images raced through her brain. Instantaneous, unrelated flashes: a man's face dominated by angry eyes and a small, square mustache; what seemed to be a low-slung, bright-red motorcar; a gray beach on which hundreds of strangely dressed soldiers raced inland; another face, this one pleasant, with a beard and gracious smile.

Clara said, "Polyester . . ." She was reading the label in a full-length flannel robe. "St. Michaels . . . eighty percent cotton, twenty percent polyester . . ." Quietly she asked, "How did you know?"

"Something's happened to me," said Elleander.

"What?"

"I seem to know things," said Elleander, watching as Fawn dressed herself in the light-blue flannel robe.

"Like polyester?" said Clara.

"Yes."

"Then what is it?"

"I don't know."

Clara, recognizing Elleander's confusion, nodded as if she understood. She faced her sister, who was draping a heavy wool shawl over the robe. "Blimey," said Clara. "Look's as if you're dressing for the king."

"It's awful," said Fawn, viewing herself in the mirror. "If anybody sees me, I'll die! How can I go out with no hat? Shoes . . ."

"You've got to, hat or no hat. Mr. Lethaby will sort it all out —money, clothes, the lot."

Clara opened a pink shoe box she had discovered in one of the drawers. Nestled inside were a pair of white shoes. "Lovely," she said. "Just the thing, and they look like they've never even been worn."

"Not those," said Elleander, taking them.

Clara looked at her queerly. "Why not?"

"They belonged to my mother."

Petulantly, Fawn threw herself into a chair. "Loony."

Elleander recalled a pair of pink fluffy slippers she had seen by the bed. She ripped off the tassels. They were at least a size too large, but Fawn put them on with no further complaints, saying, "Anything's better than staying here."

The twins embraced. Fawn opened the door, peered out apprehensively. Then with a gesture of relief, she raced, with flapping, backless pink slippers, down the familiar, gaslit stairway.

Clara, with some reluctance, closed the door, turned to Elleander, who in a flat voice said, "Panty hose . . ."

It isn't really
Anywhere!
It's somewhere else
Instead!

—A. A. Milne

22

1907

Mr. Lethaby was adept at his game. He had even, on a few occasions, taken quick, decisive aim on a crowded street at midday, bringing to bear such devious skill that no one but his target had been aware that a "shot" had been fired. That sort of thing was always a thrilling challenge, but on this particular morning, he felt the need for a more sustained experience.

It was seven o'clock in the morning. Harrison Bartlett Lethaby was dressed in his hunting clothes: a bowler hat, a caracul-trimmed gray tweed overcoat, a white silk ascot and striped gray trousers. Kensington Gardens at that hour and time of year was, except for an occasional, determined pedestrian, relatively deserted. He accepted the fact that it might very well be an hour before he found a suitable, isolated victim, but Mr. Lethaby, like many artists in other endeavors, was a patient man.

He entered the park, passed behind the Albert Memorial to make his way slowly toward Bayswater Road. He was, for all intents and purposes, a respectable, middle-aged gentleman out for a morning constitutional.

But, reasoned Mr. Lethaby, he actually was that very thing:

a respectable, middle-aged gentleman taking his morning constitutional. He had never in his life purposely caused pain to another human being; he gave liberally to his church; he paid high
wages to his employees (almost twice what his competitors paid),
and he was genuinely concerned with their welfare. His "game"
was an innocent pastime; a marvelously exciting shock to most of
his victims, but nevertheless informative . . . educational.

Five or six brisk pedestrians passed him from the opposite
direction. A single young man led by a large, indeterminate dog
came up from the rear to stumble by at a rather rapid clip.

Roughly a hundred yards from Bayswater Road, he reversed
direction. There were three figures in the near distance. The
taller of them possessed an hourglass silhouette and wore a large
hat. Within a quarter of a minute, it was obvious to Mr. Lethaby
that the trio consisted of an adult woman and two young girls.
The girls wore identical navy-blue coats and cunning little nauti-
cal hats. As the distance between them closed, he judged them
to be roughly two years apart, perhaps twelve and fourteen years
old—approximately Fawn and Clara's age. There was a look of
wealth and breeding about them. The woman, he conjectured,
was probably a governess.

As they came closer, he breathed deeply, feeling the excitement take hold. The lovely young things were holding hands,
walking in lockstep. They seemed much more childlike than his
own darling twins. Perhaps, he thought, a little education might
be to their advantage.

When just a few yards separated them, he halted abruptly,
planting both feet solidly on the ground about eighteen inches
apart. Then, satisfied that he had effectively blocked their path,
he tipped his hat. The woman seemed momentarily confused.
She stopped, held out her arm to halt the girls.

It was Mr. Lethaby's moment, the quarry was at bay! His
body stiffened against a flutter of expectation. With a broad,
sweeping gesture, he flung open his coat. Beneath it, he was
clothed in two cut-off trouser legs attached to his calves with
ladies' garters. There was nothing else—no waistcoat, no vest, no
shirt, no cravat, no undervest, no drawers. The garters were pink
lace.

The woman's rigid features collapsed in terror. He found her scream to be delightful, about an octave lower than any he had yet heard, and far less piercing. He thrilled to it as he shifted his view to the older of the two girls. Her pretty eyes were cast downward, her mouth open. (In fear or awe? Actually, either would suffice.) He thrust his pelvis forward to facilitate what he considered to be her obvious interest. She seemed rooted to the spot, her eyes locked on their target. Mr. Lethaby experienced an instantaneous shock of exhilaration. He felt his lips turn upward in a congenial smile. The delicious sensation in his loins spread rapidly, producing a glowing tingle in his fingertips, earlobes, the base of his spine. The sensation was unaffected by his disappointment in finding that the younger girl's eyes were clamped shut, her cheeks bathed in sudden tears. She was, he thought, just a little young and, unlike her older sister, perhaps a trifle unsophisticated . . . poor little thing.

They faced each other for what seemed to be ten seconds or more: a frozen tableau. Then the woman broke through her paralysis and, grasping both young girls by the shoulders, twisted them around.

They beat an orderly retreat, the woman holding her two charges to a rapid, though dignified, walking pace. Mr. Lethaby held his coat open, hoping that at least one of them would glance back for an encore. That particular desire unrealized, he retired to the sanctity of a large tree, behind which he removed the coat, reversed it to its gabardine side, and put it on. He removed the unaccustomed spectacles from the bridge of his nose and finally, with a quick, uncompromising gesture, he ripped off the heavy black fake beard and mustache.

Mr. Lethaby emerged from behind the tree, a clean-shaven man wearing a dark-brown, untrimmed gabardine coat. His late victims were still in sight, tiny figures in the distance. He watched them for a moment, thinking that perhaps someday he might acquire the courage to bring Fawn and Clara along on one of his forays. How absolutely delicious it would be to have his darling twins at his side, opening his coat . . . spreading it wide, revealing all to an innocent but hysterically appreciative victim.

Mr. Lethaby was deep into this, his latest fantasy, when he

felt a weight descend onto his right shoulder. It was a hand. It grasped firmly.

Clara Fowler pointed to the large square, glass-fronted box. It sat on a low table, was decorated with what seemed to be a number of exotic-looking drawer pulls. "And that?" she said.

"Tee-Vee," said Elleander.

"It says Sony."

"It's a Japanese word."

"You speak Japanese?"

"No, but new things seem to be in my head," said Elleander. "More and more new things every minute . . . they just come out."

"Maybe you're going balmy."

"Yes . . ."

"What kind of pictures?"

"They move."

"Like at a peep show?"

"Yes. But it talks and it's colored, as in real life."

"In that little box? It would be a bleeding miracle. I don't believe it."

"Neither do I."

"What's it say when it talks?"

Elleander flashed a tall, thin man walking eccentrically. She heard herself say, "The Ministry of Silly Walks."

"What's that?"

"A very tall man . . . with long legs . . . Monty Python."

Clara stared into the blank face. Quietly she said, "Make it work."

Elleander reached out, watched impassively as her forefinger depressed a button labeled ON-OFF. There was a click, but nothing else.

"There's no pictures," said Clara, her tone expressing disappointment.

"It needs electricity," said Elleander, "like the electrical lamps."

A little later they found some books on a small shelf built into one of the night tables. There were nine in all. Elleander read random passages from a novel titled *Humbolt's Gift*, but because of its peculiar references, she could make little sense of it. There were others: *Catcher in the Rye, The Group, Epitaph for a Spy, The New Machiavelli, The Comedians, The Guns of August.* Though she could relate to none of them, they all seemed more or less familiar, as if they were books she had read in the distant past and subsequently forgotten.

The British Equestrian Encyclopedia: 1900–1960 was a thick volume bound in dull green cloth. She thumbed through its pages with growing excitement, then lay her open hand on it, as if it were a Bible she was about to swear on.

Dimly, she heard Clara say, "There are lots of pictures in this one." The young girl was stretched out on the blue carpeting, a large-format book open before her. It was part of a set of two, the other still in its slipcase.

Elleander stood over her, looking down. The picture was of a woman christening a large ship. Bottle in hand, the subject had been frozen by the camera at the height of her backswing. "The legs," said Clara. "Look at them . . . they're exposed like in a bathing costume. I mean to say, the woman is half naked in that frock, and it's not even the seaside. Just imagine going out in the street in a skirt that short."

"It's the future," said Elleander.

"I hope so. It's bloody marvelous. . . ."

Elleander flopped onto the rug next to Clara and pulled the second volume from its slipcase. The Time-Life *History of the Second World War.* . . . She stared at the title, trying to make sense of it. Underneath, in smaller type, were the words: *Volume Two— Pearl Harbor to Nuremberg.* She flipped the pages back to front, creating a kaleidoscope of war pictures: ships, soldiers, aircraft, explosions, ruins flowed one into the other like some jerky movie montage. It was all outside her frame of reference. War was a complicated game, incomprehensible to women but played enthusiastically by men, along with rugby and cricket. She had never understood why they took pleasure in any of it.

Nevertheless, she found herself working methodically, page by page, through the book. Dumbly, she realized she was searching for something . . . someone.

She discovered him on page 88. He was walking toward the

camera, his lips turned up in a puckish grin under a ridiculous
mustache. He wore a simple officer's tunic and dark trousers. His
eyes, despite the smile, were brooding. There was a single decoration, a Maltese cross pinned just below his left breast.

Elleander stiffened, digging her fingers into the thick
woolen loops of the rug. A rush of anxiety washed over her,
draining the blood from her head. Breathlessly, in a thin, low-
pitched murmur, she spoke his name, "Hitler." Then, with
inexplicable fear clutching her midsection, she was once again
turning the pages.

She recognized the word the instant she read it: *Normandy.*
There were pictures of the beachheads. In one of them, a thousand hunched-over men wearing jaunty iron derbies were running through the surf onto an ugly gray beach. The caption read:
"June 6, 1944. Troops of the Third Infantry Division race ashore
at Beach-Sword, one of the three British landing points." Harry
. . . She searched the faces for him, but at that scale the figures
were tiny, not much larger than pinheads.

For a moment the room spun. Harry, struck down just minutes after he had stepped onto the soil of France. Who was
Harry? Then the anxious fear was gone, as if soothed by some
instantaneous sedative. Harry Morning Trasker . . . Trasker
. . . Bertram Trasker. She felt as if she had lost her memory and
was now recovering it. Her mind boiled over with partially
formed impressions, vaguely connected. Bertie . . . she had married him in 1908, one year hence. He was a handsome man, witty,
charming, with a well-trimmed beard and deep-set, expressive
eyes and . . . Her brain seemed spring-wound, running of its own
accord. Harry, her dead . . . her yet to be born son. For moments
it was clear, then not so clear.

Two and a half hours after she had left to fetch Mr. Lethaby,
Fawn returned without him. Her eyes were puffy. "He's been
arrested," she said.

Clara came to her feet in one graceful movement and embraced her sister.

"They told me at the workshop," said Fawn.

"No . . ."

"What happened?" said Elleander.

"Nobody would tell me. All they'd say was that it happened

early this morning. They were horrible—all of them!" Sobbing, Fawn wiped away tears with the back of her hand. Elleander handed her a handkerchief from the chest of drawers.

"The poor man wouldn't hurt a fly," said Clara. "It's a bloody mistake. He'll die in prison, he will. . . ."

"What are we going to do now?" said Fawn. "He was the only one who could help us. We can't even leave the flat except in these awful clothes! People were looking at me as if I were some kind of beast escaped from the Zoological Gardens." She blew her nose, clutching the silk handkerchief so as to expose a blue embroidered monogram in its corner. It read E.M. Elleander stared at it, feeling once again a sudden anxiety.

Clara sat on the love seat next to her sister. "We're in it this time—no food, no money, and not a bloody thing to wear! What's to become of us?" She looked directly at Elleander.

Elleander stared back for a moment, confused. Then, quite suddenly, she realized that for whatever reason, it must be she herself who was somehow responsible for the weird phenomenon that had overtaken them. But where to turn for help? Certainly not her father. Then perhaps her mother's ex-lover, Mr. Wells? The man was a successful author now, she reasoned, surely he had the means . . . No, not Herbert Wells, for he would introduce her to Bertie and Bertie would die in a bright-red motorcar. She felt herself drifting. . . .

The twins were looking to her for a way out. The responsibility, she realized, was hers. There was no one else. She faced them, her feet planted firmly, hands clasped in front of her like a teacher assuming control of her class. "Money," she said, "is our first priority." She paused. *Priority.* It was a word she had never used before. Calmly, she realized that, for whatever macabre reason, her vocabulary had expanded. She accepted that just as she was beginning to accept all the other strange things that were happening to her. The anxiety of just moments before was gone, though she sensed it still lurking.

Fawn and Clara stared blankly, as if waiting for her to continue. They were, she reminded herself, little more than children.

"I am going to take care of you," she said. "You've been good to me. You rescued me last night from a horrid fate and took me in. From now on, we're going to be a family . . . the three of us."

"A family!" said Fawn.

They sat in a tight circle on the soft carpet. "First," said Elleander, "we must have money." She gestured about the room. "We will sell most of this, and by tonight, each of us will have something to wear." She felt herself smiling and wondered why.

"And something to eat?" said Clara.

"We are going to dine out tonight," said Elleander, "in high style. There must be gentlemen in the West End who'd be happy to pay the bill."

"We have a few friends who'd love to," said Clara.

"And perhaps they might be willing to pay for something even more exciting than just dinner." Elleander uttered the words, not quite sure of their meaning. "Gentlemen," she said, vaguely, "who would be . . ."

"You mean whoring?" said Clara.

"Yes, the three of us." Once again, her words were involuntary, self-propelled, like a hiccup or a sneeze. Quietly she repeated them, listening carefully to make sure it was her own voice. "Yes, the three of us . . . whoring . . . the three of us . . ." This time the meaning was clear. "No! I don't mean . . ."

Fawn was saying, "Are you all right?"

Carefully, she formulated the word, "No." It emerged, "Yes, of course." She was confused, drifting again. *What red motorcar?*

"Your eyes have gone all funny," said Fawn.

Once again, Elleander heard herself laugh. "No, I'm quite well, actually." *Who was Bertie?*

"We have always been true to Mr. Lethaby," said Clara sadly.

"Poor Mr. Lethaby," said Elleander. She could think of nothing else to say.

"Are you a witch?" said Fawn.

Was she? If so, she reasoned, it would explain everything. Then she found herself thinking of Bertie and Harry again: Harry seated across from her in the Savoy Grill, handsome in his new uniform—so much like the father he had never known—Bertie, dying under the overturned bright-red Mercer. . . .

She forced her focus back to the twins. They were staring at her curiously—waiting. *Fawn and Clara, gorgeous in their new winter fashions, waving to her from the deck of the giant ship.* She would change it, make it all different. Then quite suddenly, she was liberated, in control again.

She said, "We'll do what we can to help poor Mr. Lethaby, but we must first help ourselves. Money . . . if we had a hundred pounds, I could make us rich."

"A hundred pounds?"

"To invest . . . to wager on horse racing." Elleander circled the bed to the night table, where she took a book from the shelf. *"The British Equestrian Encyclopedia,"* she said. "We have the winners." She opened the book to a page she had turned down earlier, then read in a flat voice, "April 3, 1908—Aintree Course. First winner: Grand Turk." She looked up. "According to this, the odds were . . . will be . . . seven to one. A hundred pounds will get us seven hundred, and there are the results of the other races listed here, hundreds of them. But to begin with, we have less than a week to raise wagering money for Aintree!"

"I'm sure you're a witch," said Fawn. She seemed to savor the idea.

A few hours later, Elleander, wearing the clothing Fawn had worn earlier, fetched a tradesman in furniture. She sold everything in the flat except the bed, the "tee-vee," the books and a few other small items. He paid twenty pounds cash and, as he stated, "No questions asked." By nightfall, each of them was adequately dressed.

In the cab on the way to Mayfair, Elleander Morning smiled broadly at her two new friends, then leaned back against the soft leather, taking pleasure in the young body she had not occupied for over sixty years.

23

1984

In late January, State Secretary Schmidt ordered Paul Bauer
to submit—in his capacity as future Minister of Propaganda—a
secret plan for total control of the German media to be instituted
shortly after they assumed power.

Bauer spent three nights drawing up a preliminary proposal
calling for the creation of an extensive bureaucracy with separate
departments to censor newspapers, periodicals, book publishers,

motion pictures, the theater, radio and television. The agency was planned to be empowered by an act of the Reichstag, making it illegal to disseminate news, information or "entertainment" prejudicial to the welfare or mental health of the German people or their government.

On January 24, one Martin Bormann, a retired insurance broker, filed suit against Time-Life, Inc. and the German publishing firm of Franke und Schiller. Bormann claimed libel and defamation of character. He demanded 13 million deutsche marks in compensatory damages. Later in the month, similar claims were filed by department-store owner Rudolf Hess and by the estate of Joseph Goebbels, an ex-magazine publisher.

Pickets appeared in front of two large bookstores in Berlin carrying placards reading: THE SECOND WORLD WAR INSULTS GERMAN HONOR; ANGLO-AMERICANS SPIT ON GERMAN CULTURE!; WORLD WAR TWO IS POLITICAL PORNOGRAPHY!

During the same period, the two rightist parties in the Reichstag jointly introduced a bill that would ban from distribution and exhibition any publication, film or television drama that cast aspersions on German culture or race. The next day in Frankfort, Munich and Berlin, thousands rallied in its support.

Early in February, Paul Bauer submitted, as ordered, his proposal for total press control to the party's first shadow cabinet meeting, conducted in secret at a hideaway in the forest near Rastenburg. He had purposely designed his plan to be unwieldy and top-heavy, reasoning that the idea of a complex bureaucracy would appeal to bureaucrats. He thought it ludicrous, with six departments broken into 22 divisions and 106 regional bureaus. At the meeting, Paul was applauded. Field Marshal von Seydlitz held him up as an example to the rest of the shadow cabinet, and it was agreed that he was to prepare a propaganda campaign for the coming election. The new plan was to be presented at the next meeting.

He sat now in his Uncle Rudolph's house outside Berlin staring at the March 18 issue of the German newsweekly *World View.* The cover featured a stylized illustration of a figure dressed in ornate jousting armor against a background of storm clouds and fluttering banners. Under its arm was poised a massive lance

at the ready. To the right, a cover line in heavy black type read:
FIELD MARSHAL VON SEYDLITZ, NEW HEAD OF THE NATIONAL PEO-
PLE'S PARTY.

He lowered the magazine to fix his eyes directly on his uncle
in the flesh, who stood facing him, legs apart, hands clasped
firmly behind his back. Paul glanced down at the swastika armband encircling the elderly man's arm and, despite an icy feeling
of horror, managed to smile. In a hoarse voice, he said, "Congratulations."

The field marshal nodded curtly in response. "I asked you
to come here today in order to tell you about something that
will strongly affect the future—yours, mine, and, above all, Germany's." He spoke loudly, his words clipped, as if, thought
Paul, he were addressing the troops. "As you no doubt have
concluded, the fat pig Schmidt and his cronies thought they
would control me, that I would serve as a figurehead. But I am
not a fool they can manipulate. Soon, in fact, I will be Germany! For now I have the Army, the Navy, the Luftwaffe supporting me, and the Reichsbank and patriots with power and
money. They know that we need the kind of leadership that
only I can provide. There is no room for self-interest. Most of
the others are involved in this because of what they can get
from it. I'm going to see to them just as soon as they've outlived their usefulness. The party—the nation—will be purified."
Von Seydlitz paced with rapid steps a round trip to the end of
the room, returning to the precise spot he had left. "And you,
Paul . . . don't ever forget that we share the same blood. When
the time comes, I want you by my side. Perhaps you might even
take my place one day."

"And that?" Paul tapped his own upper arm.

"The new party symbol. Armbands and banners are being
distributed to the party youth brigades. You'll soon see swastikas
in the streets all over Germany. After the election, when you
finally surface, you too will wear one. When I assume power, the
swastika will become the symbol—the flag of the New Fatherland." Field Marshal von Seydlitz laughed dryly. "I told you that
I would turn their books against them!"

My Führer, thought Paul acidly. His uncle was mad. Aloud,
he muttered, "Blood and iron . . ."

"Blood and atoms, my dear nephew. We move into a new era."

Later he sat in a café staring out the window at evening Berliners promenading in their winter finery. Did they differ essentially from their peers in Copenhagen, Edinburgh, Barcelona? An attempt to rally Danes, Scots or Spaniards to war in the name of racial superiority would surely fail. Almost anywhere else in the civilized world, such an attempt would be met with anger, derision and, in extreme cases, even revolution. Yet in Germany it was thinkable. His uncle and the others seemed to have no doubt as to its effectiveness.

He sipped his *cassis* and once again glanced down at the small pamphlet on the table: THE ELDERS OF ZION—PERPETRATORS OF THE *SECOND WORLD WAR* MYTH!

It had been handed to him in the street by a pretty young man with wild, impatient eyes, shiny black boots and a red-and-white swastika armband. INTERNATIONAL JEWISH PLOT TO DISCREDIT WORLDWIDE ACCEPTANCE OF GERMAN RACIAL AND CULTURAL SUPERIORITY!

He read on. Germany was all that stood between the civilized world and a Zionist takeover. Therefore, the Jews' first priority for its ascendancy to power was to discredit and demoralize the German race.

It went on with more of the same. Paul Bauer folded it over twice, then tore it into little bits. He dropped money on the table for his bill. Then he left the café to walk briskly down Unter den Linden, as if he were a man with a destination.

Once again it occurred to him that Frances Boardman's fears might have been reasonable. The knowledge that he was beginning to agree with her shocked him. But perhaps the Germans were special. Fanatic Arabs who were attacking Jews in Palestine were motivated by a religious and nationalistic hysteria. The Poles and other eastern Europeans harassed Jews out of ignorance and superstition. Of all the practicing anti-Semites, only the Germans might be capable of cold, businesslike, systematic extermination. Efficiency was, after all, a special Teutonic attribute. It was one of a few vital virtues his uncle had attempted, with such diligence, to instill in him when he was a child. He

recalled the others—discipline, obedience and will. He smiled
ruefully to himself. His uncle's efforts had been wasted.

Then suddenly, he found himself thinking of Lesley, missing
her. He felt a need to share it all, discuss it. Lesley, he thought,
there was no one else. How could he have been so stupid not to
have realized it earlier?

Our new acquaintance from America, Sam, a well-known novelist and essayist, laughed and said, "Those natural historical forces they speak of are a good thing to have around the place if you want to make home-made gin, but as far as history is concerned, man produces that all by himself with little help from anything, natural or otherwise. I won't take the time to argue with you about waves of civilization and culture, but suffice it to say that I have my doubts. The only thing I am certain of is that, given your average crossroads, humankind will always negotiate the wrong turn. Man is little more than an ever-increasing brood of idiots who would lose out in any test of intelligence with the food he eats, and that includes your common herring. What other creature has gone out of its way to invent the means of its own total destruction? I speak of money, politics and gunpowder—sure-fire tools to do it with. Gentlemen, in my view, history is nothing more than the chronicle of man's descent into the abyss.

> —*The Intimate Diary of a*
> *London Gentleman*
> (Chapter 6)
> By "B."
> Published privately
> Turtle Press, Glasgow
> 1910

24

1984

"Lesley . . ." It was after midnight, there was the sound of traffic behind his voice.

Breathlessly, she said, "Where are you?"

"A phone booth in Berlin."

"Paul, I've missed you terribly."

"I've been very foolish."

"Please . . ."

"Can you come to Berlin? I need you."

"Yes . . ." She thrilled to the three words.

"Now. Immediately . . . in the morning."

"I love you," she said. She would go anywhere.

Lesley Morning caught the first magnitrain of the day and was at his apartment door in Berlin at eight-thirty. Paul was wearing a blue robe and there was shaving cream on his face. He held her. She melted against him, feeling a sense of relief course through her body.

He said, "I missed you."

He sprawled onto the sofa, seeming to her drained, exhausted, as if he'd been up all night. She sat on the edge next to him, traced the length of his nose with an elegant fingertip. Quietly, he said, "You were right. Those damned books are meant to be taken seriously."

"Please, let's not talk about that. . . ."

"And the woman, Frances Boardman, I remember what she

said: 'You Germans are capable of holding the world at ransom.'
How could she have known? She said it was a possibility—a
probability—and I thought her a hysterical female, despite her
reputation.''

In a low-pitched voice, Lesley said, "What is it? What are you
talking about?" The excitement she'd felt at being with him again
was beginning to founder in a pool of disquiet.

He sat up and in flat, expressionless tones, told her everything. When he had finished, she was silent, her eyes wide in
astonishment.

Paul fell back on the sofa. "I walked all over Berlin last night
going over the options. These maniacs must be prevented from
taking power. If my uncle becomes Chancellor . . ."

"War," she said. "But it's hard to believe."

"The Second World War. It will be worse even than envisioned in the Time-Life books—far worse. Only Germany has
the atom and she'll use it, as Schmidt said, one missile at a time.
And now it's my uncle who has the power—he's to be the new
leader, the Führer! The military is supporting him and there
are others—power and money. The rockets are probably already zeroed in on Warsaw and Paris and Prague, and God
knows where else."

"I can't believe it," said Lesley vaguely.

"Neither could I at first . . . two old men talking of atomic
blackmail to regain some territories lost sixty-five years ago. Sixty-five years! It's a tired old story from the dead past. No one even
gives a damn anymore. Generations have come of age in Upper
Silesia and the Saar who don't even speak German! In the meantime Germany has developed the highest standard of living in the
world. It has been at peace since 1918 and it needs nothing. No
one but the old men even remember the Treaty of Versailles.
And my uncle goes even farther and talks of the annexation of
Austria and Trieste and of the bastard state of Czechoslovakia.
The old men are going to blow up the world!"

Lesley nodded. She was numb, unable to digest what he was
saying. It sounded almost as if he were discussing The Time-Life
History of the Second World War. She had come to Berlin prepared
to give all of that up in order to reconcile their differences; to
start anew with no preoccupation other than for the man she

loved. Everything . . . It was as if he had caught her disease. She wanted to hold him, calm him, make intimate little jokes, martinis and love. There should be nothing in their lives but each other.

"I thought of warning them through the press," said Paul, his voice strident. "An exposé; I have friends in the media. But who'd believe me? And even if they did, even if the powers that be in France and Poland were convinced, what good would it do? The chances are they'd mobilize, despite the atomic threat. They'd call on the British and the Americans to honor their mutual defense treaties. The Germans would twist it all into an act of aggression aimed at themselves and the whole thing would be accelerated. That's one of two possibilities. The other is more likely. Within hours after I opened my mouth, they'd have me in a loony bin."

Lesley had a sudden need for air. She felt flushed, as if running a high fever. She crossed the room to open one of the windows, then stood, her back to Paul, in the cooling draft. "It's so difficult to accept," she said, "like hearing about the end of the world. I just can't believe that the German people would support this kind of madness. My God, Paul, this is 1984, and Germany is a free, democratic country!"

"A democratic country with a constitution full of holes like rotten Swiss cheese. You read what happened to our Weimar Constitution in the books. You're about to see the same thing happen before your very eyes. The Reichstag will simply vote itself out of business . . . very democratically, of course. And as for the *people*, they'll applaud the process. And they'll stand up and cheer the banners and the goose-stepping goons, and they'll believe everything they're told by their new Führer. *Deutschland über Alles*, and death to everybody else! Or, as my crazy uncle tried to drum into me when I was a child: 'We must forge ourselves of blood and iron.'"

Lesley turned to him. "It sounds awful, but maybe you're exaggerating the situation and don't realize it. And your uncle; you hate him. It could be distorting your view of this. . . ." She realized suddenly that she was actually pleading for it all to be untrue; that it be an innocent misjudgment on his part, a ghastly joke they were playing on him.

"You're saying you don't believe me?" He spoke softly.

"No, I mean . . ." Lesley ran her hand through her hair and looked away in confusion. "I don't know." She felt lost now.

"Yet you believe the Time-Life books!" He laughed bitterly. "It seems to be easier for you to embrace fantasy than to accept reality." He stood up, facing her, his expression weary. "I asked you to come to Berlin because I love you, and it occurred to me that you were the only one I could talk to about this. And I desperately needed to talk. If you can't accept what I say, my sanity, my judgment of what I've been through, then it's best if you return to London right now and I'll face this thing alone . . . wherever it leads. It's simply this: What I've told you is *real.* It's not the ravings of a hate-crazed idiot and, more important, not words and pictures from a book. There are men of flesh and blood who intend to take a calculated risk that might very well blow up the world. They have the power, the plan and the will to make it happen. *They* are the reality, and they must be stopped!"

Lesley walked across the room, retrieved a pack of cigarettes from her handbag, fumbled for her lighter, took her time lighting up. After one puff, she killed the cigarette in a small crystal ashtray on his desk, saying, "I've got to give up smoking." Then quietly, she said, "I'm with you in everything you do, Paul. But had we been speaking, you could have told me about this when it started happening. I mean, you rejected me . . . it was six weeks before you phoned. Why?"

"I felt you were obsessed. I'm very serious about you. My God, you even robbed a grave! Two of them." He paused. "It was a shock. . . ." He seemed suddenly deflated.

"You're saying that you didn't want the future mother of your children to be a ghoul?" She tried to stem the tremor in her voice.

In spite of everything, Paul Bauer found himself smiling. "And I haven't even asked you to marry me. . . ."

"I know."

"But I will . . . probably."

"And I'll probably accept you." She smiled back, feeling a little better.

"I was foolish and I realized it within a week," he said. "But then something else happened—that first meeting with Von Seyd-

litz and Schmidt. I thought them both stark-raving mad, and I had
trouble taking it seriously at first. But then I realized that something must be done to stop them . . . what? I'm still not sure. But
I felt it my responsibility as a German. It was a German problem.
I had no right to bring in outsiders. And I too became obsessed,
as I thought you were." He took her hands in his, met her gaze,
a sad look in his eyes. "The books, Frances Boardman's com-
ments, all of it seemed directed against my country, its culture,
its humanity. It's not easy to say, but because of my childhood
rejection of Germany, I suspect there's some real guilt buried
somewhere. I get a little mixed up sometimes."

"I understand. . . ."

"And there was another consideration. If I were seen with
you, my uncle would have demanded an explanation. You represent the enemy. It could have spoiled everything, and it could
have been dangerous."

"But what if we're seen now?"

"It would still be dangerous. Maybe even more so, but I'd
think of something. It's just that I began to understand that I
needed you. Good God! If I can't talk to you, who can I talk to?
I love you! I want to share it all with you—everything. And last
night I saw something that I felt you should also see: the New
Order in action. So I phoned you—finally."

She held his face in her hands and kissed him gently.

There were a dozen teenaged boys dressed in military greatcoats
and peaked pillbox hats picketing each of the two main entrances
of the Ingermann department store. They wore swastika armbands and badges and carried large, professionally lettered signs.
Paul translated for Lesley: DON'T BUY FROM JEWS. JEW MONEY USED
TO DISCREDIT ARYAN CULTURE. MEYER INGERMANN PART OF ZIONIST-
JEW CONSPIRACY.

Across the street, a fur shop, its display window smashed,
was being guarded by a single policeman, while three of the
uniformed pickets stood at parade rest directly in front of him.
Naked mannequins draped in white sheets stared out blankly at
pedestrians, some of whom were gathered in a small, curious
knot at curbside. There didn't seem to be any customers entering
or leaving either of the two shops. Lesley and Paul had viewed

five other similar scenes in just ten minutes of strolling through the late afternoon shopping district.

"There are more than there were yesterday," said Paul. "My guess is that in two or three days, every Jewish-owned shop in Berlin will be under siege. They get no protection from the police until after their windows are smashed, and that usually happens late at night."

"It's awful!"

"And only the beginning," said Paul.

"Why do the people stand for it?"

"It has the feeling of being official—the uniforms and the fact that the police do nothing to interfere. People here respect 'official' actions even though they might disagree with them."

Lesley stared at one of the pickets, catching his eye. The young man turned and spoke to a companion. They both looked at her and laughed. She turned away, feeling the danger, as if she had been attempting to stare down a wild animal.

She and Paul turned to await the traffic to clear so that they could cross the street. During those few moments the picket line expanded the radius of its circle. Lesley felt a presence behind her. She turned. It was the young man. He muttered, *"Juden!"* and, clearing his throat, spat in her face.

She was transfixed, then suddenly aware that Paul had the boy by the throat and was slapping his face. In an instant, Paul was on the ground, being set upon by three of the others. Lesley fought to pull them off, grasping one by the hair—kicking, shouting. She felt her dress rip, saw one of them fumbling with a dagger.

The policeman from across the street broke it up. Within moments the pickets were on station again and the policeman was insisting that she and Paul move on.

Her dress was ripped from the bodice almost to the hem. Paul's nose was bleeding. In the taxi on the way to his flat, she held his head back, dabbing his nose with a small, bloodied handkerchief. Blood proved the reality of what they had been through. She was surprised at her calmness. It had been, she reasoned, the first battle of a war. There was no question now but that they had to fight, to do something. But what? She felt a sudden chill of understanding as the answer presented itself. The words seemed to emerge from her lips of their own volition. "Elleander Morning . . ."

Paul seemed to understand. He lowered his head to look at her, the blood dripping onto his shirtfront. "Yes," he said, "you're right. I doubt if there is any other way but hers."

The next day, back in London, Lesley watched the BBC News as a mob, numbering over a thousand, broke into a Munich bookshop, removed its contents, and used them to light a massive bonfire in the middle of the street. The police, slow to arrive, did little to disperse the crowd, many of whom were wearing swastika armbands. The BBC anchorman stated that the event was obviously staged for the media.

Within three days, literary bonfires were set in a half-dozen other cities. Most of the bookstores in Germany canceled their orders for the Time-Life *History of the Second World War* and returned their stock to the German publisher, Franke und Schiller.

On the twenty-fifth of March, a mob raged through the districts of Magdeburg-Anhalt and Kurhessen, smashing Jewish shop windows and assaulting Jewish individuals. There were a number of deaths. Observers reported that the police stood by, making little attempt either to rescue the beleaguered or arrest the perpetrators.

The Chancellor of the Republic ordered federal troops to patrol the streets of Berlin and four other cities. On the following day, the National People's party rallied a rightist coalition to demand an immediate vote on the Federal Censorship Bill. Surprisingly, it was joined in this endeavor by the seventeen-seat Communist delegation. The government now stood on the brink of dissolution.

25

1909

Mr. Lethaby was released from prison on April 21, 1909. He
had served two years and three days, to emerge an old man in
possession of the clothing on his back and five shillings in his
pocket. Nothing more.

Awaiting him on the outside, in the chilled, colorless light of
a wintery dusk, were his darling twins. They raced to him, embraced him, each in turn. In the cab he seated himself between
them, took their hands in his. He watched the ugly gray walls of
Wormwood Scrubs recede behind him into grim memory while
the twins chattered at him like a pair of excited birds. Mr. Lethaby
sighed, rewarding them with an uneasy smile. He loved them
dearly, and they were all he had. The tables had turned, he was
dependent on them now—his lovely little "nieces"—and, he
thought apprehensively, on a woman he had never met.

He found the house on Highcastle Road every bit as impressive as Fawn and Clara had described it during their weekly

prison visits. Georgian, stately, it was a house that to his eyes was enhanced rather than defiled by what he knew of its current function.

They stood on the narrow portico while Fawn pulled the bellwire. He was pleased to note that the brass was polished to a high gleam, the wood was well burnished, the stone steps as spotless as bone china.

The twins, in their usual gay manner, introduced Samuel, the butler, who seemed to Mr. Lethaby to be all that a proper butler should be, despite his unique employment. Samuel's bearing was erect, self-possessed, his livery well-fitting, his attitude toward the twins both cordial and properly respectful.

Inside they were ushered through the heavily brocaded portiere into a small reception hall furnished in the French style. Samuel took Mr. Lethaby's coat and hat while Clara fussed with his bedraggled necktie and Fawn clucked over his scuffed shoes and threadbare trousers.

Displaying the fluid grace of the best of his breed, the butler swung open a pair of heavy doors. "I'll announce your presence to the Madam, Mr. Lethaby," he said. His bow was little more than a nod coupled with just the slightest smile of encouragement.

Mr. Lethaby's first step across the threshold was to be his last for several seconds. The twins on visitors' days had spoken incessantly of their new "home," but despite this foreknowledge, a year in prison had ill prepared Mr. Lethaby for what his conscious mind insisted must be esoteric illusion.

He stood rooted. Some of the creatures were half-naked, their breasts visible beneath flimsy wisps of chiffon. There were others wearing gorgeous gowns that seemed to him to have been designed for princesses rather than whores. He counted seven in all: slim, brazen, long-legged gazelles and pink, well-fleshed nymphs sporting plump jiggling buttocks and pinched-in waists. This lewd vision was spiced with a phantom scent of exotic perfume combined with the aroma of smoldering Cuban leaf. Mr. Lethaby knew instant euphoria, sure that he had been transported directly from his prison cell to some wondrously depraved heaven.

He counted five gentlemen. One of these, just a few feet to

the left of him, seemed as overstuffed as the chair in which he sprawled, half hidden under a voluptuous bulk of female flesh. Mr. Lethaby watched as the woman laughed aloud and bit her portly companion playfully on the neck.

Finally prodded out of his delighted preoccupation by Clara, Lethaby, his arm in hers, was escorted into the room. "It's a bit early," she said, waving across at a tall, bearded gentleman who saluted her gallantly with his cigar. "Hardly anyone is here yet."

They sat on a large pillow-strewn couch. Mr. Lethaby leaned back into a well-upholstered corner. The ambience was scored by sounds of devilishly gay conversation, subdued titterings and laughter; all of it modulated by the tragic and thus incongruous strains of Puccini. The aria was being bowed by five unconcerned musicians who were partially concealed behind a jungle of potted plants in the far corner of the room.

Mr. Lethaby glanced around, appraising the furnishings. To his practiced eye, it all seemed gratifyingly lavish. In the warm glow of a half-dozen beaded electrical lamps, the artful workmanship of Louis XIV combined naturally with the casual sensuousness of a desert seraglio. There were pillows strewn about everywhere. In the far corner near the small orchestra sat an oriental booth, draped in deep purple velvet and white organdy, which, like the musicians, was all but lost in a forest of greenery.

Nearby, a male client was deep in whispered but jovial conversation with two of the women. Mr. Lethaby stared openly, his eyes locked on one of them. She was a tall mulatto with skin of rich caramel color and hair of deep ebony; exotically beautiful. She caught his eye, smiled as if in recognition. She whispered something to the man as she disentangled herself. Mr. Lethaby muttered under his breath, "A jungle princess . . . nothing less . . ."

He stood, took her hand, his eyes darting downward to admire a body sheathed in a dress of light-blue silk.

She said, "Mr. Lethaby, surely! Fawn and Clara talk about you all the time. . . ."

Clara said, "This is our good friend Alma."

"So happy to meet you," he said.

"They say only nice things about you, Mr. Lethaby." She laughed, flashing teeth that seemed like exquisitely set pearls.

"Alma is from America," said Fawn.

"Jamaica, I'll wager," said Mr. Lethaby. He squeezed her hand.

"Philadelphia, Pennsylvania," she said, retrieving her hand, then leaning forward to place a wet kiss on his lips.

During the next few minutes he met two others. Magnolia Levy was a girl just a few years older than the twins. Her physiognomy, when pressed in greeting against his, put Mr. Lethaby in mind of ripe fruit. Astrid was a stern-looking brunette wearing a restrictive corset, whose tightly formal response to their introduction led him to suspect a lack of cordiality between her and the twins.

"Mr. Lethaby?" The voice, softly feminine, came from behind him. Nervously, he turned to face it. She was wearing red, a gown he recognized as being by Poiret—perfection. She smiled sweetly at him, her eyes wide, softly questioning.

He stood as she circled the couch to offer him her hand. Her fingernails were painted the color of her dress. She said, "It's so nice to meet you . . . finally. I'm Elleander Morning."

Dazzled by her slim grace, he searched for words, could find none.

"Please sit down, Mr. Lethaby."

"Thank you . . ." He sat stiffly on the edge of the seat cushion, his eyes on her face. He had expected a much more severe woman.

She sat directly across from him in a blue brocaded love seat. The twins, standing now, ranged on either side of her, grinned broadly at him. She said, "Are you all right?"

"Yes, I'm fine . . . thank you." He hesitated, found the words. "I had assumed a much older woman."

She laughed. "The work of our twins, Mr. Lethaby." She reached out, slapped Fawn playfully on the rump. "They believe that middle age begins on one's eighteenth birthday!"

Mr. Lethaby echoed her laugh. He leaned back in his chair feeling suddenly at ease.

Within a week, he found his place. Quietly, with Madam's unspoken approval, he began looking into financial matters. With a minimum of fuss he caused kitchen thievery to be reduced to sensible, traditional proportions. He advised the purchase of an

electrical clothes washing machine to replace the expensive outside laundry service. He reorganized the primitive bookkeeping
procedure and arranged for a heavy wall safe to be installed in
Madam's office behind a large, recently purchased painting of an
accordion player dressed as a clown.

By year's end, Mr. Lethaby was overseeing the staff, which
now consisted of a butler, steward, laundress, two "upstairs"
maids, a cook, cook's assistant and scullery maid. By this time,
Elleander Morning's faith in his good judgment was total. She
accepted his suggestions for a new payment schedule for the
ladies of the house, whereby each of the eleven received a weekly
salary plus 20 percent of their fees. Gratuities, sometimes quite
substantial, were to remain theirs. Each of the ladies would make
ten to fifteen pounds a week. In no other line of endeavor could
any of them have earned a third of that. Finally, Mr. Lethaby
convinced each of them to contribute five pounds a week into an
investment trust that was to see many of them into eventual
retirement.

The ladies of the house were duly grateful. On the afternoon
of his birthday, they surprised him in his fourth-floor room.
There, one by one, in an atmosphere of strict seriousness, he
removed the little-girl clothing they had worn for the occasion.
Then, accompanied by titters and giggles, he was served tea and
birthday cake by eleven charmingly naked nieces. From then on,
he was "Uncle Lethaby," and the few years left him were to be
the happiest of his life.

───── **26** ─────

1910

As she did on most mornings, Elleander, wearing a light-blue quilted dressing gown, sat at the head of the long, well-laid breakfast table. Facing her, seated at the other end, was "Uncle" Lethaby. Between them, eleven ladies of the house sat uncoiffed in early morning dishevelment, their bodies barely covered by an assortment of expensive French nightwear. Mr. Lethaby, as always, was the only one dressed for the day, affecting the dark suit, wing collar and Etonian school tie of a broker about to set out on his daily commute to the city.

Elleander had two pieces of toast and a cup of tea. She rarely allowed herself more than that for breakfast. As a general rule, she ate lightly, habitually refusing solid food at teatime. Her lunch and dinner, though sufficient by her standards, were thought of, by the monstrous appetites surrounding her, to be

barely adequate to support life. Elleander referred to this strange
self-denial as a "diet," a term her ladies thought symptomatic of
a deep-seated mental aberration that kept their young madam
undernourished and unfashionably skinny.

For them, the abundance of good food was a stroke of fortune that little else but prostitution could provide. All but four
of the ladies were either orphans or children of the working class.
As such, breakfast in their early years had never consisted of
more than bread and tea. Lunch would usually be the same, with
the possible addition of a piece of bacon, and supper, more often
than not, gruel and tea, with perhaps the occasional added treat
of a bit of sheep's liver or spoiled mutton.

Now they sat at a breakfast table resplendent with platters of
fried codfish, kidneys, grilled tomatoes, bacon, toast, kippers,
eggs, a pitcher of hot milk, a jar of marmalade, three teapots, and
two crocks of butter with a consistency only slightly thicker than
whipped cream. They would, as they did every morning, sit there
till nothing remained.

Elleander joined their laughter as they spoke of the high
point of the previous night's activity. A member, Mr. Harold
White of the Home Office, after drinking half a bottle of bubbly,
had ascended the main staircase with the other half and two
of the ladies, Magnolia and Yvonne. In the bedroom, Mr.
White removed his clothes, downed the remainder of the champagne, then set out to impress his equally naked companions
by standing on his head while demanding their professional
participation in a series of nearly impossible acrobatic
activities.

As a result of her efforts, Yvonne, a new, "international"
member of the staff from Paris, was sporting a turned wrist,
done up in a length of tightly wound bandage. Mr. Harold
White was even now sleeping it off in one of the third-floor
guest rooms.

Elleander lowered her cup to deal with the morning post.
There were two letters by her plate: one, a bill from Miss Markle,
her dressmaker, the other bearing no return address but marked
boldly with the words PRIVATE AND CONFIDENTIAL. Unmindful of
the ongoing chatter, she slit open the envelope.

April 23, 1910

Madam:

As per your request, the subject has been under observation for three weeks, but has displayed no habits (of the kind you specified) but one, in that he has been seen each Monday and Thursday evening to leave his flat at six-thirty in order to proceed, at a brisk walk, to his club. Time en route: thirty-four to thirty-nine minutes. The return trip is always somewhat less spirited, commencing between the hours of ten-fifteen and eleven-twenty and requiring forty-five to fifty-two minutes. The subject in question deviated from this just twice, due to heavy rainfall, first on April 7, and again on April 17, at which times he reverted to a cab. With these exceptions, his route never varied. An appropriate map is enclosed.

I trust the above meets your requirements. Our bill will be posted under separate cover.

We remain at your service.

Yours truly,
Byron G. Tandy
Private Enquiry Agent

Elleander excused herself from the breakfast table. On her office desk, she unfolded the hand-drawn map. She traced, with an expectant finger, Bertie's route from his flat in Belgravia along Grosevenor Place into Victoria Street, then around Parliament Square onto the Victoria Embankment. There her finger hesitated, tapping thoughtfully. The Embankment was ideal for her purpose, even more deserted at late hours than any of the streets en route. It would be a dark night—moonless. She could lurk safely there in the shadows, awaiting Bertie on his homeward journey. With luck, there might even be a bit of fog.

She calculated the time. Eight days hence would be a Thursday, a club night for Bertie. It coincided perfectly with the fertile portion of her menstrual cycle. Her hand was shaking. She stilled it, tensing her fingers, flexing them on the map. Soon, she would be carrying their son again, and this time he would live beyond the year of the bloody landings on the Normandy coast.

Eight days later she stood in front of an ornately carved chennelle mirror, hands hanging loosely at her sides. The dress, the padded corset, the coiffure, the cosmetics had made her into everything that she was not: wide-hipped, fat-breasted, her face hardened with too much makeup. She was rounded, bulbous; a woman of soft, padded flesh. As an ideal harlot, she reasoned, she would arouse nothing but lust in Bertie; no dangerous tender feelings, no involving emotional responses. She would be, for him, a quick, satisfying fuck, nothing more.

Turning from the mirror, Elleander fought back a wave of nausea, grasped the edge of the small writing desk until her knuckles turned white. She must not, she insisted to herself, permit tears. The kohl, so painstakingly applied around her eyes, would run. She found herself, for the first time, admitting to the possibility of failure. There were, in London, tens of thousands of street harlots, her competition. A gentleman, even in broad daylight, strolling the haymarket, had to swat them off like flies . . . her sisters. She steadied herself, saying, "Waterproof Maybelline." It was, she mused, still to come, along with so much else. "Blow dryer . . ."

Elleander was on the Embankment at ten. She melted into the shadows, facing in the direction of Bertie's projected approach. A fine mist muted the lights from the nearby Strand. Would she recognize him? She closed her eyes in an attempt to conjure up his image. She failed. Only their son-to-be occupied her mind's eye. Poor Bertie . . .

It was in her dressing room on the opening night of *The Remaking of Angela* where, surrounded by congratulatory bouquets and empty champagne bottles, they had made love for the first time. She stared into the dark, featureless waters of the Thames, feeling once again the pressure of tears behind her eyelids. This time, she had assumed a role far different from that of the naive young actress who had allowed herself to be seduced. She was a whore. Gentlemen do not pursue whores.

Tonight, if all went well, she would return alone and pregnant to Highcastle Road. He would not attempt to seek out a whore, to make love to her again and again and then die.

She shrugged off the tears, breathing deeply in an attempt

to savor the damp night air. The fog was developing rapidly, softening the image of the occasional lone pedestrian on the nearby footpath. Nervously she adjusted her hat, a gigantic configuration of ribbons, bows and artificial fruit. Fawn had seen it briefly in its box early in the day, caressed it longingly, saying, "It's not you. . . ." Elleander planned to give it to her in the morning, mauve hat box and all. And of course something nice for Clara—a pearl stickpin, perhaps. The twins were her family —all she had. Someday, if everything went well, she would try to explain it all to them.

Elleander smiled grimly to herself. Clara, like any other sane person, would think her mad, while Fawn would have no further doubts about her being a witch. Was she . . . ?

She recognized Bertram Trasker's silhouette on the footpath against the warm glow coming from the Savoy's back windows. Suddenly breathless, she backed farther into the shadows. She waited interminable seconds, until he drew parallel, then passed her. Automatically, she stepped out, less than ten feet behind him. Committed, she matched his pace. He was wearing the battered old trilby, its brim pulled down to his coat collar. He carried a furled umbrella sporting a carved horse's-head handle. He had lost it, she recalled, on a holiday they would share in Paris during the fall of 1912.

It had been more than a half century. The sudden tug of realization chilled her. She slowed her pace almost to a stop. The trilby, the umbrella were real; the click of her heels, sharply defined, substantial. Her silly game had become a reality.

He hesitated, turned. His eyes were on her. She stared back, then stood in place, feeling that her heart might burst as he surveyed her body, his eyes scanning slowly upward from her feet. She battled an almost uncontrollable compulsion to turn away, to race home to Highcastle Road to live out her days, to forget Bertie, Harry, the war . . . all of it.

Instead, she breathed deeply, her first breath since he had turned to her. Then, with faked purposefulness, she stepped toward him.

"Good evening, madam." His eyes were on hers. He grinned, his white teeth contrasting dramatically with a coal-black beard.

She forced a smile, heard herself say, "It's so nice to see you again."

"To see me *again,* madam?"

"Yes, it's been a while . . . a long time." The words came automatically, as if she were acting in a play for which there was no script or director.

GOOD-BYE TO THE GOLDEN AGE OF AIRSHIPS

Thousands watch as the famous German zeppelin *Hindenburg* debarks its 103 passengers for the last time at its mooring mast in Lakehurst, New Jersey, just a few miles from New York City. The gigantic, 800-foot, helium-enflated airship has, since its launching in 1936, completed 872 trans-Atlantic voyages, providing total safety in extravagant comfort to 69,942 paying passengers.

Still in service are the 800-foot *Graf Zeppelin II,* plying weekly between Capetown and Frankfort, and the huge, 1,225-foot *Hugo Eckener,* commuting thrice-monthly between Rio de Janeiro and Frankfort. It has been announced that these two behemoths of the blue will also be withdrawn from service in early spring of 1958. The reason? High cost of competition with the conventional airlines and with the new high-speed trans-Atlantic superliners.

—London *Daily
Telegraph,*
October 5, 1957

27

1910

"How did you find me?" said Elleander Morning.

"You've gained," said Herbert Wells, "a certain notoriety. I overheard a conversation in which your name was mentioned—total strangers. I simply broke in and asked."

She stared at him. His face was that of an old, familiar friend, yet she realized that his only memory of her was of a child, the daughter of his mistress, whom he had seen just once on her twelfth birthday.

"You resemble your mother—striking. Though you're even more beautiful."

She stood, took a few steps forward, hovered over him. "I assume you've come here to purchase my professional services."

He was silent. He looked at her grimly, then glanced away. "Your friend Trasker recommended it?"

"Not quite. But he did speak highly of your . . . ah, skills." Wells hesitated, a confused expression on his face. "How could you know that Bertram Trasker is a friend of mine?"

She disregarded the question, turned away from him. A pervasive sadness seemed to have taken over her body. She felt suddenly weary.

"He said nothing to me about having mentioned my name to you."

"He didn't," she said quietly.

"Then how . . . ?"

"It doesn't matter." She seated herself primly, attempted to brighten her tone. "You've had the mother, and now the daughter has been recommended."

Wells was silent.

"I'm afraid, Herbert dear, that you're a few months too late. I no longer sell my body."

He reacted sharply to her use of his first name, capturing her eyes with his own. "You're a strange woman."

"Would you like me to recommend one of our ladies?"

"No, thank you." He held her eyes with his. "That was not my purpose."

She forced a smile. Her memory of him was extensive, hardly dimmed by the intervening half century. He had been a good friend, a kind of uncle to her. He had introduced her to Bertie, and after their marriage had been a frequent dinner guest, a close family friend. She felt a rush of affection toward him. She reached out to lay a hand on his cheek. "Dear Herbert, you've been testing me and you're confused. What did he say to you in that stuffy club of yours?"

Her hand seemed to startle him. She smiled enigmatically, sat back, waiting for him to speak.

"Bertram Trasker," he said finally. "He described your little assignation in great detail. There was nothing about his description of you that I could accept . . . you being your mother's daughter. I was right, of course." He stared at her intently. "It's easy to see that you're simply not the woman he described. And, just incidentally, he thought you totally mad."

"Do you?"

"No."

"Why not? The way I was going on, any sane person would have thought I was crazed."

"Crazed, perhaps, but not mad."

"You make a fine distinction."

"Not so fine," said Wells, leaning forward in his seat. "We've all acted crazed at one time or another—frightened, angry, desirous—to a degree beyond our capacity to act rationally."

Elleander felt a chill of apprehension. "Why are you here, Herbert?"

"Curiosity."

"Please . . ."

"It seems as if you set our friend Trasker on edge, poor fellow. As he related it to me, he said that you knew his name, his exact age and a few other things about him even more intimate: the birthmark under his beard, for example. You also spoke of his future son. On the Embankment, he had to turn his head to make contact with you. It's been my experience that prostitutes habitually approach their prospective clients from the front, for obvious reasons. It's as if you'd been following poor Bertie. And there was the matter of your accent. He's certain that he detected a Cockney flavor. I found that to be quite strange, as neither your mother, nor, as near as I can recall, you yourself, at the age of twelve displayed any trace of such an accent—quite the contrary. Then I wondered, as did my friend Trasker, why you disappeared so mysteriously from the cab. And the tears . . . He assumed you were mad. I assume otherwise. And I feel more strongly about it now that I'm here, for why should a successful young madam, proprietress of a flourishing business, disguise herself as a street whore in order to lurk about for cheap clients late at night on the

Embankment? I realize you believe all of this to be none of my business. But as a writer, my business is anything that whets my curiosity." His smile was apologetic. "I'm sorry if I've upset you in any way. I had every intention to be quite circumspect about all of this, but you very adroitly forced my hand."

Elleander felt momentarily dazed, unsure of how to react. Quietly, she said, "Surely, insanity would explain all of it. A madwoman . . ."

"No. You displayed far more method than madness. Your meeting with Trasker was not an accident, it was planned. Admit it, Miss Morning . . ."

"Elleander, please . . ."

"A lovely name," said Wells, his voice softening. "Elleander." Thoughtfully, with two graceful sweeps of his fingers, he smoothed out his mustache. "You've been very gracious and I thank you for it. I'm a total stranger on your premises, and I've been sitting here making what to you must sound like dire accusations. . . ."

"Not a total stranger," said Elleander, impulsively. The words were out before she'd had a chance to consider them. She should, she realized, ask him to leave. He had no hold on her, no right to demand an answer to his suspicions.

"Ah yes," he said. "Not quite total. We did meet once, and my affections for your mother imparts a kind of kinship, doesn't it?"

It was not what she had meant. She stared at him blankly as a broad smile inflated his face into a full moon. Then, suddenly, she was reliving that other time, all those nights when the three of them had sat over brandy until such late hours that Herbert had often been obliged to occupy the guest room. They discussed everything, and never once had she been excluded or patronized because she was a woman and therefore by definition out of her depth. On one such occasion, Bertie had accused Herbert of believing that science had the answer to all men's problems. Herbert had denied the accusation vehemently. (She recalled, too, how decades later, Wells was to call George Orwell "a shit" for having made a similar accusation on the BBC.) Elleander proceeded to advance the idea that science had indeed solved most of man's problems. The invention of steam power had brought on the industrial revolution, which continued to make such rapid social and economic changes that even the historians found it impossible to establish a perspective. And it was, she had maintained, a scientific revolution that had actually solved most of the problems that previously had besieged mankind. The rub, she insisted, was that the industrial revolution created in its wake a host of *new* and possibly even greater problems. After some discussion, both men had agreed that perhaps this was true and was a cyclic phenomenon. The resolution had been gratifying.

Wells was looking at her curiously. He said, "I'd give anything to know what you're thinking about."

She laughed. "I've been thinking about the industrial revolution and also about what a garrulous old man you're going to be."

Wells echoed her laugh, saying, "As a friend of mine once stated, 'It gets curiouser and curiouser.' "

"And I'll tell you something else." She felt suddenly lighthearted, mischievous. "Your story about a voyage to the moon was nonsense."

"Nonsense?" His smile stiffened.

"Your idea of using an antigravity substance—cavorite—pure fantasy, very unscientific. The proper way to launch human beings into space is—or rather, will be—a multi-stage rocket. The main rocket launches two others, each to fire in turn as the previous one is exhausted. The vehicle accelerates gradually so that the G forces are minimized."

"Good God! And what in the world are G forces?"

"One G is equal to the force of gravity, two Gs, twice the force, and so on. The greater the acceleration, the higher the G force. At twenty Gs, you'd weigh about thirty-five hundred pounds. You'd be crushed like an eggshell."

"Remarkable!" He paused, as if searching for words. "Where in the world did that information come from?"

"Isaac Newton, I believe." Elleander was enjoying herself, though she knew that sooner or later the game would sour. She felt a need to tell him everything. There was no one else who would believe her, or not think her crazy or, even worse, would not attempt to deter her from what she knew she must do.

"And what leads you to believe that I will age eventually into a cantankerous old man?"

"Because you have plans for a world that has no intention of following them. It will enrage you."

"You are far more than I bargained for," said Wells, as if he were speaking to himself. "Who are you?"

She laid a soft hand on his knee. "You will be a great man, Herbert, and I'd value your friendship. . . ."

He smiled. "Ah, at least we do agree on a few things."

"You must promise me," she said, "never to tell Bertram Trasker of our meeting."

"Why?"

"Perhaps in time I'll tell you why." As she spoke, she wondered what his reaction would be if he knew of her pregnancy . . . Bertie's child. She would be showing soon—another month?

Moments after he was gone, she recalled his cremation in Golders Green. He had been eighty years old, and Priestly had eulogized him as *the great prophet of our time.*

It is a matter of pride, and I must add, of comfort to me, that I will go to my reward with the knowledge that the sun will continue to find it impossible to set on the British Empire.

—Winston Churchill
1964

28

1984

Jack Burns, above all else, considered himself a professional. He was a little man in his early sixties, wiry, fast on his feet like a featherweight boxer. He was dressed somberly in a dark-blue suit and sported a brown tweed cap that no one had ever seen him without.

Now he placed a somewhat oversized attaché case on the table. "This is your bomb," he said. "It weighs just a bit over twenty-five pounds. Fourteen pounds of that is metal casing and eleven pounds is RDX, a military explosive with about twice the blasting power of TNT." He paused, seeming to relish the sound of his own voice. "It wasn't easy to get hold of."

Shulberg said, "Twenty-five pounds? How in the hell is Paul going to carry it casually without looking like a weightlifter working out?"

"Practice."

"I'll manage it," said Paul Bauer.

"But why so much metal?" said Lesley. "Couldn't you have used plastic or something light?"

"No," said Jack Burns. "The more you confine an explosion,

the greater the blast—up to a point. It gives the pressure a chance to build up. The ratio of casing to explosive in this pretty little thing is just about right for the job at hand. If the room had concrete walls and no windows, we could probably get by with a bomb one third this weight, but I don't think you're going to be that lucky. I've allowed for the worst case—a wood frame with lots of windows." He stroked the attaché case as if it were a pet dog. "That takes care of blast, but we have here something just as important—fragmentation. The metal casing is serrated, like an American hand grenade—a pineapple. When the bomb goes off, it will break up into at least two hundred iron fragments that will fly about helter-skelter in every direction." He smiled enigmatically. "You told me that there will be about twelve people in the room. Well, if the blast don't get them, the shrapnel will. They'll all be done in quite nicely; not to worry, my friends."

They were quiet. Then Lesley said in a small, husky voice, "I wish there was another way. . . ."

"There is no other way," said Paul.

Fred Hayworth said, "Is it safe?"

"It's not in the nature of bombs to be safe." Burns opened the attaché case. Inside, filling two thirds of its volume, was what appeared to be a thick, dull-gray, metal waffle. Screwed into one end of it was a metal pipe, roughly an inch and a half in diameter and four inches in length.

"Inside the pipe," said Jack Burns, "is a small glass capsule, which when broken will release enough acid to eat through a thin wire in exactly twenty minutes. When the wire is broken it will free the firing pin under spring pressure to strike a mercury-fulminate primer . . . boom. . . . Guaranteed to meet your needs. There are no ticking clocks to give it away and no batteries or electrical circuits to fail. Nice and simple it is and, if I do say so myself, ingenious." He snapped the case shut, set it upright. "On the side of the handle you will notice a pin with a knurled head. It screws out in three turns." Green proceeded to demonstrate. He held up the pin dramatically. "The bomb is now armed." Burns stood, an expectant look on his face, like a teacher awaiting questions from the class.

Shulberg laughed nervously. "A full demonstration is not necessary, Jack. . . ."

"Armed, Sidney, not primed. We don't have to evacuate the premises yet. To do that, you would have to press this small trigger underneath the handle." With some delicacy, he raised the attaché case to eye level, indicating a black plastic projection under the handle. "When you press this trigger, a small, spring-loaded lead plunger is released to smash the acid capsule and Bob's your uncle."

"And," said Paul Bauer, "if the case is accidentally dropped?"

"I would advise you to indulge yourself with a twenty-minute walk in the fresh air—just in case." He reinserted the arming pin.

Paul picked up the attaché case, tested its weight, then, grasping the handle, he walked slowly back and forth across the room.

"Right shoulder's a little low," said Lesley.

Paul adjusted, increased his pace. "It gets easier when I walk faster."

Later, when they had all left, Lesley found Paul in the library. He was seated in the oversized wing chair, his feet propped up on a hassock. Wearing the beige robe she had given him, he was reading a bound, Xeroxed text of The Time-Life *History of the Second World War*. He looked up, smiled at her ruefully.

Lesley kissed him on the cheek, saying, "I'm dying for a cup of tea and some of those shortbread biscuits. How about you?"

"Marvelous idea."

She fetched a tray from the kitchen. When she returned, Paul said, "I've been reading about Count Von Stauffenberg."

She said, "The Hitler assassination plot?"

"Yes. There's something very strange about it. I mean, it might be a coincidence, but it happened in Rastenburg, at a conference. The book doesn't make it entirely clear, but I'm left with the impression that it was a kind of headquarters they called the Wolves' Lair. It was in a forest."

"The same as you described from your first trip . . ."

"Exactly. And our secret conferences, too, are held in a forest area just outside of Rastenburg. I'm sure it was all my uncle's idea. I suspect the books have become a bible to him. They've even named the Rastenburg house 'Wolves' Lair.' It's all from the books. It's crazy." He set his teacup down on the lamp table. "But the main reason I wanted to have another look at the books tonight is that I seemed to recall reading that the assassination attempt on Adolf Hitler was made with a bomb hidden in a briefcase. It's a frightening coincidence. Here . . ." He flipped the pages back, then read, "*Colonel Von Stauffenberg had been badly wounded and possessed only one eye and one arm. His single hand had only three fingers. With these he grasped a pair of tongs and inserted the fuse into the bomb, crushing as he did so the acid capsule. The acid would dissolve a thin arming wire in fifteen minutes. He placed the bomb, now armed, into a brown leather briefcase, convinced that in less than a quarter of an hour, the Nazi era would come to an end.*"

"Same kind of bomb," said Lesley. "Acid delay—the lot."

"Ours is much more sophisticated."

"And a briefcase," said Lesley in a quiet voice.

"*Attaché case* is the more modern term."

"The similarities! It's all familiar. I mean, I remember reading it, but until now I never made the connection." She reached for a cigarette.

"You've got to stop smoking. . . ."

"But it failed, Paul. Adolf Hitler lived. I remember now, something about the heavy conference table . . ."

Once again he read, "*The time was twelve thirty-nine. Three minutes left. No one noticed Von Stauffenberg leave. A minute later, Colonel Brandt, attempting to lean forward in order to read a map, found his way blocked by the briefcase Von Stauffenberg had placed on the floor. Brandt reached down and moved it to the opposite side of a massive oak table support that spanned the width of the conference table. It was this inconsequential action that placed a shield between the bomb and the Führer, who sat less than eight feet away. Though many lost their lives, Adolf Hitler escaped with only a few minor bruises.*"

Lesley said, "Same kind of bomb, same kind of situation, same place in Germany." She felt a chill. "If your uncle lives, he will make martyrs of the ones who are killed. He'll play it to the hilt and we'll have accomplished nothing."

"It won't happen that way," said Paul. "The bomb used in the book was a baby compared to ours."

"How do you know that?"

"The officer—Brandt—who picked up the briefcase to move

it would have become suspicious if it had been unusually heavy. Ours is obviously a much bigger bomb. As Jack Green told us, there will be, in addition to the blast, a great amount of fragmentation. I trust him. Colonel Von Stauffenberg's bomb was a toy, he should have known better."

"Paul . . . you sound like you believe it."

"Believe what?"

"The Time-Life *History of the Second World War*—that book sitting in your lap." She found herself grinning at him.

He placed the book on the floor, stood up to tower over her. He spoke quietly. "I don't know. . . ."

"You've said more than once that it was only a book, a superb piece of fiction."

"I don't know," he repeated. He sat down abruptly. "But I do know that our bomb is going to work. I'm not going to make the same mistakes that Von Stauffenberg made. . . ."

29

1910

"Sherry, Major Marek?"

"Yes, thank you, madam. I presume my cigar is not offensive to you?"

"Not at all. I find it to be quite pleasant." Elleander poured the sherry.

Major Marek, recently retired from the Indian Army, was a tall man, well turned out. In his mid-sixties, he sported a full head of red hair that was thought by the ladies of Highcastle Road to be the result of frequent henna rinses. He had married well, kept a modest house and staff in Surrey and made one trip a week to London. His visits to Highcastle Road were timed precisely: arrival at nine, departure at ten-thirty. Elleander was mildly surprised to find that, at least this once, he had broken his routine. It was, at the moment, just a little past eight.

"Madam Morning." He pronounced each syllable precisely as if trying to make himself understood to a foreigner. "I've brought my nephew along this evening. The boy has just turned eighteen—birthday last week . . ."

"And you wish to begin his education?"

"Exactly."

"In that case, our Miss Fawn will make a lovely birthday gift."

"I think not. She's much too young. It's quite obvious that a much older, experienced woman would be appropriate for this sort of thing." His face took on a pained expression. "This is certainly not a frivolous matter."

"Major, I don't underestimate the importance of the occasion. Fawn is only sixteen, but is quite experienced. She is a charming girl with a lovely disposition. This is not an initiation into some sort of secret society, neither is it an army field exercise. Your nephew is not required to prove his manhood or pass a test. And it is certainly more natural for a boy to be with a young lady at least as young as himself. We don't want him to develop a taste for older women, do we?"

"Ah yes, I see. Very clever."

"I'm glad you agree, Major Marek. Above all, your nephew should enjoy his first encounter rather than be frightened by it. And in the process we will teach him how to satisfy a woman's needs. Fawn, I assure you, is the ideal choice."

"Woman's needs?" said the major blankly.

"Indeed. It is a phenomenon that will someday be quite popular." She smiled at him. "Trust me, Major Marek. This is my profession and I'm quite devoted to it."

"In that case, there is nothing more to be discussed." The major downed the remainder of the sherry. "You will, of course, add the service to my bill." He rose to his feet. "My responsibility is discharged."

"It soon will be," said Elleander Morning.

In July, when her pregnancy was confirmed, Elleander purchased a small cottage in Cornwall. By early October she was "showing." On the tenth, she left Highcastle Road, not to return until after her baby was born on February 8, 1911.

Once a week she was visited by Clara and Fawn, who stayed overnight and shopped for her in the village. From time to time

"Uncle" Lethaby, in whose capable hands she had left the business, consulted her on the telephone. Aside from that, she was alone.

When the weather was good she spent hours sitting in a secluded cove, staring out to sea. She took long evening walks on the beach. She read Conrad, Barrie, Marie Corelli, and sometimes gave over entire days to sleep. Within a few weeks she had settled into a warm, sequestered languor, aware that Harry was growing in her body. She took pleasure in the process, floating lightly on a gentle, inevitable tide.

Then one morning in December she was awakened by a severe storm whose rolling thunder and lightning flashes seemed to her like an artillery barrage. It was a gradual awakening, strangely expected, as if she had left a call the previous night. Dawn brought the realization that the holiday from herself had ended. She spent the day reading the Time-Life *History of the Second World War*. The following week, with a growing sense of isolation, she wrote to H.G. Wells, inviting him to visit her.

He arrived on a chill but sunny afternoon. Elleander watched through a window as he debarked from the station cart to make his way down the long, twisting footpath to the cottage. He was a familiar figure. It was, she realized, a strangely one-sided familiarity that saddened her. He was the reliable old friend; she the relative stranger, the inexplicable puzzle awaiting solution.

She kissed him on the cheek in greeting as he stared at her unblinking for moments. Quietly, he said, "Congratulations."

"Thank you." She took his hat, umbrella and coat.

"I didn't expect to find you with child. . . ."

"Pregnant," she said cheerfully. It was a word not used in polite society.

"I went twice to Highcastle Road to see you. They wouldn't tell me where you were."

"I'm sorry." She took his hand. "But here you are." She led him into a rustic but comfortable sitting room. The ceilings were low, supported by large, unfinished beams. Whitewashed brick walls reflected the warming glow of late afternoon sunlight pouring in from a quartet of roughly glazed windows on two walls.

Wells withdrew a small, leatherbound book from his overnight case. "A little gift." He handed it to her. "I'm certain you'll
enjoy it."

She ran her fingers over the gold-embossed title. *The Intimate
Diary of a London Gentleman.* She thanked him.

He said, "I believe you'll find the last chapter especially
interesting."

She opened it, flipped the pages. She read aloud: *"Chapter
Twenty-two . . . May thirty-first and June first . . . A cab ride shared with
a mad harridan of great beauty and sincere talents . . ."* Elleander
smiled. "I'm flattered."

There were tea and scones. They spoke of the weather and his
trip down from London. Finally, she grinned at him and said,
"It's quite difficult balancing tea-things on one's lap when there's
hardly a lap to speak of."

He lowered his teacup. "And the father?"

"One good guess, Herbert . . ."

"Bertram Trasker."

She nodded. "You must promise me you'll say nothing of
this to Bertie, or even mention that you've seen me."

"Granted." He moved to the edge of his seat, almost upsetting his teacup. "I promise . . . but why did you choose Bertie?"

"I love him." said Elleander. She had decided to tell Wells
everything. She desperately needed a confidant, a friend who was
her peer. The secret had become too much for her to live with
and it must be, she realized, Herbert or no one. Peculiarly
enough, she knew that he too was passing through a difficult
period and could perhaps also use a sympathetic ear. His affair
with Amber Reeves, a woman half his age, had become public
knowledge. His intention, despite the scandal, was to "put feeling
before convention" and continue with both his marriage and his
affair with Amber. To complicate matters, his lover was pregnant
and proclaiming that it had been her choice to bear Wells a child.
The critics, both social and literary, were having a field day con-
demning the man and his published philosophy of marriage and
sex. There were even those, a few friends included, who maintained that his creative energies had been sapped, that his career
was finished. Elleander felt a wave of sympathy. "I love Bertie,"

she repeated. "Surely, you of all people can understand that."

"Yes, of course," he said. "But still, you've seen him just once. . . ."

"I have much to tell you." She gestured for him to remain seated as she rose awkwardly to her feet to cross the room to a small cabinet under the window. Returning, she handed him a book. "Machiavelli," she said.

Wells stared at the titled embossed in white on the worn, navy-blue binding. Quietly he thumbed the pages before returning to the beginning. He read, his body rigid, as if all its functions had ceased. She watched him closely. His face was a frozen mask. At one point he raised it briefly to meet her eyes. Then he was flipping pages again, stopping to read at a place somewhat more than halfway into the book.

Twenty minutes passed before Wells looked up again. He spoke quietly, his voice breathless, as if he had been running. "I'm working on this book. As of last week, I've completed only a hundred manuscript pages!" He glanced down, reading aloud from the title page. *"The New Machiavelli . . . by H. G. Wells . . . John Lane Co., London . . . Copyright 1911 . . .* next year . . . and it's all here, word for word, published. Even the few paragraphs I wrote yesterday!"

"And all the paragraphs you've yet to write."

"It's impossible! And the pages are yellowed. . . ." He stood, facing her. "It's worn, used, old—and I haven't even finished writing it yet!"

"The book is yours," she said. "A gift. All you need do is copy out, page for page, what you haven't yet written and your manuscript will be complete."

"You must have an explanation, a rational, scientific explanation." He seemed suddenly pale.

She sighed. "Rational, perhaps, but hardly scientific . . ."

Agitated, he paced the length of the room, turned to her again. "I have never believed in that psychic nonsense that's so popular these days, and I'm damned if I believe it now!" He glared at her as if angered by a trick she had played on him.

"Please," she said. "You want to know who I am, where I come from. Your curiosity is the reason for seeking me out and the reason for your being here today. I've decided to tell you. But how? If I had attempted it a few minutes ago, you'd be gone by now, thinking me mad. But the book will validate what I have to say—it's proof in advance. The book is real, it is a solid object that exists here and now . . . hold it, feel it, read it. It's not sleight of hand or some other sort of deception, and if you can accept that fact, you'll accept what I'm going to tell you."

He seemed about to say something, changed his mind to perch himself on the arm of the wing chair facing her. "Yes, it's real," he said, riffling slowly through the book. "Perhaps we should talk now."

She placed the tea-things on the rough-hewn side table, then turned to him, smiling. Quietly, in a lilting voice, as if she were reading aloud a children's story, she said, "I think the first thing I should tell you is that I'm eighty-seven years old. . . ."

Governor General Charles De Gaulle was assassinated this morning (9:30 local time) in downtown Hanoi. Police say his car, a special, heavily armored Citroën, was struck by an anti-tank missile launched from a third-floor window of a building less than fifty yards away. Police and army units cordoned off the area immediately, but were unable to locate the killer or killers. Minutes after the act, an unidentified female phoned *Le Clarion,* a local French-language newspaper, to claim credit for the killing in the name of an underground organization calling itself Viet-Min.

—United Press
January 3, 1970
Hanoi, French
Indochina

30

1984

It was late, almost two in the morning. They were awake, side by side. Lesley Morning spoke to the dark ceiling, quietly, as if to herself. "I'm going to take no more than I can carry in a small shoulder bag: toothbrush, change of undies, a hairbrush . . ."

"For what?" said Paul.

"Tomorrow, of course. To Rastenburg."

He took her hand. "Lesley . . ."

"I think we should travel as light as possible."

"Lesley, darling . . ." He paused as if searching for words. "It's best if you don't go with me."

"Best?" Incredulous, she was up on one elbow, facing him.

"I'm afraid it's impossible."

"I don't believe you're saying that."

"I'm sorry."

She felt momentarily dazed, as if under sudden, unprovoked attack. "You mean, you're going alone?"

"Yes. It would be too dangerous."

"I don't understand. You said . . . we agreed to share everything!"

He propped himself up, facing her. "There's no need for a second person. I have a simple task. All I have to do is press the trigger, place the attaché case on the conference table and leave, as if I were going to the loo or to make a telephone call."

In a state of shock, she got out of bed and stood looking down at him in the dim light. "There could be complications; even simple plans go wrong. It never occurred to me that you would consider doing this without me."

He reached for her, brushing her naked hip with his hand as she stepped back. She said, "Paul, this is important."

"It's hard for me to think of anything more important than the way you look right now."

"No!" She felt a rising anger, took her robe from the foot of the bed and threw it on. She felt she wanted to shout at him, to grasp his shoulders and shake him until his teeth rattled. Instead, in a calm and reasonable voice, she said, "We've got to have this out."

"Okay." He lay back, hands cradling his head. "Let's have it out."

"You can't do this thing alone. I'm going with you."

"Why? You certainly can't come into the conference room with me or even allow yourself to be seen anywhere in the area. Your presence could be a disaster."

"You may need someone if something goes wrong—if you're hurt. You might even need me to drive the car . . . anything . . ."

"It's out of the question."

"Why?"

"I told you why!"

"Because I'm a woman . . ."

"Lesley . . ."

She loomed over him. "Elleander Morning was a woman . . . my grandmother . . ."

"That was different. It was 1913; this is 1984."

"What does it matter? She did it alone—the same thing you'll be doing, and for the same reason. And if she hadn't been alone, if there'd been someone to help her, she might have gotten away alive!"

"Conjecture." He fell back on the bed. "I love you, darling, but it is my country, my problem. I've no intention of exposing others to the risk . . . particularly you."

Silently, Lesley sat on the edge of the bed. She had no further arguments. She had prepared none. During the past few weeks she had not for a moment considered the possibility that Paul might go without her. Now she felt that if he took his bomb and journeyed to Rastenburg alone, she would never see him again. She suddenly felt very sure of it. In silence, she dropped the robe, got back into bed, leaving a space between them. Elleander Morning had paid with her life. Paul would pay with his . . . just like Von Stauffenberg. She shuddered. It was a cycle that she was certain only her presence could break.

She said, "Surely you must have known how I feel. Why did you wait until now, practically the last minute, to tell me this?"

"I had no idea you'd be so damned adamant about it." Paul spoke quietly. "But if you'd think about it for a minute . . . I mean, what would you be doing while I was in the meeting?"

"I'm not sure—hide in the car, the woods . . . just to be there if something goes wrong . . . anything."

He was silent for long moments. Then he rolled toward her, took her in his arms. "We'll talk about it in the morning."

"Now," she said, her voice a whisper.

"All right, then."

"All right, what?"

"You have a point." He paused, thoughtful for a long moment. "You'll come with me. But we'll have to plan this very carefully."

She was momentarily surprised, then relieved by his sudden acquiescence. She sighed, kissed him lightly on the lips. A few minutes later he was asleep in her arms.

Lesley awakened in the dark to find herself alone. She stared at the shadowy ceiling. Minutes passed, leaving her fully awake. She had assumed Paul to be in the bathroom. Now she felt a rising anxiety. She threw on her robe. The bathroom was dark, empty. She raced downstairs. He was not in the kitchen or the study. Grimly, she parted the parlor draperies. His car, a two-year-old Mercedes L310, was missing from its usual parking space in front of the house.

Paul was gone. He'd tricked her. Lesley stood in the center of the room, breathing deeply, giving herself up to an angry resolve.

Upstairs she dressed sensibly in brown wool slacks, a heavy sweater and practical shoes. In a small shoulder bag she packed a toothbrush, change of underwear, a hairbrush, a small makeup kit, sixty-two pounds in cash, a credit card and her passport.

She left a note for Mrs. Green on the hall table. Outside, the sky was lightening into a dull gray. Highcastle Road seemed colorless, done in flat, neutral tones like an underexposed photograph.

Lesley walked briskly now, pleased that she felt no fear of what might come, but only a new and deeper kinship with her grandmother.

31

1912

Trasker was surprised to find that she bore little resemblance to his memory of her. This time she wore a crisp white shirtwaist done up at the neck with an oversized travesty of a man's black bow tie. Her posture behind the oddly shaped writing desk was erect, almost stately, demonstrating not a hint of the voluptuous excess he remembered. She said, "It's so nice to see you again, Mr. Trasker."

He returned the greeting, seated himself in a deep wing chair. He noted that even her voice seemed different. The pitch was lower, the accent cultivated, the tone restrained, as if they were meeting again after a previous encounter at some innocently formal dinner party.

"I'm surprised you remembered my name," she said. "It's been two years, and our acquaintance was so brief. . . ."

"You insisted that I never forget it." He glanced around the room. It seemed a kind of sanctum—parlor, office, library, boudoir—cluttered with overstuffed furniture and potted plants. One long wall was covered with paintings, another lined with bookcases. He was close enough to make out some of the book titles and wondered at a prostitute who would read *Gibbon's Autobiography*. He said, "You've changed. I'm sure I wouldn't have recognized you as the woman with whom I shared a cab."

"You mean, the painted whore?"

He found her use of the word incongruous with her present manner and style. "If you care to put it that way," he said, feeling a vague disquiet.

"I do." She spoke softly. "I'm *still* a whore, Mr. Trasker, albeit a madam and somewhat more subtly painted than you remember, but a whore, nonetheless." She paused, turned to him, her lips now forming an innocently gracious smile. "I assume that's why you are here."

"Yes," he said. But he felt strangely awkward.

She seemed to sense his confusion. She said, "A glass of sherry, Mr. Trasker?"

"Yes, please." He had discovered her inadvertently at Aintree the previous Saturday, minutes before the next-to-the-last race. He had, at first, not recognized her, but rather found himself suddenly attracted to a stranger, an elegantly beautiful woman occupying a private box, chatting amiably with two very young but attractive ladies who seemed to be twins. Presiding over this lovely trio had been an elderly, distinguished-looking gentleman whom Trasker took to be their father.

He had stood, with his friend Jack Hall, less than ten yards from her, staring openly. There was a moment when she turned her head, surveying the crowded racecourse with wide, exquisite eyes. They brushed past his, hesitated, returned as he reached for his hat, then were gone in the instant before he could tip it.

Jack Hall nudged him, saying, "We've got a minute to get our money down."

"She is the most beautiful woman I've ever laid eyes on. . . ."

"Yes," said Jack Hall. "She is that. She's also the madam of a whorehouse on Highcastle Road. Her name's Elleander Morning."

Now, four days later in her private quarters, his glance fell on one of several unusual paintings that crowded the far wall. It appeared to represent a bizarre construction of weirdly formed beakers, tubes and retorts, all interconnected and somehow vaguely organic. He stared at it, feeling her presence behind him.

She said, "Do you like it?"

"I don't know. What is it?"

"It's by a young painter named Marcel Duchamp. I bought it in Paris last month. He calls it *The Bride.*"

"It looks like some sort of chemical process—distillation . . ."

"Precisely."

Smiling, he turned to face her. She stood just inches away. He inhaled her scent: L'Heure Bleu, his favorite. She had been wearing it that night in the cab. She peered down at him out of large hazel eyes. She was, observed Bertram Trasker, an extremely beautiful woman just past the delicate flowering of youth, entering a more hardy and robust period of full bloom. He felt a desire to reach up and touch her. Instead, he accepted the glass of sherry she offered him, then leaned back in the chair.

She turned to step away and he saw with surprise that she was wearing trousers. They were of black silk and, unlike gentleman's trousers, were fitted tightly so that the full swell of her buttocks was delineated.

She lowered herself into a red chaise a few feet from him. Astonished, he found himself staring fixedly at her legs, one folded beneath her, the other extending gracefully to the floor.

"Is something the matter, Mr. Trasker?"

"George Sand . . ."

"You mean the French writer?"

"Yes," he said. "I was wondering at your reason for emulating her."

"Ah . . . you mean by dressing as a man?"

He nodded. She said, "If that was my intention, I hope I've failed." She frowned in mock seriousness. "Do you really believe that trousers make the man, Mr. Trasker?"

He allowed his gaze to be led downward along the elegant S curve of her body. She was obviously naked under her clothing; the thin silk sheathing shaped and molded, not by the fashionable armor of a corset, but by unfettered female flesh. "You are an extremely beautiful woman," he said, momentarily dazed by his sudden desire for her.

"Thank you." She eased herself farther into the chaise. "Someday most women will wear trousers; it will be the fashion."

"An interesting prediction." He sipped his sherry, recalling that two years ago he had thought her mad. "You also predicted the success of *March Hare* even before I started writing it."

"Ah, that. You described it so well in your diary."

"The diary . . . you read it?"

"I quite enjoyed it, even the last chapter."

"You purchased a copy?" he said, the surprise evident in his voice. The lone bookseller who stocked it, a small shop in Whitehall, had sold only four copies.

"It was a gift from a friend," she said lightly.

He wondered if it was a mutual friend, one of the sixteen he had presented with books. "Who?" he said.

"Surely, Mr. Trasker, you didn't come here to ask questions."

He smiled, disregarding her evasion. "And the birthmark under my beard? Who told you of that? And there were a few other things you mentioned that night."

She glanced away. "Questions, questions . . . perhaps we will discuss it one day. . . ." She became silent, seemingly lost in a kind of pensive preoccupation.

He set his glass down, then moved to the chaise, seating himself on the edge. He laid a hand on her shoulder, feeling her warmth through the soft silk. Questions, he decided, could wait for another time.

She looked up at him. "I saw *March Hare.* "

"What did you think of it?"

"I agreed with the critics."

"Then you liked it. . . ." He realized that her opinion of his play was very important to him and for an instant he wondered why.

"It was a delight." She took his hand firmly in both of hers. *"Love . . . love . . . love! We've been hoodwinked by idiotic troubadours! Without the curse of love there'd be nothing but lust—clean, honest, forthright lust!"* She paused, cupped her face in her hands, her eyes peering at him through spread fingers. *"Ohh . . . to be able to practice what I preach!"*

Astonished, Bertram Trasker heard himself say, "Second Act curtain!"

"Barbara's speech . . . played by what's-her-name . . .?"

"Pamela Sutton."

"Very inadequately."

"You must have seen the play many times."

"One performance—opening night—though I intend to go back."

"Once? But you've got it word for word!"

"Let's just say I'm a quick study." A broad smile lit up her face in obvious delight now at his confusion.

"You are a remarkable woman . . . unpredictable."

"Yes," she said. She reached up to him, placed a caressing hand on the back of his neck. He acceded to the gentle pressure till her mouth was less than an inch from his. "Oh, Bertie . . . it was the best thing in the West End this season . . . I'm so proud of you."

Her kiss echoed the strange, unexpected intimacy of her words. It was gentle, affectionate; certainly not, he thought, the fervid kiss of a prostitute attempting to enflame the passion of a client. Her hands cradled his face, a soft fluttering tongue sought his. In moments he found himself being overwhelmed with feelings of tender regard as if she were a cherished sweetheart. Puzzled, he grasped her shoulders gently, pulling away. Her eyes questioned as he studied her face. He knew it well—too well. He recognized on her forehead the tiny scar punctuating an otherwise pristine complexion, the slight, almost oriental downturn of the corners of her eyes. He felt a sudden chill of anxiety. It was a face far more familiar than their brief acquaintance could possibly account for. In a quiet voice he said, "Who are you?"

"Elleander Morning." She buried her face in his neck.

He was aware of her parted lips against his skin as he unfastened her black bow tie, then one by one the four small buttons. Her breasts were free. He opened the blouse, exposing them completely. Though he had fondled them, he had not actually seen her breasts in the cab two years ago. Now he watched his fingers run tentatively across their softly yielding surface. She trembled. This time their kiss was an impassioned communication.

Then, while she watched through half-closed eyes, he knelt by the side of the chaise to remove her black slippers. He felt a compulsion to view her naked body, to renew an acquaintance he'd never had. The strange contradiction was not lost on him. He shunted it aside to ponder at some future time.

He undressed her, removing her trousers, her gossamer French "scanties." Elleander Morning lay naked, an offering to the tender exploration of his eyes and fingertips. He found himself awed by an exquisite body that exhibited none of the idealized rotundity of the time. It was, he observed, a body defined by long, graceful curves rather than abrupt dimpled ones: muscle-toned, taut, a body fashioned for elegant speed, like that of a lynx or a ballet dancer.

They watched each other through unblinking eyes as he removed his clothing, allowing each item in its turn to fall to the floor. On the chaise he held her, caressing the firm resiliency of her buttocks. He pulled her tightly against him as she murmured incomprehensible words into his open mouth and encircled him with her arms.

Once again it occurred to Trasker that hers were not the hasty, dissolute responses of a whore. Lovemaking . . . The thought was a fleeting one. It dissolved quickly in the warmth of an affection that in seconds expanded into a rapture so intense, he thought he might burst.

"Bertie . . . Bertie . . ." Her voice was a hoarse whisper. Then suddenly, she was silent, unmoving. Her flesh turned cold against his, her body rigid.

He raised himself to look at her. Her eyes were shut tightly, there were tears on her cheek. In a small voice she said, "Bertie, I can't . . ."

He stared down at her, his face a mask of perplexity. She turned her head away. "I'm sorry . . . please . . ." She squirmed out from under him into a sitting position. She had trouble breathing as she felt the chaise respond to his leaving it.

"Why?" he muttered.

She wanted to hold him, kiss his face over and over again, press him close to her, feel him. Instead, hating the sound of her own voice, she said, "Maybe you might like one of our ladies. I can ask Mr. Lethaby to introduce you to Yvonne . . . maybe Jennifer . . ." Her voice trailed off into remorseful silence as she turned to find his manhood collapsing into flaccid vulnerability.

In minutes, he was dressed and gone.

Blindly, she climbed the private back staircase to her bedroom. She closed the door behind her, fell into the big bed to stare up, wide-eyed, at the Union Jack canopy.

Bertie was falling in love with her. She felt certain of it. More certain, she speculated, than even he was. His touch, his voice, his entire attitude toward her were those of a man lost in much more than merely lustful pursuits. She shuddered. It would be the death of him.

Elleander Morning spent the next three days in her bedroom, fighting against herself for resolution. At dawn on the fourth day, she realized the battle had been lost from the beginning.

Over lunch, Herbert Wells, noting the weariness and depression evident in his friend's face, invited Trasker to spend the weekend at his country house in Pulham. "Perhaps a spot of fresh air might do you some good," he had said, knowing full well that the young playwright's problem was anything but pulmonary.

Now, the following evening, in the privacy of his billiard room, Wells listened as his friend told all.

"Poor fellow . . ."

Trasker spoke in flat, spiritless tones. "She is all I think about."

"Women," said Wells. The word was meant to be a serious comment. Trasker reacted with an unconvincing, derisive laugh. He paced across the room, leaned against the oversized baize-

covered table. The green light from two overhead glass lamp-
shades emphasized dark, puffy crescents under his eyes. Wells
toasted him silently with his empty brandy snifter.

"She's a whore, dammit all!"

"A madam," said Wells.

"Still a whore. She herself was very clear about it. And what
difference does it make?"

"Below your station?"

"All whores . . . and madams too, are below my station.
They're below everybody's bloody station! And please, H.G.,
none of your lectures about class and socialism. It's not her class
I object to, it's her damnable profession."

They were silent as Wells refilled the glasses. Finally, he said,
"I would wager, Bertie, that you're every bit as angry with yourself as you are at her."

"Yes."

Wells wondered how Trasker would react to the knowledge
that his pain was even less than that of the woman who held him
captive. The older man felt a compulsion to tell his friend all—
to clear the air. But he was bound by his word. And even if he
were not, how could he possibly convince him? How would he
begin? He had no miraculous books, no magic toys to use as
"advance proof." He heard himself say, "But you've only been
with the woman twice in two years . . ."

"Altogether, less than three hours," said Trasker. "It's mad-
dening."

"Steady, old friend."

Trasker drained his glass. "Elleander Morning is not an ordinary woman."

"Few women are ordinary."

"You knew the mother . . ."

"A most peculiar coincidence." Wells was quiet for a moment, then, "Pamela, too, was no ordinary woman. She wanted
her daughter to be the first female cabinet minister. She had
many advanced ideas. Good Lord! I wonder what she'd think of
her little girl now."

"Were you in love with her, Herbert?"

"It was an illicit affair."

"Were you in love with her?"

"Yes, I suppose I was."

"Elleander . . . does she resemble her mother?"

"Yes."

Trasker fell silent, as if digesting Wells' words. Then, obviously puzzled, he said, "But how could you know that? You saw her only once, as a child. . . ."

"Your description of her was quite graphic." The lie came smoothly to Wells' lips. He felt a twinge of guilt, muttered, "Mother and daughter . . ."

"Yes, it's all very strange," said Trasker blankly. "The woman knows everything about me; I know nothing about her." He hesitated for a moment, his brow wrinkling. "But I do know her . . . so much about her is familiar. I don't understand how that can be, but it's true. I know things only an intimate friend would know . . . a lover."

Wells searched unsuccessfully for a response. He had been with Elleander only three days before. They had sat in her office drinking champagne while discussing the sexual mores of the mid-twentieth century. Then later, she had left him alone for another two hours with the Time-Life *History of the Second World War.* The second, he thought—according to Elleander, the first was about to happen. Suddenly everything else was of no importance to him. He felt disconnected from Bertie's problems, even his own seemed meaningless. An entire generation of Englishmen were about to die, and despite this knowledge, there was nothing effective he could do about it. Though he would try, he knew that his warning, like most warnings, would go unheeded. The approaching horror was a juggernaut that no one had either the will nor the power to stop. Perhaps it was better to get on with it—win it.

Bertie was staring at him over the top of his empty brandy glass. With a rueful laugh, the young playwright said, "It's not every day a chap finds himself ejected from a whore's bed." They both lapsed into an introspective silence. Trasker looked down at his hands, examining them carefully. "In the cab, then, I thought she was crazy. Actually, old friend, I'm the one who is mad . . . going mad . . ."

"Nonsense!" Wells' voice was louder now, authoritative. "It

happens, Bertie, to the best of us—this awful kind of deluded infatuation."

"No, you don't understand."

"You've got to pull yourself together. There are far more important things."

"There aren't! I'm truly in love with her. H.G., believe me, I don't have any idea how or why it happened. The woman has become an obsession! She is alive inside my skin. . . ."

For the fourth day in a row, the mid-afternoon temperature was peaking at more than 80 degrees, unusual for London, even in mid-August. The oppressive phenomenon weighed heavily on Bertram Trasker. For what seemed to be the thousandth time, he glanced down forlornly at the incomplete manuscript page:

ACT THREE
SCENE ONE

Theresa's Room—Later That Night
Theresa enters, laughing

They were the same words, no more, no less, that had been there on the otherwise blank white foolscap the day before, and the day before that. Now, once again, without moving his head, Trasker shifted his view over the top of the black Simplex typewriter onto the parched garden two floors below. He felt drained. His usually sharp inner vision was blurred, leaving him incapable of constructive thought.

Perspiration soaked his collar. He removed it, then gazing down pensively at a wilted rose bush, permitted his fingers to walk across the typewriter keys: *ELLEANDER MORNING.*

He must see her, deal with her, touch her. But once again he felt the constricting fear of a final rejection. Desperately, he ripped the sheet out of the typewriter, inserted a fresh one, and he rewrote: ACT THREE.

The afternoon post included a bill from his hatter and a small, buff-colored envelope addressed in bold, simply formed script and scented with her perfume.

Dearest Bertie:
 I will call on you, Friday evening at five. Perhaps
dinner?

           Elleander

 He read the note a few times. Her desire to see him came as
a surprise. Her boldness at implementing the meeting did not.
She had, he reasoned, simply shown more courage than he.
 In the garden below, he noted an imperceptible stirring of
the leaves. The air was finally moving.

3²

1912

Elleander Morning and Bertram Trasker were lovers. Both in their own way had surrendered completely to what they knew to be an irresistible compulsion. It was a relationship neither stormy nor tempestuous, though each of them retained an unspoken reservation. This was buried deeply beneath the joy they found in each other.

A short time after the first night they spent together in Trasker's Belgravia flat, Elleander found that moving about London would be difficult for them. For the first time she preferred going unrecognized in restaurants and the theater. Bertie maintained, somewhat too adamantly, she thought, that such encounters would not embarrass him, so she insisted, and the following week they boarded the boat-train for what was to be the first of many short holidays in Paris. Within a few hours of their arrival they found an apartment in Saint-Germain. They were both delighted with it.

Its centerpiece was a gigantic bathtub. A monstrous copper monument to Second Empire French plumbing, it squatted on oversized griffin feet atop a carved marble dais. At its head loomed a bright-red, coal-fired boiler that was capable, in less than an hour, of filling the tub to its brim with warm water. They made frequent use of it, reclining together in aqueous embrace for long periods of time, sipping champagne while gazing out at the city through a sloping wall of glass. "As if," said Bertie, "all Paris is our bathroom."   ·

Now, five months later on their ninth visit, Bertie turned to her on the lumpy mattress to caress the smooth skin of her thigh. In a soft voice, he said, "I love you. . . ." She touched his face, then, with her eyes closed, ran her fingers along his softly bearded jawline. He raised himself on an elbow to stare down at her. "I realize it's an unconventional time and place for a formal proposal." He grinned. "But this is a most unconventional love affair."

She had been expecting it for weeks, at first with sadness because she knew she would decline, but lately, as they spent increasingly more time together, with a growing conviction that it might be possible. They could leave Britain, start again in some new place where the horrid events of the twentieth century would not touch them, a place where their son would not be called upon to die for his country.

He said, "I want you to be my wife."

Elleander opened her eyes to find his. The actual sound of his words seemed to nullify her fantasy. She could find no words of her own. Once again she tried to think it through. He knew nothing of her. How, she wondered for the hundredth time, would he react if she told him of Harry? And the rest of it. The sentence formed in her mind as she had spoken it to Herbert:

I think the first thing I should tell you is that I am eighty-seven years old.

"Marry me," he said.

"I don't know . . ." She stared out the skylight at a distant Eiffel Tower, that sparkled jewel-like in its recently installed electrical lighting.

"You say you love me. What other considerations could there possibly be?"

There were, she thought, more considerations than she could deal with. "I do love you, Bertie, more than you can dream," she said. "But I'm the madam of a whorehouse. I'm notorious. I've been a prostitute!"

"Then we'll leave England—get out of London—maybe to America. They're doing well with *March Hare* in New York. I can write for their theater as well as I write for London's. No one will know, and if you'd like, you can start new, as an actress. You've said you've always wanted that. You could be Ellen Trasker . . . anything you like, my darling."

"New York." She spoke softly, thinking, Harry would be an American.

"We could have children," he said. "Three, four . . ."

But, she thought, American troops had been—would also be —on the bloody beaches of Normandy. Omaha, Utah . . . She said, "I have to think."

"I don't understand." He fell back onto the bed.

"But I love you." She kissed him tenderly, her hair forming a blond tent around his head. She murmured into his mouth, "Bertie . . . just give me a bit more time."

"You're an enigma," he said, his hands on her shoulders, supporting her as she hovered over him. "Worse than that, you're a desperate disease I've contracted for which there is no cure." He laughed. "Diphtheria . . ."

They made love for hours. Then, while the Paris rooftops turned a soft, pale, wintry blue in the light of pre-dawn, Elleander watched him sleep. There had been no other men since their brief interlude in the cab almost three years ago. There never would be. She felt a flurry of confusion. She had done everything to forestall a love affair with Bertram Trasker. Her life during the past four years had been little more than a strategy designed to avoid any such possibility. It had failed. Would all her plans fail?

Until recently, she had assumed her will more than a match against "inexorable" fate. In weary bewilderment, she turned onto her side, away from her sleeping lover. She must think about it, arrive at some sort of decision. But not now.

The light had become warmer, a rising sun gilded the Paris rooftops. Bertie, she thought, had in the beginning probed almost constantly. She had found it necessary to fend off a hundred different questions. She had made light of them, adroitly changed the subject. Finally, he had stopped asking. But she knew it to be temporary. Sooner or later she would have to speak, to tell him everything . . . or . . . she shuddered and closed her eyes; she would have to disappear from his life once and for all.

They spent the next two days in Paris as they usually did, strolling the twisting streets of the West Bank, sitting in sidewalk cafés, walking what seemed to be endless miles through the Louvre galleries. On one evening they attended the opera, on the next, a performance at the Olympia during which Mata Hari danced in the nude.

On Friday morning they visited a young painter from whom Elleander made a purchase. Trasker, who had accompanied her to a half-dozen studios on previous visits to Paris, surprised her by purchasing a small canvas for himself. Later on the street, she said, "I had no idea you appreciated modern art."

"Neither did I." He pulled her close as she took his arm. "The poor fellow looked as if he were starving to death." They crossed the narrow street to a familiar café. When they were seated, he said, "Modern art? I would think the sort of things you collect would best be described as avant-garde."

"You're right, actually. Although to be more precise, you would call today's purchases Cubist." She smiled at him. "Was compassion your only reason for buying?"

He grinned. "No, not completely. Truth is, I believe I've inherited some of your taste."

"I'm pleased."

"And what of compassion on your part?" he said. "I've seen you pay some of them triple their asking price."

"Half the artists in Paris are starving."

"You're a saint." He reached out to take her hand.

"Not quite a saint, Bertie." With her free hand she poured

the coffee for both of them. "No matter what I paid, it would be exploitive." She paused, caught his eye. "The work of art you bought today will be worth ten thousand times what you just paid for it." As she said it, she realized that once again she had made a mistake. Trasker's eyes went blank. He looked away.

"Quite an astute investment. How long will it take?"

"Fifty years." She wished she could change the subject.

"Two hundred and fifty thousand pounds?"

"Perhaps even more."

Silently, he buttered his brioche.

She stared at him, echoing his silence. She felt foolish. Finally, with a weak smile on her face, she said, "I'm sorry, Bertie, I guess I allow my imagination to run away with itself every now and then. But surely you'll permit a lady the prerogative of just a little madness?"

"Just a little," he said, brightening. Then, responding to the mock-serious expression on her face, he laughed, saying, "Sometimes you almost frighten me."

"You're laughing at me, but remember, they laughed at Galileo."

"No they didn't, they just treated him abominably."

She reached across the table, laid a graceful hand on his shoulder. "But you treat me marvelously and I love you desperately."

"Marry me."

"Bertie . . ."

"I'm sure we can have it done right here in Paris . . . today."

"Bertie, why ruin a lovely relationship by getting married?"

He pulled away from her, leaned all the way back in his wicker chair. "I think that comes damned close to being the most extraordinary statement I've ever heard."

"It's not original. . . ."

He laughed heartily, saying, "I shouldn't be laughing."

"Certainly you should, it's a joke." She found herself laughing with him. "An old joke . . . no, not *old* . . . but it's never been quite this funny."

He caught his breath, sipped some coffee. "Do you know any others?"

"Yes. Why does a chicken cross the road?"

"I don't know."
She told him.

Later, strolling in the Tuleries, Trasker said, "This evening it will be a bit of Molière, they're doing him at the Comédie Française. My French is improving, I'm sure I'll understand at least a third of it."

She clutched his arm. "Bertie . . . tonight is the boat-train."

"Then let's not return to London. Let's stay another few days, a week this time."

"I must," she said quietly.

"But why? We're happy here. Why do you always insist on going back after just three or four days? Think what it would be like to stay in Paris for a week, a month."

"My business . . ."

"Damn your business!" She watched, horrified as the anger developed in his face. Transformed, he stepped back, ran his eyes derisively down the length of her body. "Bloody whore's business."

"Bertie, please."

"I'm the one who's crazy!"

"No." Elleander spoke the single word in a small voice, her eyes cast downward. She felt fragmented, as if his sudden, devastating explosion had occurred inside her own body.

His voice grew tighter, over-controlled. "I must have been mad as a hatter to think that I'd fallen in love with a whore!"

She knew she must finally tell him the truth or lose him. Their little boy living in Cornwall with his nanny—she visited him for two days every week. It was the one inviolate rule of her life. With the words on her lips, she looked up. Both Bertie and the opportunity were gone. He was twenty feet down the path, striding vigorously away from her.

Elleander stood, watching him, hoping he would glance back, change his mind, until finally he disappeared behind the trees. With a calm that surprised her, she walked purposefully to a nearby bench. She sat, her back straight, her hands folded decorously in her lap. She had never felt his anger before, neither then nor now. How long, she wondered, had the pressure been building?

The aftershock took hold and she felt tears on her cheeks. She had been weak, indecisive. She had made it all terrible for him. . . . *Mad as hatter to think I'd fallen in love with a whore!* Her strategy had worked after all. She would never see him again. It might have been better, she thought, if she had remained dead.

Nothing could have been more obvious to the
people of the early twentieth century than the rapidity
with which war was becoming impossible. And as certainly they did not see it. They did not see it until the
atomic bombs burst in their fumbling hands.

—H. G. Wells
The World Set Free
1914

33

1984

Paul Bauer had caught the first London-Berlin magnitrain of
the day. From Berlin he flew to Königsberg, where he spent the
night in a small hotel. In the early morning he drove south in a
rented Adler sedan through the heart of East Prussia. Nine kilometers north of Rastenburg he turned off the main highway onto
a secondary road. Consulting a small, hand-drawn map, he
counted the turn-offs. At the fourth, he turned left into a dense
pine forest. He was on a winding, steeply inclined dirt road. It
narrowed into little more than a track delineated by a pair of deep
ruts.

Finally, after one more bone-rattling kilometer, Paul Bauer
passed through the open gate of a high-wire fence onto a
concrete driveway. A small hand-painted sign read WOLF-
SCHANZE.

The driveway opened into a clearing. There were eight
parked cars. The house was a squat, brooding, two-story structure of gray wood. On its south side, a newly added wing clashed

in vivid white with its ramshackle, nineteenth-century parent.

Paul cut the ignition, then sat for almost a full minute, breathing deeply, allowing his tense muscles to relax. From the overnight case resting on the seat next to him, he withdrew a small .25 caliber automatic pistol. He had owned it for years, but had never fired it. He stared at the pistol for a few moments, reminding himself that to use it he must first cock it by pulling back the slide. He tried, but was unsuccessful. After a few moments, he realized that the safety had a small protuberance that locked the slide in place. Gingerly, he flicked it down. With great care, he succeeded. Then, wondering vaguely if it was still operative after seven years in the bottom of dresser drawers, he put it in his topcoat pocket.

The attaché case was in the boot, resting atop the spare tire. Pleased with his lack of apprehension, he set it upright, then, bracing it with his left hand, used his right to unscrew the small, knurled cap of the arming pin. It was loose in three turns. He pulled it out and dropped it in his pocket.

He felt disconnected from his actions, as if they had been orchestrated and he was merely playing them back—tonelessly. He breathed deeply, attempting to bring his thoughts into play. The handle, he realized, was peculiar-looking: oversized, the trigger an obvious protrusion beneath it. Priming the bomb in the conference room might draw attention to it. And there might be a noise; the sound of the spring being released, the acid capsule breaking. Impulsively, he curled his index finger under the handle. He squeezed the trigger. Other than a barely perceptible *click*, there was no sound. He was committed.

Paul slammed down the trunk lid, turned on his heel and walked rapidly toward the new wing. It housed the conference room. They would all be there by now, as he had timed his arrival a little late. Despite its weight, he carried the attaché case loosely in one hand. The acid, he realized, was even now eating its way through the thin steel wire. In less than twenty minutes the bomb would fulfill its function. There was no way he could turn it off.

The outside door led to a corridor, at the end of which was a large window. At that end, on the corridor wall to the right, was the door to the main part of the house. Directly across from it, on the left wall, was the door leading to the conference room. Reaching out to knock, Paul was aware that his hand was shaking. He was, for the first time since it all began, face to face with his fear.

The conference room was relatively small, about twenty-five feet square, dominated by a heavy oblong table. As Paul hung up his coat, Rudolph von Seydlitz, wearing black and sporting a swastika armband, nodded sourly in his direction, then abruptly returned his attention to Walter Kohler, who, as future Minister of Finance, was reading aloud from a voluminous report. Kohler was a Reichstag deputy; a small, nervous man, totally bald, affecting a black Vandyke and a monocle. His party, the DVP, occupied only 42 seats in the 586-seat Reichstag, but nevertheless was highly vocal, influential and, recalled Paul Bauer, quite adroit at selling itself to the highest bidder—right, left or center.

Paul seated himself next to his uncle. It was the one remaining empty chair. They were all present, the soon-to-be leaders of the New Order.

Von Seydlitz leaned toward him. "Where have you been?" He spoke in a barely audible whisper.

Paul shrugged, set the attaché case on the table.

"I wanted to speak to you," said his uncle, in a whisper hoarse with agitation. He was about to go on, then seemingly changed his mind, and began writing furiously on a yellow pad.

Kohler was saying, ". . . and there are others. Alfred Krupp has pledged ten million marks toward the campaign and . . ."

"What does he want in return?" This from Eric Staulpnagel, Minister of Justice in the shadow cabinet.

Von Seydlitz looked up from his writing, placed both hands flat on the table, as if preparing to leap erect. "He wants nothing in return!" His voice was strident, as if he had been personally challenged. "The Krupps have always valued a powerful Germany . . . a Fatherland as forceful as the tanks, the cannon, the missiles that roll out of their factories—a vigorous Germany proud of its blood heritage. And that's precisely what will exist after we take power. Nothing less! To even hint at an ulterior motive is an insult, not only to the Krupps and others who have extended patriotic aid, but to the German nation . . . the race.

Alfred Krupp von Bohlen und Halbach is a man of steel. We understand one another completely."

There was silence. Walter Kohler continued his report.

Von Seydlitz slid the yellow pad in front of Paul. On it was written: "You are to side with me in all disputes, especially those with Schmidt."

Paul nodded. State Secretary Schmidt was seated directly across from him. Schmidt returned his glance, a bland expression on his large round face. Then the State Secretary turned away to whisper into the ear of General von Wirsinger. The officer listened, shook his head negatively. Schmidt looked pained. As Paul watched, he seemed to develop an interest in the wood grain of the tabletop, which he traced distractedly with a pudgy index finger.

Von Wirsinger, currently Army Chief of Staff, had gained notoriety in the early sixties as the head of a military mission to train and equip the Rumanian Army. Using his tactics, the Rumanians managed to invade and occupy Soviet Moldavia, against vastly superior Russian forces, in less than ten days.

To the general's right sat his aide, a young colonel wearing army-issue eyeglasses. Paul knew nothing of him.

To the left of Von Seydlitz was Gustav Gratz, an ex-Internal Affairs Minister who, eleven years earlier, had lost his cabinet status as the result of a homosexual scandal. Since that time he had served as political analyst for the National People's party.

To the left of Herr Gratz was Dr. Josef Mengele, a short, elderly, swarthy-skinned man wearing an incongruous full blond toupee. He had, some years earlier, published a book titled *The Pathology of Race*, in which he advocated the establishment of state breeding farms, where thousands of pre-selected teenaged boys and girls of *perfect stock* could be mated at random, again and again, in order to reinforce the ideal Aryan characteristics of the German people. The book advocated a Germany that within a century could be populated entirely by a pure strain of blond, blue-eyed *Supervolk*. The good doctor was slated to function in the new cabinet as Minister Without Portfolio. Paul, recalling the Time-Life *History of the Second World War*, conjectured on the possibility of a specific utilization of Dr. Mengele's unique point of view. Perhaps, finally, he would get his farms . . . and worse.

Seated between Kohler and Wirsinger was Hermann Werner, deputy director of the SIS, the intelligence arm of the Ministry of Foreign Affairs. Paul had been informed that Werner was to replace his boss on the very day that the New Order came into power.

These, Paul thought, were the men who would, in all likelihood, be responsible for a war even more catastrophic than that which was visualized in the Time-Life books. Millions would die . . . perhaps hundreds of millions. He had, he admitted to himself, triggered the bomb before entering the house out of fear that, once face to face with his victims, he might lose courage. He realized now that such would not have been the case.

Paul Bauer looked down at his watch: 9:24. He felt himself go cold. He had squeezed the trigger minutes ago. Minutes ago? How many minutes? He had no way of knowing! He had failed to consult his watch! He steeled himself against a hard knot of panic growing in his stomach.

There were already eight cars parked in the clearing in front of the house when the Adler sedan pulled into a space between two of them. Lesley had been in the clearing for over an hour, and was now stretched out behind a thick growth of underbrush bordering the makeshift parking lot. Behind her the dense pine forest extended down to the highway below.

She shuddered with cold. She had watched most of them arrive; the last car had parked almost twenty minutes earlier. Paul was late. At first she was concerned that some minor mishap might have occurred to delay him. Then, in minutes, her imagination created horrors: *Paul had been killed, the bomb had self-detonated on the streets of London—in a magnitrain, a taxi.* . . . She tensed her muscles, breathed deeply in an attempt to grab hold of herself.

She had traveled to Rastenburg via Warsaw. It was a route that had enabled her to spend the night in a sleeping compartment on the conventional train that left the Polish capital in the evening, crossing the German frontier to arrive in Rastenburg shortly after dawn. The sky was gray, the nip of an early spring morning in the air.

The only other passenger to debark at the small provincial station had been a portly man wearing an unseasonable, heavy sealskin coat. He had tipped his hat as they stood together in the vestibule between cars, where they waited for the doors to open. He smiled, took her arm to help her down to the platform. She thanked him with one of the few German words she knew.

There was a single taxi at curbside, its driver, an old man seemingly half asleep, squatted on its front bumper. He came laboriously to his feet as she approached.

"Do you know the Wolves' Lair?" said Lesley.

The old man was bewildered. He shook his head, then tilted it, wide-eyed like a questioning beagle. "Hotel?"

"No. It's a big house." She waved her hand in the direction she thought to be north. "On a hill—Wolves' Lair . . ."

He stared at her, incomprehension dulling his eyes. Lesley felt lost.

A voice behind her said, *"Wolfschanze."* Then, in guttural English, "Wolves' Lair. I know of it, madam."

She turned. It was her fellow passenger, once again tipping his hat. "Perhaps I might help you," he said, smiling. His face was reminiscent of a favorite toy from her childhood, Mr. Potato Head, with which one created faces by sticking an assortment of odd plastic features into the meat of a large potato. His pocked skin sported an unlikely combination of tiny button eyes and a bulbous nose that overshadowed a small pursed mouth. She returned his smile, saying, "I would appreciate it if you would give the direction to the driver."

"I'd be quite happy to take you there myself."

"Thank you, but it's not necessary to go out of your way."

"It's not out of my way at all. I go in that direction." He gestured openhandedly toward the taxi, his tone now conspiratorial. "This man is stupid and would soon have you lost."

As a benefactor, he was far more likely to express curiosity than was a taxi driver, particularly one who didn't speak English. But there seemed to be no immediate alternative. Reluctantly she acquiesced.

He said, "My name is Wessel. Horst Wessel."

"Janet Kramer."

He took her arm as they walked to his car in the station's small parking lot. It was a Packard sedan of the same model year as her convertible in California. As Wessel opened the door for her, Lesley ran her hand affectionately across the roof line. She thought of her ex-husband for the first time in almost a year.

Starting the engine, Wessel said, "You like the machine? It's a Packard, American, twelve cylinders."

"Yes," she said, wondering if Ralph had married little Gloria Gold.

"There are only three others like it in all of East Prussia."

"I used to drive one," she said. "A convertible."

He glanced quickly at Lesley out of the corner of his eye as if not quite believing her. "In America?"

"New Zealand."

On the highway, Herr Horst Wessel kept his speed to a methodical 50 kilometers an hour, allowing himself to be passed at one point by a line of farm lorries. He said, "What brings you to Rastenburg—to this Wolves' Lair?"

"I'm visiting a friend."

"You have been there before?"

"No."

"It is a strange house."

"Sounds as if you know it well."

He nodded, placing a seemingly casual hand on her leg, just above the knee. "I arrange construction. . . ."

"You're a building contractor?"

"Yes. I'm sorry but my English is still imperfect." He grinned at her briefly, his hand moving almost imperceptibly upward. "The house was reconstructed—repaired—last year; new roof and plumbing and electricity. They asked me also to add a new wing to it."

She eyed his hand, clocking its movement. It would, she realized, at its current rate, reach its goal long before she reached hers. The speedometer, she noted, had dropped below the 45 kilometer mark. The road was snaking through a series of gentle curves. They were in a pine forest.

She said, "How much farther?"

"Not very far." Wessel squeezed her thigh. He chuckled as the car swerved momentarily. Then he was cupping her crotch, pressing painfully. She grasped the errant hand in hers, and as if it were an inanimate object, placed it on the rim of the steering wheel. The gesture brought about an immediate change in both

Herr Wessel's attitude and the speed at which they were traveling. He hunched grimly forward over the wheel as the speedometer climbed to 80 kilometers.

They drove on in silence for what seemed to be about ten minutes, then Herr Wessel slowed abruptly, pulling off the highway. "It's there," he said, pointing to his left at a narrow dirt road ascending into the trees.

She wondered if he was lying. He seemed capable of petty spite. With a growing sense of helplessness, she said, "Are you certain?"

"Of course . . . only a few hundred meters." He spoke sourly, not looking at her. "It would damage my tires."

Reluctantly, Lesley thanked him. She stepped out of the car, recoiling as, with a screech of tires, the big Packard careened back onto the highway and was gone.

She crossed over and entered the forest. Despite her doubts, there was no alternative. After thirty of forty yards, the dirt road became little more than a rutted track. She found herself wishing for a cup of coffee—anything. Perhaps Paul had been right after all. *Man's work.* It was also, as he had said, his country, his responsibility, and there was nothing that she could contribute. Nervously she tapped a cigarette out of a fresh pack, lit it, suddenly aware that she must shake off the debilitating feeling of insecurity or end up wallowing in it.

The primitive road twisted upward through the pines. She trudged purposefully now, fighting to keep her mind closed to everything but the goal that might or might not lie just ahead. *Wolfschanze . . .*

Behind her there was the sound of an automobile engine groaning back and forth through its two lower gears. As the sound grew in intensity, Lesley stepped hurriedly off the path into the shelter of the trees. Moments later, she watched as it came into view—a Mercedes convertible, top down, two men seated in the front seat. As it lurched past, she could see that one of them was Field Marshal von Seydlitz. Beneath the constriction of fear, she felt a sense of relief. Herr Wessel, despite his obvious frustration, had not misled her.

She reached the fence forty minutes after starting up the road. During that time, three more automobiles had struggled past her. She stared grimly at the house for a few moments, then, hearing another engine ascending the road, she moved quickly into the surrounding forest, making her way around the large clearing to a vantage point behind some shrubbery about sixty feet in front of the main entrance.

During the next half hour, Lesley watched as four more cars arrived. Paul was in none of them. The six occupants, each carrying a case of one kind or another, made their way to a doorway leading into the new wing.

Staying low, she scurried to the nearest vehicle. It was a small Opel coupé. Using it as cover, she knelt at the left front tire to unscrew the valve cap. She fished in her shoulder bag for a ballpoint pen. It took slightly less than thirty seconds to deflate the tire. Taking pains to keep the cars between herself and the house, she flattened a front tire on each of the other seven. If by some chance there were survivors, they would be incapable of pursuit.

Then, stretched out on the pine needles behind a thick wall of evergreens, she awaited Paul with a growing sense of anxiety.

The arrival of the blue Adler calmed her fears. *It had to be him.* She shivered in the damp morning air, trying to see into the small back window as the coupé was parked next to Von Seydlitz's big Mercedes.

It was a full minute—an hour, she felt—before the car door opened. She whispered his name, a barely audible prayer. It was Paul. He strode purposefully to the rear of the car to open the trunk lid. Lesley watched, her heart beating rapidly, as he set the attaché case on end and, with no wasted motion, pulled the arming pin.

Now, she realized, as soon as he closed the trunk lid, he would be passing within ten feet of her on his way to the house. She would call to him quietly, then brace herself for what she knew would be his reaction: confusion, quick anger, then finally concern. Paul loved her . . . she would explain quickly and he would understand. He would approve of how she had immobilized the cars. They were a team. . . .

She peered through the small opening in her cover, assuming he was about to lift out the attaché case. Instead, grasping the handle, he extended his index finger. She could see everything clearly. She stifled an involuntary cry as he sought out and depressed the trigger! It had happened so quickly that for an instant she thought she might have been mistaken—an aberration of vision. She replayed the unlikely act in her mind, confirming it. Then, instinctively, she glanced at her watch: 9:17:05. It was too late now to make her presence known, to use precious time while the acid ate away seconds and minutes. Why, she wondered fitfully, had he done it? In the conference room he would have been able to choose the time of his departure, triggering the bomb just before he left, allowing himself the full twenty minutes to get clear. *Now it was the bomb itself that would time his exit:* a dreadful tactical error.

She tried to sink into the earth as he passed near her. When she looked up he had reached Herr Wessel's new addition to the house. As he entered, she glanced at her watch. There were nineteen minutes and thirty-five seconds remaining.

". . . the last German election for a thousand years . . ." Rudolph von Seydlitz, the soon-to-be-Führer, was speaking. Paul barely heard him. Had it been three minutes? Five? Ten? He had never been good at judging time. He placed both hands on the attaché case, as if somehow, magically, it would inform him. Then he realized they were staring. Had he given himself away? Von Seydlitz was squeezing his upper arm, saying, "Are you unwell?"

He thought quickly. "Yes. But I'm sure it will pass." His answer might give him the opportunity to leave—to be sick in the bathroom.

"I hope so." His uncle seemed annoyed. He had, thought Paul, little tolerance for weakness. "Herr Gratz has asked you if you have any further plans for the campaign."

"Yes," said Paul, fishing for an idea. "We must buy an opinion poll." He was thinking fast.

"Nonsense," said State Secretary Schmidt.

"Hear him out . . ."

"I've done some preliminary work on this. For a hundred and fifty thousand deutsche marks, I can guarantee—"

"We're already showing forty-four percent in the real polls," said Gratz.

"That's a plurality," said Paul, making it up as he went along.

"I'm speaking of an absolute majority—better than that—sixty percent. There are still two weeks to go in the campaign. If we give up seven percent to the Social Democrats, we will lose." *They would talk him to death—literally.*

"A false poll is meaningless, Herr Bauer," said State Secretary Schmidt. "Your indisposition must be affecting your powers of logic."

"No," said Paul. "Counterfeit votes will generate real votes. People like to be on the side of the winner . . . votes are power and our people respect power." He wondered if he was right. *But it didn't matter—were there seconds or minutes left?*

Mengele leaned forward, pointing a bony finger at Bauer. "The young man is absolutely correct! The Jew Gallup in America invented the opinion poll as a means to herd sheep, to manipulate public opinion rather than reflect it . . . a psychological weapon developed by the Jews to subvert their so-called democracies to their own use!" He glanced around the table for confirmation. A grin of triumph was marred by the peculiar triangular gap in his front teeth.

"But," said Gratz, "if it gets out that we've bribed a poll taker . . ."

"We simply deny it—emphatically," said Von Seydlitz. "We accuse them of defamation—libel. And we prove that it is not we who have committed this sin, but the Social Democrats. We threaten to sue, and then we put a few thousand of our people in the streets to demonstrate . . . rage and righteous indignation!"

"I'm sure it won't come to that," said Kohler.

Others joined the discussion. As it moved away from Paul, he battled an overwhelming compulsion to bolt, to run from the room—from the house, from Germany. He had never been a good judge of time, *but surely what seemed to have been an hour must have been at least twenty objective minutes! Logic would indicate that the firing-pin spring had been slack or the acid adulterated or the wire too thick. A dud! A failure.* But even now, in the grip of fear for his life, he didn't want failure.

General von Wirsinger and his aide had moved to Paul's side of the table. The general was in deep, whispered conversation with Von Seydlitz. Paul stood, moved back silently to make room for them as the aide began unrolling a large map. Across the table, Kohler was standing, speaking of constitutional procedures required for the Reichstag to vote itself out of existence.

Paul was sure there were no eyes on him as he slipped out the door into the hall. His first priority was to get free of the potential blast area. Next he must return after the explosion to make sure there were no survivors. He shuddered. If there were, he would have to use his pistol. No living martyrs, he thought; it could start all over again. At the outer door, he suddenly recalled that his pistol was in his topcoat pocket. The coat was hanging in the conference room on a hook just inside the door. Dumbly he reversed his steps. As he was about to re-enter the conference room, he was brought up short by the sheer mindlessness of his action. He turned once again, wondering if perhaps fear had robbed him of his reasoning power.

He had taken three steps toward the exit when he heard the door open behind him. Startled, he glanced over his shoulder. Field Marshal Rudolph von Seydlitz was standing in the partially open doorway to the conference room. He was cradling the attaché case in both arms.

"Paul!" The older man's voice was high-pitched, strained with incredulity. "I moved it to make room for the map. It's heavy . . . too heavy." His eyes were wide, unblinking.

Bauer, an incongruous smile on his lips, spoke calmly. "Set it down gently, Uncle, and leave . . . quickly."

"A bomb. Why?" Von Seydlitz shifted the case to his left hand. In his right, a pistol. Quietly, conversationally, he said, "Why?" Bauer took a step toward him. "Uncle . . ." He crashed into an invisible wall as a figure flashed past him, blond hair flying. He was on the floor before the sound of the gunshot registered . . . an explosive agony in his upper torso. Then, nothing.

Lesley Morning's watch read 9:22:20. Keeping her head down, she got into the front seat of the Adler. The key was not in the ignition. Paul, she reasoned, must have dropped it into his pocket after opening the trunk lid. She sat quietly, slumped back in the seat, aware now of the fact that she was hungry. Bacon and eggs, she thought. The eggs up, perfect white circles with large, bright-yellow bull's-eyes dotted with black pepper; the browned edges crisped into a slight upward curl, the bacon, lean, aromatic, still sizzling from the grill. She peered over the right-hand door-frame, willing Paul Bauer to emerge.

He didn't, but to the right, a giant in shirt sleeves stood in the open doorway to the main part of the house. Lesley dropped quickly behind the car door, then reached up to the rear-view mirror. She had to twist it to the vertical position in order to turn it far enough, but finally she had him. He was standing as if at parade rest, staring out at the pine forest and the low hills be-yond; a scaled-up, oversized working model of a man with a monstrous, cinched-in belly and the enigmatic face of an Easter Island stone carving.

She prayed that Paul would not emerge while the brute was standing there. She stared at him in the mirror, counting sec-onds, betting with herself that he would re-enter the house in ten seconds . . . twenty . . . thirty-five . . . an attempt to ease an anxiety that she knew could soon grow into a deadly state of panic. There was no action she could take other than to check her watch again. Only forty seconds had passed since she had last done so. The slow passage of time would aid Paul . . . if indeed it was also passing slowly for him. Nervously, she chided herself for thinking nonsense.

9:25:25. The man was joined by an equally overscaled haus-frau in a bright print dress. Lesley could make out the incompre-hensible, though well-defined sounds of guttural German. She seemed to be scolding him. They were, she speculated, house-hold staff. Were there others? The possibility of witnesses, fol-lowed by arrest, imprisonment flashed through her mind. She discarded the thought an instant after it was formed. There were immediate, more important problems. Paul's life hung on a thin wire that by now was eaten more than halfway through by relent-less acid. She sank lower into her seat, flushed, her cheeks burn-ing as if she had been inflicted with a sudden, explosive fever.

9:28:40. In the mirror, the man and woman were gone. De-spite its open windows, she found the car interior unbearable. She felt the need to take some action, to leave her sanctuary and in some way be useful.

She slid under the wheel and out the door, standing erect for the first time in over an hour as she surveyed the length of the house across the car top. From its corner to her right, a thin line was etched against the sky. Lesley stared at it for almost a minute, then made her way behind the parked automobiles to the end of the clearing, where she raced across the open space. A pair of black wires, twisted together, emerged from a hole in the siding near the ground and ran upward to the level of the second floor to a small black junction box out of which were fed two other lines. One of these entered the house under a nearby window, the other was strung out 30 feet to a pole slightly taller than the pine trees surrounding it. From there, she reasoned, it was fed down the hill to the highway, where it joined hundreds of other telephone lines . . . if indeed it was a telephone line and not a power cable. She suspected, however, due to some experiences with electrical extension cords and lamp wires, that power lines would be much heavier.

Kneeling down, she wedged two fingers under the entwined pair. She pulled, creating some slack. Then she grasped and tugged, loosening a staple. A foot of wire now hung a few inches out from the wall. Lesley rummaged in her bag, hoping to find something she could use as a tool. The best she could find was a metal nail file. It barely marred the tough insulation.

Frustrated, she lit a cigarette. Then, acting on impulse, she applied the lighter flame to the twisted wire. After a few seconds the plastic insulation flared with an acrid blue flame. When she withdrew the lighter, she found the insulation charred. Using the nail file, she scraped it clean, revealing two strands of bright copper wire. They were, she noted, touching. Aloud, she whispered the word *short circuit,* and hoped she was right.

Lesley felt a momentary sense of accomplishment, a pride in her work. The household staff would be unable to phone the police after the blast and there were no cars in which they could give chase. She and Paul would make good their escape and live happily ever after.

Nervously, she checked her watch. 9:36:10. With a sudden rush of anxiety, she stepped out from the side of the house, sighting down its length at the door in the new wing. Paul had less than a minute left! She found herself walking rapidly in full view, praying silently that the acid might be imprecise or that Jack

Green had allowed some leeway without telling them. She counted in cadence with her increasing pace and soon she was running and down to twenty seconds.

If she could get into the conference room in time, she could call out a warning—save him, even if it meant sparing the others. Damn them all! The world would only get what it deserved. She ran even faster.

At the door, time had run out. She flung it open. There was a short corridor. Paul Bauer stood with his back to her. Facing him from less than three feet away stood Rudolph von Seydlitz, the attaché case cradled to his chest, an ugly pistol aimed at Paul's head. The gun wavered as the startled field marshal reacted to Lesley's headlong rush through the door. For an instant his eyes locked with hers. Then, a split second before the gun went off, she ran into him at full speed, her outstretched hands striking the old man in the face and neck, throwing him off balance. He cried out in surprise, reeled backward, dropping the attaché case. She struck him again, this time with her shoulder. The impact propelled Von Seydlitz through the gaping door into the conference room. There were startled faces peering out at her as, with no wasted motion, she picked up the attaché case and, using both hands, hurled it in after him. She slammed the door shut.

Paul was stretched out on the floor. She hovered over him. "It's overdue," she said, her voice strident, breathless. "We've got to go!" She reached down. Her lips continued to move, but soundlessly now, as the blast slammed her downward across his body, driving the wind from her lungs.

Fine white plaster dust filled the air. There was an acrid odor of high explosive. A man was screaming in regular, rhythmic cadence. Then, after less than half a minute—silence.

Lesley felt battered, stunned—her ears stuffed, as if she had descended rapidly from a great height. Dimly, she looked around. The cement-block wall next to her was still intact, though a few feet farther on, the door and part of the wall were gone. Wessel's construction methods had saved her.

She moved her body tentatively, surveying for damage. The muscles in her neck and shoulders seemed strained. There was blood. A little of it was hers from a small cut on her arm. But Paul was alive, breathing erratically. She kneeled, brushed the rubble from his clothing, then located the wound just below his left shoulder. It was clean, a small, neat hole. She removed her sweater and, balling it up, stuffed it under his jacket in order to apply pressure to stem the flow of blood.

She must move the car nearer to the house. Drag him to it . . . somehow. But the car keys were not in any of his pockets. His missing topcoat was the only other possibility.

By the portion of the conference-room wall that had been blown out, a dead man lay sprawled amid the ruin. His belly had been torn open, revealing a reddish-brown pulp. Lesley fought back the acrid bile rising in her throat, held her breath to avoid the foul smell as she stepped over the corpse into a charnel house.

They were all dead, their broken bodies strewn about haphazardly. What was left of Field Marshal von Seydlitz lay sprawled across the splintered remains of the conference table. His head was partially severed from his body, its eyes rolled up, its lips puckered as if awaiting a kiss. A swastika armband was grotesquely in place on an arm that was missing half its length; dangling shattered white bone and bloody tatters of muscle and tendon.

She felt faint, once again almost overwhelmed by a wave of nausea. Dimly, she sensed she was standing on something soft. Stepping back, she glanced down to find it was a disconnected hand, palm up, its fingers extended as if attempting to grasp her foot. Clamping her eyes shut, she fought back a scream, permitting it to emerge as a series of sobs. When she opened her eyes, she found them miraculously focused on Paul's beige trenchcoat. It hung with a few other coats on the undamaged wall to her left.

Tensing her stomach muscles and gulping lungfuls of air, she half-staggered across the room. Paul's coat seemed to her to be the only object in the room still intact. She found the pistol in the right-hand pocket. Fumbling beneath it, she felt the keys. As she did so, she was startled to hear someone shouting in German.

Lesley swiveled around in horror, half expecting to see one of the corpses sitting up. It was instead the giant she had seen standing in the front doorway less than ten minutes before. He seemed in apoplexy, his face a muddy beet color, his eyes bulging in rage. Grasped in his huge hand was what she assumed to be a submachine gun, its muzzle pointed threateningly at her mid-section. He was repeating the same short German phrases over and over again, gesturing roughly with the gun.

Her right hand in the topcoat pocket transferred its index finger from the key ring to the trigger guard. Her face an expressionless mask, she squeezed. The bullet struck just under the giant's chin, throwing his head back. The second shot penetrated his belly, leaving a small black hole in his shirtfront. With a groan, cut short by a sudden spurt of blood from the neck wound, the big, ugly man slid down the cinder-block wall to sit ponderously dead on the rubble-strewn floor. Lesley turned away, surrendering finally to nausea.

When she got to him, Paul was regaining consciousness. She leaned close, speaking his name. His first words were in German, then, suddenly aware of her, he caught himself in mid-sentence. He tried to sit up. She helped him. He said, "Seydlitz . . ."

"Dead," she said, "with the rest of them." With a tentative hand she brushed his hair back. There was a large bump just behind his hairline. The hair was sticky with congealing blood.

His voice was low, the words slurred, unevenly spaced, as if he were having trouble choosing them. "How are you here . . . ?" He winced painfully, glancing around. "I didn't know what time it was . . . my watch." He looked down as if to make sure it was still there. "But the bomb went off anyway." He shuddered, closed his eyes for a moment, then opened them again as if seeing her for the first time. "Lesley. What are you doing here? How . . . ?"

She got him to the car. The big woman in the print dress was standing in the main doorway. Next to her was another, half her size. Lesley fired two shots into the air. Both women disappeared immediately into the house, slamming the door behind them.

As she wheeled out of the clearing and onto the descending dirt road, Paul placed his hand on her shoulder. He said, "You did it all."

"Yes," she said.

"Like your grandmother."

"Yes." Her eyes were tearing, blurring the road. "How many times does it have to be prevented?"

"What, darling?"

The steering wheel seemed to ground her to reality. "The Second World War." She grasped the wheel tightly in both hands, knowing that when she finally relaxed her grip, she would shake apart.

On the highway below, he said, "Where are we going?"

"Home," she said.

When they got to Königsberg, Sid Shulberg and Freddy Hayworth were waiting for them just as they had promised her.

Screen credits for winner of 1980 Acadamy award:
best costume design

COLUMBIA PICTURES
presents
THE GERALD MOSS–IRWIN STEIN
production of

THE MEN OF ANDERSONVILLE

—cast—

George Conway .... Jack Lemmon
John McElroy .... Lazlo Butrik
Captain Henri Wirz .... Anthony Quinn
Clara Barton .... Natalie Wood
Ransom Powell
(Little Red Cap) .... Mickey Rooney
President Andrew Johnson .... Jason Robards
General Sherman .... George C. Scott
General "Pap" Thomas .... Henry Morrison
President Jefferson Davis .... Ronald Reagan
Surgeon Joseph Jones .... Franklin Tig

◆ **34** ◆

1913

    Elleander offered him a small humidor. Wells chose a cigar
that she clipped for him with a silver tool. She said, "Harry looks
more like his father every day."

"Bertie would be delighted if he knew," said Wells, releasing a perfect smoke ring. He always felt comfortable in the large, cluttered room Elleander called her sanctum. One wall was bookcase, the others were covered with paintings she had bought back from numerous trips to Paris. Wells at first had thought them formless, almost incomprehensible. She had once mentioned that a few of the canvases would one day have a market value exceeding a million pounds. He thought the idea obscene. It was one of the few things she had told him of the future that he never quite believed. Nevertheless, in recent months, Wells had found himself drawn to a few of them, particularly those two paintings that were rendered in tones of blue by an artist Elleander had described as a young Spaniard living in Paris.

He watched as she walked across the room, her floor-length dress swirling in white and gold spirals around her body. He said, "To gild refined gold, to paint the lily, to throw perfume on the violet . . ."

"What's that, Herbert?" She poured two brandy and sodas.

"Shakespeare, referring to you in that dress."

"How sweet of him, and of you too, dear Herbert." Elleander handed him a glass, then kissed him on the cheek. She perched on the edge of the desk, sipped her drink. When she lowered the glass, her smile was gone. She said, "I almost told him."

"Why didn't you?"

"He walked away, just in time."

"You had almost six months, Elleander."

"Yes . . ."

Wells raised a forefinger, his voice that of a stern teacher lecturing a difficult student. "After you and Bertie became lovers you should have told him of his son. In fact, I can see no reason why you couldn't have told him everything, just as you told me. And please, Elleander my dear, let's hear no more about your fears that he might think you mad. I've grown tired of that idea and I'll wager you have, too. You could have shown him the very same evidence you showed me—those war books, the Derby winners, that thing you call a tee-vee set, the lot. Sooner or later he would have accepted it, just as I did."

Elleander walked to the window, gazed out at Highcastle

Road. There were new crocuses blooming in the window boxes across the way. Spring, she thought. There was to be but one more and then the world would change forever. She said, "You're angry with me."

"Yes. He too is my friend and because I gave you my word to remain silent, I've had to stand by and watch him suffer."

"I'm sorry . . ."

"No doubt."

"I was afraid for his life."

"From what you told me, his death would have occurred months ago. There was no motorcar accident—you thwarted history."

"Fate."

"Whichever you prefer. Nevertheless, the day came and went."

"We were in Paris at that time. I kept him in bed all that day and night. My only fear was that the roof might cave in or lightning might strike."

"Lucky devil." Wells released a cloud of blue cigar smoke, which for a moment hung in the air in front of him, obscuring his frown. "So why didn't you tell him after that? And why don't you give up all of this and marry him? He still loves you."

She shrugged, saying, "Where is Bertie now?"

"In Paris, finishing the play."

"In our flat," she said softly. "Taking solitary baths."

"He loves you and he'll be returning soon. You can still explain it all to him—or I can." Wells smiled. "We can yet be that happy trio you told me about."

"No." She turned from him, fighting a sudden, weary hopelessness. "Bertie and I will never see each other again."

"Are you still in love with him?"

"Yes. I will always be. But there's something else . . ."

"Another man?"

"A war."

Wells was silent for a moment. Finally he said, "Of course. The inevitable war. It's all happening just as you said it would."

She recalled his attitude in that other time when he had favored the war, justified it, served as a catalyst for war hysteria.

"Every sword that is drawn against Germany now is a sword for peace. . . ." And in a shilling pamphlet he had coined the term that was to become the American justification: "The War That Will End All War." Only by winning it, he had argued, could mankind achieve everlasting peace and the utopia that only he, Wells, saw so clearly.

But this time his attitude was totally different. He had listened to her carefully as she described the horrors of the Western Front and the corrupt peace that followed it. In a quiet voice, she said, "Nothing can stop it. Even if there were some way to prevent the Archduke's assassination, it would accomplish nothing. Some other event would surely replace it." She took his hand. "You've got to stop your warnings. A year from now, after it begins, your writings on the subject could very easily be distorted, turned against you. You could be denounced as an enemy sympathizer. It would be the end of your career, or worse."

"But how can I keep silent?"

"It's no use, H.G. They all want war. Both sides think it will end after a month or so of fighting and then all of Europe's problems will be solved. All the border disputes will be resolved, the map will be redrawn, power and markets redistributed . . . the Americans will call it 'the war to end all wars.' You and I are the only people on earth who have any idea of the horrors in store for poor old Europe, and we are powerless." She moved back, leaned against the desk again, her arms folded in front of her. "The first modern war. The first universal killing machine."

Wells seemed to shake himself. After a moment, he said, "But you and Bertie . . . life goes on. I don't understand."

"The first world war. There'll be a second—even worse—as you read in the books. Forty million dead, most of them noncombatants: Russians, Chinese, Jews, Britons too . . . and Captain Harry Morning Trasker. I can prevent all of it."

Wells leaned forward in his chair, his face a noncommital mask. Quietly, he said, "How?"

She disregarded the question. "With Bertie in my life I simply wouldn't have the will. And if I did, and he knew of it, he'd try to stop me and would most certainly succeed."

"How?" repeated Wells.

"A simple murder, no more . . . a single assassination. I've had it worked out for a while, a few years, actually. All I seem to lack at the moment is the pistol . . . and the courage. You can help me acquire both those things, Herbert."

35

1913

Elleander came awake to the happy trill of female laughter
coming from the street below her open window. It was Fawn's
laughter. She rolled over on the huge bed that was a ship, dimly
aware that something must be funny. Then Magnolia Levy's voice
cried out, "It's beautiful. . . ."

Elleander placed a pillow over her head. It muffled the
words, making them unintelligible, but did little to quiet the
sound. There was, she began to realize, a gathering in front of
the house. She sat upright, squinting into the brilliant spring
sunlight streaming through the window, while her feet fumbled
for slippers.

She stood, reaching for a robe, her naked body still warm

from sleep. There was a chorus of voices from the street, Samuel's deep, resonant tones rising above the others. "Never have I seen anything like it. . . ."

At the window, she stared down for seconds, suddenly oblivious to the sound of voices. Elleander came fully awake, her body rigid, her breath suspended.

In the cellar she found the ax used to split firewood. Calmly she grasped the long wooden handle, hefted it. She breathed deeply, feeling nothing but the cold strength of her purpose.

A group of her ladies was passing through the hall—Yvonne, Alma, Magnolia, Jane, others. Their chatterings ceased as Elleander passed through them, unseeing, ax in hand, her hair unkempt.

Then, seconds later, on the portico, she was face-to-face with Bertram Trasker. He was speaking to her. She stared at his mouth, hearing only half his words ". . . had to come back to you . . ." Bertie's hands were on her shoulders, grasping. ". . . love you . . ." She looked into his eyes as his face grew rigid with dawning incredulity. "Elleander . . . !" She pushed past him.

The red motorcar stood at the curb directly in front of the house, gleaming in the morning sunlight. Low-slung, it was built for speed, out of steel, brass, wood and leather. Its two bucket seats were perched out in the open, near the rear of the chassis, looking as if they had been added as an afterthought. The twins occupied them. Fawn was hunched forward behind the great wooden steering wheel like a child playing at motorcar racing. They shouted a greeting, waving playfully, then froze when they saw the ax.

The first blow smashed into the radiator. The twins fled through a cloud of hissing steam. The second obliterated one of the large carbon-arc headlamps and the third sliced the tire and severed spokes in the right front wheel.

As Elleander raised her ax again, Trasker arrived to grab her upraised arm. She twisted. He reached out with his other hand to restrain her, but succeeded only in grasping a handful of dressing gown.

She was aware that Bertie was shouting at her. From somewhere nearby she heard a woman shrieking, then her own voice, shouting incoherently as she struggled to retain the ax.

Finally, he grasped her around the waist. Her arm was weakening. Desperately, she brought her knee up sharply, felt it sink into the softness of his groin. The effect was immediate. She almost dropped the ax as he released the pressure. In an instant Bertie was doubled up at her feet. Groaning, he squirmed his way to the steps, where a half dozen of her ladies rushed to his aid.

Once again she wielded the ax, ravaging the bonnet, cutting its leather strap. The next blow revealed the engine. She smashed the carburetor, then, moving quickly rearward, she attacked the small circular windscreen and the right rear wheel. With one blow, she sliced through the petrol tank just below the seats. The pungent fluid gushed out, forming a pool under the car.

There were strong arms around her, pulling her back. It was Samuel, her butler. She ceased struggling as he lifted her off the ground. Quietly, in conversational tones, she said, "A match . . . please, Samuel."

"Afraid I don't have one, madam."

She was in his arms, being carried toward the house. She glanced down. Bertie was seated on the steps. He was breathing heavily. Their eyes met momentarily, his full of pain. He looked away quickly. The ladies made room for them as Samuel climbed the few steps into the house. She felt exhausted, drained of everything but a dim sense of victory. As the door closed behind them, she heard Uncle Lethaby say, "Inside, ladies, before the coppers arrive."

"I've got to talk to you," said Wells. "It's urgent." He spoke quietly, his voice slightly more than a whisper. It was less than a week after the incident with the red Mercer. They stood in the rear of the theater. There were actors on the empty stage, rehearsing.

"Is something wrong?" said Bertram Trasker, a note of concern in his voice.

"Yes, terribly wrong," said Wells.

Trasker gestured for him to follow. They walked quickly down the left aisle to a door that led backstage. There they halted, faced each other beneath a circular iron staircase that led up to the dressing rooms.

Wells said, "It's about Elleander Morning."

Trasker turned away. "Sorry, old chap. I've no interest in even hearing her name."

Wells gripped his arm, a look of wrathful impatience on his face that was so ferocious it caused Trasker to recoil as if he were about to be struck.

"She is," said Wells tightly, "about to do something very foolish, very dangerous. You're the only one who might be able to stop her."

"Why me?"

"Because she loves you!"

Trasker's response was barely audible. "Nonsense . . ."

"I've been your friend for many years." Wells tightened his grip on Trasker's arm. "God knows I've heard you out many times. If that is of any value to you, you'll now hear me out. There is no time to waste."

Bertram Trasker stood silently for a moment, staring glumly at Wells. Finally he nodded.

In the dim backstage light, Wells showed him a snapshot of his son Harry. Then he told Trasker everything he knew about Elleander Morning.

Mother, may I go out to fly?
Oh yes, my darling daughter.
But do not go too near the sky,
And when you fall, hit the water.

—Nursery rhyme parody,
1910–1913

36

1913

Winston Scott Corbett leaned back against the spindly un-
dercarriage of his aeroplane, sipped his tea and daydreamed of
being the first aeronaut to cross the Mediterranean. Marseilles to
Tunis, two continents, 480 miles over open water! He would be
the first to do it—a giant step beyond Blériot's cross-channel hop
of four years ago. It would be the making of him and of British
aviation in the bargain. Beat the damned Froggies at their own
game and the bloody Heinies, too! The British lagged shame-
fully. The government . . . those idiots in Whitehall would continue in their refusal to take the aeroplane seriously until they had
their noses rubbed in it. And everyone knew there was going to
be a war. A new kind of war in which the sky would be a battlefield. But in the meantime a cross-Mediterranean flight would
get the bastards to sit up and take notice.

First he would need money—five hundred pounds to trade
his little 50-horsepower engine for a modern 7-cylinder, 80-
horsepower rotary Le Rhone. And money for a hangar and spare
parts at Marseilles. And a mechanic and fuel . . . He needed a

sponsor; the *Daily Mail* or some other newspaper, an industrialist, even a whiskey distillery. He would see to it . . . soon.

A loud voice from the open tent flap said, "Sir, may I ask if this is your machine?"

Corbett glanced up to see a tall, bearded man, partly silhouetted against the glare. He nodded, thinking it was just another tourist.

"I would like to hire it," said the stranger as he stepped forward.

The young airman took his hand. "Well, that's possible. Who sent you?"

"No one. I haven't much time, you see, and I heard there was an aerodrome just outside of Dover."

Corbett stood up. "Where do you want to go?"

"Paris."

"That's a good distance, almost two hundred miles."

"Can you do it?"

"I've never taken a paying passenger that far."

The man was obviously agitated. "Just tell me if you are willing to fly me to Paris. If not, I'm sure there are others on the field who will."

"It will be expensive."

"Money is no object. Yes or no?"

"One hundred pounds." Corbett crossed his fingers behind his back. "In advance."

"Agreed."

"When do you want to leave?"

"This very minute. I must catch up with someone who's on her way to Vienna. She has a four-hour head start—the boat-train. Can you do it?"

Corbett, excited by his good fortune, entered into the spirit. "If we allow her an hour to get to the channel port, four hours for the crossing, and another two or three hours for the train to Paris—that's seven or eight hours. With a bit of luck and a tail-wind, I can get you there in under three, in time to meet her train. There's an aerodrome just outside the Bois de Boulogne."

His passenger wrote out a check, then helped Corbett fuel up. Together they wheeled the little monoplane out onto the tarmac. The young aviator had recently added a tiny wicker seat in the canvas fuselage. He helped this, his first passenger, into it. He advanced the magneto, then swung the propellor over. The game little Gnome engine caught immediately, exuding heavy blue smoke and firing off a series of loud bangs that momentarily startled the passenger.

Corbett climbed into the tight-fitting front cockpit, as the engine finally calmed itself into a steady, rhythmic rattle. He swiveled around to hand his passenger a pair of goggles and a limp inner tube while shouting over the engine, "Have you ever flown before?"

"No, I'm afraid not."

"Well then, a few rules: First, keep your feet on the strut, we don't want them going through the canvas. Next, if it gets bumpy, hold on tightly—anything you can grab. Do you swim?"

"Yes . . ."

"Then you'll have plenty of time to blow up the tube if we go into the water."

They bumped across the grass, picking up speed. The tail lifted. Then suddenly their progress was smoothed. They had left the ground and were riding on a cushion of air. There was a momentary precipitous drop, perhaps four or five feet, and then they were over the row of tents lining one side of the aerodrome.

In the distance, the gray water of the channel. In minutes they were over it. A thin aerosol of castor oil blew back in their faces, coating their goggles. Corbett wiped his off with a rag he kept for the purpose. He ripped it in half, turned, and grinning encouragement, passed a piece back to his passenger.

The castor-oil lubricant used in modern engines was often a source of embarrassing accidents. On a long flight such as this, an "accident" would sometimes take effect before the airman could reach his destination. A standing joke maintained that this effect was at least partially responsible for aviation's preoccupation with speed. Corbett wondered if perhaps he should have warned his passenger.

The Morane Saulnier was flying heavily due to the weight of the passenger and the full petrol tank. A fast ascent would put undue strain on the engine and use valuable time. However, height was important. It was only recently that pilots had begun to appreciate it, finding that it allowed more maneuvering room in emergencies. Corbett compromised on a shallow climbing angle that would have them at a comfortable three thousand feet by the time they crossed the French coast.

A half hour after leaving Dover, the air became choppy as they approached land. Corbett turned southeast along the coast until he sighted what he took to be Boulogne. Then he turned inland, searching for the railroad—all tracks led to Paris—a simple method of navigation.

Suddenly, with no warning, the clear blue air grew savage. The little machine dropped as if suddenly weighted with a ton of rocks. It struck bottom with a jolt, then shot up again. Corbett fought the controls valiantly as a sudden cross-wind caught him. The aeroplane banked wildly, losing flying speed. It was headed into a side slip that would lead into that most deadly of aeronautical maneuvers, from which no pilot had ever recovered—the spin. Acting solely out of conditioned reflex, Corbett pushed the stick forward, sending the Morane Saulnier into a dive.

A few moments and a thousand feet later, Corbett pulled out slowly, his air speed restored, the air once again relatively smooth. He drew a deep breath of relief, then turned to encourage his passenger with a thumbs-up gesture.

The rear seat was empty.

Corbett took his machine down to a hundred feet, flying a search pattern over a wooded area. After ten minutes, he gave up.

Once again over the Channel, Winston Scott Corbett reached into his pocket for the hundred-pound check. He stared at the signature for a few moments: B. Trasker. He dare not cash it; there would be inquiries. He ripped it into a hundred pieces, released them bit by bit into the slipstream. No one had seen him with his mysterious passenger. There was no connection.

But the poor bastard should have held on as he had been told.

37

1984

The man standing next to Rose Parker in Lesley's doorway was of medium height, but his erect bearing seemed at odds with a worn-out face. Lesley guessed his age to be about seventy. She was to realize shortly that she had underestimated by more than a decade.

Rose's eyes dipped to Lesley's belly. She looked up, her face flushed. "I didn't know you were, ah . . ."

"Pregnant," said Lesley, smiling broadly.

"Congratulations."

On the telephone the previous afternoon, Rose Parker had told Lesley that her "employer," Mr. Stahlmann, wanted to arrange a meeting. He had, she said, something very important to discuss.

"Well certainly, Rose, but what are you doing in London? I thought you'd be touring the world."

"We were, you see, but the first time I mentioned your name, he just insisted on coming here."

"Do you know what he wants to speak to me about?"

"Yes, miss."

"What, then?"

There was silence on the other end of the line for a moment, then Rose spoke very quietly. "Your grandmother. You see, he knew her."

Now, Rose made the introductions, then left, saying, "I'll go chat with Mrs. Green and leave you two to your business."

Lesley took his hat and coat. He smiled shyly, saying in the voice of a younger man, "Mrs. Bauer . . ."

"Mr. Stahlmann." She returned the smile, her eyes dropping to his diamond stickpin. She had never seen one before in real life. It secured a striped tie. He wore a conservatively cut gray suit that fit him as if it had been personally tailored, its elegant lines marred only by the bulge of a small package stuffed into a jacket pocket. Mr. Stahlmann was well turned out; an old-school gentleman.

"Rose is a lovely woman," he said.

"How did you meet?"

"She placed an ad in a personal column in New York. I was very lucky. Then we corresponded for a few months and I came over here. I'm retired, you see, can go and come as I choose. I wanted to travel, but it's very lonely by yourself—haven't been anywhere at all since I went to America in 1924. But now . . ."

Lesley seated Mr. Stahlmann in the red leather wing chair. She readied the tea-things, feeling vaguely discomforted by his sudden silence. Over a church steeple of bony fingers, his eyes, shifting back and forth in their deep, wrinkled sockets, followed her about the room. Perhaps, she thought, he was just a harmless old eccentric with an overactive imagination. She smiled at him weakly, hoping for the best as she sat down.

Stahlmann's attention remained riveted on her face as he picked up his teacup from the cocktail table that separated them. "You look exactly like her," he said, his words flavored lightly with a Teutonic undertone. "It's amazing. Of course your skin is much darker. The sun . . . women in those days hid from it. She had a small parasol."

"It was a very long time ago," said Lesley.

"Sixty-seven years." Then he was silent again, stirring his tea abstractedly, the spoon dwarfed in a large hand punctuated with liver spots.

Finally he said, "You see, I read somewhere that you had something to do with those Second World War books. Adolf Hitler, she shot him . . . it's all too complicated, too mixed up together to be an accident, a coincidence. Your maiden name and hers are the same."

"She was my grandmother."

"Ah yes, the minute I set eyes on you I knew there had to be blood between the two of you." He set the teacup down and leaned forward in his chair. "When Rose told me about your father and you and the house, I could hardly believe it. After all these years . . . her granddaughter . . ."

"You knew that we look alike . . ." Lesley spoke in a small, nervous voice. She felt a growing excitement. Stahlmann was a ghost, a messenger from the past. She said, "You really did know her?"

"A short acquaintance." He paused, picked up the teacup again. "And the man she shot, the artist Adolf Hitler, I knew him too, in 1912 and '13. I was surprised when I saw the books. It was the same Adolf Hitler, they had him down perfectly; his background, his art work, his early days in Lintz and Vienna before the Great War. In the pictures he looked much older, but he had the same little mustache. If he had lived, I'm sure he would have looked exactly that way. Then I read your name, *Morning,* in a newspaper article about the books. . . ."

For the first time, Stahlmann turned away from his hostess. He gazed at the Picasso hanging on the far wall. "Lovely," he said. His voice was low-pitched now, the words slurred together. "He wasn't what you would call a close friend, just an acquaintance from the working-class beer halls. He was strange, not really like the rest of us—moody. He never drank beer; with him it was usually mineral water. Sometimes we would laugh at him, behind his back, of course. But when I stop to think about it, we were all a little afraid of him . . . except for Plumb. But Plumb was an ox, an insensitive ape who feared nothing. We would sit for hours in the taverns guzzling beer—none for Adolf, of course. Ah, but such beer! Today it's all canned dishwater. I was the youngest, by far. I felt flattered to be included in the group. We argued politics and sometimes we talked about our adventures with women, mostly lies. . . . Excuse me, Mrs. Bauer, but Vienna was still Vienna." Stahlmann's thin, old man's lips curled once again into a brief smile. Lesley attempted to respond in kind but found it impossible. It was as if her facial muscles had atrophied.

Stahlmann leaned back in his chair. "When the subject of women came up, Adolf would turn away. Some of us thought he might be, you know, queer. As for politics, he was a sort of Pan-German. He hated almost everything: Austro-Hungarians, Jews, Franz Josef, Slavs. Had he known, for instance, that I was Jewish, he would not have sat at the same table with me. In those days I kept it from everybody, even myself. We were, according to him, well-meaning but misguided—Social Democrats, Trade Unionists, Marxists, and so on. I was an anarchist. . . . Foolish youth . . . not a single one of us could have imagined the horrors that lay ahead. I was still in my teen years.

"I was called up in 1914. Less than a year later I was wounded in Poland. After a few months' recuperation, I was lucky to be attached to a garrison unit in Vienna. But it was a different city. The light had gone out . . . it has never been turned back on."

"When did you meet her?" said Lesley, her heart racing.

Stahlmann seemed not to have heard her. "The trial was delayed," he said, his eyes locked on the ceiling just over her head. "The Archduke was dead, the Great War had begun. It took only two days to convict her. She offered no defense. The newspapers talked about a crime of passion. Ridiculous! But the Austrian courts had a gallant attitude toward that kind of thing. I'm sure that if Elleander Morning had gone along with them, spoke of her passion for the victim, sobbed throughout her testimony, cried female tears, threw herself on the mercy of the court, she probably would have escaped the death penalty. But even so, during most of the Hapsburg reign, not a single woman had ever been executed, no matter what the sentence. This didn't happen with your grandmother. The war was on, she was a enemy alien. No one gave a damn, probably not even her lawyer. Or maybe he was called up right after the trial and couldn't do anything."

Stahlmann sighed. "Your grandmother had no friends in Vienna."

He offered Lesley an unfiltered Camel, then, using a small wooden match, he leaned forward to light it for her. Grinning, he said, "When I was a young man of sixty, the doctors told me to give up these things or I'd be dead in a year. Now they're gone and I'm still at it."

"As far as they were concerned, she was just a nonentity who had shot another nonentity," said Lesley. "She was all alone."

"The newspapers said she was an English prostitute."

"Madam," said Lesley, remembering Fawn Fowler's emphatic words. "She was the most distinguished madam in all of bloody England!" She felt a sudden anger and the fullness of dammed-up tears. Vigorously, after only a single puff, she ground her cigarette into the ashtray.

"I'm sorry," said Stahlmann.

"You haven't told me how you met her . . . where . . ."

He started to speak, hesitated. Then he looked directly into her eyes. "That morning in Popples—I was a waiter there—he would come in from time to time in the morning. He liked the atmosphere, you see, and I would arrange for a second cup of coffee at no charge. Well, I had just served his order when she came in. She was limping, her hat was on crooked, her skirt was ripped almost to the knee. I remember it all so well. She took a table just a few yards from his. When Adolf saw her, he seemed annoyed. He told me she had followed him all the way from the Meldemennstrasse.

"I took her order . . . she was a beautiful woman. Then later there was the sound of two shots. From where I was standing, I could see that Adolf was dead in his chair. She was freshening her makeup—in those times, women didn't do that in public. I must have been in shock, paralyzed. I didn't realize what had been going on until she was only a few feet from the door." Stahlmann's voice faded. He looked away from Lesley, sipped his tea.

Lesley slid forward to the edge of her seat. "Tell me, please, Mr. Stahlmann."

"I knocked her down."

Lesley went numb. She wanted to speak but could find nothing to say.

"I came here to tell you all of this," said Stahlmann, "because I didn't want it to die with me. Now I'm finding it difficult
—almost impossible. Maybe it would be better if it did die with
me. . . ."

"No," she said.

Stahlmann stared at her unseeing, his vision turned inward.
"The garrison unit I was attached to in Vienna consisted mostly
of men who had been wounded. We all considered ourselves
fortunate. It was easy duty after what most of us had been
through. Then one day we were asked to draw lots. There were
six of us chosen from my company. A terrible thing—some of us
would have rather been back at the front. But orders were orders.
This was the Austro-Hungarian Army, not the French. We were
issued rifles, each with a single round in the chamber, and we
were told that one of them was loaded with a blank cartridge.
None of us would ever know for sure. Each of us could believe
he was innocent, or at least that's what they tried to tell us. Then
they drove us out to the prison, where we stood at ease in the yard
for about twenty minutes before they brought her out. It was
early, the light was a kind of grayish blue . . . false dawn, chilly.

"Elleander Morning was the most beautiful woman I had
ever seen. She was dressed for a fashionable garden party—a big
flowered picture hat, long dress, nipped in at the waist, gloves,
pretty shoes, everything white and lace. It's all still with me, down
to the last detail. She was carrying a parasol—it was furled up at
the time. She was between a matron and the prison director.
Behind her stood a priest and then about four others, all official,
all in lockstep on parade. But Elleander Morning was out of step
with them. She was promenading, not marching . . . a charming
woman strolling the Rialto . . . your grandmother.

"Nowhere during the war did I see such courage in the face
of death. At the wall she turned to our captain, smiled, and asked
him for a cigarette. He was embarrassed—confused. Women did
not smoke in public in those days. He had not prepared himself
for the tradition of the last cigarette. There was an awkward delay
while our sergeant was summoned forward to offer his pack. The
captain was very nervous; your grandmother steadied his hand
while he held the match. She thanked him with a little smile and

he responded with an awkward show of heel-clicking. When it came time for the blindfold, she refused.

"I fought to make my mind a blank. It was the only way I would be able to carry out the final order. It was a futile effort. There was a ringing in my head and I felt I was going to be sick.

"Then, as the sun peeked up over the horizon, your grandmother opened her parasol. The chaplain closed his Bible and he and the captain made their way toward the left flank of the squad. A little cloud of dust sprang up around the prisoner's feet.

"I found it painful to look at her, but forced myself to do so. She stood, all alone now, the small lace-fringed parasol protecting her from a weak, reddish sunrise. Elleander Morning seemed to me a lovely lady in a beautiful white dress, posing for a picture. It's an image that will stay with me to the grave." He paused.

Lesley wondered if she could bear hearing the rest of it. She felt she must tell him to stop. Instead, she said, "Go on, Mr. Stahlmann."

His voice was low, the words precisely spaced. "She was a perfect target. I prayed to God I had the blank cartridge. The captain called, 'Ready arms!'

"It seemed like an hour before the second order was given. Perhaps the whole thing had been called off and we would remain frozen in position like toy soldiers. Then finally, he gave it, his voice cracking like a teenager's. 'Aim!' I raised the big Mauser to my shoulder, sighting at a point just below the prisoner's left breast. The front sight just wouldn't stay there—it wavered. I was an expert shot, a marksman, steady as a rock, but the muzzle of my rifle insisted on straying upward. Then the unconscious action became conscious. I placed the sight an inch or two above Elleander Morning's left shoulder. I would not fire a bullet into this woman's body. I was a soldier, I had never shirked from duty to my country. I was not an executioner . . . not a killer of defenseless women.

"Then . . . 'Fire!' I felt the rifle butt pound into my shoulder. All six had gone off in the same split second."

Lesley stood, breathed deeply, hoping it would bring her heartbeat back to normal. She said matter-of-factly, "It was all over."

"No," said Mr. Stahlmann. "Your grandmother was still there. She was standing erect, holding the parasol. Her eyes were shut."

"Oh my God . . ."

"When she opened them, she looked at each one of us in turn, just ran her eyes down the line, looking into our faces.

"The sergeant called us to attention. He consulted with our captain, who seemed very agitated and was twisting his sword point into the ground till I thought he would snap it off.

"The two of them stood before us. The captain lectured us on our duty to the Empire. He seemed flustered, almost incoherent. When he'd finished his little speech, the sergeant dressed us down, threatening court-martial. He passed out six new cartridges. This time there was no blank—if there ever had been.

"We repeated the ritual. Again I fired over her head. But this time someone on my left—one man—had decided to 'do his duty.' She recoiled from the impact and in a second was on the ground, her eyes closed tightly from the shock. The left side of her body—her dress—was turning from white to red. But she was alive. She opened her eyes as our captain approached. He was drawing his pistol, cocking it for the coup de grace. I could see that she was in pain . . . *Gott!* She looked directly up at him, held out her right hand. There was just no way the captain could refuse her. She was a lady seeking aid from a gentleman. He took her hand in his and helped her to her feet. I remember the dainty white lace glove . . . her hand seemed so small. She stood, without the parasol, now, slumped a little to one side. Her left arm hung useless, the blood was dripping steadily from a wound high on her chest. There was a small red pool at her feet.

"Our officer raised his Luger to within an inch of her head. She shut her eyes again. She was whispering to him, swaying, as if once again she might fall to the ground. They stood in place like that for what seemed a half-minute . . . a whole year of half-minutes. Then he looked away. He turned his head from her. The muzzle of the Luger dropped to her cheek . . . awful. I raised my rifle. . . ." Mr. Stahlmann paused, breathing heavily as if he'd been running. He looked directly at Lesley with moist eyes. "I'm sorry." He made a visible effort to grab hold of himself, then continued, the words strung together. "I lined up the front and rear sights in a split second . . . steady as a rock. I don't remember hearing the shot, but it caught her an inch below her left breast. She was dead instantly."

Lesley was strangely calm, as if she'd been drugged. In a voice devoid of emotion, she said, "More tea, Mr. Stahlmann?"

"No, thank you." He stood forlornly, staring down at her. "If the captain had pulled the trigger with his head turned that way, she probably would have been wounded again . . . horribly. A slow, terrible death . . . that beautiful face . . ." The old man took a neatly folded linen handkerchief from his breast pocket, wiped his face with it as if he'd been perspiring. "It has haunted me for over sixty-five years. Maybe this is the end of it, finally."

Lesley felt a sudden chill, as if she had been packed in ice. She tensed her shoulders, clasped her hands together to still the trembling. The old man was looking at her curiously as if he were expecting a question. Instinctively, she took his hand, squeezed it tightly.

He withdrew a package from his jacket pocket, laid it on the cocktail table. "This is for you, Mrs. Bauer."

It was wrapped neatly in brown paper and done up with white string. She was aware that her hands were shaking. She said, "I'm sorry. Could you unwrap it?"

Wordlessly, he broke the string, then ripped the paper away. It was a white slipper. He held it in the palms of both hands, cupping it as if it were some living thing.

"That morning in the prison yard," said the old man, "I picked this up and hid it under my tunic. In the confusion, nobody noticed. In 1924, when I went to America, it was one of the few things I took with me."

At the door, she kissed him on the cheek. He said, "They have ways now of telling whether it's going to be a boy or a girl. . . ."

"I have my own way, Mr. Stahlmann. It's going to be a girl."

He smiled. "Ah, then I would be willing to wager on the name."

"You would be right," she said. "Elleander Morning Bauer."

When she was alone, she went into the master bedroom, sat on the edge of the giant bed-that-was-a-ship, removed her shoes. Gently, she ran an index finger down the length of the slipper to the base of its graceful, two-inch heel. She turned it over, noting a few scratches on the sole. It seemed now part of an ensemble that had been chosen for a single wearing. The thought chilled her momentarily, then she smiled to herself. Without further thought, she slipped into it.

It fit perfectly. She hobbled about in it. Then for minutes she stood in front of the full-length mirror in the hall. Finally the tears came.